THE RAVEN'S BALLAD

EMMA HAMM

For every little girl who dreamt of being a witch someday

PROLOGUE

Once upon a time, in a forest of emerald leaves, a woman ran away from home. Not because her home was dangerous or unlikable, but because adventure beat deep in her heart. She raced through the forest, over hills, beyond the dales, until she grew too tired to continue.

The young woman fell asleep on a bed of verdant moss, unknowing this particular place was home to a powerful faerie. He was a ghastly creature covered in feathers with clawed hands and a warped face. The beast looked upon her and thought, *This pretty little thing would look lovely at my dinner table.*

Faeries are not kind, and he could not allow a human to enjoy his home's splendor. So while the young woman slept, he wove a spell that changed her form into that of a swan-like woman. Feathers dusted her shoulders and trickled down her arms like a mantle of snow, her hair turned white as pearls, and her eyes blue as ice.

She awoke amid a banquet. Faeries danced around her, feathers, horns, and fur decorating their bodies until she couldn't discern which were fae and which were beasts.

Delighted by what she thought was a dream, she danced with them until the sun rose.

Exhausted as she'd never been before, the young woman stopped to watch the sky turn violet, then pink, then vivid blue. She sighed in happiness, thanked the faeries for a wonderful night, and turned to leave. Only then did she realize there was no way out. A glass wall stood between her and freedom.

The beastly faerie emerged from the shadows, shaking his great cloak of black feathers and holding out a clawed hand. "I must bid you to stay with me, pretty thing."

"And if I wish to leave?" she asked.

"I would rather you be guest than prisoner."

"Then I have little choice." She took his hand and promised to stay with him for all eternity. In return, he gave her a kingdom of goblins and trolls. She strode through the darkness, her subjects bowing to her as she went, and stepped into a castle made of obsidian stone. Everything the eye could see was hers as long as she never stepped beyond the glass wall.

For a time, she was pleased with her new abode. She ordered his people about and they called her queen. Her feathered husband grew into a kind man, and though he never said he loved her, he was pleasant enough. She found herself much happier in this faerie realm than she had been in her own home.

The glass reflected a world around them that was both beautiful and dangerous. She spent hours watching deer run by, their images warped and glimmering with rainbows. Many times, the young woman reached for these strange visions only to have them disappear the moment her fingers touched the shimmering barrier.

Curiosity bloomed in her breast until she could stand it no more.

She stepped beyond the glass wall.

The city of faerie beasts crumbled behind her, turning to ash and dust in her wake. She turned and tried to catch pieces in her hands, but it was far too late.

On the wind, she heard the voice of her beastly faerie husband. "You've destroyed us all."

CHAPTER 1
THE RAVEN KINGDOM

"May the goddess bless you," the sluagh murmured.

"And you, my sister." Aisling reached for the thin, wooden bowl the bird-like creature held out. She sipped the sweet tea. Honey, lavender, and periwinkle burst on her tongue, the flavors focusing her mind and easing the tension in her spine.

She'd gotten into the habit of performing this calming ritual with many of the sluagh each evening. They were a naturally restless bunch. The desire to grow their ranks nagged their minds, and Aisling had found distractions were the only thing that helped ease their torment.

Many of the sluagh souls used to be human. She'd discovered quite a few remembered their past lives, although most weren't happy lives to remember. Those who were involved in the rituals had some form of magic in their previous lives. A few of them were witches, some were women who had wanted to be witches, and others were simply pleased to have a new distraction.

The sluagh in front of her was a quiet female. Her face had

recently warped into the bird-like beak that marked her people. The dark bone split her face in half, skin peeling back as though she was shedding. Aisling remembered her face from only a month before, a rather haggard human face, but still clearly female and a new soul gathered by the sluagh. The only feature that looked familiar now was her eyes. The change appeared painful, and yet, the sluagh had all assured her they couldn't feel the transformation.

The creature's body had darkened to a dusky gray, lifeless and dull. Flaps grew from her wrist to her waist, creating a wing-like appendage that folded in rest. Like most of the sluagh, she'd given up on wearing clothing. Her breasts hung limp, skin sagging and body lacking any sense of fat or muscle. She was bones contained by flesh that slid over them like molten lava.

Her hand was steady when she reached for the bowl. "Go with happiness, my queen."

Aisling reached out and ran her hand over the sparse hair on the top of the sluagh's head.

The female stretched like a cat, pressing her head into Aisling's palm. They were rarely touched, even by each other. They found themselves disgusting, and many had expressed their concern at having Aisling touch them at all. She was too precious, their Raven Queen. She shouldn't be touching something so tainted by dark magic.

Each time, Aisling showed them the eyes on the palms of her hands and reminded them that she, too, was born of dark magic.

She passed by the sluagh and ducked into the cave where the rest were waiting for her. The long train of her gown slithered behind her. Black lace scratched along the stones while the inner lining of silk softened the sound into a melody of movement.

Her heart gave a squeeze of happiness the moment she cast her gaze upon the ranks of the sluagh. They sat with wings folded, claws gently placed on their knees, in a large circle around a pit filled with faerie lights. It was a picture of relaxation and restraint. She couldn't have been prouder if they had started turning back into the human souls they should have been.

Aisling walked to an open spot in the circle and settled between two of the leathery creatures. The one on her right, a youngling if the smoother skin was any indicator, shifted its pinky just enough to graze the black lace of her dress. She suppressed a smile, placed her hands palm up on her knees, and let her eyes drift shut.

Lemongrass and lavender hung heavy in the air. The subtle touch of smoke filled with magic brushed along her back. There were more in this cavern than just the sluagh, and more in the Underhill than just the creatures who were banished here.

She'd felt this magic many times before. It wasn't a dangerous creature or even something aware of itself. Aisling had tried to speak with it, but it always remained a silent presence, something she couldn't quite harness, and certainly not something cognizant. Instead, she'd come to realize this magic was simply Underhill itself. The land liked to take part in the ceremonies.

The sluagh next to her rocked to the side. Others followed, gently shifting back and forth in a wave-like rhythm. A quiet hum began from deep in their bellies, over and over until their sound filled Aisling with peace.

She breathed in once, twice, three times and then let her mind clear.

"Into this smoke, I release all energies that do not serve me."

The sluagh repeated her words, some still humming, and the words became a song.

"I release all negativity that surrounds me and all fears that limit me."

Over and over, they repeated the words until she felt tension release. The magic of the room snapped, a nearly audible sound like a thread tearing.

The ogham marks on her arms, those that spelled *Raven Consort* in the ancient language, burned. She'd come to think of the familiar ache as a sign that the sluagh wouldn't hurt anyone or themselves. Their anger, their rage, was released.

She let out a quiet sigh. "So mote it be."

Resounding echoes of her words filled the cavern. Most of the sluagh remained still and silent with bowed heads and calm bodies. These were the ones who would remain in the cave for a long time, sometimes never leaving unless they were called upon. Some of them had trouble controlling their desire to consume fear, others wished to devour souls so badly they remained in the cavern to prevent themselves from harming others.

When Aisling stood, a few of the younger sluagh did as well. They would wander the labyrinth of Underhill, searching for any who might have fallen into its depths.

She twitched her skirts to the side and ducked out of the cavern. The ceremony wasn't much, but it was something she could do for her people before her own curse caught up with her.

Barefoot, she padded down the crumbling stairwell to the next that arched up and ended in midair. Aisling didn't hesitate at the peak. Instead, she kept walking and let the magic of Underhill carry her to the underbelly of the stairwell. She descended, upside down to those who were on the other side, right-side up for herself.

The first few times she'd attempted this, her stomach had rebelled. Now, she was used to the oddities of this place. The stairwells made little sense. The place made little sense. Still, it was home, and that was good enough for her.

An ache laced up her arm. Aisling winced and touched a finger to the ogham marks. "Still burning?" she whispered. "Why's that?"

They rarely burned for more than a few moments after their morning ritual. Lately, they'd been itching more and more. She didn't know if that was a good sign or a bad one.

"Mistress!" The shout trailed through the air, zinging past her head like an arrow. "Mistress of —"

"Please don't call me that." Aisling turned and waited for the sluagh to catch up to her. They had taken to calling her "Mistress of Darkness," which she thought all too ridiculous. She was mistress of nothing if they didn't want her to be. She'd come from nothing and would return to nothing. A title such as that was a slap in the face to her history.

This sluagh was one of the eldest. There were holes in the leathery wings that drooped around its shoulders, tattered edges flapping in the gentle breeze. The lack of breasts suggested this one was male, although the drooping skin hid any physical features that might have belayed the truth.

It huffed out a breath and held out a hand once it reached her side.

"Hello, Connor isn't it?" she asked, hoping she was correct.

"Aye, mistress. 'Tis Connor."

Thank goodness, or she would have been embarrassed. Although Aisling had been the Raven Queen for months now, she had yet to learn how to tell the sluagh apart. The older they got, the more they looked like each other. They were all leathery puddles of flesh, bone, and hungry eyes.

She sank into a shallow curtsey and eyed the sluagh whose hands were twitching. "Can I help you?"

"No, no, of course not, mistress. I wanted to voice my concern about Samhain this year."

"Perhaps you should speak with the Raven King, then. The Wild Hunt is not under my control."

"My concern for you is why I have requested your time, mistress." Uncomfortable, he listlessly moved his hands. "It's just...many of us have heard whispers in the darkness, an old voice that has long since been thought of dead."

Yet another dead god? Aisling wasn't certain how many of those she could survive in a lifetime. She knew well enough to listen when someone claimed an ancient voice was speaking.

Holding back a sigh, she nodded. "Do you know who is speaking?"

"The oldest of the sluagh claim it is..." He hesitated, then swallowed hard. "Carman."

Aisling had heard of the woman, although the old myths were vague and unlikely to be true. "The first witch?"

"Ancient mother and crone of all magic," the sluagh

agreed. "She has been speaking with the elder sluagh."

"What has she said?"

"That the time of magic is returning, and she shall call upon us to rise."

"Upon you?" Aisling repeated. She didn't like that thought. No one could call upon the sluagh but the Raven King or Queen, yet this whispering voice held a sway over her people. At least, so it seemed. "Tell me about Carman again, the truth, not the human myths of who this creature was."

The promise of a tale was a tempting treat for most of the sluagh. Their knowledge was vast, and this particular creature was one of the oldest. He straightened his spine as far as it would go and blew out a long breath.

Claws clacking, he began. "Carman was a goddess who came from Athens. Her skin was made of burnished gold, her hair the color of the blackest night. She rode a chariot with wheels aflame. Three sons arrived with her, Dub the Black, Dother the Evil, and Dian the Violent.

"She needed only her sons to lay waste to Ireland. Everywhere she touched, the land died. Fruits shriveled on the vine, crops withered and dried. Her magic was so powerful even the greatest druids couldn't defeat her. Her actions caught the attention of four Tuatha de Danann. They rode on the winds to battle her and her sons.

"Even they were challenged by her magic. Her sons, however, they could defeat. Here is where the human myths differ. They claim Dub, Dother, and Dian were banished, and that Carman then died of a broken heart."

The sluagh leaned closer as if someone might overhear his story. "It's not true, mistress. They couldn't banish the three

16

boys any more than they could banish their mother. Carman had tied herself to this land by sapping all the power from Underhill itself. Instead, they imprisoned her *here* with the Underfolk."

That was a bit more problematic. She had always thought there was more to this place than just a home for the forgotten creatures. Aisling had never thought it was also a prison.

Carman, *the* Carman, was hidden somewhere deep within this place? Aisling hadn't even seen the extent of the kingdom. The sluagh insisted there was far too much to see, and those who wanted her attentions would come to the crumbling keep. If there was a goddess imprisoned on the outskirts, shouldn't they check and make sure the bars remained sturdy?

The sluagh leaned back and shook his head. "I thought you ought to know, mistress. We will remain as we always have, ensuring you and the king are safe. There are some..." He licked his lips. "I would suggest keeping an eye on all the sluagh, for the time being."

"Thank you for your concern," she replied. "I'll pass this information along to the king. There's much for us to discuss."

If they even had the time. Her mind troubled, she watched the sluagh turn and pick his way across the stairways again.

The last time Bran and her had an evening together was during a storm. If the moon was visible, then he was a raven. If the sun was out, she was a swan. It didn't matter where or when; their curses always pulled them apart.

She picked up her skirts and raced down the stairs, making her way toward the deep lake in the center of Underhill. He waited for her there, as he did every night, and she didn't want to waste the precious moments they had.

17

Her feet pounded across broken stone and slippery moss. Should she tell him everything? Would the sluagh admit such thoughts to him or only to her?

The horizon seemed to part in front of her, revealing the pond where she spent her days. It was large enough for her, but not so large she could call it a lake. The waters were deep, so deep no one could see the bottom. At least, not without a spell to breathe underwater.

Above all else, she viewed it as yet another means to an end. Both Bran and she had informants spread across both the Unseelie lands and the human worlds, each trying to discover another clue that might help them. They desperately needed to break their curses, if only to rule their people better.

She stopped at the water's edge, her toes touching the cool water. The hemline of her gown grew sodden and heavy, there were plenty of others for her to ruin. Now, she just had to wait for that time between time, when the sun and the moon disappeared from the sky and allowed dusk and dawn to be born. The moment when she could finally see *him*.

Warm arms wrapped around her waist, tugging her back to a broad chest that felt like home.

"Raven queen," the deep, buttery voice growled in her ear. "You shouldn't be out of the castle without a guard."

"I already have a guard with me."

Bran chuckled. Rustling feathers tickled her ears, and the last bit of his magic faded away until his arms wrapped around her without the barrier of silken stems. "I don't count as a guard, Aisling."

"I wasn't talking about you." She paused as he pressed warm lips to her neck. "I can take care of myself."

He grunted, then turned her around. He slid his hands up her arms, drawing them around his neck so he might pull her closer. A long sigh escaped his lips, dancing across her own. "I've missed you, witch."

An aching pang echoed through her chest. Gods, she had missed him as well. This curse was worse than all the others they'd suffered together. They were so close, and yet always so far away.

Aisling tucked her face into the hollow of his throat, breathing in the musky scent of man, wine, and wilderness. The moonlight would touch her skin soon, and then she would be ripped from his arms. For a few seconds, she could stand here with him at her side, pretending she was happy.

"Where'd you go, witch?" he murmured, stroking his fingers through her hair. "I've but a few moments with you each day. I won't waste them, even with your thoughts."

He cupped the back of her head, cradling her as if she were a fragile creature. And in this moment, she felt as though she were. The constant battles exhausted Aisling. The fighting to remain normal, the desperate desire to be close to him, yet not able to *see* him for more than a few minutes a day.

Bran pressed his lips to hers in a kiss that sucked the air from her lungs. She clung to the lapels of his black jacket, holding on for dear life.

He delved into her mouth, licking and biting at her lips until she sighed against him. All her frustrations and fear melted away into the heat of his body, the warmth of his adoration, and the gentle manipulations of his fingers as he dug them into the small of her back.

The hairs on her arms raised, and a tingle of magic spread

from the top of her head to the tips of her toes. She pulled back, eyes still squeezed shut, and shook her head. "Less time than usual, it seems."

"We'll break your curse," he replied, stroking a hand over her head, tangling his fingers in the ends. "Give me time. There are hundreds of faeries who could help us. I just have to find the right one to bribe."

"You shouldn't have to bribe anyone." Faeries were notoriously difficult to deal with, and he would need to give them a reason to help. She only hoped it would be sooner rather than later.

"Our world works differently." Bran stepped back, his fingers sliding down her arms and lingering at her palm until he let them fall away. "I wish it didn't."

"So do I."

Magic slithered up her legs in the cold caress she hated so much. It was a familiar feeling by now, months of this change didn't stop her disgusted reaction. Her teeth clenched, her thighs trembled, and she fought against it with all she had. Yet, she still walked backward until the water touched her knees.

Fighting did little good these days. The magic had sunk deep into her skin until it was a part of her even when she wasn't at the lake.

Aisling felt her muscles shift, her bones break, her hair shrink until every inch of her being shattered and reformed. All at once, she was something new. Something exhausted and tired and ever so dangerously weak.

She lifted her head, long neck stretching up, and met Bran's sad gaze. He ran a hand through his hair, fingers catching on black feathers, before he cleared his throat. "Soon, Aisling. I'll fix this."

He cast her one last look before turning to make his way to the castle. The sluagh could not be without a leader for too long since they dissolved into madness without something to focus on. They would cut free from their ties, become loosed upon the human realm, and feast upon souls as their whims desired. The world would not survive it.

Aisling paddled away from the shore, making her way to the other side. Bran might rely on faerie magic to save them, but she wasn't the type to wait. Faeries could take hundreds of years to make their decisions. She didn't have that much patience.

When she knew he had crested the stairs and was too far away to see her, Aisling paddled faster to the opposite shore where a small black smudge waited for her.

Ever faithful, her familiar waited to prove himself yet again. *Lorcan*. The strange witch who had saved her life countless times and turned himself into a cat while doing so. His paws stamped the ground, alternating each side, while he glowered at her as though she had done something wrong.

She probably had. He didn't like to wait. Aisling had told him countless times she had little control over the change, but he didn't want to hear it. It was always, *change faster, some of us don't have the luxury of time.*

As soon as she was close, he opened his mouth in a hiss. "What took you so long this time?"

"Lorcan, please don't start."

"I could see you on the other side, you know. I understand you miss him, you can't just...canoodle while I'm right here."

Aisling lifted her head and honked, her new body's version

of a laugh. "Canoodle?"

"Well, maybe not quite so bad. Understand the importance we meet as soon as possible, especially on days when I'm returning from the human realm! I might have information that can help you break this new curse."

"And do you?" She swam in tight circles in front of him.

Lorcan lifted a paw and licked it. His eyes narrowed, tracking her every movement, before he begrudgingly admitted, "No."

"Then why should I rush to see you?"

"Don't give me sass, young lady."

At the very least, she knew her relationship with Lorcan wouldn't change no matter what form she was in.

Aisling gave another coughing chuckle and spread her wings in a stretch. "Have you made any progress at all, or were you sleeping in the sun?"

"There were a few helpful toads, but I figured you wouldn't want to get any more warts, witch."

"So no?"

Lorcan sighed and laid down on the small stone ledge. The white star on his chest blazed for a moment before he lowered his chin to the stone. "It's as if no one has ever heard of the Raven Queen. The king, yes. There are hundreds of legends about him, his wrongdoings, everything in between. A queen? No, she never existed."

"It has to all tie back to her, to the one in the lake underneath the Unseelie castle," Aisling murmured. "I can feel it started with her."

"It'll be difficult to talk with a dead woman," Lorcan grumbled. He rolled onto his back, letting the sunlight play across his belly. "So you might want to think of another way to fix this."

"Wasn't that why I sent you to the human realm?"

"I thought it was to indulge myself on fat mice and pretend starling wings were ravens cracking between my teeth."

She splashed water up onto his ledge with her wing. The cat let out a low hiss and rolled a few times until he was far enough away from the offending liquid.

Glaring at her, he stamped a paw on the ground. "There's no reason for that."

"Entertainment."

She floated away from him, letting eddies of the lake pull her away.

Lorcan could understand animals, being one himself, and she found the change had allowed her to do the same. Humans? They still couldn't understand a word she said. It was frustrating. She could hear what they were saying, and yet, no one understood her hoarse honks.

Speaking with animals had been fun for a few moments, now, she wanted nothing more than to speak with faeries and humans again. She sighed. Her wings drooped and her neck slowly curved down.

"Things aren't going well then, I assume?" Lorcan asked.

"Nothing has changed, if that's what you mean." Nothing would ever change. She couldn't touch him more than a few minutes a day. They couldn't rule together the way they were meant to, and it didn't seem to bother him.

"He's still trying, you know."

"So he says," she murmured.

"Not says. I've seen the effort he's putting into this. He

hasn't forgotten, and he will not let you rot as a swan forever, Aisling."

She wasn't sure how much she agreed. Bran, while understandably distracted, seemed more interested in shirking his responsibilities than helping her. It was in his nature to detest everything that had to do with being a king. He'd never wanted the role, and having it thrust upon him only made things worse.

Aisling shook her head. "I can't leave them like he does. I understand the faerie courts require his presence and he needs to be in the mortal realm to search for a counter curse, but the sluagh need *someone*. If we were both gone, they would completely unravel. Even now, they hold their minds together by a thread that I have to repair every morning."

"And you have to be that person?"

Someone had to step up and be the adult. Aisling was the worst person to do it, though. She knew how to take care of children, not fully grown faerie creatures.

As people aged, they expected others to help them. They thought a kind gesture was owed to them, no matter where they were or what stage of life they were in. Children always viewed kindness for what it was.

The sluagh were much like the children she so adored back in the human realm. They thanked her, they bowed when she walked into the room, they even whispered that she was a famed Tuatha de Danann who had cast her gaze upon them as a blessing. They desired things that adults desired: luxury, respect, honor.

And they didn't seem to understand she was just as cursed as them.

"Ah," Lorcan said with a quiet purr. "You're worried he isn't interested in you anymore."

Normally, she would deny the emotional attachment to another person. Bran had wiggled his way under her shield, and now she didn't know how to get him out.

Aisling's feathers ruffled. "He's still interested, but...I don't know. I can't describe how it feels to watch the person you" — she paused — "adore, be human while you aren't."

"You don't have to describe that feeling to me. I've lived it for many years."

She glanced at her oldest friend. "You don't mean—"

"You?" Lorcan laughed, his voice booming across the lake. "*Never*. Of course there was someone before you, foolish thing. And she was as lovely as the day is long."

"Lovely? I don't think I've ever heard you call anything *lovely*."

"Well, she was." His eyes glazed over, as if he was staring into the past. "Her hair was copper as a fire and her eyes were green as grass. She was the only woman to catch my fancy."

Aisling floated closer. "What happened to her?"

"I don't know. I turned to witchcraft and had to leave the village where I grew up. She stayed behind since her father was a traditional man. Never saw her again."

It was a story she'd heard from countless witches. The humans saw them as dangerous creatures who could hurt them. In reality, most witches lived very lonely lives. They desired the darkness only to ensure their solitude wasn't disturbed.

Silence stretched between them. Aisling didn't know what to say and assumed there weren't words he cared to hear.

Instead, she let him have a moment of quiet before she brought up yet another concern.

"The sluagh hear a voice whispering to them," she said. "They claim it's Carman."

"The first witch?"

"One and the same."

Lorcan sat up. He gazed at her severely before yowling. "Carman is dangerous news, little witch. If it's the truth…"

"I want no one getting nervous yet. It has to be the truth before we involve anyone else." She stared up at the castle, wondering just how many of the sluagh had heard this witch's voice already. "I need to find out how many of them have heard her."

"If any of them have, it's bad news. That witch nearly destroyed everything before your ancestors stopped her."

"I'm not related to any of the ones who stopped her."

And she wasn't certain that Badb had agreed with her siblings when they tried to prevent Carman and her sons razing Ireland to the ground. The war that would come afterward likely would have fed Badb's blood thirst. Even her sisters, the Morrigan and Macha, would have become involved at that point.

The Tuatha de Danann who stopped Carman also saved their people from a civil war, one that might begin again, even without Carman stepping a foot back in the human realm.

"Is *she* here?" Lorcan asked.

"According to the sluagh, this is her prison."

"That's more dangerous than we were expecting Underhill to be." He stood, then stretched out his front paws. "I'll trust you to figure that one out. The rest, you leave up to me."

She lowered her beak and stared at him over her black bill. "Which means you'll be sleeping in the sun for the next few days, is that right?"

"Well, there's rarely sun here, and even then it's very weak. So I have to spend more time to get the same amount of exposure."

She splashed him again with a honking laugh and floated into the center of the lake. There was much for her to think about, and plans to be made.

Aisling hoped she could find proof of Carman's existence before the witch caused any more trouble.

CHAPTER 2
FAMILIAL TIES

Bran touched a finger to the crumbling bannister as he walked up the stairwell to his private quarters. The sluagh trailed behind him, whispering behind their hands that the *king* was here. He'd arrived, they were saved, they could finally be happy.

The weight of their expectations pressed down on his shoulders so thoroughly he couldn't breathe.

Was being a king supposed to be easy? He'd always thought it would be. His father lounged in the throne room all day, having food hand-fed to him by slaves and daughters who doted upon him. His mother watched the proceedings of her people, only interfering to scream at them until they raced away in fear.

That was what he knew a "ruler" to be. He'd never thought it would be like having thousands of children all scrambling for his attention.

One of the sluagh tugged on the sleeve of his coat. "Sire, if I could have a moment?"

He paused, looked down at the ugly creature, and nodded.

"What is it?"

"We'd like to have more time with you."

"Why?"

What remained of the sluagh's brows crumpled in confusion. "To...be with you?"

And therein lay the problem. He didn't know how to *be* with them. He'd never had friends, the Unseelie didn't have those kinds of relationships, and he didn't trust himself not to insult one of them. Or worse...

Turn into his parents.

He couldn't tell Aisling. She'd think less of him for these thoughts since she believed him capable of more than he gave himself credit for. Was he capable of what she expected?

He didn't' know how to be a king. He didn't know how to be a man who *loved her*, let alone someone who could take care of an entire kingdom.

Bran shook his head at the sluagh, slipped out of its grasp, and left them alone on the stairs. The dark stain of their numbers lingered for a few moments in his wake before he heard them patter in the opposite direction.

He didn't want to be their leader. He hadn't asked for this, for any of it, and now with a kingdom at his feet, all he felt was that he wasn't worthy of them.

The crumbling halls tilted in front of him. They listed to the side, or perhaps, he listed to the side as he fell against the wall. Pressing a hand to his throat, he willed his body to take in a deep breath. His mind was screaming. Not words or any sensible emotion, just screaming that something was wrong, that he was dying, or someone he loved was dying, and he couldn't stop the thoughts from threatening to drown him.

Logically, he knew it was panic. His body was convinced the end of all things barreled toward him at top speed, and he could do nothing to stop it.

Stumbling down the hall, he reached his door flustered and out of breath. He pressed a hand against the cold wood, shoved hard, then let his body fall through the opening.

Fists pressed against the floor, he forced his lungs to inhale. One breath, two, over and over until he could at least think through the dangerous red haze in his mind.

The world would not end because he was a king. The sluagh would not be released upon the human realm to feast, as they were want to do.

Was it that which bothered him so much? The responsibility of an army that could decimate not just the human realm, but the faerie courts as well?

Aisling would tell him that was a foolish worry. The sluagh didn't want to hurt anyone. They were still good people under the garbs of darkness and shadow. Unlike Bran, she didn't feel their hunger, didn't listen to their innermost desires.

She didn't know every time she walked into a room, they all turned to stare at her because they wondered what her soul would taste like.

He constantly battled against them, telling them to calm, easing their minds like she tried to do. They didn't want their minds to ease. There would always be a part of them that wanted to be released from their bond to the Raven King so they might devour the world.

Their creator was long since dead, a millennia passed since an ancient god birthed them to end the world. The Tuatha de Danann had bound them to whatever poor soul was titled

Raven King. That much Bran knew. The rest of their story had been lost in the wake of a hundred wars where the sluagh had splattered the world with blood.

A prophetic image in his mind revealed the world as the sluagh wanted. Nothing but dust and ash remained in his beloved Otherworld, and still, it was the human realm he worried about most. The faeries would fight and die gloriously. The humans would die screaming in their beds as their worst nightmares were yanked out of their souls. Then they would be turned into monsters who lusted for more souls.

Anxiety pressed down on his shoulders again, the weight unbearable. His shoulders quaked and his fingers shook where they pressed against the cold stone floor.

He couldn't do this. He wasn't the man for this role and yet, here he was. Forced to take care of them, forced to remain away from the only person who might have eased his worries and convinced him that things weren't so bad.

No. He would suffer this fear in silence and alone. Aisling had already suffered enough.

Something shifted out of the corner of his room where a mirror stood alone. A portal back home, just in case the Unseelie might need him.

One of his sisters stepped forward, her head cocked to the side awkwardly, almost as if her neck had been broken.

Bran forced himself to look closer. It was important to know which one she was. Some of his siblings might try to kill him in a moment of weakness like this. Others might simply laugh at him.

"Isolde," he said, coughing and sitting up onto his haunches. He stayed kneeling on the floor in front of his most dangerous sister, watching as she shuffled into the room.

If he was forced to choose between his siblings, he would choose her again and again. She was the most trustworthy of his dangerous family. Not the least bloodthirsty, by any means, but at least she didn't hide her intentions.

Isolde was the oldest and had lasted as his father's plaything for centuries. Spiderwebs of blue veins laced underneath her paper-thin, pale skin. Her neck stayed at that angle because it *had* been broken, countless times. It was her lips that always made him uncomfortable.

Sometime ago, when they were just children, their father had sewn her lips shut. Fifty years later, he'd allowed her to speak again. The scars still mottled the blue-tinged mouth.

Her eyes, however, his father had left sewn closed.

"Brother." Her voice rasped through the air like the rattling of tree branches on a cold, winter's night. "You have fallen."

"I can still stand."

"Can you?" She stepped closer, her hand finding the post of his bed.

She had aged, he noted. Her pitch-black hair was now peppered with silver, unusual for one of their people. Perhaps not for her. She'd suffered more in her lifetime than a thousand faeries combined.

Bran stayed where he was. Though Isolde liked others to think her weak, he knew there was an iron bar in her spine far stronger than any of his other siblings. If she wanted to attack him—and there was always a part of the Unseelie that wanted to attack—she would with a vengeance he could not stop.

"Why are you here, sister?"

"I heard tell there was a new Raven King. Father won't stop

talking about you," she replied. A soft chuckle escaped her shivering lips. "Although, it is our brothers who are far angrier. I think, perhaps, our parents are proud of you."

Repulsed, Bran swallowed the gorge rising in his throat. "I've never sought their praise."

"No, you haven't. Even as a child." Isolde sank onto the edge of his bed. The billowing edges of her ragged, white nightgown caught like a web around her. "And yet, here you are."

So, she wasn't here to pick a fight with him. She would have attacked by now. Bran still carried a few of her scars on his ribcage. His shoulders sagged in relief.

"Are you here as a sister?" he asked. "Or as a foe?"

"Father does not know I'm here."

A riddle for an answer, so like all his sisters who gathered information in the Otherworld and placed it in a library for safekeeping. He understood what she meant. "Then you know more about my place here than you're letting on."

"I always know where you are, little brother." An unusually soft expression crossed her face. "You were always my favorite."

"And you were mine."

"I'm sorry for the pain you suffered in the dark castle," she whispered. "I never got to tell you that, but I think it's important you know. I recorded every beating, every whipping, and I placed it in a black book at the highest bookcase within my section. No one else has ever seen it. I know every tear you shed, every lash you bore. Everything, little brother. I have witnessed it all."

To have been recorded in such a way was the greatest

honor one of his sisters could have given. Shock stole the words from his lips. He stared at her, knowing she couldn't see his expression or his appreciation. What had she suffered? What did he not know about his own family?

Bran cleared his throat. "Thank you."

Isolde nodded her crooked head.

Silence stretched between them, and he'd forgotten how uncomfortable their family was. There wasn't a support structure of any kind. They didn't want to help each other. They didn't really care where the others were or how they were. For his sister to be here at all was uncharacteristic and odd.

He slowly rose from his knees and stood. "Was there something you wanted?"

"I want to help you, brother."

"I don't need your help. The Unseelie ways no longer rule in Underhill." It felt so good to say the words.

His entire life, Bran had waited to renounce his people. He didn't want to be a wandering fae with no connection to court or family. He didn't want to be Unseelie any longer. Their meandering eyes, hatred of everyone and anything, but mostly, how they never seemed to care about each other as much as he'd hoped they would.

He had a chance to build something else here. Something that he believed in, that would make people's lives *better*. The problem was that he didn't think he could.

Isolde reached into the folds of her dress, pulled out a black book, then held it out to him. "I think, perhaps, this will help."

What was his sister's game? He didn't recognize the tome, wouldn't anyway since he was never in the libraries for very long. When he took the offered piece, magic laced through his body like a lightning strike.

Bran stroked the soft, leather cover and stared down at the simple journal. "What is this?"

"It's yours."

The words didn't register for a moment until he realized she was saying this was *his* book. Every tiny detail of his life that Isolde had meticulously recorded. He flipped it open in the middle and read a particularly nasty moment when his mother had flayed the skin off his back.

This was *him*. Every instance, every detail, pieces of his life all written down from cover to cover by a sister he hadn't known cared.

The dark memories threatened to rise up over his head like a wave and drown all the good he'd put back into the world.

A chilled, frail hand covered his, forcing the book to close. "This was your history, and I give it to you only because the chapter thusly must close."

"What?" He looked at her eyes, sewn shut for centuries, and realized she saw far more than she ever let on.

She smiled with scarred lips. "Burn it, brother. The Unseelie Prince is gone, and these memories have no use here. Become the Raven King in his entirety. Learn who that person is. Your past and your future should not mix."

It was a rare moment of kindness that she showed him, and he would not let it go to waste. Bran nodded, turned, and tossed the book into the fireplace behind him.

Watching it go up in flames felt like the start of something new.

CHAPTER 3

OF RUMORS AND MYTHS

Aisling floated between dreams and the real world. Her mind wandered through thoughts, trying desperately to place them in the drawers they needed to be in. She didn't sleep at night anymore. She had to be awake for the sluagh and all the responsibilities that came with being the Raven Queen.

As a swan, there was too much to worry about. Wild animals found her thick wings interesting, and even the Fae stared at her breast with a hunger in their gaze that wasn't sexual.

The sun burned behind her eyes, keeping her half awake when all she wanted was to sleep.

Water rippled, waves caressing her side, as someone or something stepped into her lake. Usually, Aisling would dismiss such subtle movements. She knew what they were. The sluagh often visited her, keeping their distance but letting her know she wasn't alone. Sometimes, a deer would wander past her lake and pause for a cold drink. These were sounds she was familiar with.

Again, the water trickled as if it were being poured from a

vase or goblet. No animal could make that sound, which meant someone was trying to capture her attention. The sluagh left her alone. They knew this was her sacred time, thought that she was a swan to connect with nature since none of them had been alive when there was a Raven Queen.

That left only one person who would dare to bother her when the moon hadn't yet risen, a faerie who constantly gloated that he'd bested them. Aisling opened one eye and glanced across the wide expanse of the lake.

A man crouched at the edge, a gold goblet in his hand that he dipped into the lake. Black hair spilled over his shoulders to his waist, nearly touching the water as he bent down. His clothing was impeccably made, emeralds sparkling on his lapel and down his waistcoat. Broad shoulders tapered to a narrow waist, and crushed velvet pants hugged his long legs.

He might have been handsome if pale scales didn't stretch up out of his collar.

She paddled closer, dipping her head until her beak nearly touched the water. How dare he? The previous Raven King, the one who had cursed both her and Bran to this ridiculous life, all because he didn't want to be stuck in this kingdom anymore.

He had no right to be here.

The sluagh still whispered his name in fear that he would return to the throne. *Darcy*: descendant of the dark one. And now she knew why he was named thusly.

An ancient tome had revealed his story. He was born into a family of Unseelie who were part snake. They devoured their prey whole, enjoying taking their time in torturing all whom they ate. He had not been a good Raven King. In fact, he was worse than any in history.

She clacked her beak in warning. He wouldn't dare come too close to her, or she would bite his fingers so hard they would snap off at the knuckle.

Darcy lifted his head. His eyes were the color of sunlight filtered through leaves, slitted pupils contracting when he saw how close she had gotten.

"Aisling," he said with more warmth than he should. "My sweet queen, how have you been?"

She beat her wings against the water, rearing up. He had no right to call her his queen, let alone address her. He'd left their people, the sluagh, the dullahan, the dearg due, in the hands of Bran and herself with little guidance. She'd had to pick up so many of the pieces he'd left behind.

Perhaps he understood what her movement meant because he leaned back away from the shore. The goblet dissolved into nothing in his palm, magic glimmering on his fingertips like gossamer threads. "I see you remember me."

Of course, she remembered him. How could she ever forget the man who had doomed her to a life such as this?

"Good. I thought I would stop by and see what you've done with my kingdom." He glanced around, and a broad grin revealed pointed teeth. "It seems like you've done nothing thus far."

She was going to bite him. She was going to beat her wings against his skull until those sharp teeth rattled out.

"I came by to see your husband. Or wait, he's not your husband, is he? You're just his consort, or a king's plaything, whatever it is you tell yourself to justify the insult." He paused and glanced back at her. "I also wanted to see you. The rumors really are true, aren't they? The Raven Queen always suffers with the king, no matter what form she wears. Strange. I didn't know the curse would be quite so powerful. Here you are, a swan instead of a woman. Unless that's by choice?"

She hissed at him.

"Not by choice then." Darcy chuckled. "Well, that's new then. You'll want to hear what I have to say to your... We'll call him 'king.' I apologize for making you leave your lake, little swan."

She didn't want him to see how awkwardly she walked on land. It was yet another weakness he could exploit.

She also wanted to hit him.

Aisling narrowed her eyes and watched him saunter away, his hands loose at his sides and entirely too comfortable in this kingdom of broken souls. This wasn't a place he could play in, nor was it a place for him to rest his head. The sluagh were *afraid* of him. He'd done enough damage already.

Anger burning hot in her chest, she paddled to shore and clambered out of her lake. Giving herself one quick shake, she sprinted forward and took to the air.

Wind whistled through her wings like a shrieking banshee. Stealthy she was not, but that didn't matter to her. She wanted Darcy to hear her, to know that he was about to be hit by powerful wings and an angry woman who despised him.

He ducked at the last second, however, one of her outstretched wings still clipped him on the top of the head. Enough to mess his perfectly smooth hair.

That was a win.

She landed ungracefully, breathing hard and hissing through her beak.

"Trouble in paradise?" he asked, chuckling as he walked

by her. "That's the Raven King's curse, you know. Happiness will forever elude him, and you are his happiness. You know who's enjoying life to the fullest?" He pointed at himself. "Me."

She hated him.

A slow, sluggish crawl of magic dripped down her long neck, and she knew the sun had set below the horizon. Aisling glanced over her shoulder at the streaks of pink. She wouldn't be able to follow Darcy now. She'd have to wait until the curse ran its course.

Footsteps crunched away from her. He picked his way through the rubble and large chunks of stone with a familiarity that she hated. He had been king of this land for too long. His mark would forever linger upon its people and the land itself.

She wondered if he had caused much of the rubble during his reign.

A line of heat filtered down her arms, sticking to her fingertips and ripping at the feathers until a few floated to the ground. Gasping, she tried to see through the sparks in her vision. It would be over soon, the pain was fleeting, and then she would be herself.

However, it was difficult to think through the pain. Her face ached as her beak melted back into a face. Sinuses expanding, white hot agony spread behind her eyes and down her throat.

She tilted her head back and let out an aching call that turned into a human moan. The magic released with a pop. Aisling sagged to the ground, her muscles feeling as though they'd turned to liquid.

Every evening she endured the same brutal transformation. Every morning she wondered if she could continue in such a manner for much longer. She dreaded every waking moment.

As always, warm woolen fabric draped over her shoulders. The quiet voice of a sluagh murmured, "Mistress, are you well?"

Not at all. She still couldn't breathe normally, but Darcy had a head start on her and she refused to miss anything he had to say to Bran. Pushing herself up, she rested her weight on her forearms and let her head hang. Brokenly, she responded, "I will be. I must get up. Help me."

"Was that...?" The sluagh paused before licking its beak and then reaching out its hands for her to take. "Was that the old Raven King?"

"It was."

"Why is he here?" It pulled her to her feet, ducking underneath her arm and tucking the fabric around her nude form. "Has he come to take back the throne?"

"Never," she spat. "He's back to see what trouble he might rouse before returning underneath whatever rock he crawled out from."

"I don't know, mistress." The sluagh started the shambling journey toward the stairs that led to the castle. "He's never returned before. Why is he here now?"

"We must hurry. Bran will turn back into a raven soon. We don't have much time." She looked at the horizon and prayed for the moon to rise slowly. She needed to speak to Bran, about more than just this.

They hurried up the stairwells, leaping over areas where the stones had completely fallen and crawling over pieces that were precariously hanging over the edge. Aisling held her breath in moments like this, still too weak to stand on her own and fully aware that the sluagh she leaned against was very fragile.

Finally, they made it to the castle.

"Mistress?" the sluagh asked, "are you well enough to stand on your own?"

Of course, the creature wouldn't want to see the man who had tormented their species for so many years. She straightened, holding her own weight and catching her balance.

She was strong enough to do this. Aisling tilted her chin up, squared her shoulders, and walked down the great hall that led to the throne room. Cobwebs covered the ceiling, and vines grew in from the shattered stained-glass windows. Her home had always been something similar to a dying creature. Broken at the edges, somehow still struggling to hold onto life.

Voices lifted from within the throne room, angry and raised in great shouts that didn't bode well. She was likely going to have to stop yet another battle. Aisling sighed, gathered her wits, and shoved open the door.

The two men stood on either side of the throne, their arms gesturing wildly as they shouted. She could only catch snippets of what they were saying.

"You have *no right* to return—" Bran growled.

Only to be interrupted by Darcy who threatened, "That is a borrowed throne boy—"

"Did you think I would let you—"

"*Let* me?"

"I will throw you out by your—"

"I'd like to see you try!"

Aisling stomped toward them and held up both her hands.

"Gentlemen!" Her shout cracked through the room and rose into the rafters.

They both paused and turned to stare.

Silence rang in her ears, and she let out a happy sigh. She'd gotten used to the peace of Underhill. Even the sluagh were careful to remain respectfully quiet in their every action. For the most part, the throne room was quiet and calm.

Until the two of these men had decided they needed to have a shouting match that made her skull ache. Aisling lifted her hands to her temples and rubbed the sensitive spots. "What are you doing here, Darcy?" she asked. "It's not to check in on us. We all know that's a veiled lie. You might as well get it over with."

"I so thoroughly enjoy annoying the Raven King. Perhaps he can feel for a few moments what I've lived through for a thousand years because he refused to take his rightful place as my heir."

"It wouldn't have changed anything," she replied with an angry huff. You still would have remained in the same role you hated so much. Out with it."

He bristled, some of the scales on his face lifting in anger. "Do you have to ruin everything, witch?"

"When it comes to you, yes. I don't trust you as far as I can throw you."

Bran stomped forward, his boots cracking against the floor. He reached forward to catch the drooping fabric revealing her shoulder and carefully slid it back into place. He touched a finger to her chin. "Clothing, Aisling?"

"Missing currently. I didn't want to clean up Darcy's blood tonight. There's far too many more important things for me to do."

"You might have left him to rot. I would have taken care of it on the morrow."

"My knight in shining armor."

Darcy made a gagging sound. "Are you two always like this? It's disgusting. You see each other for less than fifteen minutes a day. I'd think you would forget about each other."

"We see each other for less than fifteen minutes a day," Bran repeated, staring into her eyes with a heat she had missed dearly. "We've learned to make the best of those fifteen minutes whenever they are given to us."

She might have melted if she didn't disagree with him. They weren't making the most of the minutes, or perhaps not in the way she wanted to. There was always something to talk about. The sluagh were like children so she and Bran were rarely alone. She *missed* him.

Darcy let out a loud chuckle that blasted through her with the chill of a winter wind. "Say that one more time, Raven King, and I think she might just tear out your heart. Do you want to hear why I'm here before you turn into a bird, or would you rather leave me alone with your delicate wife?"

Aisling rolled her eyes and ignored him licking his lips like an animal. The man was all bluster with no action. He'd proven that when he put on a show for the Unseelie Queen and gotten them all into this mess.

"Out with it," she growled once more.

"Fine." Darcy strolled toward the throne and tossed himself down onto the black velvet. He hooked a leg over one of the arms, bouncing his foot with a familiarity that set her teeth on edge. "You've been summoned."

Bran scoffed. "I wasn't aware anyone could summon the Raven King. Who dares?"

"There is only one whom you answer to as the Raven King. Midir and his wife Etain lead the Wild Hunt this year, and they have called for you."

"They call for me?" Bran lifted a brow. "Why?"

"They'd like the Wild Hunt to come early this year. And why wouldn't they when a changeling child of such a high family with a good reputation was found to be lurking outside our kingdoms?" Darcy flicked his gaze to her. "All the Tuatha de Danann grow concerned."

Aisling growled, "What dangerous things changelings are. Forgotten faeries cursed to live in human lands because no one here wanted them. Whatever would they do if they were left to live their lives in peace?"

"Easy there, little witch. Those are fighting words, and trust me when I say you don't want to fight with Etain and Midir." Darcy swung his leg off the throne arm and leaned forward. "They've sent me with a message. They'll waive your curses for the length of time it takes for you to lead the Hunt. The sluagh are invaluable in sniffing out changelings, and they can take as many souls as they wish."

"They can halt our curse?" she asked.

"For a time, although it'll be easier with the new moon arriving. Your husband won't turn into a raven when the moonlight hits." Darcy shrugged. "You'll still turn into a swan. No one knows where that part of the curse came from, or who even controls it."

Aisling's mind raced to keep up with what he was saying. They could exist without the curse of the Raven King for a few nights. They could be together more than fifteen minutes, and all they had to do was give up the sluagh for a short time. Aisling and Bran would still be with them, still watch over the creatures she now thought of as her children, but they would have to free them upon the human realm.

The sluagh weren't faeries. In fact, they had all been human at some point in their life. Many secrets and myths existed about their kind, only one that she knew of remained true.

There were three ways to summon the sluagh to the human realm. The first was a war. The second was the Wild Hunt. The third was the crushing weight of sadness that humans frequently claimed was a person dying of a broken heart. In truth, it was the sluagh who stole them away to become bird-like monsters trapped for all eternity to hunt down human souls.

It was a sad existence, and not one she wanted to see thrust upon any others. No matter how much she desired to be with Bran for a few nights.

"Bran," she muttered, "we cannot release them."

"We aren't releasing them," he replied. "We'll be watching them every step of the way."

"I won't see changelings hunted down like animals."

"We don't have a choice." His voice was firm, his decision already made without asking her opinion. "Midir and Etain are known throughout all the Tuatha de Danann. They are fair and just. They won't harm the changelings, only bring them back to our land."

"Can you be certain of that?" She searched his gaze for the truth and found that he didn't know the answer to her question. His expression answered her question without a word. Bran couldn't be certain of their intent. No one could. They were still Tuatha de Danann, and every single one of their kind had their own agenda. The Unseelie and Seelie Fae could not control the beings who had created them.

Angrily, she turned toward Darcy and pointed at him. "Are you finished?"

He held up his hands. "I'm the messenger, darling. It's not my fault you were summoned. I even suggested that I would lead the sluagh to allow the lovebirds a little more time to settle in."

"Good." She gritted her teeth and felt power build in her palms. "Then begone from this place."

"You wouldn't dare banish me."

"Wouldn't I?" Aisling brought her hands together in a loud clap that shook the foundation of the castle. A small puff of smoke remained where Darcy had sat on Bran's throne.

The owner of said throne let out a soft chuckle and shook his head. "Did you really need to be so theatrical about it?"

"I don't want him anywhere near us."

How could he not care that Darcy was here? The man shouldn't be allowed to even look at another sluagh for the rest of his life, let alone all the other forgotten creatures here. Aisling's gaze caught on a shadow that moved along the wall.

The dearg-due woman was terrified out of her wits. Her eyes were bright red, fangs poking through her lips, and still she cowered against the wall. The previous Raven King had reminded the inhabitants of all the torment they had lived through in their human lives.

This was why they were banished. The Underfolk weren't faeries; they weren't human. Instead, they were magic-touched creatures who were warped so drastically from their original form that they couldn't remember who, or what, they were.

Her heart twisted.

"I won't use them," she whispered. "I can't do it, Bran. They're too important to me now."

"We won't be using them." He touched a finger to her chin, tilting her head so that she looked up at him. Even as she met his gaze, black feathers formed from the top of his head, falling to cover more and more of his body. "We're setting them free to be who they truly are."

Someone had said that about Aisling once. They'd said to leave her alone, let her stay in the witch's hut with no one to help her. That's who she was, a witch, and witches were always lonely.

She hadn't chosen the life of solitude and had tried for so many years to speak with someone, anyone, who would listen. They always said the same thing. "Witches choose to be alone. It's who they are."

Bran's form melted in front of her, his body shifting into that of a raven. He gave her one last look and brushed a gentle wing over her cheek before soaring up into the rafters and disappearing out a window at the peak of the castle.

If only she could go with him.

The temptation of sacrificing the sluagh, even for a few moments, just so that she could spend time with him burned through her. She hadn't been able to truly *be* with Bran in so long. She didn't care about the physical part, although she missed that as well. Aisling just wanted to hold him, to feel his heartbeat against hers without fear of him turning into a bird in her arms.

She sighed and turned on her heel. There would be time for such thoughts later. For now, she needed to calm their subjects who were terribly afraid.

The moon touched the horizon, casting a silvery glow over Underhill. The crumbling stone steps became gilded in its light, and the castle's windows cast a warm glow from deep within the ancient building.

Aisling touched a hand to a dullahan's shoulder. He'd asked for council with her, instead, he simply sat on a stone bench with her and watched the wind blow across the lake's surface.

He hadn't wanted much, he told her, just a few moments of peace. That was what she brought to her people, although she didn't understand how. They liked to be in her presence, particularly when alone.

The time had come for her to change back into the hated form that had changed her life. She didn't allow any but the sluagh to watch the transformation. She didn't want them to know how painful it was.

The dullahan stood, carefully cradling his head in his hands. They were strange, headless creatures, and she'd grown used to the way they always tucked their skull underneath their arms and spoke easily enough. One didn't look at the dullahan's headless bodies. She always looked them in the eyes because that was the only way to be polite.

"Thank you, mistress," he murmured, bowing before turning away from her.

"The pleasure was all mine."

He was already too far away to hear her. She'd found the dullahan's were, strangely enough, the shyest creatures in Underhill. They terrified humans every All Hallow's Eve, but returned to their home as quiet, unassuming men who were painfully embarrassed of their strange looks.

A shadow flew toward her on the horizon. She'd seen him flying closer, his form growing bigger until she'd known it was past time for her to ask the dullahan to leave. Though Bran was certainly understanding about much, he would want their alone time before she changed back into a swan.

She stood in front of the bench and waited for him to reach her. She pushed down her black silk skirt, which slithered down her form to pool on the stone ground. It was a shame she'd waste such splendor during the change.

Bran flew in front of her, changing midair, and landed on the shore of her lake. With the sun setting behind him, he looked like a curl of smoke from a flame. And she, the lover of smoldering coals.

His black wings folded into a dark cloak around his shoulders, crushed velvet covering his torso and black pants hugging his strong thighs. He smoothed a hand down his chest and gave her a devastating smile that made her breath catch.

"Hello, witch," he purred.

And just like that, she remembered what it felt like to fall so deeply in love that she could no longer see the light.

Bran stepped forward, and her eyes traveled up the regal length of his neck to the shadow just underneath his chiseled jaw. As if he read her mind, he cupped the back of her neck and pulled her forward.

She nestled into the hollow of his neck, where all her worries ceased to be, and blew out a breath. They were going to be fine as long as they were together.

"I missed you," he murmured, pressing his lips against the long column of her neck.

Preferring to tackle issues head on, she shook her head. "We cannot allow the Wild Hunt to use the sluagh. Not this year, Bran, they're far too fragile."

"We don't have a choice."

"There is *always* a choice. I refuse to believe this Tuatha de Danann have enough power to force us to do anything. You and I are royalty now. They have to ask us before they take any of our people, and we can reserve permission this year. They need time to build up their trust in us and in themselves." She pulled back to stare up into his dark eyes. "They're more than just monsters. I know it."

He tucked a strand of inky dark hair behind her ear. "I already told them we'd do it, Aisling. The sluagh have long been a part of the Wild Hunt, and I will not refuse anyone the use of them if I am there. More than that, I long to have a few moments alone with you again. More than just a stolen heartbeat."

"I do, too, but we can't put them through that."

Bran guided her back to the stone bench and settled her onto its cold surface. He joined her and held her hands carefully against his heartbeat. "It's not the sluagh that are bothering you. I know you too well, witch, or have you forgotten that we traveled across the Otherworld together? I've seen you fight bigger beasts than this."

He'd seen right through her, even when she hadn't realized a deeper worry burned in her stomach. "The changelings," she whispered.

"We have to hunt them down."

"We *don't*." She didn't understand why the faeries always treated their lost kindred like animals. They were still faeries. She should know — she was one of them.

Bran squeezed her hands. "I know this is hard for you to understand, Aisling. It must seem strange to you that we hunt down creatures who we've sent away. It's the royals responsibility to take those faeries, who should never have been sent to the human realm, and bring them home."

She'd spoken to other changelings before. They were terrified of the Wild Hunt, where great beings hunted down their kind and dragged them back to the faerie realm. The human world was forgiving of those who were different compared to the faerie realm, where they would either be torn to pieces or forced into slavery.

"We both know that's a lie," she replied. "Do you really think they're going to be welcomed home with open arms? What do you do with the changelings when you return?"

"They're given up to their respective courts, who return them to their rightful place in society. We can't change the opinions of faeries who only believe changelings are good for slavery."

"You lived in the Unseelie court. You've seen what your

own parents do to changelings returned to them. Bran" — she licked her lips — "the faeries aren't sent home. Not when there are so many more uses for creatures no one wants."

He stood abruptly and began to pace in front of her. "What do you want me to do? Stop the Wild Hunt? Even I'm not capable of that Aisling, you have to know that."

"I'm asking you to give the changelings a fighting chance! Don't send the sluagh out into the human realm where they will certainly find these creatures. Let them try and hide. It's the least we can do for them when it was *our* families who sent them out there on their own in the first place."

She could hardly breathe for fear he would deny her. The faeries would go, regardless of whether she traveled with them.

Underhill was far more frightening when she was here alone. She blew out a breath, watching the struggle in Bran's gaze, and knew what he was going to say long before he said it.

He dropped to his knees in front of her, pressing his forehead to her thighs and shaking his head. "You're asking too much. I don't know how to describe this to you in a way you'll understand, Aisling. I cannot say no to the Wild Hunt."

"It's been done before."

"*Never.* To do so is to go against the very fiber of who and what I am. I know you did not grow up here." He looked up, his eyes dark and tormented. "You are a wild flower they transplanted into a place where it could grow and form the most beautiful blooms I have ever seen. You are not truly faerie, and you cannot understand what it is you ask."

"*Please.*" She tried one more time, knowing he would never give in.

Bran compressed his lips into a firm, white line. "The best

I can offer is that you come with me. If we find any of the changelings first, they could have a place here before anyone else can claim them."

It wasn't ideal, but it was a start. The poor creatures would be condemned to a life of twilight for the rest of their lives. It was better than whatever the courts had planned for their own people.

She could only imagine the horrors faeries utilized to punish their own people. The clanking sound of chains filled her mind with ghoulish memories.

Bran straightened, and a mischievous light returned to his eyes. "Besides, what better opportunity than this to steal faeries from other courts? I think ours is far better."

"I think so, too."

He pulled her close to his side, and together they watched the sun set. A tingle of magic ran down her spine, and as always, she fought against it for as long as she could. Until the power of her curse ran through her body and crushed her very spirit.

CHAPTER 4
Entertaining The Courts

The sluagh maid tightened her corset with a brutal twist that left Aisling gasping. She placed a hand against her belly and glared at the other woman in the mirror.

"A little more delicately, if it pleases you," she growled.

The sluagh shook her head. "The whale bones have been passed from mistress to mistress. Each one is ensorcelled to help you through any battle. The Wild Hunt is dangerous, my queen. I would not have you harmed."

"I'm not helpless," she said with a snort. "I wasn't before I was your queen, and I'm certainly not now."

"I don't doubt that. A little bit of help goes a long way."

She was right, of course. That didn't mean Aisling needed to like it. She gritted her teeth and allowed the woman to continue strapping the midnight dress to her body like some form of ethereal armor. And in a way, it might have been. Aisling didn't know much about faerie armor.

They were going to meet the leaders of the Wild Hunt, the creatures who had decreed that her own people, changelings, were little more than animals to be hunted down in sport.

Aisling already hated them.

And perhaps that wasn't fair. They had their own reasons for enforcing such rules, but they were rules she simply could not agree with. She'd argued with Bran again. He said it was becoming far too frequent an argument for him to be comfortable, and she should let it rest. She couldn't change the world simply because she didn't agree with it. Faeries were a stubborn lot, and he was doing the best he could. They would save whatever changelings they could. In the meantime, she had to play along with the part.

"Trust me," he'd said, swinging her in a circle before putting her down again. "Like you did before. Remember the library? My sisters? This is my world, Aisling. I know what I'm doing. I wouldn't lead you wrong."

She couldn't help feeling as though he still might not understand this world as much as she did.

Or perhaps he didn't understand its people at all.

The sluagh behind her let out a soft sigh that sounded like the wind and then stilled. Was she breathing? Aisling counted her own breaths, waiting for the sluagh to inhale.

When she didn't, Aisling slowly turned around and stared into eyes she didn't recognize. The sluagh were all very similar. Their eyes were entirely black with no emotion in them left at all.

These eyes were blue as the sky on a clear morn. They stared back at her with no recognition, blinking slowly as if they were trying to bring her into focus.

"Who are you?" Aisling asked. "And why are you here?"

"I wanted to see you." The sluagh's beak was open but didn't move as though it were speaking. Instead, its mouth was left agape while another voice spoke from the empty chamber of its body. "I wanted to see the famed Raven Queen."

"I'll ask you again," Aisling repeated. "Who are you?"

"I think you know. You've known the moment you stepped foot in Underhill that something was different here. That there was more hidden in the depths of this world than the sluagh and their king were letting on."

Aisling swallowed and held her ground. "Carman."

The sluagh remained still as death. Its chest did not fall nor did its fingers twitch. Even the eyes remained locked in a forward direction. Perhaps the witch didn't have as much control as Aisling thought. A body was simple to direct like a puppet. This body had someone else in it, and she knew without a doubt that the sluagh fought for control.

She just had to distract the witch long enough to give the sluagh a fighting chance. Or perhaps, for a banishing spell to work.

"You have no right to be here," she said quietly. "You were banished long ago."

"Banished?" A laugh boomed from the open mouth of the sluagh. "Not quite, little girl, but you will learn my story soon enough. Haven't you heard? I'm the mother of all witches. I felt your soul enter this place, and I knew you would be my successor."

"I have no need of another crown."

"Every woman needs more than one crown, my dear. We were made to bear life, more than that, to bear witness to all wrongdoings. I decided long ago that if we were to carry the weight of the world, then we would also decide its punishment."

Aisling shook her head. "No one should be able to decide the fate of the world. *No one.*"

The laugh this time was edged in darkness. Aisling scooted back until her hand pressed against the mirror at her back. A spell danced in the edge of her mind. A simple one, one that she hadn't practiced in a long time, one that would free the sluagh. She'd give it a little more time to fight, but not much longer.

Carman could find out too much if she remained here.

"There will always be someone trying to decide the fate of the world. Do you think there isn't one out there already? I say, who better than you or I to make these decisions? We have lived the lives of these changelings." At Aisling's flinch, Carman gave a gleeful whoop. "You thought I didn't know? Aisling, child. I know everything about you."

"How do you know that? How do you know where we are going?"

"Everything that happens in Underhill happens because I approved it. Don't think for a moment that the magic running through this place isn't directly tied to me. I created Underhill. I am its lifeblood. They thought it would be my prison. Instead, it became my kingdom."

She'd had enough of this witch's poisonous words. "I have no use for you, nor do my people. Return to whatever hole you crawled out of."

"I just have one more question for you, witch. Why haven't you told the Raven King about me?"

Aisling hesitated because she didn't have a response to that question. She'd had ample opportunities. She should have told Bran the moment she found out, but simply…couldn't.

The sluagh's expression changed, slowly as if time had

nearly stopped. As Aisling watched, it raised a brow. "So you see, little girl? Perhaps you believe in my words after all."

Aisling slammed her hand flat on the mirror behind her, and the spell flew from her lips. "Begone, demon, for you are not wanted here. I banish you to return to your cage. You are *not welcome here.*"

Power flowed through the eyes in the center of her palms and slid into the glass. She knew, if she turned, that she would see Carman's true face. The woman was standing in front of her, not the sluagh.

Magic such as possession was dark. It should never be used, even by witches. She'd never even heard of someone breaking this law.

Bodies were sacred to pagan witches. It was a temple that each person should take care of, but witches would never force their conscious mind into another's. To violate a person in such a way... It was black magic of the worst kind.

Claws skidded down the hallway outside her room and screeched to a halt. Lorcan dashed into the room in a flurry of fur and bared teeth. "Where is she?" he shouted as he entered.

Carman was already gone. Only the lingering scent of absinthe betrayed that she'd been in the room at all.

Lorcan's ragged breath filled the room. He rushed to her side and plopped down next to her foot, sniffing the air until his whiskers bounced. "Was she here?"

"Yes," Aisling replied, still staring at the sluagh who had yet to reanimate itself. "She was. Talking through this sluagh."

He hissed. "Then they've been talking before. She wouldn't have the energy to actually possess something. This one has been listening to her whispers a little too closely for comfort."

"What do you suggest I do with it then?"

"Get rid of it. Carman is like an illness. She'll spread from this one to the next, whispering in their minds and turning them against you. It's what she did before, and she'll do it again."

Aisling finally stirred. She looked down at her dearest companion in shock. "Are you suggesting that I kill her?"

"You don't know the stories of Carman, I do." When Lorcan shivered, the fur along his spine rose. "She wasn't just a terror for the faerie realm. She wanted all the human witches to unite under her. She wanted them to bow down and become a new realm, a third world, living here, where they would be able to attack both the humans and the faeries. It was a dark time for our people."

"Did she succeed?" she asked. "Even the slightest amount? I can't imagine witches joining together. We're too solitary and our magic too volatile."

"Where do you think most of these sluagh came from?" He looked up at her, his luminous eyes reflecting the light behind her in a burning green. "She sent the horde out for the witches who wouldn't join her, and then she turned them into the wandering dead. These creatures were the first who either joined her or were forced to. Her power and control still lingers here. Never forget that."

Gods, she hated it here. Aisling wanted a simple life. Was that too much to ask?

She sighed and walked up to the sluagh who was still as stone. Placing a gentle hand on its beak, she whispered, "Your services here are no longer necessary. Thank you for all that you have done. Rest now."

It let out a quiet sound, like that of a peaceful end. Aisling let its lifeless body drop to the ground and tried to tell herself it was for the best. The sluagh wasn't even itself anymore. Carman had taken everything it used to be and twisted all the good into something bad.

Still. It didn't feel right to take its life away.

Lorcan rubbed against her leg. "Come away from this, Aisling. The others will take care of it for you."

"I don't want them to see it." They didn't deserve to stare at their fallen comrade and wonder what had happened. Aisling was a paragon to them. The kind woman who had fallen from the sky to teach them what it meant to be people again.

Instead, all she'd done was kill one of their own.

Lorcan dug his claws into her foot. "This wasn't a sluagh anymore, Aisling, at least not one of yours. Carman had already twisted its mind, and it would have done anything to follow its new mistress. Do *not* let this linger in your thoughts."

She nodded in response, she would let this stay with her. The death would remain as another black mark on her soul.

A soft sigh blew out from the cat at her feet. Lorcan knew her far too well and understood this wasn't something she'd wanted to do. Letting the souls go from the sluagh army was as good as a permanent death. They disappeared. Not to heaven, not to hell, nowhere at all. They were just gone.

There was no time to deliberate on these thoughts. She had to rush to meet Bran at the portal that had opened in the great hall. The Wild Hunt waited for them.

"I can't afford to be weak when I join the Hunt," she whispered. "I don't know how to banish these thoughts, either."

Lorcan touched a nose to her leg. "Let me help."

61

"You want to poke around in my head?" She hated the mere thought of it. Aisling had spent much of her life trying to forget memories, but she'd never allowed anyone to actually *take* them.

"The Wild Hunt admires strength above all else." Lorcan met her gaze with wide eyes. "You'll already have a hard time chasing down changelings."

She knew it was a bad situation when even the cat was worried about her. Sighing, she nodded. "Fine. Only for a small amount of time. I want these memories back."

He dug his claws farther into her foot, raising a bead of blood that rolled to her instep. "Earth, air, water, fire, hear this spell and my desire. This memory which haunts her mind, release her now for thus I bind."

Aisling waited until she felt the strange, sleepiness overtake her. A wisp of darkness poured out of her nose, the black fog swirling in the air and funneling toward Lorcan who guided it to her nightstand. He nudged it toward a small empty vial that used to hold her perfume. It funneled into the jar in a swirl of color and darkness. He picked up the stopper in his mouth and carefully closed it.

"There," he muttered. "Gone for now. I'll put it back where it belongs when you return from the Hunt."

She felt strangely foggy. Aisling touched a finger to her forehead and shook her head. "A memory spell?"

"Taken away with your consent. You know I'd never do that without permission."

She did, but what had he taken away? Her natural curiosity nearly got the better of her, Lorcan had always been good at reading her mind. He gave her a censoring look and muttered a spell that hid something in the room.

If Aisling really wanted to, she could have negated the spell. Becoming the Raven Queen had given her certain powers that made her far stronger than ever before. Her mind wasn't just a wealth of knowledge, but also a deep pool of ancient, wild magic that needed no words, no spells, just the will of a strong woman.

"The Wild Hunt awaits," Lorcan reminded her gently. "As does the Raven King."

Bran. The reason why they were going to this forsaken place where they would hunt down people just like herself.

Aisling set her teeth and strode forward. Though she was afraid, she refused to let it show. If they could help the changelings somehow, then this would be worth the trip. It had to be. There were far too many people who needed her.

She strode through the halls with sharp footsteps cracking in the empty palace. A few sluagh peeked out through doors and then quickly shut them as they saw the thunderous expression on her face.

Such reactions were precisely the reason why she shouldn't be leaving. There were still so many who needed to understand that she wasn't like the previous Raven King, and neither was Bran. They wanted to *help* the remaining sluagh return to their previous state, although they had yet to figure out how. No humans should be doomed to live among their ranks if they didn't wish to.

A memory wiggled in the back of her mind, the tails of it hanging like tattered curtains. It wasn't quite something she could pinpoint, a sick feeling the moment she thought of releasing the sluagh.

Her heart beat faster and her palms grew sweaty. What was the memory Lorcan had taken? What did it have to do with freeing the sluagh souls?

She rounded a corner, her thoughts distracting her, when a warm hand cupped her elbow and slowed her rapid speed.

"Easy, little witch," Bran said with a chuckle. "We don't have to charge to the Wild Hunt as though we are leading the entire troop."

"I don't want to do this, Bran."

"Neither do I." His eyes filled with shadows, dark and sad. She'd seen them many times since cursing him. He was plagued by demons she was only just discovering. Even now, he hadn't told her his story.

Not a single word had passed between them of his tale. She knew he had been the Raven King's successor his entire life. She knew he hadn't spoken with his family in a very long time, something his mother hated and his father ignored. There were siblings, but he didn't speak with them either.

Bran was a complicated man who held his cards close to his chest. Fifteen minutes a day wasn't enough to push him for further details.

She met his dark gaze and tried to understand what he was thinking. "Then why are we doing this?" she asked. "We're the king and queen of Underhill. Are we really at their beck and call?"

"Our titles aren't exactly...recognized." He rubbed the back of his neck. "Our subjects are the fallen fae, the ugliest that neither court recognizes, or the sluagh who are really human souls twisted by a faerie curse. It's not exactly a faerie court, Aisling."

"Then why even call us king and queen? Call us the lord and lady of misfits for all I care. They shouldn't give us the honor of the name if they don't intend to recognize it."

She bristled at the mere thought. Faeries had always considered themselves better than her. They looked down their nose at changelings, even ones like herself with infinite power and potential to be so much more than just a forgotten child.

At least, so she thought. She wanted to believe her abandonment could have been a misunderstood memory now that she'd met her sister. Elva had given her a considerable amount to think about. And it wasn't just that her family might not have wanted to give her up, but perhaps they also had missed her.

Bran snapped his fingers in front of her face. "Where'd you go, witch? We've got far too much to do for you to be wandering off in your mind."

She lashed out and grabbed his fingers, digging her nails into the soft skin at the back. "Don't snap your fingers at me like I'm an animal."

"Then don't forget I'm standing in front of you." He used her grip to tug her forward into his arms.

The soft sigh that brushed over her lips was one of pure pleasure. One of his hands slid over her shoulder and traced the bumps of her spine. He settled in the curve of her back, his thumb tracing a circle on her hip.

"There's so much more I'd rather be doing with you," he whispered, leaning down to press his lips to the hollow of her ear. "Instead, we're going to be fighting in the Wild Hunt."

"Who says we have to fight?"

"We always fight." His chuckle vibrated through her, an

answering call lifting from deep within her belly.

They argued about anything and everything they could, only because it felt right. She got a thrill every time she bested him. Likewise, he felt the same. They were competitive creatures by nature. The battles between them were long and hard-won.

The portal cracked behind them. Aisling glanced over his shoulder to see the strange spell that had opened in the middle of their home. It was an impossibly beautiful thing, unlike any magic she'd ever seen before.

Silvery like a fogged mirror, the magic was as tall as Bran and as wide as a doorway. It glistened as if it were liquid metal and shifted with ripples at the slightest breeze. The fluid magic solidified at the edges, creating a hardened shell like the frame of a painting.

It cracked again, a fissure breaking from one corner to the other.

"The portal won't stay open forever," she whispered. Her fingers dug harder into Bran's hand, pulling him closer to her side. Her heart beat faster at the mere thought of being in the presence of so many lethal fae.

"Are you ready to face them?"

"Never."

He tugged her closer, pressing her entire body against his, as if he might absorb her fear. She wished it were possible. He'd dealt with them his entire life, knew what to expect, how to act.

Aisling felt as though she were blind.

"I won't let them touch you," he muttered. "Don't you dare worry about that. They won't lay a finger on you. You're no longer a changeling. You're the queen of the Underfolk and ruler of the mighty sluagh. You are my second in command. They wouldn't dare lift a hand to you."

He thought she was worried about herself? Aisling let out a soft snort. "I can take care of myself, Bran."

"I know you can. Sometimes, you shouldn't have to." He pulled back, keeping ahold of her hand. "Let's join the Wild Hunt, my queen."

She followed for the promise of warmth and happiness at his side, regardless of where they were. He would protect her, he would believe in her, but most importantly, Bran would never think she was something other than what she was.

They stepped to the portal and, as one, moved through the fluid. She felt the pull of magic as it yanked on her clothing. It touched her throat, and she understood the unspoken threat. It didn't want her there. It tasted the changeling on her skin while whispering a promise that she wasn't welcome, that she would remain alone for the rest of her existence.

A sharp tug on her hand pulled her through the magic, and she stumbled out. Bran caught her, steadying her against his side before he ran a hand down her hair.

He pulled her close for a seemingly romantic moment, then whispered in her ear, "Did you feel that?"

She nodded into his shoulder. There would be faeries staring at them. All the courts wanted to see the new Raven King and his queen. Already, she and Bran were putting on a show.

He let out a soft growl. "So the games began before we even arrived. Keep your wits about you, witch, and don't stray from my side."

"And if I do?"

"I'll be honest, sweetheart. I have no idea what they want from us. This isn't just about the Wild Hunt, it's something far more than that. Everyone wants to show how powerful they are. There's war brewing on the horizon again. I don't know if that's between courts or... within. Stay close to me and don't make any deals with faeries you don't know."

As if she would know any of the faeries here. She'd only met a few lesser fae, boggarts and hobgoblins that wanted to help her with her magic in return for a first-born child. Tuatha de Danann and high fae were far above her rank as a changeling witch.

She held her breath and stood on her own. Aisling squeezed her eyes shut for a moment to steel herself for what she would see, then she turned to face the hordes of faeries that awaited them.

Her eyes were assaulted with colors, textures, and glimmering creatures that all seemed impossible. They filled the clearing to the brim, almost rivaling the stars in their glamorous forms. The Wild Hunt called upon only the best of each court. Aisling now knew what that meant.

The Seelie faeries were bright and blindingly beautiful. Their hair was the color of gold, their skin alabaster. Some were as dark as night, their eyes gleaming like moonlight on her lake, others were pearlescent, glowing beings. Each more beautiful than the last.

The Unseelie faeries were dark, their features warped by animalistic qualities. Feathers were common among those who had answered their brethren's request. Some wore scales like a second skin. It was the giants far in the distance, seated at overly large thrones they had brought with them, that caught her attention.

"Bran," she whispered, "your family is here."

His expression darkened. "Of course, they are. Even if mother and father cannot hunt with the rest of us, they would want to see the spoils. Blood calls to them. My siblings will hunt for my family, and they'll likely kill a few of the changelings, only to claim it an accident."

Aisling steeled herself for another meeting with the Unseelie Queen. Bran was affected by the Raven King's curse and therefore handsomely decorated in raven feathers. But his parents and the rest of his family?

She shuddered.

They were part human, part spider. Neither of his parents wore clothing. His mother preferred to drape the long, tangled strands of her hair over her chest. She reclined far away, her pale skin meeting the bloated belly of the spider seamlessly. Even from this distance, Aisling could hear the scratching of her legs as they shifted with her excitement.

"All right," she said. "Let's go see them."

"See them? I have no intention of speaking with my family. Come with me. There's someone I'd much rather introduce you to." He held out an arm for her to take and smiled. "I'm not throwing you to the wolves just yet, witch."

There were few people here she could guess he wanted her to meet. Elva wouldn't be here since she was still on an island training to become stronger. Even her own family would likely be safely tucked away in their Seelie homes. Who else could there be?

Curiosity coursed through her veins. She tucked her hand into the crook of his elbow and grinned. "Lead away, Raven

King. You've intrigued me."

"As always."

He drew her through the crowd, pausing only a few times to make introductions. She didn't remember the names, or even the faces, of the faeries around them. It didn't matter in the end. Aisling wouldn't see them again any time soon, nor did she really care to allow them space in her mind. They cared not for her. She wouldn't care for them.

Finally, he drew her through the crowd and deep into the heart of the Seelie court where no Unseelie would go. Aisling felt thoroughly out of place in their beautiful number.

Bran glanced down at her and grinned. "What is it, Aisling?"

"Hm?"

"I don't think I've ever seen you look so uncomfortable before."

She stared at a woman who passed by them. She wore no clothing. She didn't have to. Her entire body glowed so brightly that no one would have seen the skin underneath it. The ephemeral creature was one she'd never even *heard* of before. Surely, there must be a legend of something like her?

"Aisling," Bran said again, another laugh bursting forth from his chest. "You have to stop staring at them."

"It's impossible not to stare."

"You're one of them." When she finally turned back to him, Bran touched a finger to her chin and tilted her head up. "Even among their ranks, you still stand out."

"Hardly." She felt like a weed in a garden of perfect roses. No one would ever notice her when there was so much beauty surrounding her. Oddly enough, it eased her mind. She didn't want to be noticed. Here was the best place to hide.

"You are a black orchid in a bed of a hundred white roses." He reached down, lifted her hand, and pressed it against her lips. "My poisonous flower."

"Stop being so romantic."

"You don't like it?"

She did. Too much.

Aisling was uncomfortably aware they had been together in human form for longer now than they had in months. He was right here, touching her, and she couldn't think.

Even as he guided her through the crowd, his warm palm grazed her back constantly. Sparks of energy traveled from his fingertips through her spine until she couldn't even think straight. She wanted him. More than she'd ever wanted anything in her life.

Bran let out a ragged breath. "Later, my dear Raven Queen. Now, I want to introduce you to the only person I've ever called 'friend.'"

That caught her interest. Aisling raised a brow. "Who might that be?"

"Surprised you, have I?"

"I didn't think you were capable of friendship."

"Most people are far beneath me for such a trivial thing but…he's different. *She's* different."

"A couple then? I wouldn't have thought you to be interested in such things." Aisling's chest burned at the thought. She wanted him to desire a relationship, a family, a place to call home. That was a conversation for another time.

He seemed to think so as well. His brows drew down for a moment before he shook his head. "Allow me to introduce you to Eamonn, King of the Seelie Fae, and his lovely wife, Sorcha."

The woman's name felt familiar, as if a ghost had passed through her mind. Aisling turned around and stared at the couple who had walked up behind her.

The man was incredibly handsome in a dangerous way. His jaw was strong, his hair wheat-colored and shaved on either side. He'd braided it into a long tail that swung to his waist. For a king, he was modestly dressed. A simple tunic and trousers adorned his body. A sword hung at his hip.

It was the woman who captured her attention. Hair like fire, freckles dotting her face, a proud expression and vivid green eyes that Aisling remembered all so well.

A grin spread over her face, and she shook her head with glee. "Midwife? I hadn't thought you'd catch yourself a king."

The calm expression on the redhead's face changed into that of complete shock. Her jaw dropped open, and her eyes widened. A barking laugh split her lips, and she blurted, "Witch? Is that you?"

Bran narrowed his eyes, and his hand on her arm tightened. "You know each other?"

"Know each other?" the Seelie Queen said with another laugh. "She's the only reason I'm here. When I was trying to capture the attention of the fae to bring me back, a plan which didn't work in the slightest, your witch was the one who helped me. I never thought *you'd* come here, though! You seemed so against it."

Aisling shrugged. "Neither did I. This wasn't where I wanted to end up, but apparently it's where my fate rested."

Eamonn wrapped a meaty arm around Sorcha's shoulder and stared at Aisling with an intense, blue gaze. "Who are you?" His bright blue eyes trailed down her body, and Aisling had the distinct feeling she was being weighed and measured. "I'm afraid I don't know this story."

Aisling opened her mouth to respond, hesitating when Sorcha beat her to it. "It's not a story I thought I'd ever have to tell you. When you were ignoring my existence and stuck in your foolish war with your brother, I was trying to find a way back to the faerie realm. This woman helped me, although I'm afraid I've forgotten your name already."

Unsurprising, considering the life story that Sorcha hinted at. Aisling had found herself intrigued by this human woman's life. When she'd helped her through the portal, she had sensed there was something more to her. Not quite faerie, certainly not human. Perhaps, if she was nice enough, Sorcha would tell her the story in its entirety.

Shaking her head to clear the thoughts, she smiled at the couple before her. "Aisling. And no longer just a witch, I'm afraid. My true name is no longer spoken. I was Seelie Fae. Now, I am the Raven Queen alongside Bran."

Eamonn's expression darkened as he cast a look at Bran that would have seared flesh from bone if possible. "Your doing, I presume?"

"Not everything is my fault," Bran responded with a laugh. He held up his hands. "She chose this life. I gave her an out. It's not my fault if the woman is a glutton for pain."

Aisling elbowed him. "Hardly. You wouldn't have been able to rule the sluagh without me, and I certainly have no interest in remaining in the Seelie court now that I've been found out."

"Found out?" Eamonn repeated. "How so?"

"I was a changeling." The words still stung. She didn't know how to explain it in a way that didn't make her seem lesser in their eyes. The Seelie Court in particular liked the age-old practice of sending away their "ugly" children so they wouldn't have to look upon them. The custom made her heart burn with anger. They had no right to send their children away. No one should hate their children that much, or value beauty over their own blood.

Surprisingly, the Seelie King made a disgusted face and squeezed his wife's shoulder. "We're working on changing the old ways, but it's not as easy. Changing a millennia of traditions takes nearly as much time. I apologize that you've experienced such horrible things. We can't erase those memories. I do hope, at the very least, someone has tried to rectify the issue."

"I haven't seen my family if that's what you're asking."

Bran shifted next to her. The nervous twitch made her pause, but it was the Seelie King who narrowed his gaze on him.

Eamonn grunted. "Something you want to share, Bran?"

"I don't appreciate the tone, Eamonn," he replied.

"You just look like you've been up to something I wouldn't approve of. I know that expression."

"I'm a king now. A little more respect is in order."

"Or what?" The Seelie King took his arm back from his wife and straightened. "I've bested you before."

"When we were children. I don't remember you besting me since our voices deepened."

Sorcha stuck out an arm and laughed. "I'm glad the two of you haven't changed at all. Neither of you is the better warrior. You both fight very differently. Stop arguing, you fools." She winked at Aisling. "Who is your family, if you don't mind me asking?"

"Ilumin and his wife. My sister is Elva, although she has left the Seelie Court and sought training with Scathach and her women." An icy chill fell between the two couples. Aisling frowned and looked up at Bran whose face had turned white. She licked her lips. "I take it that wasn't the right thing to say?"

Eamonn grunted. "It certainly lowers my opinion of a man I thought had better judgement."

"You're back to making snap decisions about people without assessing the situation, I see," Bran growled in return. His hands curled into fists, and Aisling saw the shadow of feathers forming.

"Should I not when you chose the *sister* of the woman you—" He paused, his eyes flicking to Aisling.

So, he was worried about what she did and did not know. As though Bran had chosen her simply because she had a connection with Elva.

Aisling had known of Bran's fascination with her sister. Their relationship was complicated, and yet not something she couldn't ignore. People had history, gods knew she did, and Bran had made it perfectly clear that his past would remain in the past.

They might not understand it, but Aisling always had.

She met the Seelie King's gaze without flinching. "I know of Elva and Bran's history. The past is something we must forgive if we wish to move forward in our lives."

The darkness in his eyes cleared like clouds drifting away to reveal a clear blue sky. "Wise words from a witch."

"It's my experience that most things a witch says are wise."

"Perhaps I haven't been listening to them correctly then."

Bran's hand settled on her back, and Aisling felt as though she had somehow won a battle. The tension in the air eased. Eamonn and Bran drifted into a conversation about their courts, how Bran was feeling as a king, how Eamonn was handling his own people.

She cared little for their conversation. Politics always bored her. Aisling wasn't cut out to be a queen like that. She wanted to talk about her people or how these two had ended up together when they were clearly such different people.

Most of all, she wanted to understand how this strange red-headed creature in front of her had become a queen.

Sorcha shifted and met Aisling's stare. "You have questions for me?"

"Mind reader, are we?"

"Something of the sort." Sorcha held out her hand and took Aisling's. "We're very similar, you and I. Two beings who aren't quite faerie any more, but aren't so far from it either. You'll find the courts are much more welcoming than you would imagine."

"I hope so."

Aisling looked out over the crowd and doubted they would accept her the same as Sorcha. She remembered the way the feisty midwife had been. There had been something commanding about her even back then. Now, she had fit into the role of queen with ease.

The mass of faeries around her wouldn't accept one they had already tossed aside so easily. Aisling had been unwanted the moment she'd been brought into this world. Until she had accepted witchcraft, and suddenly everyone wanted a spell.

What did they see when they looked at her? A tattooed freak who now controlled the most dangerous army the faeries had? Or did they see something to pity?

She shivered, her mind flitting between the possibilities until it was almost too much for her to bear.

Sorcha squeezed Aisling's hand and let it drop. "You'll get used to the stares and the scrutiny. Perhaps the best advice I can give you is not to care what they think. You're a queen, and no one can take that away from you now."

"Did they try to take it away from you?"

"They tried for only a heartbeat and then realized their fault. Eamonn and I have done much to change the Seelie court, but there will always be more that we cannot change with speed. Generations of darkness have bred within both faerie ranks. We do what we can to ease the pain of those who have been harmed by such darkness."

It felt like a lesson as well as a promise. For once in her life, Aisling actually believed a faerie royal.

She frowned then nodded firmly. It was a promise she hoped to give to her own people as well. They would get through the Wild Hunt first, then she would make certain the sluagh and the other faeries under her care felt the same protection.

A sick feeling in her stomach warned that she might not be able to.

CHAPTER 5

THE WILD HUNT

Bran set his eyes on the armies of faeries before him, marveling at the movement that mimicked ocean waves. How long had it been since he'd been in an army? Centuries?

Unseelie faeries were no stranger to war. They'd all fought amongst each other more than they needed to. He grew up with a sword in his hand and a knife in his belt. Those were the conditions his young mind grew with. This shouldn't bother him as much as it did.

He stared at all these faeries, bloodthirst running through their veins, as they prepared to hunt down the same kind of woman that he'd fallen in love with. It didn't feel right anymore. Not just for her, for the creatures he was preparing to loose as well.

His gaze found her, not far from him in the crowd and backing away with the rest as he prepared to summon the sluagh.

The wind pushed her dark hair in front of her eyes, a strand catching on her nose and obscuring her eyes from his vision. Tattoos trailed up her arms, the ogham marking her as the

Raven Queen.

Every time he saw them, heat trailed down his spine. It coiled at his hips and spread throughout his body like a beast he couldn't recognize. He adored those marks because they told the world what he couldn't yet.

Aisling was, and forever would be, *his*.

A wave of restlessness washed through the faeries watching him. They wanted the Wild Hunt to begin. They desired to see the fog-like body of the sluagh army, to unleash it upon the world and hunt down all the creatures they deemed unworthy.

He couldn't back down now. He'd already agreed to this, no matter how much it pained him to do so.

Letting out a soft breath, Bran tilted back his head and let magic rush through his body.

The Raven King's power was still foreign to him. He'd lived with something similar most of his life, the rush of flight, the rustle of feathers, the hum of ancient knowledge whispering in his ear, but it was amplified now by the thousands. He became more than just Bran, hundreds of souls who had been here before him, each darker and more dangerous than the last.

He was thirsty for blood, ached for more power, desired that which he could not have. The power of the Raven King was more than just dark. It was a consuming madness.

A familiar, cool wind brushed against his skin. The madness was soothed in the wake of Aisling's magic as it always had been. Just a simple touch from her, and it all disappeared.

He understood why so many of his successors had spent their entire lives searching for their consort. She was a rare beauty that made him so much stronger just by existing. He simply wished he understood how.

With the madness abating for a moment, Bran brought his hands forward. The shadow of feathers stood out on his fingers. They remained underneath the skin, waiting for a moment when he would release them and become the bird once more.

"Sluagh," he called out. "I summon you to my side. The Wild Hunt awaits."

A deep rumble shook the ground. They rose from underneath the surface, hundreds of blackened souls, now nothing more than mist. They wouldn't return to their bird-like forms until they had found prey upon which they could feast, or until they returned to Underhill with Bran and Aisling.

The black mist gathered at his feet, swirling in eddies all around him. He looked down into the shifting mass and tried to pick out faces he might recognize. No matter what, they did not reveal themselves.

Was this what it was like to be king? Or was he little more than a fraud?

The dark mist parted as a graceful woman stepped through the mass. His breath caught as Aisling's silk gown rippled through the darkness. Without fear, she walked to his side and reached out a hand.

"Well done," she said quietly, as if even loud words might provoke him. "Our army has arrived."

Bran glanced up at the other faeries and felt the darkness in the corners of his mind flare its wings. They were all afraid of him. Even the Unseelie stared with horror in their eyes, pulling back when he made eye contact.

He wasn't a king. The glorified title was an insult to the

power he now controlled. And he understood why they were so afraid.

Bran had never been particularly responsible. He was known as the prince who made trouble knowingly. He wanted to annoy people, to put them in situations where they had to react poorly. He knew too many secrets because of his history, and they wanted him to disappear. Not to gain even more power.

Anger boiled his blood until they all turned a shade of red.

"Bran," Aisling murmured again. Her cool hand slid over his bicep, down his forearm, and closed around his clenched fist. "I don't know what's going through your head, I need you to remain calm. You cannot abandon me to all these faeries' mercy."

That was right. He wasn't here because of the Wild Hunt. He was here to take care of her.

The anger disappeared again, settling beneath the surface of his mind. The mere thought of her worried or uncomfortable banished all the dark thoughts for good.

He blew out a breath. "I'm still here."

"Barely," she replied with a snort. "That was a close one, Raven King."

He wouldn't tell her how close. That would only make her even more nervous. Bran loosened his fist to interlock their fingers. "Never so close that you couldn't pull me back."

"Don't put that on me, Bran. I won't always be here to help you."

He saw the struggle in her gaze, but refused to believe her words. There wasn't anyone who could take her from him. He would make certain of that.

"Come," he said quietly, tugging her toward their mounts. "The Wild Hunt must begin. We've stalled them long enough, and the sluagh grow hungry."

He brought her to their beasts, strange creatures shaking in excitement. Hanging pieces of flesh decorated the horse's bones, much of their previous form had long since rotted away. They weren't a named species and rare even in the faerie world. In Underhill, they had found a place to flourish.

A glowing red eye rotated to watch them approach. Aisling avoided eye contact with them, but Bran enjoyed meeting their strange gaze. They were his favorite creatures in Underhill. Misunderstood, odd, still alive no matter how much life had tried to ruin them.

He held out his hand for her to take. He gently helped Aisling up onto its back, then slid his fingers down her spine and stroked a hand down either side of her dress, making certain she looked the part of queen.

A firm pat to her leg marked her as ready. "I'll be by your side the entire time," he advised. "Keep your eyes forward and don't watch anything that becomes too hard to watch."

"Remember your promise," she replied. "If there are any…"

"I will do whatever I can. I don't break my promises to you, Aisling." He let the unspoken words hang in the air between them. He might not break a promise to her, but he damned well would for the rest of them. She was more important than the faeries here, so even though he couldn't stop the Wild Hunt entirely, he refused to put her in any more danger.

Her eyes stared into his, and he marveled at her composure. Her fear had been there for only a moment before she hid it behind a well of strength so deep he was certain he'd never see the end of it.

Patting her leg once more, he then turned and lifted himself up onto his own mount. The strange beast shied underneath his movement, huffing out a breath then stamping its foot on the ground.

He couldn't see the leaders of the Wild Hunt. They would be at the front of the army, those who would ride through the skies as a symbol more than a soldier who would actually do the hunting. They would enjoy the spoils at the end when everyone else had already done most of the work.

Bran and Aisling were in the middle of the pack. His sluagh would find the changelings and any other human souls they desired. Humans were a small price to pay to find all those who had escaped the faeries.

Changelings were wrong. No faerie should end up stuck in the human world, and any family who abandoned their child knew better than to leave them with those the faeries deemed "lesser." Humans didn't know how to raise their kind right.

Though Aisling didn't agree with him, Bran had been raised this way. Faeries in close contact with humans meddled. It was in their blood to do so. They couldn't be trusted with such fragile creatures as humans.

A quiet mutter started in the crowd and, as one, the mounts they rode rushed forward. A portal opened in the distance. The horses knew where to go. They could smell the battle on the breath of the faeries, could see the portal was the next obstacle. Hooves pounded the ground like a drumbeat in his ears.

Black mist congealed around him and Aisling, protecting them from any harm that might come. The shadowy form of the sluagh coiled around his throat, then burst forward in a fluid thrust as they struck the portal like hitting water after leaping from a cliff edge.

He let out a whooping call and then burst free into the human realm.

Whipping around, he turned so he could watch Aisling's expression as she rode with the Wild Hunt the first time. She stared at the clouds beneath them with shock clear on her face, then her eyes turned toward the stars that burned like a thousand candles. Her expression softened into awe, the beauty he had known she would appreciate overwhelming her.

Gods, he loved to put that expression on her face. And she wore it often now. Underhill was so very different from the human realm where she had spent her entire life. There were more wonders that he could still show her, but didn't want to overwhelm her too fast.

They had time. They had all the time in the world.

The black mist surrounding him suddenly changed. The air crackled with energy, and he knew they had found their first changeling. The entire army surged forward as one, horses neighing, battle cries striking the air like a raised fist.

He hadn't thought it would feel like this. The emotions of the sluagh bled through his connection, and suddenly he felt everything they did. The changelings were an abomination that needed to be hunted, and the humans were even worse.

He could feel hundreds of lost souls dotted across the rolling green plains beneath them. Every soul called out to him. The dying light of their happiness meant they were food for the sluagh. They could be devoured, added to the collective, and then they would be happy.

A small part of him marveled at how convinced the sluagh, and therefore himself, were in their conviction the souls would be happier. If only they could feed off of the hurt and anger that made these humans upset, then they wouldn't remember...or perhaps they just wouldn't be able to feel such emotions again.

He ached to show them what life could be like in Underhill. Sure, their bodies would change into monstrous beings, yet, they wouldn't care anymore. No part of their previous life would affect their happiness with the sluagh.

"Bran," the melodic voice called out to him, whispering against the gale of human souls. "Bran, come back to me."

Again, she pulled him from madness back to her side.

Bran shook himself, horrified at the direction his thoughts had turned. He had known the Wild Hunt would be dangerous. That he might think things that weren't his own thoughts. He didn't know it would feel like this.

No wonder so many of the Raven King's had lost their mind. This was impossible to fight against without his anchor.

He reached out for her, holding out a hand as they surged through the sky and plummeted toward the land. Her cool fingers grasped his, and together they made their way to the hunt.

Reaching deep into the powers of the Raven King, he coiled his grip around the sluagh one last time before he unleashed them onto the world. "I release you," he cried out. "Feast upon the souls you deem fitting and find the changelings for us. We shall bring them home where they belong."

In his mind, the sluagh cried out in glee. They fled from his side, parting into many waves of darkness that flowed over the land and disappeared from view.

The faerie bands split up. Some even mixed Seelie and Unseelie, past grievances forgotten in the adrenaline surging through their veins.

He hung back, waiting to see who would pair up before he nodded to a family group he recognized. It was mostly Unseelie, faeries he knew and trusted, with a few Seelie fae he didn't know. Bran trusted the other's opinions, however, and they were a family whose children stretched between both courts.

"We go with them," he said, nudging Aisling's horse in their direction.

"Any particular reason why?" she asked.

Not really, he knew she wanted an answer to ease her nerves. "None of them are considered royal. They're here to drink more than to hunt, and they used to be friends of mine. They'll be a little more respectful than some of the faeries we might pair with."

"Enough said."

They rode toward the others, and Bran winced as the stark differences between them stood out. These faeries, even the Unseelie, were pristine in their clothing. Not a single moth-eaten hole or frayed edge marred their opulence. Their steeds were a sight to behold, well-groomed and perfectly bred.

In comparison, he and Aisling were shabby and gray, strange creatures out of a haunted home rather than royalty. No wonder the others didn't respect them.

An Unseelie looked up, scales covering one half of his face, and grinned. "Bran! I didn't think you'd be gracing us with your presence tonight. I thought you far more likely to join the royals."

"The apple doesn't fall far from the tree," he grunted in response. "I've never been one to enjoy the company of royalty."

The faeries let it slide, taking it that Bran wasn't hiding anything. He shouldn't feel guilty about that, but the reality was that Aisling couldn't be with the other faeries. Not just yet.

She was too nervous, and it showed. The Unseelie found weakness in others as a challenge. They would tear an open wound in her soul until it was raw and bleeding. While the Seelie found something to exploit until she was no longer useful and then would eventually crush her underneath their heel. Either option wasn't something he was willing to watch her go through.

The snake-like Unseelie cast his attention to Aisling and grinned. Fangs poked his bottom lip. "And who's this? Haven't seen her face before, and here I was thinking I knew all of Bran's conquests."

Aisling arched a brow. "All of them?"

"Well, it's not like there were that many. A private person, Bran is. He's far more likely to take off and disappear for centuries rather than bring a lady back to his family."

"Ah, that would be why then."

The faerie tilted his head in curiosity. "Explain."

Aisling grinned, the expression feral and foreboding. "I'm no lady."

A surge of pride seared Bran to the bone. He tilted his head back and let out a booming laugh that made a few of the faeries flinch. It took everything he had not to drag her across the rotting horse and feel her lips against his.

Instead, he gestured at her pridefully. "There you have it. I wouldn't bring a lady home. Such a rose would wilt in the darkness of Underhill."

The scaled faerie bowed on his horse. "It's an honor to meet you then, mistress. May you rule as the Raven Queen for many more days to come."

Although Aisling might shrug off such a compliment, Bran knew what it was. The faerie had given her a significant honor. Very few would wish another to remain on a throne. The Tuatha de Danann were bloodthirsty creatures, always looking for the next way to grab their own power.

He'd essentially told Aisling she was the better choice for the position. Very few would admit something like that.

Cold magic touched his neck, drifting down between his shoulder blades and spreading icy fingers through his body. The sluagh had found a changeling nearby. They whispered in his ear how much they wanted to destroy it. How such a creature deserved to be punished for lingering in the human realm, when such a life was wrong...wrong...*wrong.*

"Go ahead of us," he heard Aisling say. "I'd like a few minutes alone with him before we hunt."

"What a woman," someone called out, laughter bubbling like a brook. "Enjoy yourself Bran, but not too long. All the good ones will be taken!"

He held himself in place as the others raced away, though every fiber of his being brayed that he should hunt with them. He wanted to find the changeling, to tear it limb from limb, to make it bleed so much that the metallic taste coated his tongue....

This wasn't him. These weren't thoughts that had ever gone through his mind before.

Dark power tangled in his mind like a spider weaving a web. He was trapped in the shadows, his mind fracturing beyond hope of repair. Until he felt the cool touch of Aisling's hand on his brow and heard her voice whisper in his ear.

"Where is the changeling, Bran?" She was more than just Aisling, more than just a witch. She was his queen, his everything, his all. "Find it and bring it to me."

Find the changeling. That was everything he wanted. Every fiber of his being vibrated with the need to do just that.

The horse between his legs seemed to know what he wanted. When the beast surged forward, Bran gathered the reins tight.

He could feel the frantic heartbeat of the changeling as it realized it was being hunted. The creature knew exactly what tonight was, and yet it still remained outdoors. What a foolish thing it was. Did it not know the Raven King hunted on this night? That the sluagh thirsted for its blood?

Branches scratched at Bran's cheeks. He and his queen raced through the underbrush, flushing out a changeling who took flight. It ran on human legs, having not been taught how to shift its shape so it could fly away to safety.

His blood boiled beneath the surface of his skin, and suddenly all the power inside him burst free. Feathers flowed over his hands, then shifted into shadows that consumed. Bran melted into the host of the sluagh and became one of them, racing at the forefront of their mass.

The branches in front of him parted, and he saw the changeling as it ran. Fabric fluttered behind as it darted through a clearing.

Foolish, again. Didn't it know he could see it perfectly

now? That it would take so little for him to grab it?

He materialized in the center of the clearing, dark magic billowing out from around him. It burned behind his eyes, and he wondered if they were completely black as well.

The changeling almost ran into him. It fell to its knees as it tried to stop, whimpering and crying out for mercy. It would find none from him. Not tonight, when the hunt ran in his veins and the sluagh howled in his mind. This was a night for feasting, not for sparing lives.

"Stop!" A shout rang through the clearing, chased by the thundering of hooves.

He looked up and saw a banshee riding toward him. Bran shook his head. No, not a banshee. A beautiful woman with magic sparking on her fingertips and a dead steed between her legs.

His power-crazed mind hardly recognized her, but a quiet voice inside him whispered that she was everything he'd dreamed of. That she had fought long and hard to be by his side. That she was the only person in the world who could stay his hand with a single word.

So he let her. Bran hesitated, though it made every inch of him ache.

She thundered up to his side and dismounted with a natural grace that spoke of strength. Fluid and calm, the woman stepped to his side and placed a hand against his arm. Her dark eyes flashed. "This one is mine, remember?"

Though he didn't want to let the changeling go so easily, he inclined his head. What would this woman do? Would she tear the shivering creature to bits with her bare hands? A flash of heat made him shake.

The woman didn't do anything as he thought she might. Instead, she knelt at the side of the changeling and reached out a pale, long-fingered hand. "You're safe now," she murmured. "I know the Wild Hunt is a terrifying night. You shouldn't be outside."

"There's nowhere else to go," it spat, still shaking in fear. "What else would I do? No one would let me into their homes to pass the dangers."

"I cannot save you the fate of a changeling caught on the Wild Hunt, instead, I will offer you a choice. You can go with the other hunters, or you can come to my kingdom."

"Your kingdom?" The changeling looked her up and down. "What's your kingdom?"

"Underhill, where the sluagh live and all the rest of the Underfolk."

"You're the Raven Queen?" It looked up and caught Bran's gaze, then blanched when Bran bared his teeth in a feral grin. "And the Raven King?"

The woman chuckled. "It's not as bad as you might think."

Aisling. The voice whispered through the darkness and reached into the depths of his mind. He knew her name. Not just that, he knew who she was.

And just like that, the curtain of darkness parted. Bran shook himself, embarrassed that he'd allowed himself to fall so far into the tantalizing power of the Raven King. It wasn't right for him to scare a creature like this.

He looked at the changeling now, really looked, and felt guilt lance through his body as sharp as a spear. The creature was little more than an elderly man. His body was thin and wiry, sagging flesh loose from recent starvation. A shame, because his face was that of an attractive man.

Faerie, he reminded himself. This was not a human, although he looked particularly convincing. This was a faerie who had been cast aside by his family.

"How long have you been here?" Bran asked, kneeling as well. "You don't have the look of a child."

"I was a child when they first left me here," the changeling growled. "I'm older now."

"Old enough to have evaded the Wild Hunt for many years. Why did you allow yourself to be captured now?"

Aisling hissed out a breath. "Bran."

The changeling lifted his hand. "It's fine, mistress. He's right. I've managed well on my own for many years, and I'm tired of running. Tired of living with humans and watching their ways eat away at my flesh. I'm sick, and I'm dying. I'd like to return home now."

Bran chewed his lip. The changeling's thought process was understandable, but that wasn't quite how it had worked. By remaining for so long, whether they were aware of their bloodline or not, the faerie had broken numerous faerie laws. Faeries were not allowed in the human realm, regardless of who brought them there. His return to the faerie realm would not be with any sense of welcome, only with punishment.

Perhaps the changeling knew that, though. Their gazes met, and Bran saw understanding in the male faerie's eyes. He knew that there wouldn't be any fanfare and there would likely be a trial.

"I want to spend the rest of my days on the soil where I was born," the faerie said. "It doesn't matter if that's behind bars.

It's still where I was meant to be and where I was cast away from."

Bran dipped his head. "Then I bid you flee, changeling. Run through the dales, and the Wild Hunt will catch you. They will return you to the faerie realms where you will be tried by the court you would have resided in. Your fate is their decision, and I cannot sway them once you choose this path."

"I wouldn't want to sway them, Raven King."

Aisling made a soft sound and touched the faerie's shoulder. "Are you certain of this? Underhill has many rumors about the dark creatures who live there. We're trying to make it a comfortable place for people like us."

"Us?"

"I was a changeling, too, before Bran found me." Her gaze softened, and a small smile lit up her expression. "We don't always have to be the ones who are hunted. There's a place for us now. I've made sure of it."

The changeling smiled in return. "I have no doubt that you've done your best. Our people will never be welcomed or accepted by the other faeries. We were cast aside for a reason. Most of the time it's because we embarrassed our families or we weren't what they wanted. That kind of slight on their honor cannot be forgiven."

"It's wrong," Aisling whispered.

"Life usually is," the changeling replied. He leaned forward as if to touch his hand to Aisling's shoulder, then stopped at the last moment "We learn how to manage ourselves and others simply because we must. Faerie honor is a delicate thing. They take it seriously, and it's very easy to break the rules. Rules are what they live for. Otherwise, they would take over the world."

Bran hated that he agreed with the man. Faeries were not kind creatures, though many myths claimed they were. Even to each other, there was more bloodthirst and anger than genuine feelings of appreciation or love.

Wasn't his own family a perfect example of that? He hadn't even known what a kind touch felt like until he'd been thrown into a training ground with Eamonn. The then Seelie Prince had helped him up off the ground and hadn't slapped him again for failing.

It was life. But it wasn't a life that Aisling understood.

Paying back the favor Eamonn had shown him, Bran stood and offered the changeling his hand. "Stand. May your feet be swift and your luck be well on this night."

The changeling allowed himself to be pulled up and ran a hand down his mud-smudged shirt. "Thank you, Raven King. And you, mistress."

Aisling stood, disappointment shining loud and true on her face. "Are you certain of this?"

"I've never been more sure of anything in my life."

It killed Bran to watch Aisling's eyes tilt toward the ground so she didn't have to see the changeling race away from them. She'd done everything she could to help the man, but that didn't mean he was going to accept her help.

In a way, this had gone exactly how he expected. Faeries, even changelings, had more pride than they deserved to have. They wanted to fix their lives on their own. They wouldn't take help if it was offered so blatantly, and even if they didn't know someone was trying to help them, they likely still wouldn't take it.

Aisling remained at his feet on her knees in the grass. Her black gown had turned sodden with dew, yet she didn't react. She stared at the ground.

He waited until the changeling disappeared from sight then sank down beside her. "We cannot save them all, Aisling."

"I just wanted to save one." The defeat in her voice made a crack run through his heart. "Why wouldn't he let us take him home?"

Home. The word sounded all the sweeter coming from her lips.

When was the last time anyone called Underhill home? Bran doubted it had been done in centuries, or perhaps not ever. This little witch had no problem wandering into the strange world with all its terrible creatures and saw it as a place she could enjoy.

Her shoulders shook and pulled him out of his own head. Bran reached out an arm and tucked her into his side. "Hush now, witch. Some changelings don't want to be saved."

"How is that possible? They've been alone their entire lives. Why wouldn't someone want a single moment when they aren't the only one who cares whether they live or die? I can't understand."

She was projecting. Damn it, he didn't know how to fix this. So he pulled her closer and pressed his lips against the top of her head. She wrapped her arms around his waist, tucking herself into the hollows of his body.

He wondered if it made him a sick man that he liked her where she was, the feeling of her breathing against his side, the way she fit him perfectly, even when she was upset like this.

"Not all of them are like how you were. Some changelings

never know what they lose," he replied. "Some of them only know the human realm and care little to know what the faerie lands are like."

"Not that one."

"No"—he chuckled—"not that one. He seemed to remember the faerie realms all too well. But some people don't hold a grudge. Perhaps he looks very different under that skin he was wearing."

Aisling slapped a hand to his chest. "Looks don't matter, Bran. No matter what, they should have stayed with their families. They should have been loved no matter what they looked like or how they ended up."

She wasn't wrong, at least in the human sense. They were far kinder to their offspring than faeries. Tuatha de Danann were brutal. They knew who was going to grow up to be a warrior, a beauty, a king. If their child was anything less than that, then it wasn't worth wasting all the effort to raise them.

"I never said it was a foolproof way to live, little witch." He pressed his lips against her head again, silky strands sliding against his cheeks. "Faeries are hard to understand, especially for those who have soft hearts."

"A soft heart?" She pulled back to give him a disbelieving stare. "No one has ever accused me of that before."

"That's because I see through you."

She was kinder than she wanted anyone to know. Deep within the shadows of her heart, Aisling was a woman who wanted to heal the world. She just put up thorns so no one knew how much it hurt when she failed.

When she snorted, he touched a finger to her nose and flicked the end. "Don't snort at me just because I'm right."

Her brows drew down as the fight rose deep inside her. She wanted to argue, and damned if his heart didn't start beating faster for the fight she would put up.

Aisling opened her mouth, then stilled as the braying of hounds filled the clearing. The Wild Hunt had caught up with them, a few hunting parties passing each other. Some of the faeries let out whooping calls, others cried out how many they had caught, some just brandished bits of fabric that once belonged to changelings.

He knew what they would do with those they captured. They were likely in cages at the camp in the clearing, their screams and cries for help lifting into the air. His mother would chortle with glee. She'd stamp her feet to make them more afraid, and they all knew she feasted on fear more than physical food.

Aisling shivered and pressed her face to his shoulder. "I don't like this place, Bran. I want to go home."

"I think you've made enough of an appearance."

He thought. Some of the other faeries might mark her absence as a slight upon the other courts, but he was beyond caring. Let them think she had run away in fear. He'd brawl with any who tried to mar her name.

For now, he would take her home. He only hoped she wouldn't do something foolish when he left her alone again.

CHAPTER 6
JUST ONE NIGHT

Aisling held herself together until Bran nudged her through the portal back to Underhill. Once through the pulling magic, she fell onto the stone floor. Her knees struck the hard surface painfully, but the pain didn't register.

The changelings. They didn't want to come with her. They wanted to remain hunted or afraid rather than return to this place with the Raven Queen.

Was it so bad here?

She lifted her head and stared around the great hall, unable to see what others saw. There might be cobwebs in the ceiling, the spiders kept the entire place free of bugs. The floors were cracked, though still shone with ancient beauty and splendor. The windows were shattered, but that meant a breeze caressed her sweat-covered face.

How could anyone see this place as monstrous? Beauty covered every ancient, damaged surface from a lifetime of hard use and love. These were good things.

"Mistress?" The voice came from the rafters, and a sluagh dropped down in front of her. "Are you all right?"

No, she wanted to shout. She wasn't, and wouldn't be for a very long time. Her own people didn't want to be with her. They should have been like a family. Changelings should stick together, and she'd always thought that they would. Now she had proof faerie blood ran far stronger than make-believe ties.

Aisling dug her fingers into the stone floor until her nails screamed in pain. "I will be fine."

"How may I help you?"

You can't, a scared side of her whispered. The sluagh meant well, but all they would do is remind her that she was alone. That there was no family who would take her…

"Mistress." The sluagh knelt in front of her and touched a finger to her chin. It tilted Aisling's head up until she was staring into the strange face. This was an elderly creature. The beak had split its head nearly in two, bone gleaming in the dim light. Not a single hair decorated its head, and skin sagged from its cheeks. Black, beady eyes stared into hers.

She blew out a breath. Even in the strange ugliness, she saw the beauty in this creature. There was kindness in its eyes and a heart that beat strong and true within its breast.

The sluagh tsked. "You've been working yourself too hard, mistress. I'm glad you're back. We've all missed you."

"I haven't been gone long." She frowned and shifted, pulling away from the sluagh's hand. "Why aren't you with the others?"

"Some of us didn't want to hunt."

The words vibrated with something Aisling couldn't

name. It tasted like a lie, yet sounded like the ringing peal of truth. She frowned. "I didn't think it was possible for the sluagh to remain in Underhill when their king has called upon them." Even as she said it, the words seemed even more unusual.

The sluagh's eyes cast to the floor, and it scuffed a foot against the stone. "We consider ourselves loyal to you, mistress, and the Raven King has no hold over us."

It should have terrified her. The sluagh were not meant to serve anyone other than the Raven King. That's how it had always been. Their loyalty was a curse, not a choice. And yet...

Aisling straightened her spine and stood. She might not have family among the Fae, but she'd made a family here that meant far more.

"I missed you as well," she said, holding out a hand for the sluagh to take. "How many more are there?"

"Just a few, the numbers grow every day."

"Are you unsatisfied with your king?" She frowned at the thought. Bran was a good man; she'd seen him do wonderful things to help others. She was rarely in his presence when he had a chance to be king. Was he perhaps not as good as she thought?

"No mistress, the king has been very kind. It's just that..." The sluagh rose from its crouch and twisted its fingers together. "You were like us. A witch in the human realm and now something more. You're just like us."

Gods, was she really? Aisling looked the creature up and down, then sighed as she gave in. She *was* just like them. Though her outward form might not be as ugly, she was still the creature faeries wanted to forget existed.

They wouldn't let her change that.

Aisling flexed her hands, then let out a long breath. "Shall we prepare dinner then? The king will not be returning tonight."

"We've already eaten, mistress, I'd be happy to awaken a cook for you."

"There's no need. It won't be the first meal I've cooked for myself." And an opportunity to feel like she was herself again.

Aisling took five steps before a portal opened up on the other side of the great hall. Much smaller than the first, it vibrated with a familiar magic that she had felt many times. The edges were feathered with darkness.

"Bran?" she asked. No one stepped through.

She frowned and nudged the sluagh behind her, then tried again. "Bran?"

Someone stumbled through the portal. Long legs, flailing limbs, and with scraggly hair in front of their face, she couldn't hazard a guess at who they were. They fell onto their hands and knees in front of her, breathing hard and shivering in fear.

Thin fingers reached out for the hem of her dress. The quaking creature lightly touched her dark skirt and whispered, "Raven Queen?"

She let out a low breath. "Yes."

"He said you would be waiting for me." The creature looked up, and Aisling saw it was a pretty little pixie. Her spiked hair and leaf-shaped growths on her face were discolored, but she was alive. "Are you really going to help me?"

He'd managed to save one for her. Aisling's heart squeezed. "You're welcome here for as long as you'd like."

"I don't want to go back there."

"You don't have to." Aisling crouched so she was eye level with the little pixie. "Would you like something to eat?"

The pixie shook her head. "I don't know what I'd eat here, mistress."

"We aren't so far away from the world that we cannot grow food. Let me give you honey and bread. That should tide you over until we can find something more suitable for you."

Aisling's chest swelled with pride when the pixie looked at her as if she had saved the creature's life. She planned to do that, just not quite yet. The little thing would learn what it meant to be part of the Underfolk. They would become a family, and no one would ever cast them aside like something used and broken.

She reached out an arm for the pixie to tuck herself under. As they made their way out of the great hall, she looked at the sluagh over her shoulder. "Stay here?" she asked quietly. "In case there are more of them."

What had been a dejected look in the sluagh's eyes changed to that of respect. "Yes, mistress. And if more come through portals?"

"Bring them to the kitchen." Aisling let out a little laugh. "Bring them all to the kitchen, and we will feed them. Let them know what it is like to have a full belly once again."

Maybe it was foolish, but she felt hope for the first time in a very long time.

The last changeling snuggled underneath the blankets Aisling laid over its shoulders with a soft sigh. This one was the youngest by far, really just a little girl and nothing more. She was slight, lacking any weight on her body that left her cheeks sunken.

She had survived the Wild Hunt, and now she had a place where she could be safe for a few moments longer.

A total of seven changelings had stepped through Bran's portals. They were all officially part of the Underfolk now, although Aisling didn't know what she was going to do with them. There was enough room in the palace, though it was falling apart at the seams. She would need to find someone to start repairs immediately, especially if there were going to be children around.

Her mind bubbled with the possibilities. She could talk to the other sluagh, see if they remembered any skills from their time as humans, and if they would like to teach the others. They could make this place more than just a resting ground for the unwanted or a cage for the armies of the Wild Hunt.

They could make this a home.

She left the tiny bedroom and closed the door gently. Pressing her forehead against the cool surface, she let out a tiny, happy laugh, so small she didn't even recognize what it was.

They'd done it. Although the Wild Hunt had been a horrifying thing, a terrifying creation of the faeries meant to punish, maim, and hurt... They'd really done something more than just sit by and let it happen.

Arms curved around her waist and tugged her back against a strong chest. "Are you happy, Raven Queen?"

"More than I could ever express." She turned in Bran's arms, pressed her face against his neck, and chuckled again. "I hardly can believe we've actually done it. The changelings are *here*, Bran."

"Not all of them." Darkness crept into his voice with a hint of regret. "There were far more than I'd like to admit who were sent back to the courts."

"Se saved some. Not all of them, that would have been impossible. Seven changelings have lives that actually matter now, lives that can be whatever they want, however they want." Aisling pulled back, staring up into his dark eyes and seeing the world trapped in their depths. "You did this for me."

"How could I do anything else? You wanted this to happen, and you're right. This was the only future for them. They deserve more than a trial or to be set loose in the Otherworld with no one to guide them."

He tucked a strand of hair behind her ear. This man, this impossible, strong, kind man meant more to her than anything she'd ever had in her life.

He had put himself in danger for her. The other faeries could have stopped him, or worse, fought him for the rights to keep these changelings. But he hadn't cared.

Even the dark power of the Raven King hadn't stopped him. That had to mean more than just a passing fancy or a man who found her a good equal to rule his kingdom.

Blowing out a breath, she reached up and ran a finger down his jaw. Aisling had waited a long time to tell him the words that would split open her chest and reveal far more about herself than she had ever dared with anyone else. And perhaps it wasn't the right moment, would it ever be?

"You look troubled," he said, frowning. "What is it? Did I forget something?"

She let out a ragged chuckle, "No you foolish man. You haven't forgotten anything. It's perfect, all that you've done for me, for them, today."

"Then why do you look like I stuck a dagger between your ribs?" He reached between them and ran a hand down her side, as if checking for an unseen pressure that would cause her pain. "There's nothing here, my queen. You have no reason to look so sour, and I'll be angry if you've changed your mind about the changelings. It was more trouble than you could guess to get them here and —"

She pressed a hand against his mouth and blurted. "I love you!"

Bran froze under her touch, then his eyes crinkled at the corners as they always did when he was smiling.

She frowned. A muscle on her jaw ticked as the smile spilled down his face, curving his lips under her hand and then bubbling in his chest until she could hear his laughter.

"It's not funny, Bran," she scolded. "I really do. I haven't said anything before now, and I don't appreciate it that you're questioning me. I love you, despite all your flaws, and they are numerous!"

He reached up and pulled her hand away from his mouth. "I know."

"You know what?"

"I know you love me. I've known for quite some time now." He ran a hand over his dark hair and grinned. "How could you not love me? I'm devastatingly charming, far more handsome than the rest of the men you've met in her life. And besides, I'm better than anyone else you've ever met."

"And so gods-damned arrogant."

"The arrogance is a bonus. You'll never have to worry that my self-esteem is too low."

She rolled her eyes, trying to build a casing of ice over her stinging pride. "I just thought you'd like to know. I was obviously wrong."

If this was how he was going to be, then she wasn't going to waste any more time here. She struggled to untangle herself from his arms, but Bran simply tightened them. He allowed her to turn around until her back was pressed to his front, then rested his chin against her shoulder and waited for her to stop struggling.

Aisling let out a huff of breath and finally relented. "What? What else do you want?"

He pressed his lips to her cheek, then breathed, "I love you too, you know."

Pride stinging, she sniffed. "Of course, I do."

"Really?"

"Really."

"Then why were you trying to get away like I had set you

on fire?"

Because she hadn't wanted to face the possibility that he might not have loved her back. Because the mere idea of a future like that was enough to make tears build in her eyes. She would have stayed with him, she couldn't live without him. It would have been a very lonely future and one she wouldn't like.

Letting go of her anger, she sagged into his hold. "Oh hush, you ridiculous man. Can't you let me win just once?"

"Never. It's too much fun to tease you instead."

His arms tightened around her waist, and Aisling let him hold her. His words rolled over and over in her mind. *He loved her.* It felt almost too good to be true.

The Raven King was a story she had told many children, and one she had listened to countless times herself. He was a paragon. The kind of faerie who helped children like her, who hadn't had a home or anyone else to call their own.

And now, she'd captured the Raven King's attentions and made him fall in love with her. Life was strange like that.

Blowing out a breath, she wiggled to get his attention. "You really love me?"

"So much that sometimes it hurts to breathe. I don't know how you forced your way under my skin so firmly, witch, but I can't let you go now. I love you more than life itself, more than this title, more than the kingdom. I'd burn the world to the ground for you and build it back into the one you wanted if I could."

Why was he so perfect? He always knew the words she wanted to hear when she was just a mess at his feet.

"Let me turn around, Bran."

"I like you this way."

She huffed out an angry breath. "I want to kiss you."

"And I want to annoy you. It seems like only one of us is going to get what we want, and I'm bigger and stronger. I'll let you guess who is going to win."

"Can you take this seriously for a moment?"

"There's no such thing as seriousness in our life, my love."

She spun so quickly in his arms that he didn't have a chance to catch her. Aisling crashed against his chest and framed his face with her hands. Feathers poked her palm, their ends prickling. "Say that again."

"Seriousness?"

"*Bran.*"

He grinned, all pointed teeth and otherworldly face. "My love." He leaned forward and pressed a kiss to her forehead. "My love." Another kiss landed on each eye. "My love forever."

His lips met hers, and he sank into her like the breath of life. She couldn't inhale anything other than his wine-drenched scent. She dug her fingers into his broad shoulders, so beloved and so strong. He carried the weight of her world on them and didn't even flinch.

"Take me to bed, Bran." She shivered. "This is our one night together, and you came home early."

He swung her up into his arms. "With pleasure, my queen."

Aisling could only hear the drumming of her heart as they raced through the halls. His breath fanned over her face, drugging her with his masculine scent. How long had it been since she'd had complete access to his skin? To touch as she wanted?

Too long.

When Bran kicked the door to their bedroom open, it slammed against the wall with a resounding clang. She tilted her head back and laughed. It was reassuring he needed her as fiercely as she needed him. Their lust for each other hadn't dulled in the absence of time or space.

The black curtains surrounding their bed seemed to cast the entire room into darkness, as if the moon rose in the horizon rather than the sun. He laid her down on the down-filled mattress, crawling up her body with a dark look in his eyes.

He'd always hunted her like prey when it came to the bedchamber, and she lost herself completely as her soul tried to run from his. She would always be afraid of what he'd do to her. Of what loving him could do to her.

Warm hands ran up her thighs, dragging the silken fabric of her gown up her legs. The slow slide of heat mixed with the decadence of silk made her gasp.

Bran leaned down and pressed his cheek to her knee. "I missed this," he whispered against her skin. "I missed *you*."

How did she tell him she'd felt empty all this time? That not just her body, her heart, ached for a connection with him that was more than a few passing words? More than just the concern of a people, of a kingdom, the needs of a woman who desperately wanted to drink in his breath like the finest of wines?

She reached down, grabbed a fistful of his hair, and gently guided him up her body to settle him into the crook between her legs. "I will always miss you," she rasped, then dragged her nose along his jaw. "Even when you are standing in front of me, I miss you."

"Wild thing," he replied with a chuckle.

Aisling felt her heart begin to pound once again as he shifted. He rolled his body against hers, relearning the shape of her and allowing her to get used to the shape of him. He was strong and lethal in every movement, long and lean as well.

He reached behind his head and pulled off his shirt in a graceful movement. Every beloved line of him was revealed to her greedy eyes.

Framed by black velvet curtains, his body seemed to glow. Aisling reached out and gently traced a finger over the starburst scar above his heart. *Her mark.*

Bran caught her hand and held it close to the thundering beat inside his ribs. "Not a regret in the world, mo chroi."

Her breath caught. "Not a single one?"

In one smooth movement, he tugged her dress up and over her head. His gaze raked over her bare body, leaving a heated blush in its wake. "You are the reality of all my forbidden longings. Never once in my life would I regret finding you."

His lips pressed against her throat before dragging down her body and finding the hidden hollows that made her gasp and squirm.

Her mind fracturing with pleasure that overwhelmed her, Aisling traced the muscles that bunched in his shoulders. Every flex rocked through her, every kiss made her toes curl, and every long lick made her breath catch in her throat.

He touched her like a starving man, and she the banquet laid out before him. Aisling couldn't think, couldn't *be* anything more than the writhing creature trapped between his claws.

The sounds she made were ones she'd never heard before. The primal growl of a snarling beast, the whimpering cry of a trapped animal, and the whispered call of a woman who desperately needed him.

Only once she'd fallen over that eternal ledge over and over again did he slide back up her body. She opened her eyes and met his gaze, watching as he licked his lips like a leopard who had finally sighted his next meal.

There were no words between them, but they'd never been all that good for talking.

He slid his hands into the tangled length of her hair, tugging until she tilted her head back and bared her neck for his lips. Tongue stroking the vein on her neck that beat fiercely, he slowly slipped inside her.

Aisling was overwhelmed, stretched farther than she thought possible, and it was still not nearly enough. She held onto his back, traced the bumps of his ribs, and sighed against his shoulder. Tangled together as they were, it was impossible not to feel the shudders running through him.

"You are..." he whispered, pulling back enough to stare deeply into her eyes.

"What?"

Bran shook his head and swallowed. "There are no words."

And damned if that didn't send her over the edge again. He drank deeply of her body, her soul, and every inch of her that she didn't know existed. Moving within her with a singular goal, Bran plunged over the cliff edge with her.

He sighed into her shoulder, shifting them both so he could hold her close to his heart. Together, they slid into sleep with their fingers intertwined.

CHAPTER 7

A WHISPER IN THE DARK

Aisling paddled through the lake, icy water chilling her webbed feet. It would be winter in Underhill soon. Snow would fall from the sky and pillow the earth with a pristine, untouched blanket. And yet, she still couldn't force herself to enjoy the beauty and the crisp quality of the air.

There were more changelings showing up every day through the portals Bran had left open. They reached out for her with their minds now, or some contacted the sluagh directly.

Bran was losing control over his famed army. The sluagh disappeared constantly. Some of them found changelings or returned with new human souls already added into the midst of their black cloud. Others never returned at all.

These were the ones she worried about.

She began to ask the sluagh directly if they were hearing voices other than hers or Bran's. And it seemed as though they were lying to her. Each always said there were no other voices, even the sluagh who had told her about Carman's voice in the first place.

She couldn't go to Bran with a rumor. They had to be

honest with her, to say one more time that the ancient witch was trying to contact them.

The changelings were distracting her, however. They cared so much they had a home. So many of them wanted to help rebuild the palace. Others wanted to create homesteads away from the crumbling walls, to rebuild an entire populace of people deep inside the earth.

Bran hesitated to keep them here as more and more joined their ranks. He worried too many changelings would capture attention and start another war. He wanted them to return to the courts they had been ripped from, to do what the faeries had wanted to do.

Give them justice or give them death.

Aisling couldn't believe those were the only choices. She wanted to keep them close to her, to give them the lives they should have enjoyed long ago.

She refused to believe it was an impossible task. Every night when the moonlight touched her skin, she raced back to the palace to help them with whatever she could. If that was spells to strengthen the walls, then so be it. If it were carrying sheets of fabric to help create the temporary housing, then she was the first in line.

She couldn't say the same for Bran.

He looked at all her proceedings as if she had done something terrible. His eyes would widen and his mouth compress into a hard line. "The faeries won't stand for this very long," he had growled. "They're going to want them back. We can't keep them forever."

"I can save them. Why wouldn't they be able to stay here? They aren't hurting anyone, Bran."

"Of course, they aren't hurting anyone, though they could. They don't know our ways, and that's dangerous."

"Neither do I." Her eyes had flashed in anger, and her heart beat fast. "Am I a danger, Bran? Am I also part of the problem?"

They hadn't spoken since their last argument, and she couldn't blame him. Both had said things out of anger they didn't really mean.

Once upon a time, they might have made up because they would be thrust together in an impossible quest that forced them to work side by side. Now? They only saw each other for fifteen minutes before their curses ripped them away from each other.

The low rumble of a purr stretched across the water. Aisling lifted her head and saw Lorcan stretched out on his side, his favorite perch nearly obscured by his dark fur.

She drifted closer to him and called out, "What are you doing here? I thought you weren't going to return for a few more weeks at least."

"A little birdy told me you had returned home early from the Wild Hunt and you were saving changelings now. Do you really think that's wise?"

"Why is everyone asking me that?" she grumbled. "Even Bran doesn't like the idea. I thought he would be the most welcome to it, considering he *brought* them here in the first place."

Lorcan slowly lifted a paw and licked it. "He would do anything for you, even go against the laws of the Fae. Foolish woman, don't you know he's mad for you?"

"Not mad enough to let the changelings remain here."

"That's because the faeries will attack Underhill instead of the human realm next. You have too many creatures here that aren't supposed to be, and..." Lorcan flexed his paw. The sharp claws glinted in the sunlight, reflecting magical sparks over the lake. "Well, it's not pretty when the faeries decide someone has taken something that is theirs."

"Changelings are faeries. They cannot be owned by anyone just because their family didn't want them."

"I didn't say it made sense. Faeries rarely do, which is why I've always told you to stay away from them."

Aisling let out a honking laugh. "A little hard to do when I'm one of them, Lorcan."

"All I'm saying is that you're inviting too many eyes that will watch you like a hawk when it spies a mouse." He gave a little shudder. "And I've tangled with enough hawks to know you don't want their eyes on you."

"I've used many hawk feathers in spells before, and I don't intend to let them take away these changelings. They're my family now, Lorcan. My *family*." She swam closer. "Don't you remember what it was like when it was just you and me? How badly we wanted to have someone other than just each other?"

"I haven't forgotten anything, Aisling. I also remember the family we wanted never came. You and I were all that was for each other. I take care of you first, and anyone else who comes into our life had better have a damned good reason for being there."

Their story was painful from the first moment they drew breath and hadn't gotten much better when they found each other. She shuddered every time she remembered the amount of rats and bugs they'd survived on, and this was before Lorcan had been a cat.

Back when he was a gangly teenage boy, their lives had been far more difficult. No one wanted two scraggly children around. If they did, then it was for payment neither Lorcan nor her were open to paying.

They'd found food at farms that had dumped the slop to their pigs. They'd cast spells by moonlight only, sometimes on small nubs of candles they had found thrown out by inns. Even then, it was hard to do magic when everything around them was falling to pieces.

She sighed and brushed a tip of her wing against the water. "Have you found anything else out about...this?"

"Your curse?"

Aisling hummed out a yes.

"Not really. Too many people think that it's tied somehow with Carman, and we both know that's a dead end. You can't talk to the dead witch, and I can't find her."

"She's here, though. Somewhere."

Aisling didn't want to talk to the dead witch either. There was something infinitely dangerous about the idea. The witch wanted more than just a conversation. She wanted something Aisling knew wasn't on the table for payment.

What could something like that want, anyway? Carman was dead. Or at least, that's what the rumors said. A dead woman couldn't come back to life, and her soul could only have so much power. Even the darkest of magic said that was impossible. Death was death.

So what did she want? Or was she not as dead as everyone seemed to think?

Lorcan shifted, slowly getting up to his feet and stretching. "I'd tell you to reach out to her through another sluagh if I didn't think you would have to kill it. That wouldn't end well in the slightest. That poor sluagh would be dead on the ground, and I'd have to pick you back up. I refuse to do that."

"What?" Aisling flinched back. "A dead sluagh? Again?"

"Oh, that's right. I never gave you that memory back. On your desk in your room, there's a silvery memory. You can probably drink that again, but you shouldn't do it while Bran is around." Lorcan's face scrunched up. "He'd yell at me again, and I don't like it when he yells. My ears are sensitive."

Gods, had she killed a sluagh? Aisling wanted to rush back to her room and drink the memory immediately. How could she promise them she would watch out for them when she had killed one of their own kind? What kind of queen did that?

"Damn it, I can see you spiraling already. Aisling, pay attention to me right now. I have something important to tell you."

She shook her head, snapping her beak wildly before focusing on the cat. She could do this. She could pull herself back together and not get lost in the what-ifs. The vial contained all the information she needed to know, and one day wasn't that long to wait.

"What other declarations do you have to make?" she snapped.

"Just that I think you should talk to Bran sooner rather than later. I came back because I overheard an Unseelie talking about something that was rather troubling."

"Which was?" Aisling hated it when Lorcan had a secret. He always tried to dangle it over her head, and her patience was running thin.

"They said there was a war brewing." Even the cat didn't

hesitate this time. His voice shook with concern. "A war within the Unseelie court. That one of Bran's brothers decided he wanted the throne sooner rather than later."

"Why should I care what the Unseelie Court does?"

"Because technically Bran is part of the Unseelie court. They could call him to war any second."

CHAPTER 8
THE UNSEELIE WAR

Aisling swept into the main hall, magic tingling along her arms and back. The curse didn't want to release its hold on her. As with every day, she fought against it. Moonlight had touched her skin so she was human for as long as it was here now.

Her feet pounded on the ground as she ran to Bran's side. He hadn't come down to the lake, and she already knew why. Lorcan had told her enough. Bran needed to hear it from her lips.

What if he didn't know? What if he hadn't heard yet that his family was falling apart at the seams and was trying to tear each other to pieces? And could he even stop them?

She ripped open the last door and thundered into the throne room where she skidded to a halt.

Bran sat upon his throne, head in his hands, legs spread wide. He slumped against the royal seat as if the world had ended.

"You know," she said, her voice carrying throughout the hall.

"I already heard."

"I'm sorry. I don't know how to help, but if I can in any way, you know that I will."

He held up a hand. "There's nothing you can do that I would ever ask for. My family has always fought between each other. I just didn't..." He paused and cleared his throat. "I never expected it to come to this."

"Can't you talk some sense into them? The Unseelie court cannot go to war within itself."

"Don't you think I've thought of that?" Bran looked up. His eyes were sunken into his face, bruised and dark from worry. Sweat stained his brow, and she was certain he hadn't slept in days. "The Seelie court will take advantage of this. I've already tried to contact Eamonn. He's not interested in speaking with me on the matter. This will tear not only my family apart. It will tear apart the entire Unseelie kingdom."

"What can I do?" Aisling couldn't think of anything. The moment Lorcan had told her, she'd started the flight back to the palace. Every bit of her wanted to help, but the Unseelie were as foreign to her as the rest of this world. They wanted to fight with each other, so be it. They would fight, and the consequences of the royals' choices would spill throughout the Otherworld.

He shook his head again, limp against the throne. "There's nothing you can do. Our world is about to change, and not for the better."

"Can you appeal to your mother? Certainly she won't want to fight against her own child. She fought to get *you* back, and she made it quite clear you are her least favorite."

"Thank you for bringing that up."

"Don't make me feel guilty for that. It's the truth, and you know it." Aisling walked up to his side and knelt at his feet. "You have to do something, Bran. They're your family."

"And they are fools."

"And still you blood."

He reached for her, scooping a hand under her chin and cupping her face. "Your heart is too big. You shouldn't give them any pity. They've made a bed they must now lay in."

There was something in his eyes that she'd seen before. A regret, but also the lust for adventure. "You've already done something, haven't you?"

Bran lifted a brow. "And perhaps you know me far better than I give you credit for."

"What have you done?"

He sighed and ran a hand over his head. "I've spoken with the council of the Wild Hunt. They're the only ones who can lift my curse, although they cannot lift yours. They have agreed to remove the Raven King's curse for a few weeks, enough to let me travel to the Unseelie court to try and talk some sense into my family. The council sees what I do. This could bring about a new era in the courts that we don't want to see come to life."

"Weren't the leaders of the Wild Hunt this year both from the Seelie Court?"

Bran nodded.

"Then why would they allow you to help the Unseelie court? It doesn't make sense, Bran." She worried they were playing him as everyone else had done.

He blew out a breath. "There must always be dark and light in our world. If you take away the darkness, then there is nothing left. The Seelie court requires us to exist to remember their own values. Otherwise, the entire court system shatters."

"Why wouldn't Eamonn talk to you then? It benefits him to stop this madness."

"It does. Hhe's likely trying to figure out what he will do if the war begins regardless. For all his intelligence, Eamonn doesn't think I stand a chance at talking some sense into my family." Bran hesitated, a muscle on his jaw jumping. "And he might be right."

She squeezed his knees, then smoothed her hands over his thighs in hopes that it might comfort him. "I believe in you, my love. Certainly they will listen to you. You're the Raven King. There's more to you than just the Unseelie prince now."

"It depends on who started this war. I don't even know which brother is fighting for the throne. Some of them have tried before and failed but...I suspect it is my eldest brother. And if it is, then this will be much harder."

Aisling racked her memory for the name of his eldest brother and came up short. She couldn't remember who he was, or if Bran had even spoken of him.

"Your eldest brother?" she asked. "Who is he?"

"A fool," Bran spat. "Far more interested in power being given to him than gaining it for himself. He's been tempted by many powerful people before, but he's weak on his own. If he's trying to take the throne, then someone else is behind him."

Aisling could hazard a guess who that was. He darkened their doorstep enough for her to hate him already. "Do you think Darcy could be behind all this?"

"I don't know. I wouldn't be surprised to see the previous Raven King with my brother." Bran sighed. "I have to go to them. Tonight. I don't want to leave you and this entire kingdom all on your own but—"

She interrupted him. "We'll manage. I'd rather go with you, though. Your family is not particularly kind to you, and I'd much rather be there to help you."

"Who else would control the sluagh?" he asked. "You have to stay here. I know they've already formed more of an attachment to you than to me."

"That's not entirely true."

He shifted his hand to the back of her neck and pulled her forward. "I'm not jealous, witch. I see why they'd prefer you over me."

Bran pressed his lips to hers, tasting her for a long moment before groaning against her lips. She wished they had more time together. That they might have another night where they could dream at each other's sides. Even if she turned into a swan at the first hint of sunlight.

"I'll take care of everything," she whispered against his mouth. "Just come back to me in one piece. Please."

"Help me get ready?"

She knew what he meant. The Raven King's armor could magically appear on his body any time he wished, and there was something calming about strapping it on him. She knew that he would be safe if she placed everything so that it covered every piece of him that might be hit in battle.

And she knew he would battle soon.

Without a word, Aisling stood and held out a hand for him to take. He let her pull him from the throne and guide him through the hallways of their home. The sluagh parted like a wave in front of them.

Dark eyes watched them with interest. She wondered if

they knew what was going on. The creatures were highly intuitive, or they had access to both her and Bran's mind.

They always seemed to know what their royals were thinking. If she was hungry, a sluagh appeared with a plate next to her. If she was thirsty, water would appear at her side, sometimes without her ever seeing them enter. She wondered if they knew her better than she knew herself.

Then she would wonder why they served her. Aisling hardly thought of herself as a good person or as someone worth serving at all.

She pulled Bran to their room and nudged the door open with her foot. When they first had arrived, Aisling assumed Bran would want his own room as they had in the Palace of Dusk. It wasn't unheard of for couples to remain in separate facilities. In fact, most people would have chosen to do so.

Not Bran. He wanted her close to him, even if that meant he simply slept in the same bed as her. The longer they were in the room together, the more she understood why he wanted her to live that way.

Aisling glanced over at the black silk sheets and felt a smile spread across her lips. How many times had she lain there, inhaling his scent and breathing out a sigh of happiness? Just knowing that he still lived had helped her these many nights alone. When they did get a few moments together, that bed had kept them safe from the world. They'd loved and lost in this room. Sometimes together, sometimes apart.

She pulled him to the corner where an armor stand stood empty. Pointing at it, she lifted a brow. "Would you like to do the honors, or should I?"

"I believe I can still manage." Dramatically, he cracked his neck and focused on the stand. In seconds, the armor of the Raven King appeared upon it.

Aisling gave it a severe glance, checking over his magic. He'd done well enough. Not a mark on it from the teleportation.

The entire set was a black, intimidating thing. The pointed helmet gave the impression of a raven, while the breastplate mimicked black wings arching back over the shoulders. Black leather padded his legs, while gauntlets gave his fingers claws.

She hated the sight of it. It had remained in the castle for only a few hours when they arrived here. Bran had cleaned the room of the previous tenant's things while she had stared at the beastly thing.

Aisling knew what it meant. Darcy, the old Raven King, had made it very clear he enjoyed battle. Blood had been his harvest and his feast. He wanted to devour the world if he could along with the rest of the sluagh, and the power that gave him was only one of his favorite things.

She'd asked for the armor to be removed immediately. Bran had done so, and though she didn't know where he had put it, she knew it was far away from this place.

Now, it had returned, and she hated it even more.

Without a word, she stalked toward it and pulled the breastplate from the stand. "Turn around," she murmured.

Bran did so without argument. The clothing on his body disappeared with a whispered spell, leaving only a thin shirt and comfortable pants.

Her heartbeat quickened at the sight. Love for him bloomed deep in her soul, and it wasn't just the physical reaction to seeing him like this. It was more than that. Something she'd never felt in her life.

The armor clanked in her hands as she rounded to his front. She placed it on his chest, then took his hand and forced him to hold it in place while she returned behind him to begin tying the straps.

"What do you think you'll find?" she asked.

"Bloodshed. My family at each other's throats, yelling most likely. If they haven't started tearing into each other, I'd be surprised."

"Do they do this often?"

"Around every century, although it's never turned into a civil war." He shifted, hefting the chest plate higher when she finished with the first strap. "We aren't particularly loving."

"I could have guessed that. You haven't invited any of them to the castle, nor do you speak of them often."

"Do you speak of your family?"

He had a point. Neither of them liked to bring up their pasts, although she was curious about his. Bran hadn't ever spoken of it.

"No," she replied. A swift tug to a strap had him wincing. "You know enough about my family already. Why would I talk about them when you know them far better than me?"

"Low blow," he growled.

"Well, you did try to marry my sister."

"I thought that didn't bother you?" Bran craned his neck to look over his shoulder. "I made it clear I'm not interested in her anymore. I'm far more intrigued by you, witch."

"I'm an intriguing person. I won't argue that." A part of her still wondered.

Did he want the Seelie bride with her long golden locks and her pretty voice? The life he would have had with Elva, her sister, was far different than this. Instead of gardens filled with golden wheat, balls with gowns, and gorgeous people, he had a dark castle with damned souls.

It must be hard for him to think about all that and not regret his choices.

"Aisling," he murmured, turning and brushing her hands away from the metal feathers of his armor. "That is in the past."

"What is that past?" she asked, searching his eyes for an answer she knew he would not give. "You haven't said a word to me about anything, other than you aren't close to your family. I *know* that. It's not a secret. I don't know *you*."

He brushed a strand of hair behind her ear. "You know me better than anyone else."

"And that is still only a small piece of who you are. The Raven King. A man who can somehow ask people to remove his curse and they'll take it away. You haven't found anyone who can remove mine, not a single person who understands how it came to be."

"I'm trying to—"

"Are you?" The words blurted from her mouth, and she hadn't realized how much the wound had festered until she said them. The curse ripped her away from the changelings, the sluagh, *him*, every single morning. And she was still struggling to deal with the pain.

He stepped back from her, a frown marring his beautiful face. "Of course, I'm trying to break the curse, Aisling. I've been doing my best."

His raven eye whirled in its socket, looking anywhere but her.

The air whooshed from her lungs. "You're lying."

"I'm a faerie, Aisling, I can't lie."

"Then you're hiding the truth. I can read you like a book, Bran. You aren't trying as hard as you can to break this curse. Why aren't you?"

He ran a hand over his head. "I have other responsibilities now. I'm a *king*. I'm more than just Bran, more than an Unseelie prince. There's so much to do here. You cannot condemn me for trying to learn how to take care of these people, to care about someone other than myself. I'm fighting against every single thing that's been taught to me. I'm Unseelie. We're selfish. We're not supposed to take care of anyone other than ourselves."

"I'm not asking to come first, Bran, I'm asking for proof that you have attempted to even find a spell, the history of the Raven King's consort. Anything."

He remained silent, and his eyes continued to stare above her head. It was the only answer she needed.

"Why?" Aisling asked, her voice thick and her soul weary. "Why aren't you trying?"

"I am." Bran's voice cracked on the words. "We can't have this conversation right now, Aisling. I have to go."

Why did it always happen like this? The moments when she was just breaking through, he always had to whisk off somewhere to save someone else.

There was a war, she reminded herself. One that would affect all the faeries if she didn't let him go. She couldn't be the selfish creature she used to be, because she was now a queen and so many people relied on her.

She hated it. She wanted to go back to being the witch in the bog who looked out for herself and no one else.

Aisling nodded and reached forward. "Turn around. I didn't finish yet."

They remained silent. The only sound was the tightening of leather and clanking of metal as she made certain each individual piece would keep him safe. A voice in her ear whispered to leave one piece loose. Just give someone the opportunity to hurt him, like he was hurting her.

She wasn't that person anymore. She couldn't be.

Aisling sighed and patted his shoulder. "Done."

"Are we?" He turned, his heart in his eyes. "I promised you the world, witch, and all I've handed you is hell."

She wouldn't speak of this. Not now. Aisling reached up and placed a hand on his cheek. "Come back to me in one piece, Unseelie. I'm not done with you yet."

Bran stepped back with a troubled look on his face. He searched her eyes for something, then firmly nodded.

A portal opened behind him. Black tendrils of magic reached for his shoulders and caressed his arms. They pulled him through the murky darkness.

Then, he was gone.

Bran shoved through the magic of the portal, stepped into the Unseelie castle, and sucked in a deep breath. Why did it always have to happen like that? Damn it, he should have been able to stay with her. To reassure her that he wasn't interested in her family.

That was *why* he hadn't told her about his past. He didn't want her to know how much he had changed just by knowing Elva. That she had torn out his heart when she chose someone else, and then his world had crumbled around him.

He wasn't proud of his history. He'd been a horrible person, before and after Elva, although much worse after her.

Bran had seen the world as a place where people wanted to hurt him. Any kindness suddenly looked tainted, as if he were merely a stepping stone to the next best thing. And he'd hurt a lot of people.

Memories played through his head, visions of blood, gore, and violence.

A lot of people.

He shook his head firmly. He couldn't get stuck on all the things he'd done. His family would scent that like blood in the water and tear into him instead of each other. As much as he wanted to distract them, he wasn't willing to sacrifice himself to do so.

Growling, he stalked through the halls of the Unseelie castle. They were dark, as usual, lit only by torches on the wall that cast everything with a red hue. Not even the goblins were out and about. Usually that meant his mother was on a killing spree.

He hoped she was only killing the lesser fae. If she'd torn into his sisters again, then he would have to step in far more than he had planned on.

The door to the throne room was ajar. Light spilled through

the small crack, already a terrible sign. Neither of his parents were fond of light. Their arachnid eyes were sensitive to anything bright, even more than that, they hated to be able to see each other completely.

Though they valued ugliness in their children, they still saw the same thing the Seelie did when they looked at each other. They were monstrous beings. Creatures that could only remain in the dark.

He slipped through the small crack and stepped into the place he most hated.

His mother lounged on the throne, silent. His father stomped past some of his children. All eight of his legs moved separately, but it was his flailing hands that made Bran wince. The King of the Unseelie liked to hurt people. He liked to feast upon pain, whereas his mother enjoyed fear. Together, they were a dangerous pair.

Bran glanced up at the cobwebbed ceiling. His sisters hung there from giant hooks in their backs. Blind eyes roving as they tilted their heads, trying to track where their father was so they could lower or raise themselves accordingly. Of all his siblings, his sisters had learned how to hide themselves.

He was surprised they'd come out of their library. It didn't bode well for any of his brothers.

Three of them were lined up in front of the throne. Shoulder to shoulder, they left their back to their mother and stared at a single sibling who stood in the center of the room.

Eion was the closest in age to Bran, that was where their similarities ended. Some speculated that he wasn't even the Unseelie King's child. By looks alone, he certainly stood out.

Red hair cascaded from his shoulders in a great mane. His

skin was so pale Bran could see his veins even from this far away. Slitted eyes watched the proceedings with far more intelligence than his other brothers.

He wore nothing more than a kilt, black with a ragged edged. Muscles shifted on his chest, and Bran observed that he was much larger than the last time they'd seen each other. Eoin had been building his body to be the perfect weapon. Always a bad sign with one of the Unseelie.

So, his youngest brother had finally grown up.

"This will not be forgotten," his father growled. "Of all your brothers, it will *never* be you who sits upon this throne."

"I'm the only one who should be your successor." Eoin's voice had deepened, too. It cracked through the throne room like a powerful whip. "My brothers lack what it takes to be king. They will run this kingdom into the ground. I will not stand by and watch them."

The Unseelie King reared back onto four legs, the others waving in the air as he prepared to attack his own son. Bran had seen the aftermath of such anger before.

Stepping forward, he cleared his throat. "I believe they already have a king for a son. So you are wrong there, Eoin. My kingdom is prospering."

Eoin's shoulders tensed. "Hardly a kingdom in anything but name."

"And yet, the name is all that matters."

His mother leaned forward on her throne, hair sliding away to reveal pale breasts. "My son! You have returned to us."

As if he would ever return for anything less than a war. Bran scowled at her. "To stop this nonsense and talk some sense into all of you. Have you forgotten what the last civil war did to us? To *all* of us?"

"Bran..." She slumped back in her throne like a petulant child. "That's such boring talk. I'd much rather you pick a side and fight with us. Like the old days when you were still my favorite boy."

She referred to a dark time in his life, one he had long ago refused to acknowledge. "Enough, mother."

"This does not concern you," Eoin snapped. "Go back to your hole in the ground."

"Oh, if only I could, brother. I didn't want to come here and fix what you have broken."

Eoin lunged forward, only to be stopped by their father screaming, "Both of you! Enough."

Bran had heard that tone of voice too many times in his life to not flinch. He shifted back, baring his teeth in anger. He was an adult, damn it. He shouldn't be so afraid of his father shouting. *He was also a king.*

His father stalked forward, the talons on the ends of his legs clicking on the floor. "You were not invited here, forgotten son. I have no interest in seeing you."

The words stung more than they should have. "I'm not letting you start a civil war with each other and tear apart this world. The Seelie have prepared for something like this for a very long time. They will take everything we have here and turn it into whatever they want. They will feed upon our civil war." He met his mother's gaze. "You know this, as well as I."

"I lived it," his mother replied. She shifted one of her legs, rubbing it against another one. The rasping sound of hair and arachnid skeleton reminded him of his childhood spent hiding from this monster of a mother. "The Seelie like to think we're scared of them. We're not."

"You cannot control what happens if there is a civil war. While all of you are distracted with each other, they will swoop into this kingdom and take it back."

"They can't take back anything that wasn't theirs to begin with," his father growled.

"They can. All of us were just Tuatha de Danann, and then they left. Now we're here, split into two groups who hate each other because of our differences, and you are all squabbling like children!"

Eoin began to laugh. He tucked his hands behind his back and shook his head. "Brother, there are three kingdoms. The Seelie who are the good faeries. The Unseelie who are the bad faeries. And the Underfolk, who no one cares about at all."

How dare he? Bran whipped around and pointed severely at his brother. "I do. And you should, because they are good at what they do. Or do you no longer wish to have the Wild Hunt? If I remember correctly, you weren't even invited this year."

"For no reason other than an old prejudice."

"No. Because you are unpredictable and you cannot even follow Unseelie traditions."

"When have you suddenly cared for rules, brother? You always did lean toward Seelie, but pity for the weak? The changelings are brought back to their own courts for a reason." His brother sneered.

"You don't get to kill them just because you want to."

Eoin had always done that, even as a child. If Bran had a puppy, Eoin would kill it. When his mother brought in a new maid, Eoin would lacerate her skin with a knife until she left. He was the perfect Unseelie child.

Mad.

His brother shook his head. "Oh, Bran, you never were able to understand exactly what we're meant to be. I can. Which is why I say again, Father, I am the only one of your children worthy of that throne. If you won't give it to me, then I will take it."

Bran wanted to kill him where he stood. He was a *child*, despite all his centuries of life. No one this arrogant should ever be king.

Had he ever been like this? He knew the answer was yes. He'd been the worst of them all, trudging through the castle and striking the hobgoblins whenever he wanted to. That was why he had left this place.

The Unseelie castle was toxic. Everyone in it was unhappy, angry at the world, and wanted nothing more than to hurt everyone they loved. It was dangerous for him to even step foot in here with memories riding in the forefront of his mind.

Eoin conveniently forgot that only their father could declare a war. A usurper could try, of course, but few of the Unseelie would be so foolish as to fight against the current king. It was why his parents had ruled for so long. No one dared anger them. No one dared rise up against them.

Before he could scold his brother for such words, the sound of clapping filled the throne room. Stomach dropping, Bran turned to see yet another wraith step out of the shadows.

Darcy. The previous Raven King was looking far too good these days. The scales had completely grown back to rise over his throat like personal armor and covered his hands in pale green.

He finished clapping and shook his head with a fanged

grin. "It's always so lovely to see families getting along. Mine never liked each other that much. I'm glad to see that family tradition has spread all the way up to the royals."

Bran bared his teeth. "What *are* you doing here?"

"Well, I'm here to support your brother. I also think there are very few people who could do your father and mother justice in their old age. And I don't think any of your family could appropriately represent them. Other than Eoin, of course."

"What do you get out of this?" Bran stepped closer to the other man. "You aren't here because you like any of us. You aren't capable of that. So there's something else afoot."

"You think you can read my mind? You're nobody in this world anymore. The Raven King has no respect, no power, and no control over what happens in any of the faerie courts. The sooner you realize that, the better." Darcy spread his hands wide. "I'm full of knowledge on how to run your kingdom the right way. Perhaps you should ask me."

Perhaps he would kill Darcy instead.

His mother stood, and everyone in the room fell silent. They all knew how dangerous the Unseelie Queen could be. And more than that, how unpredictable she was.

He'd long admired her ability to silence a room with a single movement. She had not only the respect of her people, but their fear. They didn't know what she would or could do. No one knew if the queen had magic at her bidding, or if she was just a malformed faerie who hadn't learned much of the dark arts. Regardless, no one wanted to find out.

She left the throne and walked toward him, her feet tapping in a rhythm that raised horrible memories. Bran swallowed hard when she paused in front of him.

"My son," she said quietly, tucking a hand under his chin and lifting his face so he had to stare up at her monstrous form. "I have missed you a great deal, and all the ridiculous things you do while you're here. Do you think I forgot the performance you put on last time? And that little girl who you made a queen?"

"Her name is Aisling."

"I don't care what her fake name is. I know her true one, and you won't fool me that easily." She ran a nail underneath his eye, delicately pressing it against the thin skin. "You aren't here for us. You never have been. Why don't you tell me what you want, Raven King?"

Bran swallowed hard. "I don't want to see a war open up and everything else spill into my kingdom."

"You're trying to be a good man? Well, you'll have to try harder than this, little boy. You have too many black marks on your soul to ever be thought of as good."

"I was once. I can do it again." He'd given up all this, tried to be Seelie, all for Elva, because that was what she'd wanted.

"I remember how much you changed for the last woman you thought you were in love with. A shame really, you would have made an impressive Unseelie if you hadn't fallen in with the wrong crowd. We know how you work. You try to convince someone you are exactly what they want. A shapeshifter, if you will. This one will give you up, just like the last one did." She released her hold on his jaw and touched a finger to his nose. "And then you'll come crawling back to me. Like you always do, my predictable, foolish son."

"Not this time, Mother."

"No? What changed? You're still with a woman who is arguably out of your league. You have too much responsibility, so you've been avoiding it. And should I mention the curse? I've heard you've stopped asking around entirely on how to break that. I wonder why?" She grinned. "Is it, perhaps, because it was becoming too hard for you to figure out? So you grew frustrated and gave up?"

"Stop it."

Eoin stomped his foot on the ground. "Why does the conversation always turn to Bran when he's here? I'm threatening a war, and you're talking about his love life?"

The queen held up her hand. "Silence, Eoin. We're not talking about you right now."

"I will destroy all your supporters and take this kingdom through bloodshed if I must!"

She narrowed her eyes, and the entire room trembled. "And I said we're not talking about you right now. Would you like me to start?"

"No," Eoin said, backing away slowly. "No, Mother."

"Good. For a moment I thought you wanted me to be angry at you." The words were more of a threat than if she had pulled a knife. The queen never got angry. Bran had seen her hunt, feast, and feed, but had only seen her angry once.

They'd had to rebuild the castle after what she'd done. He would never forget the blood and gore splashed on the walls. How the entire castle had been as silent as a tomb in the wake of her wrath.

When he shuddered, the movement brought her attention back to him.

"So," she said. "Have you given up on this new, little toy?

Or are you going to waste even more time trying to convince her you are more than just an Unseelie? My boy, you are part of us just as we are part of you. Acting like a good man isn't going to change that."

"I will break her curse. I will have her at my side like a queen should be." Bran said the words, though he wasn't certain he actually believed himself. There was more to the curse than he could have ever imagined. It was so intricate, so hidden, that there wasn't anything he could do. And failure wasn't an option. Unseelie failed.

He couldn't do that to her. Not after everything she'd done for him.

Darcy chuckled, catching both Bran and his mother's attention. "This is lovely and all, but you do realize I know how to break her curse, right?"

"No, you don't," Bran grumbled. He rolled his eyes, knowing that the other faerie was simply trying to get attention. He probably knew the same amount that Bran did, which was very little.

"I do. I was the Raven King long enough to do my own research. The consort's curse is an old one. You already have everything you need to break it."

"You wouldn't tell me anything even if you knew how to break the curse."

"Consider it a gift for taking me out of that cursed kingdom. You did me more favors than I could ever say. I wouldn't have been able to align myself with an Unseelie prince and take the throne, for example." Darcy nodded at Eoin. "Sorry, it's not like you didn't guess I wanted it for myself."

Eoin shrugged. "I figured. We'll deal with that mess once

we destroy my family."

"I like a man with ambition." Darcy sauntered forward, his hands stretched out by his sides. "I'm not lying to you Bran. I do know how to save your lovely lady, and I'd very much like to tell you. There's a soft spot in my heart for her. Not many women are so feisty."

"You want something in return." It wasn't a question. Bran was certain this was a trap.

Darcy shook his head firmly. "No, of course not. I simply want to make sure that your little witch is the happiest she can be."

"Why?"

"I already told you. There's something special about that one. She's beautiful, she's powerful, and she isn't afraid of anything. Qualities like that are rare in a woman. Perhaps someday she'll bear you a child, and then I can have one of my own."

Bran made a disgusted face. "I wouldn't let you within sight distance of my children."

"Perhaps that's what I'll ask for then."

"My firstborn is off the table."

Darcy shrugged. "Then consider it a gift."

What was this dangerous man hiding? Bran narrowed his eyes. "What is it then?"

"The Raven King needs to have his consort become more powerful. I'm certain you've already seen what that power can do, how tantalizing it is. But, when she's a swan, that power goes away, doesn't it?"

He'd felt the change before. It wasn't completely gone, a fact he didn't want Darcy to know, it certainly waned as soon as the sun came up. Guarded, he nodded. "It does."

"The curse is a way to make certain that the Raven King doesn't become too powerful. It keeps him in his place, you might say. The Raven King has always had a hard time loving anything other than himself. It's why we're always Unseelie. Now, it seems like you might love this woman."

Again, Bran nodded.

Darcy smirked. "Truly love her? Enough to save her no matter what the cost?"

"I'd give my life for her, willingly and without question."

"That's good. That's very good to hear, because you're going to have to do just that to break her curse."

"What?" Bran hardly had time to think before Darcy gestured with his hand and Aisling stood in his arms. A cloak covered her body, and she struggled hard. He could see her face, that beloved face and the angry expression on it that always made his heart pound.

A knife appeared in Darcy's hands and a mad expression made his slitted eyes glint in the dim light. "Just how far would you go to save her?"

When Darcy drew the blade across her throat, Bran didn't think. He charged forward, ripped her out of Darcy's arms, and blasted him back so far his spine cracked against the wall on the other side of the throne room.

Blood splattered Bran's fingertips from where the blade had touched Aisling's throat.

"Are you all right?" he asked, frantic that he was too late. He cupped her face and tilted her eyes up to look at him. "Aisling, my love, answer me."

Darcy called out, "Say you love her! And the magic will

know that you've declared yourself to her."

Her eyes stared up at him, confused and angry. He didn't know how to explain himself or his family. There weren't words to justify what had happened to her. Now and throughout the entire time he'd known her.

Instead, he leaned down and pressed his forehead to hers. "I love you."

Her hands beat at his chest.

"No, Aisling, stop it. I love you more than life itself. I pledge myself to you and only you for the rest of our existence."

A crack of magic struck him in the center of the chest, so agonizing it nearly knocked him to his knees.

Was this the curse breaking? Why did it hurt *him*?

Darcy's laughter filled the room, and Bran realized how much of a fool he had been. He'd trusted a faerie, yet again, who wanted nothing more than to destroy him.

His mother made a disappointed sound and walked back to her throne. "You're too young to be a king. This is why we wouldn't ever put you on our throne, foolish child."

What had he done? What had Darcy made him do? With shaking hands, he reached up and pushed the hood of Aisling's cloak back.

Golden hair spilled out, glittering like freshly hewn wheat. She shook her head, pointing at her throat.

"Elva," he whispered.

"Isn't that who you wanted?" Darcy called out. "After all this time, your perfect woman is now handed to you on a platter. Go ahead, take her. You've already pledged yourself to her, after all."

"No. My words weren't for her."

"It's far too late to change your mind, I'm afraid." Darcy pushed himself away from the wall and laughed again. "Now, your little consort is free. She's no longer tied to you, nor is she tied to Underhill, or feeding you her power. And that means I'm going to take her and show her what a real king can do."

Bran released his hold on Elva and whipped around. "You wouldn't dare."

"Try to follow me without the massive power of the Raven King. It'll take you a while to draw up the runes and chase me back to your kingdom." Darcy shrugged. "You always were a little slower at magic than the rest of us. By the time you make it, your little consort will be gone and your castle empty once more."

A portal came to life behind him, the red sludge familiar dark magic. Darcy stepped through it and disappeared.

Bran let out a shout and ran toward the portal, but it closed before he reached it.

"Damn it!" he screamed, punching a fist against the wall where Darcy had leaned.

With the previous Raven King gone, his spell had shattered. Elva let out a croaking sound. "That bastard took me from the isle without any difficulty. What is he? How is it possible he got around Scáthach's wards?"

He pressed his forehead against the wall. "Does that matter right now? He plans to kidnap your sister."

"Then you should be building your portal, Bran."

The Unseelie queen laughed. "Naive little Seelie girl. He's not going to do anything at all. It's far too hard to save her now and so much easier to just stay here and give it all up."

He shoved back from the wall and pointed severely at his

mother. "You knew. You knew this entire time that there wouldn't be a war. You *baited* me."

"Perhaps," she said with a shrug. "I like to see what you do. You've yet to prove yourself to be Unseelie, not completely, and I worry about you, child."

Eoin finally spoke up, pushing out of the shadows and stalking toward their mother. "I will raise an army and prove you wrong—"

"Enough!" their mother shouted. All eight of her legs rose and then thumped hard against the ground, the echo of talons reverberating throughout the throne room. Bran's ears screamed in pain, and he clapped his hands over them in hopes that he might drown out the sound. When the ringing stopped, he heard his mother growl at his brother, "The Unseelie are ruled by the most feared faerie in all the kingdom. They fear *me*, little boy, not you."

Bran lifted his hands, magic pulsing through his veins as he began the spell for a portal, though he was weaker than before.

Let his family argue.

He was going to save Aisling if it took his last breath to do so.

CHAPTER 9
HOW A FAERIE LIES

Aisling touched a hand to the child's arm, gently moving it in a large circle. "You see? It has to be perfect for the spell to work, then you can do anything with it."

"I don't know how to make a perfect circle, though."

"Keep practicing. Hold your arm straight as an arrow and move nothing but your shoulder. It takes a lot of work to be a witch, trust me, it's worth it."

The little changeling girl scrunched up her face and continued etching the large circle on the dining hall floor. Each time she drew it the wrong way, she would scuff it with her shoe angrily before starting again. She had the making of a good witch. It wasn't going to come easy to her.

Some people were like that. Others were natural witches. Aisling saw a bit of herself in the child, though. No matter how hard it was, she would do her best to learn the ways of witchcraft.

She straightened and placed her hands on her hips, looking out over the crowd of changelings with a smile playing over her face. They were happy here. Learning, teaching, growing with each other as a new family.

Aisling hadn't realized how much she had missed this, the feeling of comradery between so many different types of people. Unseelie and Seelie fae shook off their old ties and simply became *changeling*. They were all cast aside by those who should have loved them. Yet, all of them agreed that this family was the one they would choose.

Hope bloomed in her chest. She couldn't remember the last time she had felt like this. The incredible feeling was so pure, so untainted, that it filled her near to bursting.

One of the older changeling's walked by her and pinched the fabric of her sleeve between his fingers. Fur covered his face and body, horse-like features unusual to her eyes. Even the deep pools of his gaze were animalistic, like she had never seen before.

"Mistress," he said, his voice deep and hoarse. "I wanted to thank you again."

"You're welcome here for as long as you wish." She tried to remember his name, but couldn't find it in the long list of changelings who now inhabited the castle. So she grinned and shrugged her shoulders. "I'm afraid I cannot remember if you were one of the few who wanted to stay or leave."

"I'll find my way back to the Unseelie court eventually, mistress. For now, this place is safe to lay my head, and I'll never forget that."

"You're always welcome back, you know." The words were one she wished someone had said to her whenever she was in a safe place. No one wanted to harbor a witch more than a few moments before they would force her to leave. "We won't turn you away, even if you leave."

His eyes filled with tears that did not fall. "You're an angel, mistress. A guardian sent to look after us."

As he walked away, she let the words roll in her mind. An angel? Goodness no, she was a witch, and even Aisling knew that was the exact opposite of what he thought she was. A guardian?

She quite liked the thought of that.

A crowd of changelings clamored in the halls; even the dining chamber was nearly filled to the brim. She didn't know how many there were now. No one could keep count. The sluagh were at their wit's end trying to make sure that each and every one were taken care of.

Aisling caught the hand of one bird-creature walking by. "Do they all have rooms?" she asked.

"It seems so," the sluagh croaked. Its brow furrowed. "We cannot be sure. They keep walking through portals from countless places."

"Watch the floors tonight. If you can spare a few of your own, I want to make sure none are sleeping near hearths. They deserve a bed."

The harried expression on the sluagh's face didn't change. "Aye, mistress, I'll make sure of it. Eventually we'll run out of rooms."

Aisling hoped they would. That would mean she'd saved countless changelings. They were here, where they would remain safe and out of sight. No faerie could harm them here. Not while the sluagh army remained on their side.

"Mistress!" a soft voice called out from the other side of the dining hall. "We have something new to show you. Come, come!"

147

A smile split her face, one so unfamiliar that it almost made her uncomfortable. "What did you learn?"

She could get used to this. The quiet living of a woman who took care of her people. They weren't monstrous. They weren't broken. They were just creatures who needed someone. For once in her life, Aisling realized that being a queen wasn't quite as terrible as she'd always thought.

No one forced her to remain. She *wanted* to be here, for them, for someone other than herself.

The thought was liberating. She'd finally managed to do something more than just healing boils on the town fool. Magic had a use here, far bigger than a small town's worries. She could help people.

When had she ever wanted to help people?

She stepped one foot forward, and the world exploded in her face. A portal opened in the center of the dining hall, cracking a table down the middle and sending shards of wood flying through the air. Stone shattered. The remaining glass of the ceiling caved in, daggers raining down upon them.

With an angry scream, she opened her arms wide and brought her hands together in a great blast to surround them all in a bubble. Wood turned to slivers, glass turned to powder, and stone turned to dust.

Aisling crouched with a knee on the ground, hands held out and black magic writhing through her fingers. Anger boiled in her chest. Her heart thudded against her ribs while a voice in her head screamed out for justice and for bloodshed.

Slowly, she looked up.

Darcy looked back at her with glee in his snake eyes. He licked his lips, then gestured behind him for the portal to close.

"You've gotten stronger," he admired. "I hadn't thought that was possible."

She ignored him and looked out over the crowd of people. Horror made their eyes large, while fear made them shake. They were stuck in place by her shield, but she could tell most of them wanted to run.

They should. This was not going to end well, and she didn't want them to see just what kind of justice she was going to mete out.

Aisling let the shield slip out of her fingers. The magic poured off her and struck the ground in a black sludge that sank between the cracks of the stone floor. "Go," she told the changelings and the sluagh. "I will take care of this man who dares step foot in our sanctuary."

They ran from the room as Darcy chuckled. "Sanctuary now? Funny, most people would call this a prison."

"Perhaps when you ruled here. We saw a greater purpose for these people and these lands."

"A purpose? Other than being the ones to hunt down all that you love?" He pressed a hand against his chest and stepped toward her. "I always knew you were a remarkable woman, but I didn't think you were so capable of forgiveness. It's an unusual trait for an Unseelie fae."

"I'm not Unseelie."

"Ah, yes, of course. You consider yourself to be one of the Underfolk now? Is that it?"

Aisling held up a hand. "Don't come any closer."

She didn't want them to think he was welcome here. After all that he had done, how could he consider that entering the castle in such a way would leave him in a good light? She wanted to destroy him. And she planned on doing so immediately.

He cocked his head to the side, eyes following her movements. "Do you think you could attack me? Is that what you're planning, little witch?"

"You can no longer call me that. Your Highness is acceptable."

Again, he licked his lips. The green scales on his throat flared with some strong emotion. "I think I'll call you Aisling."

She'd never felt her name slide down her spine like cold water. There was something different about this visit. He wasn't teasing her, or trying to make her angry just to see what she would do. Something dark lurked in his eyes and the way he held himself.

Foreboding made her shiver. "What are you doing here, Darcy?"

"Did you feel something shift?" He took another step closer, his foot crunching on a piece of stone that pulverized under his heel. "Just a few moments ago. A snapping feeling perhaps, or something like power flowing back into you, where it had been stolen without your permission?"

"I don't know what you're talking about."

"Perhaps you were simply too powerful already to feel the difference. Unusual, but even better for me when I take you."

Aisling frowned. "Take me?"

"Yes, Aisling. Your consort has made his choice very clear. He no longer wants you, so I've come to take you with me. I've a home with people who will appreciate you, and I certainly plan to treat you better than he ever could."

What was he going on about? The man was clearly mad,

although she hadn't seen him this bad before. It meant he was unpredictable, and that made her all the more nervous. Darcy was bad enough on most days.

She took a step back, closer to the doors behind her, and tried to think of a plan that would get her away from him without giving away what she was doing. "Darcy, I think you should go."

"I'm not going anywhere without you."

"And I'm not going anywhere at all. If you lay a hand on me, I will remove it."

He let out a laugh that shook the rafters. "Ah, that's what I appreciate so much about you, witch. You don't know how to feel fear, do you?"

It was running through her veins like a river. She held her hands in fists so he couldn't see them shaking. How could he say she didn't feel fear? It was in everything that she did. That only meant she would force herself through it.

Someone like him couldn't understand that.

Aisling glanced up. Her gaze caught on the remains of a chandelier hanging onto the ceiling by a small chain. If she could get him to stand under it... Well, it was a long shot. He likely would see what her plan was long before she could get him there. It was worth a try.

She looked back at him quickly. "What do you mean Bran chose another?"

"Stings, doesn't it? I know the feeling well. The woman I was in love with, the one who was promised to me before all this" — he gestured around them — "also left me the very first moment she could."

"Bran wouldn't leave me." She stepped back, watching

him intently as he followed her movement with his own body. "He loves me."

"Unseelie don't know how to love. But the words are poetic, aren't they?" Darcy ran a hand through his hair and down over the scales on his face. "Now, I know you don't mind men who look a little less human than others. I can assure you, my animal side is far more pleasant to touch than the scratch of feathers."

Just a few more steps, and he would be exactly where she wanted him. "Who did he choose?"

"Who has he always chosen? Fate is a circle. It goes round and round, but we always end up exactly where we began." Darcy's eyes narrowed, and she knew he was enjoying these words that still ached in her chest. "Elva, the pretty little golden thing that every eligible faerie wants to get his hands on. Do you know they loved each other long ago? He might have told you it paled in comparison to what he feels for you, I can assure you it doesn't. I was there, and I saw all that happened between them."

Two more steps, she thought. Two more steps, and then she could shut him up forever. "I don't believe you. How did you trick him into choosing her?"

"I didn't have to trick him. All I had to do was give him the choice. Her or you." His expression twisted into something pitying and sad. "He's always wanted her, Aisling. The sooner you believe that, the faster you can heal."

She knew he was lying, but something still settled nervously in her gut. She hadn't ever questioned what Bran felt for her. Their feelings ran deep beneath her feet like the roots of an ancient tree. They were subtle, and some people couldn't see them at al. Yet,they were there, feeding everything around them. Sometimes she could feel the leaves raining down on her head.

Believing Darcy's words would be foolish. He was a trickster. She'd learned that a long time ago, and there was a reason why he told her this. There was something hidden in the words and she didn't have time to figure out what they were.

"And if I believe you?" she asked, keeping her eyes locked on him. She wouldn't look at the chandelier above them, not yet. "What then?"

"Come with me, as you should have long ago." He took another step forward and then he was exactly where she wanted him. Darcy shifted a stone away from his foot, smoothed a hand down his shirt, and then held it out for her to take. "Let us be the most powerful couple the faerie realms have ever seen. With our magic combined, we could rule not only Underhill, but the Unseelie court as well."

"Ah," she replied. "You want to take a throne."

"I want to take *every* throne."

"You can't do it without me."

"I can find another, but I want you to sit by my side. Your knowledge of magic far surpasses any other. And your beauty…" He paused, his eyes drifting shut for a small moment as if he were savoring her memory.

Lips curling in disgust, she threw up her hand and let out a bolt of magic that struck the chandelier chain with a loud clang. Aisling spread her palm wide and assisted it in falling. She had to make sure it hit him, no matter the cost.

His eyes snapped open, a shield surrounding him so quickly that she didn't see it until the metal struck it. The blast echoed, and the chandelier ricocheted toward her.

She threw herself to the side, the ragged edge that could have sliced her in half narrowly missing her. It struck the wall and left a hole in its wake. Dust billowed down upon her, stone raining in chunks as the room shivered then held. Gasping, she placed both palms on the ground and pushed herself up.

The dust would hide her for a few moments only. That was her last chance to escape him, and she had failed.

"Aisling," he called out, laughter in his voice. "An admirable attempt. If you think that was the first time someone tried to kill me with a chandelier, you would be wrong."

She had to think. No one was immortal though he had lived a very long time. She had to be more creative than a regular parlor trick. Faeries constantly tried to kill each other, but there had to be a way they hadn't thought of. Something dirty, something not quite so showy.

A large rock rolled toward her hand. Aisling blew out a breath. Sometimes, the old ways were best.

She snatched it off the floor and stood shakily. All she needed was for him to get close enough, and then she'd bash his brains in. She'd seen a man do it before, back when she lived in the swamp. It looked like a lot of work, but if it would shut the man up for good, then she was happy to suffer the consequences.

Darcy whistled. The sharp sound blasted around the room, ringing from every corner. "Come on then, witch. I don't have all day to hunt you."

"Why's that?" she called out. "Is Bran following you?"

"I told you he's made his choice."

"Then there's no reason for you to be so worried."

The mist next to her swirled with movement. She spun and lifted the rock, only to find nothing behind her. So, he knew where she was. He was simply toying with her.

"I'm not worried at all. I can take you whenever I want you, Aisling. And I do want you, because I want everything that Carman has shared with you."

Aisling frowned. "Carman? What does she have to do with any of this?"

"Everything. Did you think you weren't directly connected to her? That's where the raven consort's curse comes from. You and her are linked."

He knew something that he wasn't sharin. If she was lucky, she could use his arrogance against him. "I'm linked to no one but Bran. If you take me, he will find me."

"I'm sure you'd like to think that. Carman is alive and well because *you* are alive and well. That's why no one can figure out how to break your curse, little witch. Because the most powerful witch to ever live is keeping you alive. So that she can stay alive."

It wasn't exactly what she wanted to hear. Carman was dangerous. Aisling couldn't argue she was infinitely more powerful now than before she had been cursed. She'd hoped it had something to do with being the Raven Queen, and in a way, it did. But it wasn't what she wanted.

Connections were strong between witches. They could call upon each other when something was wrong, sometimes even forcing the other to appear beside them. Why hadn't Carman done that if all he said was true?

"Is that your plan then?" she asked. "You want to use me to get to Carman?"

155

Darcy's breath fluttered against the back of her neck. She felt the heat of him blanket her spine, and he leaned down to press his lips against the hollow of her shoulder. "No, little witch. I'm not using you to get to Carman. I want you to *be* Carman."

"Well, that's too bad. I will never be anyone other than myself."

She brought the stone in her hand up and caught him at the temple. It struck hard, bone meeting rock in an agonizing crack that made her wince even as she lunged away from him.

Darcy let out a howl that vibrated with magic. The floor and ceiling shook with the power of his rage, and Aisling knew she didn't have much time. She had to get out of here, but as it always did, magic leaked out of her as fear took its place.

More power filtered through the room behind her. What was Darcy doing now? Had she failed? Could he really steal her out of her own castle so easily?

It wasn't his dark-edged magic that touched her shoulder, nor was it a faerie portal as she was used to. Instead, magic as cool as a forest spring slid over her arm and a hand linked fingers with hers.

She looked down in shock and saw black tipped fingers threaded through her own before she was yanked through the portal.

CHAPTER 10
In The Depths Of Underhill

Bran finished the last etched rune on the floor and blasted the circle with so much power that it made him faint. He let out a ragged breath. The runes glowed dark red, sinking into the floor and opening a way for him to return home.

To her.

He only hoped he wasn't too late. When he stepped forward, a hand landed on his arm.

"I don't have time," he growled.

"Bran, wait." Elva tugged harder. "You don't know what you're leaping into. She could already be gone, or they could still be fighting for all you know."

"I can't leave her there. She can't think I abandoned her so easily."

"Would she believe that?" Elva stepped in front of him, blocking his view of the portal. "The sister I saw on the isle, even wounded, would never have second guessed your feelings for her. She won't believe his lies, Bran. So you need to think of a plan, or you're jumping in blind. You'll get yourself hurt, or worse, killed."

"No one can kill the Raven King." The ferocity of his growled words startled even him. Bran believed them wholeheartedly. He'd felt invincible ever since the curse swallowed him whole.

"Are you so powerful?" she asked. "Because I don't think you are. Not anymore. He took away much of your power, and I'm sorry for that. Everyone still needs you. Your *people* need you. You aren't just Bran, anymore."

Gods, how he hated that. He wanted to be free to find the woman he loved and hold her against his chest once again.

He hadn't said it enough. There wasn't enough time in the world to say the words as many times as she deserved. They had danced around their feelings for such a long time that it would be his fault entirely if she believed the poisonous words Darcy spouted.

He was a fool. How many times would he have to realize he was nothing but a fool?

Elva cupped his cheek, forcing him to focus on her. "If you're so set on saving her, then I'm not letting you go alone."

"What stake do you have in this?" He wanted to shout that she was the reason why all this had happened in the first place. It was her fault that Aisling was in trouble, and he'd somehow severed the strange bond between them.

Bran also knew that this was all his doing. He'd been the one who didn't look close enough and only tried to save the woman he loved. He should have known Aisling wouldn't let herself be captured by such a fool. She had more luck than that.

"I have every stake," Elva snapped. "She's my sister. And I haven't been very good family to her my entire life. This will make up for that."

"I don't think anything can make up for that." He strode forward, hovered a foot over the portal, and did not look back at her. "If you want to help, I won't stop you."

He plunged into the portal and stepped into his own throne room.

Chaos was everywhere. Debris spilled out from the dining hall, and sluagh wailed all around him. Their screams made his ears ache, but he continued through their masses toward the only person he was interested in seeing.

Darcy sat on the Raven King's throne once again. One leg hooked over an arm of the chair, he bounced his foot and waited for Bran to reach him.

A sluagh grabbed his arm. "My king, the mistress, she's—"

"I know," he growled and shook off the creature.

Another latched onto the other arm. "That man on the throne—he's not coming back, is he?"

Hands grasped his leg. "Highness, save us. You cannot let him come back."

"The mistress, where is she?"

Over and over again, they asked him questions, swarming around his arms and legs, tugging him down among the masses. And through it all, he kept his eyes on the man who sat upon *Bran's* throne.

He wouldn't be like Darcy. He wouldn't brush them aside because he was angry. Aisling had taught him better than that. Instead, he let out a snarl.

"Let me go," he warned. "I will answer your questions soon, first I intend to tear that animal apart limb by limb."

His anger poured into them, and it gave them strength.

Their hands fell from his flesh, and they turned toward the previous Raven King with anger as their power. The sluagh melted from their bird-like forms and shifted into a dark mist that gathered around Bran like armor.

Darcy let out a chuckle. "So, you still have some of your powers, I see. Pity. I thought maybe you would learn how to be Unseelie again without leaning on what should have never been yours."

"Where is she?"

A knife appeared in Darcy's hands. He twirled it between them, the metal flashing in the torchlight. "Yes, Unseelie Prince, where is your wife? I desperately wish to know where she is considering you traded her to me."

"I traded no one," Bran growled, stalking toward the throne.

"Funny, I remember it differently. You promised your everlasting love to another woman. That seems like you don't want Aisling at all."

Words shriveled on Bran's tongue. Not from guilt or fear, but an anger so powerful that it turned him into little more than a weapon the sluagh could wield. They ate up his emotions and reflected them back a thousand-fold. He became little more than rage incarnate.

"You can't fight him, Bran," Elva called out. The sound of a sword pulling from its scabbard reached his ears. "We need to know where he took her."

"Did I take her?" Darcy replied, the grin on his face only incensing Bran further. "Or did she somehow slip out of my hands?"

Bran snapped his teeth. "I don't need him to talk. I'll find her without his help."

"I don't think you will."

"Bran," Elva said once more, "we need to know what he knows."

"He knows nothing," he spat. "The only thing he knows how to do is hide the truth. This man needs to be punished, not listened to."

"And we will punish him. But not until he tells us where she is."

Unable to think clearly, he shot out a hand. The sluagh slithered across the floor and snaked around her. The dark mist traveled up toward her mouth. "I need you silent," Bran said. "Your words have no place here."

Darcy placed his hands on the throne and slowly leveraged himself to standing. He clapped, the sound echoing in the silent hall. "You've finally come into your own, Raven King. I always knew you would accept the darkness and snap eventually. Unseelie enjoy such power. I certainly did."

"I'm nothing like you," he growled.

"Oh, you are. Look at you. Taking what you want, so easily, because all it would take is a snap of the fingers and I would be gone. The sluagh are your army, and you can use them in whatever way you want." Darcy hopped down onto the floor, arms spread at his side. "By all means, use them to destroy me. Or, perhaps, you could use them to find *her*."

The words filtered through the darkness in his mind. *Her*. Aisling. The woman all this was for.

The woman who wouldn't want him to be a monster.

He shook his head to clear the evil thoughts, held out a hand, and sent the sluagh swarming around Darcy. The man began to scream as they ran up and down his sides, slicing into flesh along the way.

Bran closed his fist, and the sluagh paused. They held Darcy still, his face the only thing not covered by the quivering mist.

Sauntering forward, Bran made his way to Darcy's side and held up a single finger. "First, never question my feelings for that witch. She is mine and mine alone." He held up another finger. "Second, if you think I can't punish you for this and find her at the same time, then you are a fool." Bran held up the last finger and grinned. "Third, you should never have challenged me when she wasn't here to keep me a good man."

He brought his hand down, and a small portion of the sluagh broke away from the others. Their mist shot through the ceiling while the rest closed in on Darcy and fed upon his screams.

Aisling stumbled through the portal and landed hard on her knees. How long had she been in there? It felt like days, although she suspected it was only a few hours.

She dug her shaking fingers into the gray, lifeless dirt beneath her that seemed to go on forever. This wasn't a place she recognized, although she doubted it was an in-between place, neither real nor fake. It felt *real*.

The earth crumbled beneath her fingers, cracking and breaking with the simple movement. This was a dead place.

Blowing out a breath, she slowly pushed herself up onto her haunches and searched for the person who had helped her. The person who had *saved* her.

A dead tree stood in front of her, far too familiar for comfort. The rattling branches still held the screams of her ancestors in their bark. The hanging tree always seemed to show itself to her when her life was about to change.

Was she to hang now? Would she finally join the hundreds of souls who were trapped within the earthen tomb?

A shadow shifted at the trunk, the shape of a man forming but not stepping out so she might see him.

"Who are you?" she called out. "Show yourself."

"I'd rather not." The voice was gravelly, harsh, as if the man hadn't spoken in a very long time. Perhaps it was one of the sluagh, an ancient that hadn't stayed with the others. Or worse, yet another creature who had hidden themselves deep in Underhill and now wanted her help.

She stood and winced when her muscles seized. The portal travel hadn't been comfortable this time, though the magic had felt far kinder than others. "Where are we?"

"We're still in Underhill."

She looked around at the gray landscape, the sparse dead trees surrounding them, the brambles far in the distance. "I've never seen such a place in Underhill."

"It's a very big kingdom."

Something in her mind slid into place at the words. "Show yourself to me."

The shadow sank back to the tree. "No, I'm afraid I can't do that."

"Can't or won't?" She stepped closer, squinting her eyes to try to make out his features. "Step forward, faerie. You saved my life, and I would like to know who my rescuer is."

"Aisling," the voice sighed. "Are you sure about this?" When she didn't respond, the man stepped out of the shadows and let a spear of light show his face.

His high brow was smooth and blemish free. A hawk-like nose gave him an aristocratic look, while his full lips jutted forward in a pout. Dark hair fell to his shoulders, curling at his ears where gray hair dusted the locks. His square jaw and long neck were not that of a warrior or a farmer, but an artist.

Or perhaps, a witch.

Her breath caught in her throat, ragged and aching. Pressing a hand against her chest, she stumbled a few steps forward then paused. "Lorcan?" she asked. "Is it really you?"

The cat turned man lifted his shoulders in a shrug. "I didn't think it would really work. Now that it did, I've changed my mind. Being human is much worse than being a cat."

"You-you—" She waved her hands up and down, gesturing at his body. "You look older."

"I am older."

"I don't remember your nose being that big."

He frowned and touched a hand to his face. "I suppose not. They say that keeps growing as you age."

Aisling let out a sob, then pressed her hands to her face. Muffled words poured between her fingers. "I don't know what you did, or what deal you made. I'm so glad you're here."

The tension in his shoulders eased, and for a moment, she

saw the man she remembered. Not the cat at all.

Begrudgingly, he lifted his arms. "Come here, Aisling. Let me hold you for once, take back a little bit of masculinity now that you don't have to pick me up."

She laughed through the tears that fell from her eyes and raced toward him. He lifted her up so she could press her face against his throat to let out years of frustration and sadness. She'd felt so alone for such a long time, and yet he'd always been there with her.

Her familiar no longer, Lorcan had finally joined her and become a man again.

"Why now?" she whispered against him. "Why now, after all this time?"

He shook his head. "You needed me. And there's far more at work here than just an Unseelie trying to capture another throne after being forced to give up his."

"Darcy?" She pulled back to meet Lorcan's gaze. "I don't think he's really something to worry about. He's all show, but he won't hurt anyone. Not if I can help it."

"He wasn't lying when he told you about Carman," Lorcan replied. He set her down and placed his hands on her shoulders. "You're in grave danger, Aisling. That woman is directly tied to you, and you aren't just a witch. You're a changeling, with so much more magic in you than any human could hope to have. She's coming after you."

Aisling shook her head. "No, it's not possible. She's dead or imprisoned."

"That doesn't mean she can't reach you. Witches are far more capable than that." He stepped back and gestured to the tree. "I've been talking to them, and they're all worried about what this change is going to bring."

"Change?"

"Carman is awake, Aisling. She's sensed you, talked to you, and she wants to take back her crown as queen of witches, mother of darkness, all that is evil in this world. And she's going to try and use you to do it."

Aisling stumbled back, staring up into the branches of the hanging tree. "I won't let her."

"I don't think you have a choice."

She gazed into the small fire Lorcan had started. Shapes formed in the depths of the flames. Faeries dancing to the beat of a drum she thought might be her heartbeat. Aisling couldn't really tell, her mind whirling too much.

"Why can't I go back to the castle?" she asked for the fifth time. "Bran could help. He's the Raven King. Of all people in Underhill, he's the one who can actually make something happen. He owns Underhill."

"And you are the Raven Queen, yet Carman can still use you without any problem." Lorcan looked up from where he lay on the ground. "Do you really want to risk her getting claws sunk into Bran as well?"

He had a point. If the witch queen could control Aisling,

she didn't want to know what kind of hold the creature had over Bran.

"Can we at least send him a message? He probably thinks Darcy managed to steal me away or that I'm dead." Aisling ran her hands over her arms, trying to warm her chilled flesh. "I don't want him to worry."

"I know, you love him, blah blah blah." Lorcan rolled over onto his side and met her gaze across the fire. "You have to stop worrying about him so much. He's a grown man."

"A very powerful Unseelie who can control the sluagh like an army," she corrected. "He's not very good at controlling that power either. He uses me to help ease the burden of all the previous Raven Kings who want him to do very evil things."

"Then let him. It's in his nature."

"We aren't evil because we're Unseelie or Seelie fae. It doesn't work like that."

Lorcan rolled his eyes. "That's not what I meant, and you know it. I'm not saying that his species makes him naturally inclined toward evil. I'm saying *he* leans toward evil. Bran's a bad man who wants to do a little good in his life here and there to balance it out. You can't force him to be good simply because you think your morals are right. Let him be who he is supposed to be."

"He'll kill them," she whispered. Needing a distraction, she picked up a stick and poked the fire. "The changelings, I mean."

"Do you really think he would? You left him alone with the Wild Hunt, and look at what showed up? Hundreds of them."

"Because I asked."

"You don't give him enough credit," Lorcan replied. "He would have done that without you is my guess. He sees them as people, too, where most faeries just see them as property. Bran's never been like the rest of his family, which is why they have such a hard time understanding him."

"Perhaps you're right," she murmured.

He'd done so much for her, and still she thought of him as "unseelie" before she thought of him as Bran. Old habits died hard, she supposed. Aisling worried that if she wasn't at his side, he would walk in the footsteps of all those who had gone before him.

The Raven King was not a good man. He wasn't even a kind man, if the rumors and legends were true. He wielded the sluagh like a blade, made their lives horrible because that was what he was supposed to do.

Bran wasn't like that. He softened when he saw the sluagh. He told them stories while she wasn't there, built their confidence and helped them stand on their own two feet. These were the reasons why she adored him so much.

And still, she judged him for something he couldn't change.

She slapped her hands to her thighs and stood. "That's it, I'm telling him."

"No, you aren't."

"I listened to your reasoning, and I don't agree with it. I'm telling him where we are and asking him to let us handle it."

"As if he'll do that!" The fire spat, red light reflecting in the depths of Lorcan's eyes. "You know he'll be here in an instant if he knows our plan."

"We don't have a plan." She lifted her hands, a spell already dancing at her fingertips. "And Bran specializes in not having plans."

Lorcan lifted his own hands. "Have it your way." Before she could whisper her own spell, he blurted out, "Magic burn and magic bite, take her tongue with all my might."

A burning pain sliced through her mouth. Eyes wide, she lifted a hand to touch her mouth where a thin trail of blood leaked out. The sudden absence of a large piece of flesh made her gasp out a breath. Bubbles blew through the liquid sticking to her teeth.

Aisling curled her fingers into fists.

He didn't even look at her. Instead, he stared up at the night sky and held up his hand. Slippery and glistening, her tongue gleamed in the firelight. "You won't get it back until you agree with me."

She wanted to shout at him that he'd crossed the wrong woman. That she would destroy him with a single thought, with all the power of the Raven Queen flowing through her.

Even more concerning was his knowledge of this magic. He hadn't done this before he was a cat.

Or had he?

Snarling, she wiped away the blood and drool on her chin before reluctantly nodding and gesturing with her hand.

"You sure?" he asked.

Again, she nodded.

Her tongue disappeared from his hand, and her mouth filled with flesh once more.

She gasped out a breath and touched her tongue tentatively to the roof of her mouth. "I will skin you alive if you *ever* do that again."

Lorcan snorted. "Can we talk about Carman now? I know you don't want to think about it, but I did spend an entire week with the hanging tree to garner some information."

The acidic taste of a grudge burned her throat. She didn't want to talk about Carman. She wanted to launch herself across the fire and wring his neck. Stealing her tongue? When had he learned how to do that?

He was right. Carman was a larger issue than him not wanting Bran to know where they were. She'd get to the bottom of that soon enough. For now, they needed to figure out where the true danger was.

"She wants to use me." Aisling flinched. "What exactly does that entail?"

"Likely possession, although I don't know how she would get past your wards."

Aisling looked down at her fingers. The black tips that she'd once thought of as chains now reminded her she was more protected than she had originally thought. "Ah yes, these." She lifted her hands and wiggled her fingers. "Care to explain how you got yourself a matching set?"

He shrugged. "Some of the other witches thought it might be nice to support you."

"Lorcan."

"And it was a good idea to carry the same spell in case Carman tried to use me to get to you." He rolled his eyes and let out a frustrated breath. "We don't even know if it's going to work. Only that Badb gave you these to keep you hidden from faeries, so maybe it'll work on the witch queen."

"That might be wishful thinking," she replied. Could something that had hid her face from faeries really do anything against a witch? "You were able to see my face without any issues. I'm not sure this spell really works like that."

"At the very least, we put a little extra into it." Lorcan rolled to his feet, strode to her side, then crouched next to her and held out his hands. "Take a look."

She grasped his fingertips and turned them toward the fire. On the inside edges was a fine webbing laced in white ink. It looked familiar in a way, like a prayer rather than a spell.

"What is it?" she asked.

"An old protection spell, used by the very first of our kind. Blood magic."

She shuddered in disgust. "I'm not interested in adding it to mine."

"You don't have a choice. I'm doing it if it helps keep you out of that witch's clutches."

"No, Lorcan. I don't meddle with blood magic."

"Too many people are afraid to use a power they consider to be stronger than any other. Blood magic will save your life, because it *is* your life. Now give me your hands."

He'd have to tie her down and cast his spell quickly with the mood she was in. Aisling crossed her arms firmly over her chest and shook her head. "No, Lorcan. You don't know if it will even help. You've already taken my tongue tonight. Push me again, and I will prove how powerful I can be."

Lorcan lifted his hands and stepped back. "If you don't want the added protection, I won't force it. It's a foolish choice, Aisling."

She shook her head and didn't respond.

He didn't get to decide what was smart and what wasn't. Blood magic terrified her, always had. She didn't want to cast a spell that tied her lifeforce directly into its function. What kind of fool did that? If the spell failed, it would drain not just her magic or energy from the world around her, but directly from what kept her alive.

No, she would never use blood magic.

Huffing out an angry breath, she cracked the stick in her hands. Splinters dug into her palms. "So what does the hanging tree think we should do? All those centuries of spirits, and the best they can come up with is blood magic?"

"Not quite."

"Spit it out."

Lorcan eased back onto his haunches. The fire reflected banners of red light in his eyes, but she saw far more than that. She saw the collective experience of her ancestors. Of women and men who had swung by a rope around their throat, of so much pain that it bubbled over into the souls that were reborn. The souls that would follow in their footsteps.

He reached out and touched a hand to her knee. "We have to kill her, Aisling. Remove her from this world as the Tuatha de Danann should have done long ago."

"They must have had a reason to leave her alive."

"Maybe they did. Maybe they just didn't know how to kill a witch for good. Maybe they wanted to see what would happen if they left her here. We all know how much the faeries like to play. Regardless of their intention, it's our role now to save them. To save everyone from this witch."

"You want to kill the mother of all witches?" She shook her head. "That's impossible."

"There are a few here who remember the old days. We'll visit them first, and they'll tell us exactly what we have to do."

"Who? Who knows anything about Carman?"

"The banríon bean sidhe."

Aisling shook her head. "The Banshee queen is impossible to find. We don't even know if she still exists in Underhill."

"That's because no Raven King or Queen has ever searched for her." Lorcan squeezed her knee. "Do this with me, Aisling. Trust me on this."

He'd never done her wrong before. Aisling gave him a nod and watched as he made his way to the other side of the fire once more. He laid down and shut his eyes, leaving her to dark thoughts that swelled like the crest of a wave.

Aisling shivered as a cold wind crept over her arms, and she swore the wail of a hundred raven queens wavered in the air. It was almost as though they were telling her to turn back now.

CHAPTER 11

A JOURNEY MADE ALONE

Bran slumped on his throne, leaning an elbow on the edge while cupping his head in his hand. The sluagh cleaned up his mess quietly, not wanting to disturb him, but not wanting to leave the blood and gore slicking the stone floor any longer than it needed to.

He'd lost control. More than that, he'd used his own people as a weapon. When had he become that kind of Unseelie Fae? He'd always thought to be a king who saw the sluagh as something more than a sword or blade.

Instead, he'd used them much the same way his predecessors had.

A scuffle near his elbow made him lift his head. One of the sluagh knelt beside him, male or female, he couldn't tell. Its big eyes glowed in the dim light.

"Master?" it asked quietly, voiced pitched low and calm.

"What is it?"

"Thank you." Reverently, it reached out and touched a hand to his boots. "We've desired to destroy that monster many nights. All our dreams are filled with the sound of his screams for mercy now, and that is a very good thing."

At the very least, he'd freed them from a demon who plagued their nightmares. He gave the sluagh a curt nod and flicked his fingers. It raced back to the others, picked up the rag it had left on the floor, and scrubbed with renewed vigor.

Warmth bloomed deep in his chest. They were pathetic creatures, but they were his. He'd been gifted a kingdom of people who were afraid of every shadow. Now, they had finally taken their retribution and perhaps could heal. The sluagh deserved more than just fear, and no one had ever offered them anything else.

Elva strode into the throne room, a cloak firmly wrapped around her shoulders. Was it cold in the castle? Bran couldn't remember the last time he'd felt cold, or warm for that matter… He furrowed his brows. He should be able to remember that. Temperature was something people remembered easily since it was part of basic bodily functions.

When had he lost that?

She'd braided the long tail of her hair, a few golden curls escaping the weave. Each ringlet framed her lovely face, enhancing her beauty and also making her appear more out of place.

Underhill was a home for the forgotten and the ugly. The children no one wanted or cared to remember existed. She should be in the Seelie Court with fields of wheat surrounding her. Just as Bran remembered her from so long ago.

Elva met his gaze and made her way to his side. "Your castle is falling apart."

He lifted a brow. "I don't remember you being so forward."

"As I said before, a lot has changed since we were

children." She swiped a nervous hand down her stomach as she said the words.

"Not so much, I think." He glanced away from her blinding beauty, choosing instead to stare at the dark shadows of the sluagh lurking in the corners of the room. They waited for a single word from him, an order, some reason to exist. Gods, it was too much.

Elva glanced down at the sluagh on their hands and knees, blood splattered up to their elbows. "Was killing him absolutely necessary?"

"Absolutely."

"She won't like it, you know. And now we have no way to find her."

"I don't need him to find her," he growled. Agitation stirred to life. His thighs twitched, and he drummed his fingers on the arm of the throne. "The sluagh will find her."

"Are you willing to take that risk? Truly?" Elva clenched her teeth, the muscle on her jaw bouncing. "It could take them weeks to find her. Underhill is endless."

"How would you know that? Is this your kingdom now as well?" The words came out too harsh.

An answering rage bloomed in her gaze, and she cocked her head to the side. "Well, you did pledge yourself to me. Again. Does that not give me some claim to this kingdom?"

He abruptly stood. Though his pride was stinging, Bran logically knew she was simply lashing out because he had. It wasn't fair to punish her for words that came from a place of pain. He didn't know how to stop. *Couldn't* without the cool water of Aisling's magic lapping at his wounds.

Bran stepped down from the throne, then strode until he

was so close to her that their toes touched. To her credit, Elva didn't back down.

"You have no claim to this land, no right to stand on its shore, and no place in this kingdom," he growled. "You may be my queen's sister, but that does not mean I cannot destroy you as well. I want that to be very clear."

She licked her lips. "Bran, she's my sister. I know you think I don't love her, or that I don't feel as deeply as you. I've had so many years stolen away when I might have learned who she was, listened to her stories, found out what kind of food she liked. There is so much I want to know, and I can only do that if she's here with me."

His jaw ached as he clenched his teeth together tightly. The words were in the air in front of them, yet, he couldn't register them. All he could think was that she wanted to stop him from doing things his way, the only way he knew how to control.

"Bran," she repeated. Elva didn't reach up to touch his chest or move at all. Instead, she remained perfectly still, a woman who knew she was in the presence of a predator too powerful to kill. "I know what it feels like to lose everything. She's not dead. We would know if she was. We'd feel it. So I need you to listen to me. There is another way to find her. One that doesn't require your sluagh to search every inch of Underhill for her soul."

He almost didn't hear the words. His memory was filled with the tiny moments he'd forgotten to tell her that he appreciated. Small things, like the way her dark hair would stick to her lips when she was muttering spells. The way her hands gracefully traced the air with runes because lifetimes ago she was a dancer. And the beautiful poetry of her body underneath his hands late at night.

The words eventually sank into his mind, and his eyes snapped up to Elva's. "Another way? Is that so?"

She nodded. "Aisling is still considered a changeling. The Wild Hunt could find her."

"I refuse to call another hunt and then chase her down like an animal. The sluagh would just as likely kill her as they would rejoice in her finding. They aren't themselves during a hunt."

"No, they aren't. The leaders of the hunt could find her without any issues." Elva took a deep breath. "You could petition them for their assistance."

"Midir and Etain owe me no favors. They despise my court for all the darkness in it, and they have no interest in entertaining me. Once the hunt is done, their use for me ends," he replied with a huff.

They were as old as faeries could get, and old prejudices ran deep in their veins. They saw Underhill as a kingdom of mistakes. Proof that faeries weren't as perfect as they liked to think, and therefore something that needed to be hidden.

Elva shook her head. "Midir and Etain are no longer the leaders of the Wild Hunt. That honor was passed on to the people who will spend the rest of the year planning for their first time in leading the sacred festival."

"Who?"

"The Seelie King and his druid queen, who perhaps will understand the suffering of the changelings a little more than the previous leaders."

Blood froze in his veins. Eamonn had agreed to lead the

hunt? Knowing what he did?

Bran didn't know if it was anger or sadness that locked his muscles in place. His age-old friend had never hurt him before, but this seared deep into his bones. Eamonn knew who Aisling was. Had Bran not made it clear enough in their first meeting? And certainly he'd heard the story from Sorcha herself. The witch was not just a witch. She was a changeling who had feelings and memories.

He couldn't allow someone so close to him to lead the hunt. Not when it would destroy her so.

Elva stepped back, her lips parting in surprise. "I had forgotten you and the king used to be friends."

"Still are."

"Even after everything that happened?" Her brows lifted. "Eamonn was banished for his deformities, and his brother took the throne. I don't care what the Seelie King looked like. I care that he didn't even try to take it back for centuries."

"You're holding a grudge for that?" he asked. "Eamonn did what he thought was best for his people. The Seelie court likes to brainwash its people, as you well know. He'd been told he was nothing more than a shadow in his own home. Did you really think he would rush back just because one Seelie faerie was being mistreated by his brother?"

She shook her head. "I thought he would rush back to save his kingdom."

"It wasn't his kingdom anymore. He didn't view them as his people. Only as the misfits on the isle of Hy-Brasil needed him." Bran gestured around them. "Similar to this. It seems we both ended up on thrones that are moth-eaten and destroyed. A shame he let go of something so splendid to take back what was his."

Old memories filled Elva's gaze with darkness. He'd seen such a look before. She wanted retribution, revenge, destruction, and an ending that would satisfy her bloodlust. She'd likely not get it. The previous Seelie King, and Eamonn's twin, was banished to the human world forevermore.

It was unlikely the spoiled faerie had done well.

To distract her, Bran took a deep breath. "What would you have me do then? Beg on hands and knees that Eamonn and Sorcha tap into a power they haven't used before to find a single changeling and then *not* send the hunt after her?"

Elva shook herself clear of the old memories and glared at him. "Yes. That's precisely what I'm asking you to do."

"It's too dangerous."

"When has danger ever stopped you before?"

Magic pulsed deep in his navel, and he realized the boon given to his curse had ended. The sun set on the horizon, and with that darkness his form would disappear. Sadly, he looked at Elva and held his hands up. "I am running out of time."

"Then let me speak for you." She reached for his hands then clasped them delicately in her own so his clawed hand wouldn't break the delicate skin of her wrist. "They are dear friends of mine as well. You don't have to do everything yourself."

He felt the curse churn in his belly and could only nod. They didn't have the time to wait, and he knew she was right. The sluagh couldn't find her in the ever-growing outskirts of Underhill.

Black and angry, the curse burst in his belly, and he

shattered into a rainstorm of raven feathers. Letting out a croaking call, he signaled Elva to start moving. He would follow her on wing to the castle of the Seelie Fae.

Bran dove through the white mist and spread his wings wide to slow his descent. The Seelie castle was just as he'd remembered it. The high spikes rose into the air, glimmering gold in the sunlight. White marble made the entire thing blend into the clouds as if it were seated in the sky itself.

Green gardens spread all around it. Mazes where faeries raced through the high walls, their laughter bubbling up as they tried to catch each other. Large blossoms, far bigger than anywhere else in the world, filled the air with their cloying scent. He had once wanted to live here more than anything he'd ever desired. And yet now, he looked at its splendor as dull and shallow.

Elva stepped through the front gates, entering the castle and waiting for a chance to petition the king and queen for a few moments of their time.

He clacked his beak. Foolish woman. She always forgot that he wasn't a patient man, and he had no interest in making it easier on Eamonn and Sorcha. They would come to him, and he would force them to understand what he wanted them to do.

Speak for him. He hadn't been in his human form long enough to tell her that he didn't let anyone put words in his mouth other than Aisling. He'd simply have to show her that the Raven King needed no one to assist when he asked another king for help.

Soaring through the air, he found the window he was looking for.

The king's bedroom was usually in the center of the palace. That was far easier to defend should there ever be an attack, and the king could easily flee into the many passages that led deep into the belly of the castle.

Of course, Eamonn had no interest in being a pampered king. He'd fought countless battles, likely still trained even without Bran to give him a wallop over the head, and would want something that would please Sorcha.

And she would want to see the entire kingdom at her feet.

Bran carefully hovered in front of the window, cocking his head and narrowing his eyes as he searched for any clues. The room was as splendorous as he'd ever seen. Pastel paintings depicting forest scenes covered every inch of the white marble walls. Gold filigree framed the ceiling while strands of gossamer hung around the giant bed with its golden four posters and cream sheets. A large mirror hung above the headboard, gilded edges so pristine they almost glowed.

These weren't the details he was looking for however. Bran noticed instead the herbs hanging in the corner, a brush with strands of bright red hair and, of course, wrinkled bed clothes.

When Sorcha had made her way here from the human realm the first time, Bran had been with her. She'd come across on a ship destined for the faerie world. She had no idea he was faerie and likely thought him a pet of the captain. She'd quickly realized that he'd watched her journey carefully, knowing she was going to be the one that won Eamonn's heart.

Long ago, he'd been a romantic. Bran landed on the gilded windowsill and tucked his wings against his side. When had he lost that romantic side? Perhaps Aisling would enjoy it once and a while.

He reached forward and slid the top part of his beak through the window. Carefully, he felt around for the latch and then flipped it up. Simple enough, he'd have to chastise Eamonn for having such a ridiculously easy room to break into. Anyone could have done this if they could make the climb up to the highest tower.

Did they think they were in some kind of fairytale?

He rolled his eyes and nudged the windows open, then hopped down onto the desk abutting the opening. They had to come to bed soon. The night might be young, but they wouldn't stay with their people for much longer. Elva was far too late, and they would ask her to come back tomorrow. She'd grow angry, likely throw something, and that temper tantrum might make Eamonn and Sorcha remember her.

The snapping of his beak warned that he was getting a little too worked up. He remembered Elva as a ridiculously foolish young woman. She'd changed since then, trained to be a warrior, so he shouldn't judge her so harshly.

A soft exclamation from the hearth made him pause. He spread his wings wide and hissed at the maid who had entered the room.

Her arms were filled with laundry, and she still tsked when she saw him. "Shoo," she said. "Get out, vermin! How many times do I have to remind them to close the damned window? They'll let in all manner of beast."

Gods, how he hated it when a faerie didn't recognize its own kind. What kind of creature was this anyways?

He looked the maid over and would have sneered if he could. The pixie was a familiar face, one he had thought would remember him. Her leaf-shaped face was deep red at the tips above her forehead, changing into an almost flesh color by the time it reached her pointed chin. Bright purple dragonfly wings spread wide behind her.

If he remembered correctly, her name was Oona. She had served Eamonn since he was a child, had even willingly been banished with him to an isle far away from her home. Apparently, he'd thought it a smart idea to keep the sharp-tongued woman in his employ.

She'd hated Bran back on the isle, and he didn't think that would change any time soon.

The pixie gently set the laundry down on the end of the bed and waved her arms. "Go on with you. Shoo!"

He snapped his beak at her, set a foot against the side of a stack of paperwork on the desk, and threateningly shifted.

"Don't you do it."

As if he wouldn't take the chance to mess with something Eamonn owned. Hissing, he shoved the paperwork slowly toward the edge of the desk.

"I'm warning you bird. I will pluck out your feathers and serve you on the table tomorrow."

She wouldn't. She didn't like cooking living animals, like all lesser fae. Oona and her kind existed on little more than honey and cream, sometimes bread if they were lucky.

He let out a huffing chuckle and carelessly pushed the paperwork onto the floor. It fell in a shower of vellum and papyrus, satisfying as it hit the ground in quiet patters.

"*Oh.*" Oona moaned. "That's it, out you go."

Croaking angrily, he flapped his wings, picked up a pen in his mouth, and threw it at her. How long would it take for this foolish faerie to realize he wasn't just any old raven? Hissing angrily, he continued snatching anything he could off the desk and tossing it at her head.

The words coming out of her mouth might have made him blush if he were in a human body. His hiss quickly turned into a cackling laugh as he kept messing with her. When had the pixie learned such language?

It certainly wasn't from the Seelie court. They'd hang her up by her toes if they heard her using such language. He had a feeling it was likely from his very own old friend. Eamonn had always been particularly creative in his swearing, and Oona was using that to her best advantage.

She chased him around the room as he slowly destroyed it bit by bit. He hopped over the bed, head bobbing for momentum, and snatched up the teacup left on the bedside table.

Oona pointed at him. "Don't you dare."

On the other side of the bed, she could only yell at him as he held it precariously over the edge.

"Don't!"

She managed to surprise him when she leapt over the bed and landed in the center. Unable to help himself, he muttered a quick spell that tangled the blankets up and over her. Wrapped securely in the center, she swore a blue streak as he let the

185

teacup fall out of his beak and shatter on the marble floor.

He'd missed being Unseelie so much.

Laughter filled the room from the doorway, interrupting their entertaining battle.

Eamonn leaned against the door jam, large arms crossed over his barrel chest. He wore the uniform of the Seelie king. Gold overcoat spilling like liquid over a cream-colored shirt and soft leather breeches that were tucked into black knee boots that shone in the candlelight.

His face was free of crystals now, although a faint white scar still ran down his eye and around his throat. He'd kept his hair cut like a heathen, something Bran was certain made the Seelie faeries skin crawl. Shaved on either side, he braided the long length from his forehead to the tail that swung at his hip.

"Bran, have you terrorized my staff long enough?" the Seelie king asked.

Oona squeaked from her place on the bed. "Bran? That Unseelie rascal I used to chase out of Hy-brasil?"

"One and the same, my dear."

She huffed out a breath. "I should have hit him with a broom."

Bran narrowed his eyes on her and contemplated another spell that would have set her skirts on fire. See how she liked chasing him out then.

Eamonn shook his head forcefully. "Easy, pixie. He's not a man to trifle with anymore." He looked over at Bran and lifted a brow that had a bisecting scar. "Release her, Raven King."

His feathers ruffled, he still muttered the counterspell under his breath. Let the pixie do whatever she wanted. If she tried to hit him with a broom, then he would absolutely set her skirts on fire.

As she untangled herself, Bran realized he hadn't felt like himself so thoroughly in a long time. Perhaps the last moment had been when he and the witch were on their adventure together, disappearing into the wilds of the Unseelie kingdom, bantering back and forth.

He wished for that time back. When they both weren't drowning under the responsibilities of a kingdom and a curse that clawed at their backs.

Oona stomped to the door, pausing to glare up at her massive king. "I don't like him, and I don't want him here any longer than he needs to be."

Eamonn held up his hands. "I'm certain he's here for a reason, not to visit. The Unseelie have rarely been the kind for house calls."

"Good, because I refuse to feed him." She glared at Bran over her shoulder. "Or anything else for that matter. And you can clean up after yourself. You've made a mess of this room, young man, and I am thoroughly disappointed in you."

He clacked his beak at her, somehow managing to make a kissing sound through the hard surfaces.

"Oh, you!" She left the room in a huff, but Bran saw the smile she tried to repress. For all that, she was a stubborn little thing. Oona liked it when someone teased her.

Eamonn carefully shut the door behind his maid and then turned back to Bran. Laughter still danced in his eyes, the smile giving way to a contemplating frown. "Why are you here?"

Bran lifted his wings in a shrug.

"Bran."

Again, he flapped his wings, severely pointing at the

darkness outside and then tucking his wings back to his side. Had Eamonn really forgotten that Bran was cursed as the Raven King? He couldn't talk during the nighttime, not unless someone lifted his curse. Which, sadly, Eamonn now had the ability to do.

He watched as the Seelie king gave him a quirked grin. There was no pleasure or happiness in that expression, only pity that Bran had seen before and hated.

Eamonn lifted his hand and snapped his fingers. The curse fell from Bran like shackles hitting the ground with loud thumps. He slid from the bedside table into a crouch, feathers shaking from his body and landing onto the floor in a blanket of darkness.

He pressed his fists onto the stone, grinding his knuckles before looking up. "I hate that anyone has such control over my curse. That should be mine and mine alone."

"And yet, it is not. You'll have to give up that pride Bran, or you'll lose your mind." Eamonn gestured toward a pair of seats next to the fireplace. "Since you're already in my bedroom, shall we?"

Bran slowly stood. His body creaked with the pain of transformation, but he didn't let any of it show. Eamonn would be understanding of the weakness since he'd lived his own life in discomfort. His curse had been that crystals grew from every wound that split his skin until he took the Seelie throne and the curse was lifted.

Sinking into the seat, Bran let out a frustrated sigh. "How did you know I was here?"

"I know everyone who enters the castle, who they are, where they came from." Eamonn shrugged. "And I might have had someone watch you for a while now. I've been curious to see how you perform as a king."

"Doubted me, did you?"

With a wave of his hand, Eamonn summoned two glasses filled with amber whiskey in either hand. He handed one to Bran then held the other aloft in a toast. "Perhaps. I never thought you had the makings of a king, but you've proven me wrong. Congratulations on that."

The toast was an insult. Bran's lips twisted to the side, and he downed the whiskey without returning the gesture. He didn't need to follow any of these ridiculous Seelie customs, not while there was more on his mind. "I see you've taken up magic again. I thought you were far more interested in brute force."

"A redheaded lass convinced me it might be a good idea."

"She's convinced you of a good many things, it seems."

Eamonn grunted. "A good woman does, although not all of us appreciate it. Where is your little wife, Bran?"

The words stung. "She's not my wife." Another thing he'd never asked her to be, or do, or even told her that he desired. Bran's chest tightened at the thought of binding her to him for all eternity. He wanted that more than anything, but he also wanted it to be her choice. She needed to be certain she loved him, to be wooed, to have the life she wanted before he tried to change more things.

Eamonn watched all the emotions dance across his face, and Bran let him. There was more to this story than just asking Eamonn to repay old debts.

For all that he was a king, and a good man, Eamonn always fell for a story of unrequited love. It was why they had become friends so long ago. Bran was the boy who never got the girl, and Eamonn wanted to somehow change that.

Ever the fixer, Eamonn was a perfect choice for the Seelie King.

"She's gone," Bran said quietly.

"Left on her own terms?"

"The previous Raven King tricked me, forcing me to choose Elva because I didn't recognize her and then tried to steal Aisling away from me."

Eamonn frowned. "Why?"

"I don't know. I think it has something to do with someone waking up in Underhill that no one wants awake." He scratched the back of his neck. "Other than some people who might have made a deal with said awakened."

The frown deepened, old wrinkles showing on his face and severely marking his cheeks. "Is this someone I need to be aware of?"

"Possibly."

"Bran."

He huffed out a breath. "Carman. The old witch is back, although I believe she's still stuck in whatever prison we tossed her into."

The words acted like a weapon. Eamonn slumped back into his chair and his glass refilled with more whiskey that he knocked back quickly. "Carman. I didn't want to deal with her again in my lifetime."

"No one does. And it seems the witch wants to use Aisling as a vessel."

"We'll keep her here then," Eamonn replied. His voice had aged, deepening with an ancient power that ran deep into the earth of the Seelie Court. "As far away from that witch as possible so Carman won't be able to touch her."

"I'd agree with you if I knew where she was. I cannot find her."

"You lost the one thing Carman wants to use so she can take her kingdom back?" Eamonn pounded a fist on the arm of his chair. The fire popped, an ember leaping out and nearly landing on Bran's foot. "Bran, you've always been irresponsible, but I never thought—"

"Spare me the theatrics," Bran interrupted. "I'm fully aware of what this might mean for all the faerie courts. I'm trying to find her, even the sluagh can't manage. Underhill is a large place, far bigger than either of us have ever given it credit for. I need you and Sorcha to find her."

"What can we do?"

"Begin the Wild Hunt. Narrow it down to just her. She's still a changeling. She's never aligned herself with any of the courts and certainly can't be considered a wandering fae. Once you find her, then I can go and get her. As it stands..." He rubbed the back of his neck then blew out another frustrated breath. "I don't know where she is Eamonn, and she could be in trouble. She could be dead for all I know."

Eamonn stared into the flames. He always seemed to withdraw into himself when he was thinking, and Bran knew he was measuring every possibility.

He'd already thought of them all himself. If she was dead, then they needn't look. If she had already been captured by Carman, they'd know. The witch wasn't one to hesitate. If she was still out there, then they stood a chance. They might be able to stop whatever reckoning was coming and put a bottle back on the witch who should have been killed long ago.

Finally, Eamonn nodded firmly. "I'll go get Sorcha. She's with Elva now, and I said I'd give them time together."

Bran lifted his brows. "Elva made it here?"

"You were with her?"

"I wanted to see if I could beat her at her own game. She thought she'd speak for me." Bran scoffed. "As if I'd ever allow that."

Eamonn chuckled and stood. "Ah, Bran. You've a lot to learn about women. It wasn't me you had to convince to help you. It was Sorcha, and I have a feeling Elva's already convinced her. So you never stood a chance at besting your old love."

CHAPTER 12

THE DUCHESS OF THE DEAD

"Where is the banshee kingdom?" Aisling grumbled, picking her way over a fallen tree. Breath sawed in and out of her lungs, leaving behind a faint metallic taste. When had she gotten so out of shape? The night was young at least. She didn't have to worry about turning into a swan just yet.

Lorcan hissed a low breath ahead of her. "If I knew, don't you think I would have teleported us there?"

"Since when do you know that kind of magic?"

"I've always known it. You just don't remember because I've been a cat for the last fifteen years."

He had a point. She didn't remember him all that well when he was a human. She knew what he had looked like. His beaklike nose was a little hard to forget, but she hadn't remembered his magic. Mostly, she just remembered being hungry and wondering when they would find their next meal.

Aisling smacked at a dead branch that flung back at her as Lorcan made his way through the underbrush. "Do you even know what it's going to look like?"

"I know we're going in the right direction."

"How?"

"The hanging tree, all right? The souls happen to know which direction the banshee kingdom is in, but they didn't know how far."

It sort of made sense, considering the tree couldn't really move. It was in the same spot in every kingdom, which overlapped like the pages of a book if one were teleporting. Although, that magic had always been far too difficult for Aisling to try.

"Why are you even talking to them?" she asked. "The hanging tree has always been a bad omen for witches."

"That doesn't mean the souls trapped inside are bad. We can trust them."

"How do you know that? The dead can still trick us." She frowned. Already, she was in the same habit as long ago. Aisling hadn't trusted anyone in a very long time, had thought perhaps she'd gotten over that with a kingdom of her own. Now she realized she was far from it. That ancient wound had split open instantly and spilled its blood over every fiber of her being until she was questioning even Lorcan's decisions.

He glanced over his shoulder and shoved at a dead tree. Light spilled through the branches, revealing an opening in the tangled brush they fought. "Aisling, they're all witches, just like us. You trusted the sluagh witches, even though many of them are twisted and warped, so you'll have to trust me and the hanging tree soon enough."

She paused in front of him, staring up into his eyes. "Can you promise me that the tree isn't trying to get me into a position where I will join all the others in swinging from its branches?"

"I can't."

"Then why should I listen to you?"

"Because I will do everything in my own power to make sure that you don't end up there."

Her shoulders curved in a slump. "Fine. I appreciate the support, I guess."

"Ever the child." Lorcan nodded at the opening. "Out with you. I think we're finally moving in the right direction."

"What makes you think that?" she muttered, then stood stock still in the clearing and stared at the strange sight before her.

A meandering river split through Underhill, its waters darkened with swirls of blood. Laundry floated throughout. Shirts of men with red blooms on the chests, pants missing a leg, a dress with a bright spot of blood on the skirt.

Aisling stepped forward until her toes nearly touched the water. It was here where the clothing of every soul ended up. Legend had it that if one saw a banshee washing their clothes, it meant that person would die soon. She'd heard of it many times, but never thought it was actually true.

"The banshee kingdom?" she asked quietly.

"Yes," Lorcan replied.

She looked up at him and then in the direction where he stared. Giant carved stone hands jutted out of the earth, holding their wrists to the sky in supplication. Massive shackles surrounded each wrist that made a doorway onto a path that started in the center and snaked up a large mountain range, disappearing in the distance.

"Keep your wits about you, Aisling," he said while straightening his shoulders. "The banshee are not to be trifled with."

"I well remember the stories. I *am* their queen. They owe me their allegiance and their help when I request it."

"The banshee haven't recognized a queen in over ten centuries. You'll be lucky if they don't threaten to kill you where you stand."

She'd heard the stories before, although she couldn't remember when. The banshee had forsaken all the faeries long ago. In the beginning, they were Unseelie faeries. They had quickly despised the way the court was run and renounced their people. The Seelie court refused to welcome the pale, rotting creatures and had banished them.

Instead of becoming wandering fae with no land to call their own, they had disappeared into the wilds of Underhill, rarely heard from again. Sometimes, they could still be seen washing faerie clothing, but even that was rare now. They mostly kept to themselves.

Wasn't that what Underhill was for? All the creatures who didn't have a place in this world had come to Aisling's home for something that nowhere else could give them. Understanding, safety, hope that the world was still a good place.

She wished it were that easy.

They passed by the great hands reaching up, chained like slaves. As she drew close, Aisling realized the carvings were far too lifelike. She could see the skin texture and a faint scar on one wrist where a previous, larger shackle had marked it for all eternity.

"This is a giant, an actual giant, isn't it?" she murmured.

Lorcan looked at the nearest wrist and licked his lips. "It's highly likely. The history of Underhill hasn't been told in centuries. I don't know who he is or where he came from."

"He?"

Lorcan shrugged. "Just a feeling."

She placed a hand against the nearest wrist and blew out a breath. "My apologies, great beast. You should have never had your final resting place here. It is, and I swear to you, I will protect whatever memory is left. I won't let this final resting place be of an unnamed man who gave his life for a reason no one knew."

There was a rumble deep in the earth, and she knew the spirit of the giant had heard her. The vow tightened around her throat, but it was one she intended to keep. No one in her kingdom should ever be forgotten, especially by their queen.

They made their way down the winding path and up into the mountains beyond. Her legs burned and her tongue tasted blood again. She would not stop. Lorcan kept up with her.

Eventually the path was nearly straight up. They traveled hand over foot, their fingers grasping onto crumbling rock and feet finding notches in the stone to continue pushing them ever forward.

Aisling grew more and more worried as they traveled. The sun would soon rise, and then what would she do? They would have to pause, or she would have to fly ahead. If they reached the banshee kingdom, she wouldn't be able to speak.

Did she trust Lorcan enough to voice her concerns? Aisling

wasn't certain of it. He seemed to know what he was doing, and she had a feeling he wasn't telling her the entire truth.

Now she understood why faeries so hated humans and their ability to lie. He let the words slip from his tongue so easily without a single worry on his mind. He didn't freeze the moment a lie crossed his mind; his lips didn't seize as they tried to say the words. Instead, Lorcan could let them drift out like a steady current from the sea.

She wanted to demand that he pay attention to her. That he say every single thing that he'd heard from the hanging tree and explain further. She wanted to dive into his memories and pluck them from his skull. Force him to relive every moment over and over again so that she might see what he really meant when he said the words.

A stone under her hand broke. Frantically, she reached up to find the next handhold.

And her hand slapped down on flat earth.

Breathing hard, she looked up and saw that they had finally reached the peak of the mountain. Her breathing eased. Aisling yanked herself up and over, rolling onto the ground and lying flat for a few moments to still her thundering heart.

Lorcan joined her, crouching at her side and staring around them in shock.

"What is it?" she asked. "What fresh horror has you so afraid?"

"I didn't think they glowed in the moonlight."

She turned her head, cheek pressing again moist earth, and stared at the hundreds of banshee women who caught the bloody clothing and washed it clean in the river.

Each was more beautiful and haunting than the last. Their

hair was white as snow, touching the ground and pooling around their feet, strands dipping into the river and gently floating on top. They wore white gowns, and their pale skin glowed as moonlight stroked it.

Their cheeks were hollow, eyes sunken into dark, smudged shadows. Each banshee reached into the stream with a strength she envied and pulled out articles of clothing.

She'd always thought it would be a frightening sight. They would vigorously scrub the wool and linen, forcing the life out of it like wringing the neck of a bird. They weren't nearly so cruel.

Instead, they handled each piece with obvious care. They stroked the collars, easing the stress of life from the fabric. They smoothed hands down dresses and pressed the wrinkles out with a mere touch. Every drop of blood and dirt was washed clean with careful attention to every detail. Only then would they let it drop back into the water to continue down the stream where the person might find it later and wear it to the land of the dead.

Aisling pushed herself up onto her forearms. "Can we ask one of them where their queen is? They all look identical."

"I don't think we're supposed to interrupt them," Lorcan replied.

It seemed he might be right. None of the banshee looked up at them. Instead, they all remained dedicated to the task at hand.

Aisling frowned and stared around them, hoping for some kind of clue. There didn't appear to be a castle anywhere, nor a town or hovel where these creatures might live. Did they ever stop washing the clothes of the dead?

She eased to her feet. There had to be something here. Some kind of clue that there was more than just a river. More than just banshee who endlessly worked. She had to find something before the sun rose on the horizon and she missed her chance.

Aisling might have spent the rest of the night frantically following the river upstream if she hadn't heard one of the banshee's let out a soft keening cry. They hadn't shown any reaction to the clothing at all, not until now.

Moving slowly so as not to frighten them, Aisling looked across the river at the banshee who held an article of clothing in her hands that was eerily familiar.

The dark gown spilled over the banshee's hands and sank into the river like ink. Red blood stained the bodice, completely invisible other than the streaks across the banshee's pale hands. Beetle wings decorated every inch of the beautiful dress, carefully hand sewn like emerald beads down the waist and skirts.

Aisling let out a choked sound somewhere between a sob and a scream.

"Don't," Lorcan said with a gulp. "Don't look at it."

She couldn't stop staring because it was the most famous gown of the Raven Queen. The one she wore to court as all her predecessors had done before. That gown had never seen bloodshed before.

At least, not yet.

Aisling strode into the river before she registered her own movement. The powerful current pulled at her legs, sending shards of icy pain through her body. But she didn't stop. She continued until it reached her chest and then she was swimming through the river of death and blood until her feet touched the opposite side.

All the banshees stopped what they were doing, watching her in shock as she waded through the water. Aisling batted other articles of clothing out of her way until she stood in front of the banshee holding her dress.

She reached out and grasped it, tugged hard, and growled, "That is *mine*."

The banshee stared back at her, dark eyes wide, hands trembling where she gripped the fabric. There was uncertainty in the depths of that gaze. The creature didn't know whether or not she should let go. Perhaps no one had ever done this before. Or perhaps it would end poorly if Aisling's clothing was not properly washed. Damn it.

She'd rather stride into the otherlife with the blood of her foes on her dress than arrive clean and untouched.

A voice interrupted her thoughts, high and haunting like the wail of her kind. "You are a fierce creature, aren't you?"

"You have no idea."

"Release the dress, my sweet. The Raven Queen has come to see us, and I would very much like to hear what she wants."

The banshee released the dress, and Aisling tossed it up onto shore. There would be no death for her tonight, nor soon. She would see to it.

Climbing out of the river, she met the gaze of what could only be the banshee leader. The woman was the only one with dark hair. Black as night, it slithered down her body like snakes, undulating with her movement. She, too, wore a white gown that revealed the shadowed hollows of her body. Eerily pale, she reached out a hand for Aisling to take.

"Welcome, Raven Queen, to the Kingdom of the Banshee."

"And you are?" Aisling took the offered hand hesitantly.

"Many call me the Duchess of the Dead."

"What do the few call you?"

A soft smile spread across the banshee's face. "Aoife."

"It's a pleasure to meet you, Aoife. My name is Aisling, and I need your help." Aisling bit her lip, then added, "Not just as your queen, but as what I hope might be as a friend."

"Ah, another Raven Queen who thinks she can control us." The banshee closed her hand around Aisling's with surprising strength. Her nails bit into Aisling's wrist as she tugged her closer. "Yet another who thinks the banshee might provide some benefit when we have been forgotten for so long."

"No." Aisling shook her head. "I need your help. Carman has awakened, and I fear she will try to renew her power through me."

Aoife's eyes widened, and her grip loosened. "Then it is good you have come to me. Carman... I never thought we would hear from the witch queen again."

The curse tightened around her neck and the now familiar pain blossomed in her spine. It spread tendrils of power through her entire body until she felt the feathers wiggling out from underneath her skin.

She croaked through an ever changing mouth, "I ask protection for the day, for myself and my man servant."

"Then you shall have it."

Aoife watched with a pitying gaze as the change warped Aisling's body and thrust her back into the prison of a swan.

Exhausted, though encouraged she was moving in the right direction, Aisling waddled toward the bloody waters to await the night once more.

Bran paced the drawing room, hands behind his back so he didn't tap them incessantly against his leg. He followed the same path. First, he rounded the edge of the small sofa, then stalked past the large, stone fireplace, made his way around the twin chairs, one currently filled by Elva, around the table where tea had been set, then back to the sofa. Over and over again.

"You'll wear holes in the carpet," Elva murmured, sipping her tea delicately.

"What is taking them so long?"

"They're probably laughing behind the door because you're so worked up about this. They'll find her. They've already agreed to it."

"I don't appreciate the sarcasm," he growled.

"Why are you so surly with me and not with everyone else? They can find her, Bran. We wouldn't be here if they couldn't." She delicately crossed her legs at the ankle and leaned forward to place the teacup on the table in front of her. "Rushing them certainly won't get Aisling back any faster."

"I believe that's the definition of rushing." Heat from the

fireplace blasted out of the hearth and seared his legs. Cursing, he whipped around to find Sorcha striding into the room.

He was still pleased to see she hadn't changed a bit since he'd found her on the docks and knew there was a story to her. Red curls tumbled from the top of her head and swept the delicate swells of her hips. Freckles coated her from head to toe, while the spark in her green eyes resonated with power. She was a sight to behold, and he was glad that hadn't changed now that she was queen of the Seelie fae.

"Rushing me could end with her losing a limb," Sorcha scolded. "Besides, asking the ancestors to help isn't precisely easy."

"Why?" His voice was gruff, but the tension immediately eased from his shoulders. Words of assistance meant nothing. If she was speaking of her druid ancestors, then she would actually help.

Sorcha's lips twisted into a wry grin. "Because they don't want to help *you*."

Big surprise there. The ancestors hadn't exactly been a fan of Bran for a long time. Even the druids knew he'd forsaken his family and all the traditions of his people.

Tradition was tradition, at least to the old souls. They wanted him to follow in line the way he was supposed to. Without that, faeries were simply magical creatures running amok.

No, the druids wouldn't like the idea of someone like him existing.

With a dark grin, Bran shook his head. "Well, they'll have to get used to it. I need them to find her."

"They've agreed to it," she said. "They also said it's

unlikely they can find her without calling a true Wild Hunt. I suspect that's something you want to avoid?"

He felt as though she was prying into his soul. Her eyes saw far too much for comfort. Nearly twitching, he replied, "What would make you think that?"

"Because then all of the Unseelie Court would be looking for her as well, and it seems as though you want to keep her to yourself. Or, perhaps, that you have enemies you don't want to find her?" Sorcha's gaze sharpened. "Enemies, I suspect. Although, she's likely capable of taking care of herself."

Too well, although he didn't want to admit it. She made him feel like less of a man sometimes. Aisling would go on without him just fine.

Was that so bad, though? At least he had the reassurance that should anything happen to him, dismemberment, dethroned, murdered, maimed beyond all hope, Aisling would continue on. He didn't want her to fade into the shadows simply because he was no longer there. It didn't feel fair to him.

Even if the thought of her with someone else made him want to start a war.

"Fine," he admitted. "I have no interest in letting the Unseelie court sink their claws into her. They aren't precisely the kindest of creatures, and they're all ridiculously interested in the new Raven Queen. I don't know why."

Sorcha laughed. "You *do* know why, Bran. Because you haven't shown interest in another woman for hundreds of years. Now, all of a sudden, you're completely, foolishly, irrevocably, head over heels for a woman who spent most of her life as a hedge witch. They want to understand why you're so mad for her."

She was probably right. Faeries notoriously hated things they couldn't explain and would dedicate their lives to understanding the *why* of something. Hell, he'd done it himself multiple times in his long life.

The muscles in his shoulders tensed at the self-realization. He didn't like being picked apart in front of Sorcha, like she was pulling the flesh from his bones just to see how white they were. She already knew him as well as anyone else. She knew those bones were blackened and charred by a hundred years of mistreatment.

"Enough talking," he grumbled. "Can you just get it over with?"

Eamonn stepped out of the shadows beyond the door and into the room with his wife. "I don't like your tone, Unseelie, but I'm just as eager to get this over with as you."

Bran lifted a brow. "Care to explain, Seelie King?"

The new king's immediate wince was answer enough. Bran had suspected his age-old friend wasn't entirely in love with his new title. At least now Bran knew he was correct in his suspicion.

Becoming a king wasn't easy. Even Bran didn't like the sudden attention it had thrust upon him. Eamonn had lived alone on an isle for hundreds of years without anyone's eyes watching him. Now, everyone wanted to know what the king was doing, what his favorite dish was, what color they should wear next season.

At least Bran was more practiced at this than Eamonn.

Sorcha made her way to the hearth, gracefully twitching her skirts to the side. "I'm going to try to use the spirits to find her. If they can't, then we'll likely have to resort to other means."

"Other means?" Bran asked.

"The druid spirits are still talking about it, but most are fairly confident they know someone who can help you. Not necessarily to find Aisling. If she's out of their reach, then she'll be out of the reach of other druids. They might be able to help you stop Carman."

It was a start. Bran strode to her side and crossed his arms over his chest. "Begin."

She sighed. "This isn't a spell, Bran. I'm asking for help, and usually that requires at least pretending to be polite. Would you ask them, like a gentleman, to assist you?"

He didn't want to. It felt a little too close to owing someone a debt, and Bran didn't owe anyone anything. He also wanted to find his queen, so he crossed his arms, dug his fingers into his ribs, and nodded. "Ancient ancestors of the druid line. I seek your help in finding the Raven Queen, as she has been stolen from her home and deposited somewhere in Underhill."

Sorcha's eyelids drifted shut. He waited for a moment before seeing her entire body grow lax. She listed to the side, straightened, then opened eyes that suddenly glowed with green power.

She spoke, and her voice vibrated with hundreds of ancient souls who knew him. "Bran. Unseelie Prince. Raven King. Forgotten boy who none know. Who none will never forget. You have asked us to find your queen?"

Gods, if that wasn't the most terrifying thing he'd seen in a while. Bran lived in a castle with creatures who held their heads in their hands, but this made him far more uncomfortable. It was Sorcha's body, a woman who he remembered quite well, yet it was not the woman who talked to him.

He squared his shoulders and cleared his throat. "I do."

"We have searched far and wide. She is masked by someone even more powerful than our deep well of magic."

He looked up toward the ceiling. "By who?"

"You already know the answer to this, boy. Carman, the mother of all witches, wants no one to find your queen."

Of course, she didn't. That would mean Aisling could be saved, and she wouldn't want that. Carman wanted something with his bride, and there was nothing Bran could do about that. Aisling was on her own, at least for now. He prayed to all the ancient faeries in his line that she had the strength and the knowledge to get through this until he could find his way back to her side.

"What can I do?" he asked.

"Aisling must prepare herself to face the first of her kind. Carman will try to trick her. She will try to tempt her. Most of all, Carman wants what Aisling managed to obtain that Carman could never do."

"Which is?"

Sorcha's eyes rolled into her head, shifting round and round until they settled on Bran's raven eye. His raven eye stilled its endless twitching and focused entirely on Sorcha's.

"Aisling is a perfect blend of faerie and witch. She can control the elements, call upon all that faeries can, and also can meld that knowledge, thatpower with the dark magic only witches can control. She is the perfect weapon, molded in a body that was made to house Carman herself."

"Then we have to stop her."

"If you wish to fight the witch, then there is one who can help you."

Small blessings, he supposed. Bran didn't want to involve anyone else in this madness, but if that was what it took, he wouldn't complain. "Who?"

"Her name is Tlachtga, a druid soul who still remains on this plane. She is..." Sorcha paused, and the souls inside her slowly retreated. He watched the magic drain from her body until no one else stood in front of him than the little druid woman he'd followed so long ago. She licked her lips and shook her head. "Tlachtga is a myth, but they seem to think that she is still alive and well."

"I don't recognize the name."

"No, I suspect you wouldn't. The faeries tried to hide her from their history, mostly because she was such a powerful creature who helped them. Your kind doesn't like to admit that sometimes they need help." She reached out and placed a hand on the hearth.

It was the first time Bran had ever seen her look weak. She was such a beacon of light and power, constantly moving and asking people what she could do to help. Sorcha had always seemed less like a human and more like a deity who would live forever.

Her cheeks steadily grew ashen as she stared into the flame. He didn't know if the spirits of her ancestors were still speaking to her, or if channeling them had taken out more than she had anticipated. Regardless, he reached out his forearm for her to take. "Shall we have a seat?"

She glanced up at him and smiled as she took his arm. "I

don't remember you being so willing to help another person. Ever, really. You were always more interested in putting yourself first."

"A person grows."

"A person learns," she corrected, allowing him to lead her toward the settee where her husband waited for her. "It seems as though you've had a wonderful teacher, Bran."

He handed her off. Eamonn reached up for his wife and delicately helped lower her to the cushions. He handled her as if she were made of glass, although Bran knew her to be the exact opposite. Still, it was good to see them together like this. If only to remind himself that he'd experienced it himself.

Bran lowered himself into the chair beside Elva's and leaned forward, elbows on his knees. "Care to explain who this Tlachtga is and how she's supposed to help us?"

Eamonn manifested a glass of water and handed it to his wife. "In a moment."

"I don't exactly have moments to spare, Eamonn."

He thought his friend would launch himself across the room. Eamonn was ridiculously protective of his wife, yet she was a woman who had no need of a man to protect her. It was too easy to provoke him, and at the very least, it made Bran feel a little bit more like himself.

Sorcha placed a hand on her husband's thigh and chuckled. "Stop, both of you. Goodness, I didn't miss this. You two are exhausting."

Elva shifted for the first time since Sorcha entered the room. Teacup in hand, she delicately sipped the tea and sniffed. "Most men are, I find."

They both chuckled, and Bran tried to tell himself to grow angry at their jesting. Instead, all he could do was shrug. He knew he was a pain in most people's asses. That was his role in life. To annoy people who needed to lighten up a little bit, as well as relieve tense situations.

Sorcha sipped at the water in her hand before nodding. "Tlachtga was an ancient druidess who was far more intelligent than any who have ever lived before. Her father was an arch-druid, and he taught her everything he knew. Her power, her knowledge, is far greater than even the combination of all the druid ancestors I can speak with. She's an incredible woman and more valuable than I could ever explain."

"If she's dead, why can't you connect with her here?"

Sorcha shook her head. "It's not that easy. Tlachtga knew people would try and use her, even when she died. So she placed her grave in the highest peak she could, then bid her sons to guard her. Her energy feeds the land, not the ancestors. It was such a powerful death that her magic has bled into the human realm as well, through the very fiber that separates the Otherworld and the next."

It couldn't be easy, could it? Bran growled, "Sons?"

"Perhaps I should tell you her entire story. Tlachtga traveled the world with her father and his mentor, Simon Magus. He was a sorcerer of black and blood magic. He caught her when her father had left for a fortnight and had his three sons rape her. Broken and bleeding, she dragged herself from his home to the same peak where she is buried.

"It's not a happy tale. She birthed three sons, Cumma, Doirb and Muach, each looking like one of the rapists who had fathered individual children. And though she saw the monsters every time she looked at her own children, she still kept herself alive until their eighteenth birthday when she died. They named it the Hill of Warding, and they light Samhain fires in her honor."

Bran had heard of such tales, and they were always in threes. Black magic liked to feast upon pain. Likely, the druidess hadn't even realized she was feeding into the sorcerer's spell for all those years she kept herself alive for her boys.

It wouldn't be easy to convince her to help him, not when Aisling herself was a dark witch. Although his bride hadn't dabbled in black magic, he'd seen her do many things that a good witch wouldn't have.

"She won't like helping a witch," he verbalized. "That's too much to ask of a woman whose life was ruined by one."

"Sorcerers aren't witches, Bran. And it's been a long time."

"Wounds like that don't heal as easily as you'd think." He heard the deep inhalation of Elva beside him and wondered just how far her wounds ran. Perhaps it wasn't the same as Tlachtga. Elva hadn't been raped. At least, he hoped not. When all this was over, he intended to speak to her and figure out what had actually happened in all those years he'd been gone.

Sorcha shook her head. "She's still one of the druids. I am her only descendent, and she will help me if I ask."

"Are you willing to give that up?" Bran held up his hand when Eamonn opened his mouth. "Not yet, I'll let you have your say, Seelie King. I think we've thought of the same possibility. There may come a time, Sorcha, when you need to seek this ancestor's help. I don't want you to waste it on my queen. Tell me where she is, and I will go alone."

Elva set her cup down on the table between them. "Not alone. She's my sister just as much as she is your wife, Raven King. I go with you."

He didn't need a keeper, although it seemed as though Elva disagreed with him. He glowered at his previous love and wondered who had taught her to be so stubborn. It wasn't him. He wasn't like that when someone he loved was at the stake.

"Well," Sorcha said slowly. "At least we know that someone will be watching your back. I can tell you where Tlachtga is, but it won't be so easy to find her. If she decides to help you, then it might be more of a curse than a blessing."

He blew out a breath and nodded. "That's how it always is with druids, isn't it? None of your magic is given freely or with ease."

Sorcha shrugged. "When it's powerful magic, someone has to pay for it."

He scrubbed a hand down his face and waved the other in front of him. "Fine, that's fine. I'll meet with this Tlachtga, beg for her help, try my best to woo her, and then we'll see if she helps us at all."

"With Elva at your side," Sorcha added.

The muscles on his jaw jumped immediately. His teeth creaked so loudly that even he could hear their grinding. "Yes, with Elva. If she slows me down, then I'm not waiting."

Elva let out a loud laugh that startled him. "Oh, you pathetic little Unseelie prince. I'm not going to slow you down, but you might not be able to keep up with me."

He glared at her between his fingers. "We'll see. Sorcha, where is this druid and how long is it going to take me to find her?"

"At least a few days if you teleport to the base of her mountain. The rest is climbing. Magic won't work on that mountain unless it's hers." She waved her hand between them, and an image appeared in the air. "This is where you will begin your journey."

CHAPTER 13

A Curse And A Blessing

Magic burst through Aisling's body, coursing through her veins, cracking and realigning her spine. The agony of the change had become so familiar at this point that it almost didn't hurt anymore. She'd felt it nearly a hundred times now. Perhaps more.

Finally, the curse let go of her. Immediate relief made her sag in the water that rose up and over her head until she kicked back to the surface. Blood-red water streaked down her cheeks, shoulders, and hands. There was so much death in this river, and even that didn't bother her. She'd been around it enough in her life to know it was merely part of living.

Dragging herself out of the river, she slumped against the edge and pressed her cheek against the warm grass. In a few moments, Aisling knew she had to get up and continue her journey. She couldn't stay in one place for too long or Carman would find her.

Still…

"Bran," she whispered. "If you can hear me or feel me, please just keep doing whatever it is your doing. *Find me.*"

They'd only been gone for a few days, and she missed him. She missed the endless quips that made her angry, the ridiculous outlook on life when death was barreling down toward him. But most of all, she missed the soft way his hands would hold her, how he could bring her back from the edge with nothing more than a touch.

"Aisling?" The voice wasn't similar at all to Bran, but it still made a shiver dance down her spine.

She picked up her head and saw Lorcan standing a few feet away with a banshee at his side.

"What is it?"

"The Duchess would like to see you."

Yet another duchess involved in a curse. Was she walking the same path as she had before, just with a different danger this time?

Considering how she was alone this time, and the danger was far more personal, Aisling was loathe to admit this was a cycle. She'd helped Bran; now she had to help herself. If she'd been a bard, this might have even felt poetic.

"I need clothing," she croaked, throat still sore from holding in screams during the change.

"I have those, your majesty." The banshee stepped forward and held out her arms. A billowing white dress flowed down her hands like the white mist of a waterfall.

"No." Aisling shook her head. She pointed downstream where her own beetle wing dress lay limp on the shore. "I will wear what I have earned. I might be lying in the muck right now, but I am still a queen."

Pride shone in Lorcan's gaze for a moment before he spun on his heels and trod through the sticky river edge to pick up her fallen mantle. The gown would likely smell like earth and dirt, and wasn't that what the Raven Queen should smell like?

Her throne was not one made of gossamer and gold. It was a throne for the queen of the dead, and it smelled like a grave.

Lorcan returned to her side, reached his hands underneath her arms, and hefted her to standing. He didn't look at her overly much, only helped her into the dress that molded to her form like a glove. It was the second time she'd worn it, but then perhaps this wasn't the same one she'd worn. This gown felt like the future and radiated magic.

Beetle wings clacked against her side as she turned around toward Lorcan. "How do I look?"

He gave her a severe once over, then met her gaze. "Like a queen."

The modest corset hugged her chest and ribs, supporting her posture when she might have slumped in exhaustion. Thin, black fabric looped over each shoulder and draped over her form like a cape. The beetle wings created armor that flared out over her arms, gathered at her hips, and then sprinkled down her skirts to meet the ground.

It would have been impressive if her hair hadn't been wet and tangled. She felt as though she looked like she'd crawled out of the river already dead. And perhaps she was. This place felt like a resting ground for the damned more than it felt like a place for redemption.

"Shall we?" she asked the banshee. "I trust it's a poor idea to keep Aoife waiting."

"Yes, your majesty."

The faerie whirled, her skirts spreading like the wings of a moth, and made her way past her sisters to a path Aisling hadn't noticed before. Plain and simple, it started as nothing more than dirt until large stones framed the path through the jagged mountain top.

Large stone cairns jutted from the ground. They looked like soldiers standing at attention, dotted throughout the landscape that was barren of any greenery. There wasn't even moss on the stones themselves. Just ashen dirt and dust.

"Aisling," Lorcan murmured, speeding up so he could whisper in her ear, "I don't trust them."

"I trust no one," she replied. "This duchess has her own means that she wants to achieve. I don't blame her for that."

"I do," he grumbled. "You are the Raven Queen, and they owe you their allegiance. It matters little what someone did long ago. This is your kingdom, and they must ensure they follow the rules just as everyone else does."

"They don't seem to care for tradition." It was something she admired in them really. Aisling didn't like the old ways of the faeries, the Wild Hunt only one of the many things she disagreed with. There was a future they could all build together if they wanted to. Unfortunately, most faeries didn't.

The banshee slowed in front of them and gestured directly ahead. "The duchess awaits you there."

Aisling couldn't see where the woman was pointing to. White mist blanketed the land beyond, so thick she wouldn't have been able to see someone standing right in front of them.

"Through the mist?" she asked. "And what stands in my way?"

"Nothing but yourself, your majesty." The mist rolled toward them, and the banshee disappeared into its gray fog.

"That's not cryptic at all," she hissed. "Lorcan, how do you think we're to proceed?"

No one responded to her.

Aisling whipped around and saw nothing behind her but white. She pivoted in a slow circle, heart pounding. The mist had already swallowed her whole.

"Lorcan?" she tried again, though she knew he was gone. No one would help her make it to the banshee duchess but herself. That was what the price would be.

Aisling cupped her hands together, the tattooed eyes on her palms staring up at her. "Fire burn and magic bite, give me all that you can light."

A glow began between her fingers, growing ever stronger until she could hold her hands aloft. The magic burned through the mist enough that she could see the ground around her feet.

Aisling hadn't realized how disoriented she had become with nothing in front of her. The entire world seemed to tilt once she saw the ground again, and she nearly fell onto her knees before she righted herself.

Blowing her hair out of her face, she shook her head firmly. "This is nothing, Aisling. A little bit of illusion that you've seen before. Get your feet under you and walk forward."

Fear churned in her gut, and she refused to focus on the needless emotion. There would be time to be afraid. Now was not the time. She held her arms higher and stepped one foot in front of the other.

This test wasn't about her powers or her abilities. They

already knew she was a strong witch, made even more powerful by the gifts of the Raven Queen. She could only imagine that this was to measure her bravery and worth, just as they would have long ago when they hadn't only washed the clothing of the dead in the river, but had a choice in whether or not a human life was deemed worthy of the afterlife.

Farther and farther she strode, fear melting away with each step. Eventually, her toes kissed the edge of a cliff. Though she could not see how far down it went, she felt the stirring of the air and heard the whistling of winds far below her.

"If this is a test of bravery to see how far I'm willing to go to prove myself, it will not be leaping to my death," she muttered.

The light between her hands grew brighter. Just a little mist burned away, enough that she could see a gray metal chain jutting out of the side of the cliff.

So, this had been the warnings of the giants then. Perhaps the banshee had killed them to take their lands. Another question she would ask the duchess once all this was over.

Aisling made her way over to the chain and nudged it with her foot. It stretched from the cliff and hung suspended in the air. The links were larger than her, each metal piece at least a man's length across. Only a giant would be capable of lifting them.

She frowned and stared out into the swirling white mist. If the chain was broken, it would hang limp and straight down. It must be attached to something at the other end.

A growl burst forth from between her lips, the sound both angry and disappointed. "Is this the test you send me?" she asked. "Blind faith that you aren't leading me to my death?"

No one responded, and she had the feeling someone was listening to her. Gods, she was beginning to hate the banshees.

Carefully balancing herself on the first link, Aisling stepped onto the chain and began her slow, meandering crawl across it.

She stepped purposefully each time. The last thing she needed was to slip, and the chains were damp with dew. Cold seeped between her bare toes from metal that hadn't been heated by the sun in ages.

A wind blew toward her, pushing against the chain and making it sway side to side. Not enough to dislodge her, enough that it shoved her stomach up into her throat at the first movement.

Her heart raced at the possibilities. She could fall, and it might all be a test. There could be ground only a few steps below her and the sounds were all a hallucination, something her mind made up because she couldn't see the bottom. More likely there was a never-ending fissure far below her. The banshees wouldn't stop her plummet to death; they had never wanted Aisling as their queen in the first place.

Besides, if she fell here, the fault wasn't theirs. She had chosen to step out onto the chains. "It's a shame you can't see me now, Carman," she said through gritted teeth. "You might find yourself ashamed of the woman you want to possess."

A faint chuckle floated through the mist, and Aisling immediately regretted her words. Perhaps the witch was listening after all. And was far from disappointed.

Stones appeared before her, the other side of the chain sunk so deep into the side of the cliff they would never fall out.

Letting out a soft sigh of relief, Aisling stepped a foot onto the other edge and let the feeling of thick moss surrounding her feet ground her. Although she hadn't let fear impact her movement, she had been more frightened doing that than she had anything else in a very long time. Heights made her more than a little uncomfortable, and cliff edges she avoided at all costs.

She'd done it. She'd conquered yet another fear without letting it cripple her.

Clapping heralded her arrival at the edge of the mist that disappeared with a breath of magic that pushed it out of the way. Aoife stood on the other side, still as dark and pale as before, surrounded by a hundred banshees.

"You have made it to my home," Aoife said, her voice chiming like church bells. "I'm impressed."

"I take it not many people make it across the chains?" Aisling asked. When no one responded to her, she switched tactics. "Where is my man servant?"

"Likely still hurling curses at the mist. We wanted to speak with you alone." Aoife swept her arm back, gesturing that they should walk together. "There's much I've heard about you, Raven Queen. And I would like to know exactly why you are here."

"I told you everything already. Carman is awake, and I would like to ensure she does not hurt any more of my people." She stepped up to stride beside the duchess. Together, they walked away from the edge of the cliff where the mist still hung heavy and opaque.

Aoife let out a sound of disappointment. "I don't quite

believe you. From what I've heard, your man servant has convinced you to go on this foolish quest. You think you can stop Carman? The mother of all witches?"

"I think I stand a chance."

"As does a mouse against a cat, but we both know who usually ends up dead. Explain to me more, witch queen of mine. I would like to know exactly why you are running headlong toward your death without pausing for breath."

Aisling didn't have an answer for that. She let out a frustrated grunt and stilled her mind as she felt the dark lick of power. Aoife was trying to dig into her thoughts. Or perhaps not dig, but taste the magic that surrounded Aisling like a comfortable, warm mantle.

The banshee sighed. "Interesting. You have so much magic in you that you don't know what to do with it. Yet, you rarely use the magic. I've seen you in memories of my people, working alongside the sluagh. Cursed creatures who have no right to live in the castle, let alone be allowed to see you."

Anger made the hair on Aisling's arms stand up straight. "Who has claimed they are nothing more than animals? They are cursed, yes, humans we have forced into forms that are unnatural and frightening to the souls trapped inside them. We are the ones who hunted them, stalked them, enslaved them. Should they not have comfort? At least a little bit in their lives."

"You are not what I thought you would be, Raven Queen." Aoife pointed at the mist that swirled and solidified into that of a bench they could sit on. Together, they rested on the cold furniture. "I would have thought you to hate them."

"Why?"

"They are the perfect example of all the things you've tried to change. Sluagh are the only creatures in the Otherworld that can hunt down the changelings and bring them back home where we enslave and imprison them." Aoife cocked her head to the side. "So you see, it confuses me when you proclaim the sluagh to have rights. Do they not do exactly as we have done to them? They are the instruments upon which we harm changelings. You protect a weapon that murders without discrimination."

"A hand wields a weapon."

Aoife looked at her with a calculating expression, and Aisling knew she was being observed by a creature who had seen a millennia pass. This banshee queen was old, far older than any of the other fae she'd met thus far. Perhaps even older than Bahb herself, the grandmother Aisling had always looked up to and assumed knew everything in the world.

She cleared her throat and looked over at the banshee. "I suppose it's a selfish journey as well."

"There's more to the story then." It wasn't a question.

AIsling nodded. "I'm tired of being cursed. I know it's the way of the Raven Court, but I've never been particularly good at doing something simply because it's tradition. I want the lingering effects of this magic gone from my body. I want to stop feeling jealous of the man I love because his curse can be lifted while mine must remain."

That was the root of the problem, even though she hadn't realized it until just now. Bran's freedom was only partially taken away. He could still beg and plead for a little time. His human body was denied for him only so long as his pride remained intact.

Neither of them had a good life at the moment. At least he could somehow remain himself for a few moments longer, even if it was at the mercy of others. Aisling was adrift in a world of magic where she had so much at her fingertips but couldn't even break a simple spell.

The banshee nodded. "Ah, it all makes much more sense now. You aren't searching out revenge or power. You want your freedom."

"I want my own choices back," she corrected. "I want to be able to walk out into my kingdom and help others whether it is night or day. The chains that bind me were not faerie made. I can feel that just as I can feel you are an ancient being who might have been alive when the first Raven Queen was cursed."

Perhaps she had managed to catch Aoife in her own game. The banshee's eyebrows lifted in surprise. "You may be correct in that observation."

"Then tell me how to break the curse. Or if you don't know, tell me how it was first cast, and I will unravel it on my own."

Aoife's gaze turned sad. "You don't have enough time to unravel it, little witch. The cogs in this wheel are constantly turning, and the time has passed when you might have stood a chance against the great queen of old."

"That's not for you to decide."

She'd snapped the words, perhaps a little too strongly. A few of the nearest banshees flinched back from her side. They reacted as though they were far more used to a leader who lashed out in anger, not one who berated herself for her own foolishness.

Aisling could feel her own expression darken. She drew

her brows down in anger, clenched her fists tight, and glared at the duchess who she had a feeling liked to hurt her own people when something didn't go her way.

In contrast, Aoife seemed to relax. She melted into the misty bench. Her lips quirked to the side in a sardonic smile, and she lifted a hand. "So you are embarking on this journey all on your own? Where is your husband, Raven Queen? He should walk this path with you."

"He doesn't need to be here." The words burned her tongue. It was too close to a lie, far too close for comfort. The words twisted back on her, traveling down her throat with the acidic burn of a bitter potion.

"No?" Aoife asked again. "You're trying to break your curse, yet you do not want your king here?"

This was her price then. The banshee duchess wanted a bit of truth from Aisling, something she could lord over all the other faeries that she knew.

She blew out a breath. "The Raven King... We're both cursed. Each of us are locked in this form that's traditional for the role. He hesitates to find a cure for my curse, not because he doesn't want to break it, because" — she paused and licked her lips — "he's overwhelmed."

Aoife gave her a knowing look, catching the lie before Aisling even realized her words weren't entirely true. "You think he doesn't want to break your curse."

"I think if he knew how, he would. The Raven King holds no value in ancient traditions such as this. The weight of his entire kingdom rests on his shoulders. He worries about my curse, his own, the health of the kingdom, and welcoming the sluagh as people and not just tools. There's far more under his responsibility, and he's stretched himself so thin he can no longer see the end." The words poured like a river from her lips, on and on until she finally paused and gulped in a breath. "I need to do this on my own. I want what was taken from me, and that is something I must do alone."

Aoife looked her up and down, her gaze measuring once more, and then slowly nodded. "You are not what I thought you would be, Raven Queen. The journey ahead of you will be arduous, although I fear it will not be too long. You need time to prepare and learn, but that is not something the universe is gifting you."

"You know how to defeat Carman and therefore break my curse."

"I know a way, there are always numerous paths to the same end," Aoife said. "You will need to perform the most powerful spell Underhill has ever survived. You cannot do it alone. There are powers here, great, unspoken powers that will help you or hinder you. That is up to them to decide."

Aisling measured what that might mean. She didn't want to owe any faeries favors, but she couldn't handle this weakness any longer. It was ridiculous the way she felt like hiding because of what would happen when the sunlight touched her skin.

She hated it. Every instance of her curse that took everything from her being. The ability to speak, to touch, to feel the world the way she should be able to feel it. She deserved that back.

And if that required a few faerie favors...

"I accept," she replied. "Whatever your cost, I accept it."

The banshee's eyes widened in shock, almost as though she

didn't believe Aisling would take the leap. "Brave as well," Aoife murmured. "Or perhaps merely foolish."

The duchess reached out her hand, and a rope appeared between her fingertips. It dangled like the limp body of a snake, waving in the faint breeze. Aisling's eyes couldn't move from the sight.

There was power in the object, although she couldn't understand where it originated from. An ancient magic was woven deep into the strands of hemp. It hummed an almost audible song that sank into Aisling's veins.

"Take it," Aoife said. "It is the first part of your spell, imbued with my own magic."

Aisling reached for it, then let the strand slide through her fingers before she closed her fist around it, the rough edges biting into her skin. The rope took on a life of its own. The tail looped around her wrist four times, and then the opposite end coiled over itself when Aoife breathed out a sigh.

Aoife reached out and held Aisling's hand still. "By knot of one, the spell's begun." The ends met and tangled together, securing the rope to Aisling's wrist. "I hope you know what you've started, Raven Queen."

"I do." Still, she gulped as anxiety twisted her belly. "What is your price?"

"A message to the Raven King from an old friend." Darkness brewed in the banshee's gaze.

Aisling hesitated, then replied, "I'm happy to bring back the message."

The darkness began a chasm that swallowed the whites of Aoife's eyes. "You won't have to."

With a vicious twist, the Duchess of the Dead snapped

Aisling's pointer finger. The crack was the sound of a dry twig breaking in the forest, ringing in her ears long before the lancing pain pounded along with her heartbeat.

Bran hissed out a breath and grabbed his wrist. He'd touched nothing, but the throbbing ache felt as though he'd punched a wall.

"What is it?" Elva asked from ahead. Climbing the shear mountain cliff was dangerous enough without distractions such as this. A blast of wind shoved her hair in front of her face, the locks tangling on the roots of a tree desperately trying to stay anchored to the mountain edge.

His hand was on fire... No, not the hand. He stared in anger as his pointer finger twisted slightly. Not enough to snap his own finger, but he knew what the message was.

Someone, or something, had captured Aisling and wanted him to know they had her. How dare they? Rage burned through his lungs, making his breathing a ragged gasp of pure hatred. They would pay for this. They would feel her pain a thousand-fold if he ever found out who they were.

"Bran?" Elva shouted. "What is it?"

He looked up the mountain, his gaze searing the mountainside. He locked eyes with her and saw the exact moment she recognized his pain.

Elva frowned, situated her hold on the mountain tighter, and leaned back. "Tell me."

She was so comfortable up here, dangling on a precipice high above the land. Leather leggings helped her climb with ease, her movement unhindered by foolish skirts. The long braid of her hair waved in the wind, and she held onto the wall of the cliff with only one hand. Strong, and capable, she continued to surprise him with her endurance.

It wasn't her he wanted to look at. Even now, he saw only Aisling in the planes of her face. That her smile wasn't twisted enough, her eyes not quite dark enough, and she wasn't the woman he loved so dearly that it made his heart churn in ridiculous little knots.

"It's Aisling," he grunted, opening and closing his hand to banish the ache. "Someone is sending me a message."

"How so?"

"They broke her finger." He pulled himself up onto a ledge. His balance was slightly off, his mind not exactly with them as they made their way toward the druid's home. He needed to focus on what they were doing now, but could only think of Aisling's pain.

"Why?" Elva was only just ahead of him now. Her braid whipped through the air and nearly lashed him across the cheek. "What message does a broken finger bring other than a threat?"

"It's the Unseelie way. Sending someone home with a broken finger means they've found something I want, and I owe them a boon for losing it in the first place." He shook his head to clear dark thoughts that bubbled in the corners.

"Have you any idea who would send you a message like that?" she asked. "There has to be a few Unseelie that you know would be so ruthless."

"It's just a finger." It was so much more than *just* a finger. He had to say the words to remind himself there was nothing he could do. He might have felt her die. The burning pain through their binding curse would have hurled him off the mountain to his own demise. It was just a finger, but it could have been much worse.

A few rocks tumbled from above and struck him on the top of the head. Glowering, he glanced up at Elva where she had clearly sent the stones tumbling on purpose.

"It's more. That's my *sister*, Bran. I don't care how you're feeling right now. You don't get to play with her wellbeing just because you're distracted."

"A sister you left on her own for her entire life. You don't get to dangle that over me like blood somehow means you're more important." He climbed hand over hand until he was even with her. "Blood isn't thicker than water, Seelie fae. She will always see me as her equal and you as the woman who left her to live in the ditch."

Elva remained silent after that threat, and Bran found he wasn't interested in talking anymore. There was far more for him to think about than verbal sparring with a woman who had no right in the slightest to speak of his Aisling at all.

He told himself to get ahold of his emotions. That the druid woman wasn't going to like having a male already enraged. He would say something foolish, or worse, insulting. Then she wouldn't help him at all, and Aisling would remain on her own.

He flexed his hand again. He couldn't leave her alone, not

when there was so much riding on her safety.

The top of the cliff edge appeared next to his hand. He yanked himself up and over, crouching carefully and observing around him. Elva would make her way beside him, Bran never questioned that once, but for now, he wanted to make sure no one was going to attack them.

He'd heard of Tlachtga's sons before, although not their mother. Legend said they were warriors who could defeat even the most talented of the Fae. Neither court had bothered with them simply because they lived so far away from the Otherworld. They weren't a problem if they didn't attack the Fae on a regular basis, and they didn't.

The sons were hermits, in fact. They remained on this mountain with each other. He hadn't even heard of them bringing women here, and most would have spread such rumors if they had experienced it.

The few who had seen the sons said they were handsome beasts. Tall as trees, broad as horses, they were powerful beings who were said to be able to cleave a man's head from his shoulders in one fell swoop. Women whispered there was more to them than just warriors, although this was always when Bran stopped listening. He had little interest in the prowess of other men.

Stones scrabbled behind him, Elva sliding over the cliff and onto her feet beside him. "Anyone?"

"No." He looked out over the sparse mountaintop and saw nothing more than a simple wooden house. "Which feels strange. They should know we're here."

"I'm sure they do." Elva straightened and placed a hand on the pommel of her sword. "They're watching us. Waiting to see what we do next."

Druids. They were always calculating creatures who wanted to measure a person's worth rather than act. Bran forced himself not to bare his teeth in frustration. If the druidess wanted to speak to him, then she would. Otherwise, he needed to prove himself worth speaking with.

Grand.

"What would you suggest then?" he asked.

"I don't know," Elva replied, her eyes sweeping over the barren landscape. "I'm not precisely sure what they want from us."

"They want nothing from us. We're the ones who want something."

"They're expecting us to do something in return for information. That's how the world works. We just have to figure out what they want."

He wracked his brain for any kind of information he might have once learned about druids and their history. Was there anything he could do to bribe them? They had to want something he could manifest. He was the Raven King; anything he wanted was at his fingertips. They need only to ask.

Then it became clear in his mind. These weren't faeries. They didn't want some trinket or bauble that no one else had. They didn't want some magic that he could pull out of the air or knowledge that he hadn't yet shared.

They were druids, and druids were humans. If he'd learned anything from Aisling, they only wanted one thing that was universal to all their kind.

He smoothed a hand over his ruffled hair, then shook out the dirt that lingered on his clothing. Bran took time to pat down his clothes, making sure that he was presentable to mixed company.

"What are you doing?" Elva asked, her voice vibrating with frustration. "Now is not the time to be concerned about your appearance!"

He ignored her and strode toward the small wooden hut with purpose. His boots struck the barren earth, and he wondered for a moment how the brothers got food up the mountain. Did they not need it? It seemed as though even druids required some kind of sustenance, but perhaps he was wrong. It wouldn't be the first time. Even Sorcha was beyond his understanding now.

He lifted a fist and knocked on the door as gently as his impatience would allow. "Tlachtga, I have come from afar to sit at your table and beg your guidance. Perhaps you would allow me inside?"

Silence rang from behind the door. Elva stomped up to him, hissing under her breath, "You foolish man! You cannot simply order a druid to do as you wish! Do you want to die? Is that what this is?"

The door in front of them swung open on silent hinges. Beyond, an old woman sat in a rocking chair next to a blazing fire in a stone hearth that crackled merrily. Patchwork rugs covered the floor, and a simple table sat opposite the woman. Three men, each with different colored hair, sat around it while sharpening their knives. He recognized the lazy movements. They weren't preparing for a fight or a battle, but simply keeping their hands busy while their mother knit next to the warmth.

He hesitated. "Tlachtga?"

The rocker creaked into motion. "You've come a long way to speak to an old woman, Raven King."

Bran lifted a foot and stepped over the threshold into the druid woman's home. "It was a long way, yes. Well worth the journey if you can help me."

One of her sons, the blonde, leaned forward and placed his knife down on the table. "Mother? If I might take the woman out back, you'll be able to speak with him privately."

Elva snorted. "You aren't touching me with a single finger, big man."

He lifted his brows in response. The large beard on his face obscured most of his expression, but even Bran could see he wasn't all that impressed. "Did I mention touching you? There's plenty to keep you busy out back, though for someone like yourself, I'd suggest cutting wood. It might do you some good to work off that rage."

"I don't need to do your chores," she growled.

"Elva," Bran censored. "I believe the druidess wishes to speak to me alone."

"We came together, we stay together." Elva crossed her arms over her chest, but it didn't escape Bran's notice that she hadn't stepped into the small hut. Perhaps she felt as though she would be trespassing. It certainly felt that way.

A creak from the rocking chair made him look over at Tlachtga, and he caught the simple movement when she nodded to her son. When he stood, Bran realized the rumors were true.

This man was nearly as big as a Tuatha de Danann. Even larger than Aisling, at least seven feet in height, he must tower over human men. Though his queen was smaller than most faeries her age.

Bran nodded at the blonde man as he moved past, then muttered under his breath, "Good luck."

A flash of white split the big man's beard. "I've dealt with far more terrifying creatures than a woman on a rampage, Raven King. I look forward to this battle."

True to his word, the son did not touch Elva at all. Instead, he used his bulk to back her away from the house and closed the door behind him without a single word from Bran's companion. Strange, he had thought Elva more likely to argue with the man at least a little.

Perhaps she was losing her hatred of men. Unlikely, but Bran could hope.

"Come closer," Tlachtga said, her voice wavering on the words. "I cannot see you, boy. My eyes aren't what they used to be."

"Gladly." Bran strode to the rocking chair and sank onto the floor beside her. "I'm glad to see you, druidess. I've heard tales of your life adventures, and I believe you are the perfect person to help me on my journey."

"Such a charmer," she said with a chuckle. The remaining two sons chuckled with her.

Bran glanced over his shoulder and realized all the sons were mirror images of each other. The only difference was the color of their hair. Black, blond, and red-headed, they were all as different as they were the same. If they covered their hair with mud, he couldn't have guessed who was who.

"My boys are remarkable, aren't they?" Tlachtga asked, gesturing at the other two sons. "Cumma and Diorb, the latter has red hair. Makes it easy to tell them apart, otherwise I never would have been able to know who was who."

Diorb, the red-headed beast of a man, let out a booming laugh that shook the rafters. "And you're our mother. You'd think there were other ways to tell us apart."

"Oh, there are, but I don't want to say it in mixed company." The sparkle in the old woman's eyes spoke of a time when she had been a beauty even Bran would have chased.

"Ah," he said with a quiet murmur. "Now I see why there are legends about you, m'lady. You are a beauty indeed."

"Beauty is what always caused me trouble when I was a girl." Tlachtga reached out and smacked his cheek lightly. "And that is what causes young men to get in trouble, too. What would you ask of me, Raven King? My time is finite and precious."

Bran licked his lips. "The woman I love was taken from my side. She's lost, somewhere in Underhill, and I was told you might be able to find her. To help guide me back to her side so that I can keep her from harm."

"You wish to find a lady love?" Tlachtga's cheeks burnished with a blush. "I've always adored a love story. Perhaps because I never understood it myself, but there is something sweet about a man willing to risk everything for a woman he loves. Come. Stare into my fire, and we'll see if we can find her together."

Bran reached out to help her stand, hesitated for a moment to hold her place. "What is the cost?"

"We will speak of a price after we find her," Tlachtga replied, patting his arm with her hand. "Do not worry overly much, Unseelie. There are many things I might ask from you, but none that will harm you or your people. You've been polite, and you surprised me by acting unlike your kind. I find myself far more curious to your story than what I might get from you."

He hoped she would stay that way. Bran had a feeling that Aisling would think she was lying. Druids were capable of it, and he didn't know how to tell if their words weren't exactly what they meant.

With a gentle hand, he helped her close to the fire, though he eyed the flames cautiously. Every movement brushed the fabric of her dress far too close to the flames. The last thing he needed was for the one woman who could find Aisling to be engulfed.

"Tlachtga"—he cleared his throat—"perhaps we should take a step back."

The dark haired man at the table, Cumma he assumed, slapped a hand to its worn surface. "Mother, you didn't tell him?"

"I assumed that he knew."

Diorb shook his head. "Not everyone knows the whole story, and you're as solid as the day you were when you died. Foolish woman, he hasn't the faintest clue what he's touching."

What he was touching? Bran looked down at her and focused his own magic on the feelings of his body. He could feel the rough edges of her woolen gown against his fingertips. Heard the whispered rasp of her breath. Warmth sank into his hand from her body, which appeared at this moment to be very much alive.

He narrowed his gaze. "You aren't here, are you?"

Tlachtga frowned back at him. "I'm very much here. Otherwise I wouldn't be speaking to you at all, Raven King."

"You aren't alive." It wasn't a question. He already knew

what she would say.

"No, I haven't been alive for quite some time. I died the day my sons were born, but I couldn't very well leave them, now could I? They were giant babes. Unlike the legends say, I didn't die of a broken heart." She hooked her thumb over her shoulder and pointed at Cumma. "I died because that one split me open like he does logs. There wasn't a person here to help me, and I couldn't sew myself up. Reaching betwixt your own legs and managing a needle while trying to juggle three babes was impossible."

Bran didn't want to focus on the image she'd put in his mind. Grimacing, he slowly let go of her arm, making certain she could still stand on her own. "Not a ghost then? I haven't ever met a spirit I could touch before."

"Not quite. Druids have knowledge vastly different from your own." She gestured around them with her hands. "Everything you see here is as much a part of me as it is the land itself."

"Ah."

He understood now, although he didn't like it one bit. He reached out and grasped the edge of her dress in his hands. Carefully, Bran peeled back the sleeve of her dress to reveal the dirt filling out the rest of it.

So, she really was dead. Earth mimicked the form of a human, filled out the corpse and let it continue living as though it hadn't actually fallen to the worms. He'd never seen such magic before since it was usually performed only by necromancers, but whatever spell this was, it was an impressive one.

He bowed his head. "Golem?"

"Not so simple as that. No word of god rests underneath my tongue." She gestured toward the flame. "I am the mountain, and the mountain is me. Mother Earth gave me another chance to live and continue with my work. It also allowed my sons to live without dying on the mountain top with me."

Cumma snorted. "And she's never let us forget it."

"Hush, now."

Another light burst to life in Bran's mind. He tilted his head to the side, respect for the old woman filling him near to bursting. "The Samhain festival. It celebrates this mountain in the human realm, although it's more like a hill there. Their sacrifices each year, the festival itself, it feeds you, doesn't it?"

She stared into his eyes and magic bloomed deep in her gaze. "You see too much, Raven King."

He held up his hands. "I have no plans to stop you from doing that. I understand a hedge god when I see one. You've made yourself far more than a druid, mistress, and that is something I can respect."

"Leave it to an Unseelie to like a woman turning herself into a god." Tlachtga clicked her tongue. "No one else would let this go if they found out."

"And too many would lose a good woman because of it. If I remember correctly from my time in the human realm, you've helped the village prosper far better than the others surrounding it." Bran touched a hand to his forehead. "You've done more good than bad, druidess. I see that for what it is."

Tlachtga stared into the fire, and he knew he'd gotten through her shell. She was afraid someone was going to take her magic away. That someone would try to stop her because the Tuatha de Danann preferred to remain the only gods humans knew about.

As he saw it, there wasn't anything wrong with a druidess becoming a god like this. She was tied directly to the land and couldn't take her magic elsewhere without becoming the mud of the mountain that filled her body here.

Let her live in peace. She wasn't hurting anyone.

He turned to stare into the fire as well, then said one last thing. "If you find my queen, Tlachtga, I will offer you all the protection of Underhill should you need it. There are worse things than helping to protect a small goddess who looks after the village who helped her long ago."

Her surprise was palpable. "Thank you, Raven King."

"It's my pleasure."

Tlachtga lifted a hand and waved it over the fire. He couldn't see her magic like many of the faeries who could cast such a spell. There were no bright lights or flourish of power. Even the fire remained still other than the images that now reflected within the licks of heat.

Underhill. He saw it from above, as if he were flying over the castle on obsidian wings. The Raven King part of himself, the ancient magic that longed for death and destruction, lifted its head deep within his soul. This wasn't just Bran's kingdom, but it was the kingdom of a hundred Raven Kings who desired nothing more than to feel power at their beck and call once more.

He straightened his shoulders and forced the magic deep inside him. It would not rear its ugly head while Tlachtga attempted to help him. Now was not the time, and the ancient power *would* obey him.

Tlachtga's vision shifted, moving faster and faster until the sight of Underhill was nothing more than a blur he couldn't focus on at all.

"What are you doing?" he asked.

"I'm trying to find her. It's fairly easy to do for the dead. I can latch onto the piece of your soul that she carries with her."

"My soul?" He rubbed a hand over his chest and the star-shaped scar where she had burned a curse into his flesh. "I suppose you could say that."

"I'm not speaking of your curse," she replied with a chuckle. "That has nothing to do with the hold she has over you. I speak of your love and the dedication you feel toward each other. You are thinking of her, and she is thinking of you. It's strange, but it feels as though you both are never far from each other's thoughts, no matter what is happening to you."

It made him slightly uncomfortable how easily she read him. Bran had always prided himself on being an independent soul. He hadn't ever needed someone to stand by his side. Instead, he'd gone into the world alone and without any other to question him.

Now that he'd found her, the entire axis of his world had shifted. He *wanted* to be beside her. He wanted to experience the world through her eyes, to understand what she did, to show her off to anyone and everyone that would see her.

Even though it made her uncomfortable sometimes.

A wry grin twisted his lips as he thought of the Wild Hunt. His little witch had been a fearsome sight to behold. The Unseelie faeries had yet to stop talking about her. The sluagh whispered in his ear all the stories the other faeries spoke of. They hadn't seen her in a while, but they wanted to see her again. Aisling had left a mark on the courts with little more than a single sighting.

The Raven Queen was something to be proud of, if one could catch her. And Bran had caught her very soul with his own.

Puffing out his chest in pride, he cleared his throat and watched the flames. "Will this take a while?"

"That depends on how long you think a while is."

"I would like to see what your son is doing with my traveling companion."

"Your long lost love?" Tlachtga corrected. "There's more to that woman than meets the eye, you know. She'll be just fine with Muach. He'll help her understand there is more to life than just being a warrior."

Bran furrowed his brows. "What do you mean by that?"

"I mean her story has yet to be told, and there is far more to her than meets the eye." The strange sight of his kingdom blurred for a moment, and Tlachtga let out a low hiss.

"What is it?" He leaned closer to the fire than was comfortable, trying to see what the druidess had. "What do you see?"

She waved her hand sharply, and the fire suddenly died. In a whirl of motion that seemed impossible for a woman of her age, she snapped, "Cumma, Diorb, bring your brother and that woman back into the house. Immediately."

Her sons didn't hesitate. They raced from the hut in a sprint while their mother ran to the windows and began to cover them. She snapped the coverings shut while muttering spells under her breath. The air quickly grew heavy, weighing down on his shoulders like the hands of a hundred people.

Bran fought against it, but he was quickly pinned to the floor in a crouch. Heavy magic poured over his shoulders again and again as Tlachtga forced him to stay still. The front door burst open. The three brothers carried Elva spitting and screaming over the threshold, then slammed it shut behind them.

He didn't like seeing them handle her like that. She didn't like to be touched even by *him,* and they had history.

The anger that bloomed in his chest was enough for him to wrestle his tongue free from druid magic and growl, "What is the meaning of this, Tlachtga?"

"You tricked me," she said on a howl. "You forced me to reveal myself, and now you will pay the price."

"I have done no such thing."

She strode toward him, suddenly no longer an old hunched woman. Instead, a powerful druidess with a straight spine and power sparking on her fingertips. Crouching in front of him, she put a finger underneath his chin and forced him to look up at her. "You are working for Carman, and I do not like witches."

Bran gritted his teeth. "I want Carman out of Underhill. She is the one who hunts my Queen. If I could kill her, then I would."

Tlachtga paused. "You don't mean those words that come out of your mouth, Unseelie."

"Faeries cannot lie. You know this to be true."

She shoved his head to the side and strode back to her sons. "Put the female faerie down. I'll kill her, and perhaps that will make him talk. I want to know what Carman plans and how quickly she's going to attack us."

"I don't know anything about Carman, but if you lay a

hand on my companion, then I will tear you apart limb from limb." The magic of the Raven King seared through his veins, strengthening his muscles and making his vision spark black at the edges. "Don't test me on this, druidess."

She gave him a cocky look over her shoulder as her sons held Elva still. "You said it yourself, Unseelie. I am a goddess made by my own magic. Do you really think a faerie will be able to fight me?"

"I'm not just a faerie. *I am the Raven King.*"

Tlachtga picked up a wicked-looking blade, and Bran's vision skewed to the side. Her magic still pushed down on his shoulders, but it suddenly didn't matter. He could stand without fear of what her power might do to him. Striding forward, he let out an angry chuff of air that had Tlachtga's three sons tightening their grip on Elva's arms and shoulders.

The druidess hesitated for a brief moment, her knife hovering at Elva's throat. "You would risk everything for this one, too? Are you building a harem?"

"I'm not a Seelie king. I have no use for harems or concubines. I want my queen back, and you're going to help me get her no matter what."

"I will not help Carman's accomplices."

"And I'll say it again," he growled. "I don't work for Carman, and I want her out of Underhill for good. If I must send you protection until I kill her, then I will. I was told you could help me find my queen. If you can help me destroy the witch haunting my kingdom, then that is all the better for both of us."

Tlachtga's hand shook, then the knife slowly drifted away from Elva's neck. "I haven't heard a faerie who could lie before. I trust nothing in that has changed since the last time I was in the courts."

"I cannot lie, and I will give you a blood vow that I will not harm you or yours if you help me kill this woman." Bran held out his wrist.

She didn't wait for him to change his mind. Tlachtga whipped out her hand and drew the knife sharp across his wrist. Blood welled immediately, the strength of his words searing the vow into his own flesh.

Bran hissed out a breath. "Will that be enough?"

"For now," she responded, then put the knife down. "You want to kill Carman and save your queen? I can't promise they won't be the same in the end."

He didn't want to know what that meant. There was so much wrong with their lives, he wouldn't be surprised if Aisling had somehow managed to bond herself to the witch queen. They would fight that battle when they got there, but he wouldn't kill Aisling. Ever.

"I won't kill my queen," he said, baring his teeth. "So I suggest you come up with a better way for this to end."

Tlachtga hissed out a breath in response, nodded. "There are items of my father's that are capable of killing the witch queen, only a sorcerer's magic will do. I can give you the map on where to find them. Dig up his blade and shove it through that horrific woman's heart. That will put her in the grave for good."

"Then we have a deal."

When the three sons let Elva drop to the ground, she whipped out a leg and caught Muach at the knee. He fell with a grunt, Elva dancing out of his reach as he tried to swipe at her with a meaty fist.

Tlachtga paused, her head tilting to the side as if she were listening to something. Her expression shifted into one of curiosity, then foreboding.

"This is for you," she said quietly, a thin rope with a single knot suddenly dangling from her fingertips.

Bran took the offered gift, watching as it wound around his arm. "What is it?"

"A spell," she replied, her brows still furrowed. "It seems there's more at work here than just you." She looked over his shoulder and said, "I understand. Two parts, one for the druidess and one for the goddess."

"Who are you speaking to?" He knew there was no one standing behind him, but that she spoke to another ancient being who had reached out to her directly.

"No one," she said, then held a hand over the rope around his wrist. "By knot of two, it cometh true. By knot of three, so mote it be."

Two more knots formed on the rope, and Bran felt his stomach drop. Old magic wove through the hemp. Magic that would change the very fabric of time.

CHAPTER 14

THE QUESTING BEAST

"Lorcan?" Aisling called out, searching for her wayward companion who the banshee's had left in the mist. "Lorcan, if you can hear me, shout!"

No response. Blowing out a frustrated breath, she pushed harder with her magic at the lingering fog that clung to her hands and clothes. It pulled at her, tugging her closer and closer to the edge.

"Stop it," she muttered, batting at the strange magic with her own. "Enough. Lorcan! Damned cat, would you at least respond?"

They needed to leave. There was a long journey ahead. The map in her hand pointed to the next most powerful creature they could beg to help them. It didn't say what the creature was, but she'd handle it once they got there. Only a few creatures scared her anymore.

A searing pain sliced along her wrist. Hissing out an angry breath, she grabbed the arm where the banshee had wrapped the rope. Was there more magic at work here? Would the duchess try to drain her life as payment for her assistance?

It wasn't the banshee's magic that she felt, nor was the rope disturbed. Instead, a red welt drew along her flesh.

"Bran," she whispered. "What are you up to?"

Heat pressed flush to her side, and a masculine hand covered hers. "What's he doing?"

"Damn it!" Aisling flinched back, tugging her hand out of Lorcan's grip and pressing it against her chest. "Don't sneak up on me like that. Where were you?"

He pointed in a random direction then waved his hand. "Somewhere over there."

Her heart thundered in her chest. When had he gotten so good at sneaking up on people? She hadn't even heard his footsteps, let alone the snapping of a twig or a released breath. He'd been as silent as the grave.

Aisling narrowed her eyes. "What magic were you using? And why were you trying to sneak up on me?"

"I wasn't." Lorcan lifted his hands. The grin on his face said he was lying. "I wouldn't do that to you."

"You know I hate it when you lie."

"I'm not!"

Aisling lashed out a hand and caught him upside the head. "If I can't lie, neither can you. *Why* were you sneaking up on me and using magic to hide your steps?"

Rolling his eyes, Lorcan stepped back so she couldn't hit him again. "I didn't know if the banshee had done something to you. There's plenty of ways to control a faerie, and you aren't exactly a weak faerie anymore."

"Anymore?" she hissed. "When was I ever a weak faerie?"

"I'd say likely when you were a little girl." Lorcan pointed at her wrist. "What's that?"

"An arm."

"On the arm."

She looked down at the rope and shrugged. "A way to track a spell I suppose? The banshee duchess said we'd have to pool as many powerful creatures as possible into this spell. We're off to another part of Underhill to convince the next ancient here to help us."

Lorcan snagged her wrist and pulled it toward him. "I don't know this magic."

"That's because it's older than us and currently completely controlled by the duchess of the dead, so I would very much like to have more magic to compete with hers."

"Why doesn't it have yours?"

She blew out a breath. "We're not at that part of the spell yet? I don't know, Lorcan. I'm doing what other people tell me to do. I'm *trusting* someone else for once in my life."

"Dangerous," he said, releasing her arm. "And unlike you."

"Well, sometimes people change."

"Not people like us."

The words stung, although once upon a time she might have agreed with him. Aisling and Lorcan weren't like other people. At least, they hadn't been in their old life.

Now, she'd seen what the world was capable of. She didn't have to live in the shadows as a witch, trading for scraps of food in exchange for a simple spell. Bran had dragged her from that life, albeit kicking and screaming, and given her a throne. More than that, he'd given her a group of people who needed her.

Who loved her.

Aisling shook her head and rubbed the rope at her wrist. Before she could tell Lorcan he was wrong, that there was another way for them to live, the rope twisted sharply.

She stared in shock as two more knots wove themselves into the hemp. Furrowing her brows, she brought it closer to her face until she could see the individual strands of magic flowing through it.

Lorcan leaned closer as well. "Is that—?"

"Druid?" Aisling replied. "I think so."

"Where did it come from?"

Her wrist still stung where a line had been drawn through her skin. Uncontrollably, a smile spread across her face, and it felt as though her soul lit up from the inside out. "Bran."

"What's he up to?"

"That's what I'm wondering, but it seems like someone has fed something into the spell as well."

She touched a finger to the thread and tried to send a pulse through it. If Bran was connected to this old magic someway, maybe she could get a message to him.

"That's a bad idea," Lorcan said, interrupting her thoughts with a finger to her forehead. "We already said we weren't going to involve him. You know it's too much of a risk."

"You've always said not to trust anyone. Even you," she murmured. "How do I know you aren't the one working with Carman? That you haven't been swayed by the hanging tree and are only working to bring me to my death?"

Lorcan pressed a hand to his chest, and for the first time since he'd turned back into a human, she saw sincerity in his eyes. "You were my very first friend, and the first person to ever look at me as though I was something more than a ragged boy in the dirt playing with spells that were too big for him. The earth would have to shift and the mountains flatten for me to stray from your side."

A sharp edge of guilt tore at her heart for a brief moment before she remembered that he would be proud of her for the distrust. Lorcan had taught her from the very beginning to remember that not everyone wanted to help her. In fact, most wanted to hurt her. Questioning him was the first start to remembering all the things he'd taught her.

And she remembered those lessons like they were yesterday. He'd drill them into her every morning when they woke up. An hour of how to take care of herself, then learning spells, then cooking, cleaning, sparring, all the things that a little boy could teach a little girl so that she didn't die on the street when he was gone.

He always said he was going to leave her. Even after a year or two, he'd say next winter was the time when he was going to leave. That she would have to figure out a way to take care of herself because he certainly wasn't going to do it.

He never did. Even the times when he walked out the door, muttering how women were foolish and useless in this world, he always came back with something to eat or a new spell for them to learn.

He'd never left. Not really.

Reaching out a hand, she took his and squeezed it. "Thank you. For everything."

"Don't get mushy on me, witch. I don't want to kiss your

ass, so don't kiss mine." He smiled as he pulled away.

Together, they strode out of the white mist and into the fields beyond.

Deep channels created long grooves in the dirt, perhaps where there was once a field. The more she looked, the more details she saw of an ancient people who had made this place their home.

An orchard stood far away. The trees were overgrown, fruit weighing down branches with no leaves. It didn't seem possible there was anything growing on them for the trees themselves looked dead. She stepped closer. Blood leaked from the apples and dripped onto the ground.

"Don't touch those," Lorcan scolded, pulling her away.

"I wasn't touching them. I was just looking."

"Looking is just as bad. We don't know what kind of magic seeped into the ground here. This isn't a good place."

"No, it doesn't feel like it." Try as she might, Aisling couldn't figure out where they were. Clearing her throat, she hurriedly made her way to Lorcan's side, trying to match his long-legged stride. "What do you think this is? Or was?"

"A battlefield."

"It looks like farmlands to me."

He snorted. "The perfect place for a battle, no one would have the upper hand on land already made flat by farmers for hundreds of years. You can't hear the souls still crying out in pain? All their blood and death washes down to the banshee kingdom where their clothes will be cleaned for the afterlife. It makes sense."

In a way, but she didn't hear or see what he did. Instead,

all she heard were the wails of the banshees lifting up into the sky and tangling with the clouds.

They traveled for the better part of the night until she felt the sun rising on the horizon, tugging at her navel with magic that boiled deep in her blood. She gasped at the first ache. A spear of sunlight had touched her arm, and she looked down to see the faint outline of raised hair changing into gossamer feathers.

"Lorcan," she said. "I don't have much longer. We have to stop soon."

"You can fly."

"It doesn't..." Her stomach rolled, gorge rising in her throat even though she couldn't remember the last time she ate. "It doesn't feel right this time."

"Aisling?" He turned, then lunged forward to catch her in his arms.

She sagged toward the ground, her legs suddenly numb. This wasn't how she was supposed to change. Shifting into her swan form wasn't exactly painless. It had always been easier than changing back into a human. The curse wanted her to be punished. It didn't want to *kill* her.

Unless it did here.

Lorcan pushed strands of hair out of her face. "Tell me what's wrong. I need you to focus on me, Aisling. Something is happening to you, something that isn't the curse, and I need to know what so I can help you."

She tried to open her mouth, but she couldn't make her lips move. Instead, she drifted into darkness as her eyes rolled back in her head.

Aisling awoke in shadows. She opened her eyes and knew this wasn't the place where she had been before. Her body felt weightless, arms lifting from her side without her raising them. Almost as though...

When she gasped, fluid sank into her lungs. It didn't hurt, not here, she had felt this way before.

The faintest white glow pulsed to life behind her. The silvery touch lit the back of her hands and filtered through her fingers that cast spikes of shadows through the water all around her.

She wasn't drowning, so she wasn't really in water. No one had teleported her away from Lorcan. Memories rushed to the front of her mind. She'd been in Underhill, in that old blood-soaked battlefield where Lorcan heard souls screaming for help and the apples bled.

Carefully, she kicked her legs and turned to look at the light that had blinked into existence. Only a few feet away from her, the original Raven Queen floated in the water. Her white hair drifted like a halo around her head, her pale gown tangled around her like the strokes of a painter's brush.

Only this time, the woman wasn't trapped underneath the ice below the Unseelie castle. She floated freely in the depths of darkness, blue glowing eyes open and staring at Aisling.

"What is it?" Aisling's voice carried through the water. "What do you want from me?"

"She doesn't want anything." The voice was a sip of honey mead, the pour of wine in a silent room. "She's doing a favor for an old friend."

Aisling spun again, and there *he* was.

"Bran," she whispered.

Dark, handsome, and ever so dangerous, he floated with not a stitch of clothing out of place. Every inch the Raven King. His yellow eye whirled in its socket, the other focused on her with such intensity that she felt it to her very bones.

He didn't move. He merely opened his mouth and asked, "Where are you?"

"You know I can't tell you that."

"You can."

She shook her head, body shaking with the need to be at his side. To explain. "I really can't, Bran. This is something I have to do alone. To keep both of us safe."

His face twisted in anguish. "I need you."

The words shattered her carefully placed shield around her mind, and she floated closer. She had to. Even if she could only feel the faintest heat of his body warming the water around her, it would be close enough. "Bran, I can't risk it. We can't risk this."

"I'm sorry," he said, his voice a whisper and a hymn. "I should have seen it before. I was drowning under the weight of all those expectations. *You* are the most important thing in my life. Let the kingdom fall to ruin, I don't care. You come first. You will always come first."

"It can't be like that." Her words choked on a gasp. "The

kingdom, our people, our home has to come first."

"You foolishly complicated woman. You cannot have both! You have to come first, my love. You will always come first."

She didn't know which one of them moved, but they were suddenly in each other's arms, and heat bled out around them. Aisling hadn't realized she'd been so cold until ice no longer existed in her veins.

His hands framed her face, and he leaned so close that their lips barely touched each other. "Your namesake is watching."

"Then let her see how a woman should be loved."

He devoured her lips. Pressed his own to hers until she couldn't tell where she began and he ended, but it didn't matter. She'd give her soul to him if he asked it.

His hands traced patterns on her shoulders and down her back. Runes of protection and love that flared to life and burned as they trickled between her shoulder blades and settled against her hips. Over and over he tasted her, branded her, reminded her why she loved him so in the first place.

She had been a cracked porcelain vase, tossed aside by the world until he picked her up and knew there was use in her yet. And he was her fallen prince, ready to launch a thousand ships should her silver tongue beg him to.

His love was a heady poison that beckoned her to do dangerous, deadly, horrible things. Things that made her dark soul want to sing.

Aisling pulled back, darted out her tongue to taste merlot darkening her flesh.

He touched a thumb to her lips, dragging it slowly away before bringing it back to his own mouth. He licked the dark droplet of wine away and then growled low and deep. "I'm coming for you."

Aisling came to with a gasp, stretching her wings wide and letting out a cry that sounded like the hoarse cough of a wild beast. She wasn't human?

No, of course not. The sun was high on the horizon, filtering through the dusty air. There was no place for a woman here, not yet.

"Aisling?" Lorcan asked, racing to her side where he must have laid her to sleep. "Are you finally awake?"

She nodded her long neck. Her body felt normal. She remembered the pain of the transformation, the dark dream, and her tongue still tasted wine where Bran had left his mark.

Lorcan breathed out a relieved sigh. "Thank the gods. I thought you'd died."

In truth, so had she. Aisling wasn't sure what that small vision had been. A dream? Some kind of connection the Raven King shared with his queen? She'd never experienced anything like it and wasn't certain she'd like to again.

Blowing out a breath, she tucked her wings against her sides and waddled closer to Lorcan. As usual, he seemed to understand her need for connection. He ran a hand over the smooth feathers of her back and settled onto the ground next to her.

A small part of her wanted to crawl directly into his lap. She was *tired*. So very tired and aching, but most surprising of all...

She was sad.

Aisling burned with the need to be beside the man she loved, to live a normal life that always seemed denied to her. No matter where she was in life, witch, wastral, queen, she was still alone.

"We're going to figure this out," Lorcan murmured, still stroking her back in a soothing motion. "Nothing is the end, and soon you'll be curse free."

She wasn't so confident. There was a lot more at play than just a curse, and she couldn't control Carman of all people.

What did the witch queen want? Aisling tried to put herself in the woman's shoes though she had no idea how to even begin thinking like Carman. No one knew the woman's history, only that she'd come from warmer climates and swept through Ireland with little more than a glance. She'd destroyed everything in her path, not because they'd attacked or insulted her, because she wanted to.

Lorcan patted his hand on her head. "Come on then, just because you're a swan doesn't mean we cannot travel. The map the banshee gave you is a little deceiving."

She knew he was trying to shake her out of the strange mood she was in, and Aisling was grateful for it. She shook her head firmly, forced herself to focus on the task at hand, and got back onto her feet.

The webbed toes made walking on land hard, but she'd

never stopped doing something simply because it was hard. Feathers ruffled in frustration, she padded to where it seemed Lorcan had set up camp.

A small fire died in a ring of stones, wisps of smoke curling up in the air. Lorcan's boots were piled on top of each other, ruining the leather most likely, along with some of their other belongings scattered about the ground.

They didn't have much on this journey, she realized. Lorcan had somehow acquired a pack, likely stolen from the river, that seemed to have a few pieces of food in it.

He plopped down next to it and pulled out an apple. "Want a slice?"

Her stomach rumbled, and she honked. A knife appeared in his hands that he used to slice a small sliver off the apple, which he then tossed to her.

She'd already gulped it down and watched him eat another before it dawned on her that he was eating faerie food. She let out a panicked sound, eyes wide, trying to convey the danger he'd put himself in.

Although he was a witch, he was still human. He couldn't eat the food without being doomed to live in the Otherworld forever.

Lorcan gave her a wry grin. "It doesn't matter anymore, little witch. You're here, and that means my family is here. Why would I want to go anywhere else?"

The sentiment was not lost on her. Aisling's heart melted, knowing he'd give up his freedom, that which he valued over all else, just so that he could continue this journey without leaving her side. The man was a foolish idiot to a fault, but he was loyal.

She waddled over to his side and gave him a harsh nip on the ribs. His answering shriek of pain was enough to satisfy her before she nudged the pack and gave him a look.

"Yes, the map is in there." He reached over her head and withdrew it. "Have a look."

Lorcan spread it out on the ground in front of them, then leaned back to finish off the apple.

It looked no different than she remembered. An endless, vast landscape of barren wasteland that continued on as far as the map could stretch. There were no markers for distance and it looked far larger than she could fathom. Even the kingdoms were marked. Some labeled banshee, others sluagh, some even dullahan, although Aisling was surprised to find out they had their own kingdom. Most of them remained within the castle.

Lorcan let out a soft snort and pointed at a corner of the map. "It looks big, but it's really not. That marker there is a druid note saying that the size changes. When a person knows where they're going, the land shifts to accommodate."

She honked in confusion.

"It's a faerie tactic to hide things they don't want any trespassers to find," he replied. "Someone has to know exactly where they are going in this kingdom to get anywhere. If they know, the journey is only half a day at most, even for the outskirts. If they don't, then it will take them weeks to find the place, maybe even months. Land is easily manipulated when it comes to druid or faerie magic."

The last bit was grumbled as if he didn't like admitting it. He'd always wanted to be able to do *more* magic than the rest of the witches but was limited by his blood.

Druids and faeries were directly connected to the land.

They could tap into its magic, manipulate it, change it in ways witches could never do. Witches could control bodies in ways that faeries couldn't even imagine. Aisling had seen black magic that could sear the flesh off a person's bones and still keep them walking. Lorcan was just as capable as a faerie.

He just never wanted to admit it.

She tapped the map hard and looked up at him. He had to know exactly how far it was to get to the area the banshee had highlighted.

He nodded to her right. "It's just over there."

Spreading her wings wide in shock, she hopped in that direction before pausing. Just at the horizon was a giant tangle of brambles. A massive mesh of dead vines with deadly needles rose into the air and wickedly reflected the sun. Each glint was a reminder that any who tried to step foot in that place might never come back out.

She looked over her shoulder and honked again.

"Not a place I'm going to follow you," he replied, then turned and punched the pack to soften it. Nestling the stolen bag under his head, he leaned back and placed the sleeve of a shirt over his eyes. "You'll have to make this journey on your own, Raven Queen. That is one place I'm not interested in going."

She beat her wings hard, racing at him with all the fury her form could muster. Hissing and pecking every inch of him she could reach, she rolled him over.

The swearing coming from his mouth would have made her ears burn if she'd been human. "Aisling, stop it! I'm not going with you. That's a place you can manage all on your own. Fly over the top, find an opening, and—would you stop pecking me — get the next part of the spell!"

Another frustrated breath rang from her lungs before she stopped assaulting him. She didn't want to go in alone. That briar forest looked like it housed a beast that would eat her sooner than listen. And how was she supposed to say anything to it in this form?

Opening her wings wide, she gestured to her body.

"Yeah," Lorcan said with a scoff, scooting back to his bag and laying back down, "it looks like you have a problem."

The damned man was still far too cat-like for her liking. Narrowing her eyes, she hissed and backed away from him. If he was set on staying here, then she would make him wait as long as possible. See how he liked starving while she tried to fix herself.

She kicked the pack for good measure as she passed, apples rolling from the open top and spilling onto the barren ground. Lorcan let out a shout and tried to grab her wing, but she was already racing from his side and beating the air with them.

Lifting into the sky, she soared up to the clouds.

How dare he? After all he'd said about wanting to help her, that he would never be far from her side, he decided now was the time to laze about? This forest was terrifying, hidden deep in Underhill, and likely housed something far more terrifying than the banshee duchess.

Had she said anything about it? Aisling wracked her brain for any memory of something the banshee might have let slip. Was there an animal here? She only knew that it was as powerful and as ancient as the banshee herself.

There were a lot of creatures in history that were powerful. She could list a hundred just by herself, and those were the ones that humans spoke of. Let alone all the ones that faeries hadn't mentioned to the human realm at all.

She glided over the briar forest and stared down at the tangled nest of thorns. There had to be a way into it. A few gaps showed a path that winded through the entirety and stretched farther than her eyes could see.

How could anyone manage this?

The longer she stared, the more she realized the briar forest was a maze. Winding channels connected with each other. Glimpses of beasts waiting at the end of each tunnel struck fear in her heart. If she got this wrong, she'd definitely end up in the belly of some animal that hadn't eaten in a very long time.

She gulped, then descended closer to the labyrinth. Gaps in the tangled vines allowed her to plan out her descent into the forest, but certainly didn't make her feel any better.

Aisling spent the better part of the day surveying the entire landscape. Some of the long passages were safe. Glistening pools of water waited at the end, some with tables overladen with fresh faerie fruit. Others were a sheer drop hidden by magic until she got close enough to see the chasm.

Just as the sun dipped to the horizon and the moon peeked out, she found it. A small gap that must be the dead center of the labyrinth. Wasn't that always where the treasures were hidden? The center had to be where she was supposed to go.

She carefully set herself on top of the brambles above it and pecked at the first one. It crumbled under her beak, but not nearly fast enough. This would take days in this form.

Thankfully, the curse loosened just enough that her human skin burst forth. She forced the change so hard it happened in an instant of blinding pain that caused her to cry out. A bolt of magic shot from her fingertips, sizzled through the tangled vines, and blasted them into dust.

Aisling tumbled through and landed hard on her side. The air rushed from her lungs, leaving her gasping and grasping at the hard soil with clawed fingers.

There was something here, there had to be, and she couldn't be wheezing on the ground. Coughing a few more times, she forced herself onto hands and knees, then stared around her in fear.

The center of the labyrinth was no different from the rest. Dim light glowed from deep inside the brambles with only enough to cast long, jagged shadows. Dust hung in the air, orbs of a crumbled, ancient world. Everything seemed to be in shades of gray. Charcoal brambles, ashen dirt, iron-dark corridors stretching out in a star pattern, and the faint hint of a smoke-smudged symbol in the center of the floor.

She dragged herself closer and smoothed a hand over the hidden mosaic. An eye stared back at her, the same as the tattoos on her palms. She lifted a hand and compared the two.

Hissing resounded throughout the chamber. A voice emanated from deep within the sound, barely recognizable as words, but ones she managed to pick out.

"They're the same, aren't they?" it asked.

A shiver skated down her spine. "They are."

"I wonder why?" The creature inhaled, long and loud then snorted as though it was tasting the scent it had pulled through its mouth. "Witch? Queen? Strange combination for these parts."

"I am the Raven Queen," she said, remaining in a crouch. "I take it you are the ancient creature I've been sent to meet?"

"Sent?" Another sound rang out, this time a braying call of hunting dogs. "By whom?"

"The Duchess of the Dead."

A rattling sound came from behind her. Aisling turned with an answering hiss, but saw nothing. The creature was hiding in the shadows of a corridor somewhere, she couldn't tell which one.

The beast's voice rose again. "Have you come to steal?"

"No."

"To harm?"

"No."

"*Lies*," it hissed. "All come to steal or harm."

She placed her hand down on the symbol, pressing eye to eye and feeling power surge through her body. "You scented me. You know what I speak is true. Faeries cannot lie."

"That's all faeries do. They tell stories, they misdirect people's thoughts, and then they lie... lie... *lie*." Its voice grew more and more ragged with every word until it descended into an unrecognizable cry, like dogs who had finally caught scent of the hunt.

"*I do not*." Her voice carried throughout the corridors, echoing back upon her like a thousand women enraged that they were being questioned. "You see me, you smell me, you know I am not like the others. What more can I do to prove myself?"

And she had to prove herself. This creature was clearly the most powerful thing in the labyrinth, although she had yet to see the extent of its magic.

Her mind flashed back to the memory of Bran, of the vision he'd cast upon her. He was coming, and she didn't have much time to figure this out on her own. She had to stop Carman from getting her claws into the Raven King. More than that, she wanted to protect the man she loved who'd done so much for her already.

When the beast did not respond, she licked her lips and shifted in a slow circle. No shadows moved with her, nor was there anything in any corridor that would suggest the creature laid in wait there. It had to be here somewhere.

"I need your help," she said.

"So you *do* want something."

"Everyone does."

It chuckled, deep voice clamoring with the sound of countless animals. "You have no idea what I am, do you? A witch queen who cannot see, scent, or feel."

Power crackled at her fingertips, but she stilled the reaction to silence. She wouldn't try to threaten this beast since it didn't seem to respond well to brute force. There was some emotion she recognized in the edge of its voice. Perhaps a vulnerability that called out to her own.

"Come forward," she said. "I'll speak no longer with a face I cannot see."

"What makes you think I have a face, witch queen?" The hissed question echoed throughout the room.

"*Now.*" Her word vibrated with magic that seared throughout the room. The ball of magic burst forth from her lips, rocketed up into the air, and illuminated the center chamber. Light filtered out into the corridors, and for a split second, she saw a cloven hoof larger than her head.

The beast retreated farther into its corridor, hissing in anger. "Magic has no place here."

"Are you not made of magic yourself? An animal who can speak. Cursed or naturally born?"

The hoof kicked out at her. "Questions such as these will get you killed."

"And yet, this the question I'm asking." She lifted her hand and whispered a word of power. Her fingertips glowed in the darkness, spreading light across the room and spearing into the shadows of the corridor where the beast lurked. "Don't make me force you."

The large sigh it heaved made her wonder if someone had done this before. Was it used to such treatment? Of men or women barging into its home, forcing it to reveal the form it so clearly hated?

Pity welled in her chest, threatening to overflow from her being and spill out onto the floor in soft words of encouragement. She could not allow the beast to see her weakness. Not yet, not when there was so much she needed from it first.

A cloven hoof stepped into the light, followed by speckled legs of golden amber that ended in the hooves of a hart. Though these were strange indeed, it was the face that made Aisling wince in sympathy.

The beast's head and neck were that of a large serpent. It flicked out a tongue, tasting the air around her. Jaw opening, it hissed a long breath that ended with the sound of thirty dogs barking in the chamber.

"You're the questing beast," she murmured. "I thought you were dead."

"Lies," it repeated, head weaving back and forth as its slitted gaze watched her movements. "Mother could not let me die."

"What part of your story is true?" Aisling asked.

"All of it."

She'd heard the story a few times, although it was rarely told in these parts. The beast's mother, though never named in the story, lusted after her own brother. She made a deal with the devil to change her form, seduced her sibling, and found herself with child. Her brother discovered her deception and, in guilt, confessed to the local priest. He was then sentenced to death by his own hunting hounds. The beast was the result of such a match, cursed with a monstrous form and the voice of the pack that killed its father.

Aisling shuffled away from the creature, moving toward the center of the chamber where the eyes were etched into the floor. "Your mother?"

"Always a soft-hearted woman. A shame she was so easily taken advantage of." It stepped silently into the chamber, following her movements. "You remind me of her." There was no softness in the words, only an ancient rage and hatred reflected in the beast's eyes.

"I've never been a mother."

"You will someday, and your child will be a beast just like me."

She blew out a low breath. The words were far too prophetic for her liking, but they didn't garner the response the questing beast likely wanted. "Then I shall welcome the child with open arms. I have little issues with a child who is more animal than human."

"*Lies.*"

"I cannot lie. The dearest person in my life is more bird

than man. Even I am more animal now."

The questing beast lifted its head high and flicked out its tongue once more. The slimy appendage hovered over her head for a moment. Tentacle-like, it slithered just above her head and then split down the middle. Each forked end undulated before returning to the beast's jaws.

Aisling held her breath though the movements. Her heart hammered in her chest, but she forced her muscles to lock in place. It wouldn't intimidate her.

Like it or not, she needed this creature's help. Although, she had a hard time believing it had more magic in it than the Duchess of the Dead. The questing beast was a forgotten legend, more lore than reality. It had faded into nothing more than a children's story to tell in the middle of the night. What magic could it have?

"You taste of faeries," it said on a long sigh. "You are not a faerie."

"I am. Although, if you had asked me that mere months ago, I would have told you a different story."

Its eyes widened. If it had ears, those might have perked up also. "A story?"

So it wasn't so different from the faeries it didn't like. Aisling cocked her head to the side and gestured toward the eye on the ground. "Did you think it was luck that I matched this place? I'll trade you my story if you tell me why my tattoos are the same as that."

"I don't like games," the questing beast hissed.

"Neither do I. I do very much like a good story, and I think you might be able to tell one that would entertain me. And I'm certain my story would entertain you."

Its head shifted side to side as the beast considered her words. Aisling hoped this was the one thing that might win it over. She wanted nothing more than to get out of this labyrinth and move on. The questing beast felt very much like a waste of time. This creature was hardly sane, let alone useful in a spell that required finesse and skill.

"Fine," it grumbled. The great body brushed against hers as it lumbered past. The fur on its hide was soft, like that of a rabbit.

She swallowed and pivoted to watch as it curled around the eye in a great circle and then laid its snake chin on the floor.

"Tell me," it howled. The sound lifted up to the ceiling of the chamber and swept throughout the corridors.

And so she would. Aisling meandered over to its side and settled onto the floor beside it. She had no issues sitting in the dirt, even though the ash of a long-ago fire smudged her skin. It streaked her arms in black smudges and left a bitter taste on her tongue as she spoke.

Hours passed as she relayed her entire tale. She was nothing more than a forgotten thing, cast aside as a changeling who had then become a queen. It was a compelling tale, although she still didn't feel as though it were hers. Not entirely, not yet. She was still just Aisling, a little girl who wanted her family to love her but didn't have the faintest idea where to find them.

When she finished, the questing beast looked at her with different eyes. The pity there mirrored what she had felt for the beast only moments before she began.

"So," it said quietly, "your mother didn't want you either."

Aisling thought about it for a few moments. She'd never

put it into words how her mother must have felt casting aside a child that was no longer a baby. A child who loved her mother more than the world, who had cried out for help and mercy when they had left her alone in the forest where humans could find her, or wolves. "No," she finally admitted, "I don't think she did."

"Why?"

Aisling stared into the creatures eyes and saw it desperately desired a reason for its own mother leaving. And though their stories were very different, she also understood that need for understanding.

Reaching out a slow hand, she gently laid her fingers on top of its front hoof. The questing beast stared at the touch in shocked, tongue flicking out to taste the air, as if she might be trying to hurt it or poison it with little more than a touch.

Aisling waited until it looked up at her again, eyes wide, before she quietly said, "I don't think there needs to be a reason. It wasn't a flaw in us that made them leave. It was a flaw in them, and that takes a very long time to understand."

A wound in her heart she hadn't realized was still open finally closed. Words stitched it shut until there was little more than a bitter ache left. Something like abandonment would never completely heal, she didn't know the magic words for that, but this felt considerably better than it had before.

The questing beast set its head back on the floor and hissed out a long, low breath. "The eyes hide me," it quietly said. "They keep most people away, although there is always some soldier who finds their way to the labyrinth in hopes they might appease the great sorcerers by killing me."

"Why does anyone want to kill you?" she asked. "Why

can't they just leave you alone?"

"Because once upon a time, a man said they should. He said the world would be worse with me in it, and that man was the father of my mother. Hiding me, killing me, would wipe away his greatest shame of a daughter who didn't listen, a son who had turned to sin, and a grandchild who was nothing more than an abomination."

She realized the beast wasn't as simple as she thought. The questing beast was just a person, like her, albeit one who wore a different form.

Suddenly, the spell didn't matter that much anymore. She had been selfishly guided into this mess because she didn't want to turn into a swan. Because she wanted a few more moments with the man she loved, but there was so much more in this world that she should have been focusing on.

The questing beast was just one of many who had been cast aside and thrown deep into Underhill so that no one would remember they were alive. She could find them. Bring them back to the castle. Bring them *home.*

She squeezed its fetlock, then scooted back so she could stand. "The Raven King's castle is no longer a place where we murder, harm, or force anyone to do anything they don't want to. Even the sluagh are finding peace there now. You are welcome within my halls, and I hope you realize we will protect you."

"No one can protect me from my grandfather," it said with a scoff. "He is a sorcerer, ancient and powerful."

A protective urge rose deep in her chest. It bubbled to the surface like lava from a volcano and spilled into her throat. "You've seen what I can do," she said, voice deep like thunder.

"No one takes what is mine. I am the Witch Queen of Underhill, and they will fall beneath my wrath if they raise a finger toward you."

The questing beast looked up at her with its heart in its eyes, and she saw the world hidden in their depths.

"You wish to find Carman," it said. The words reverberated in the chamber until it felt almost as if the world held its breath in the silence that followed. "The first witch queen, and the woman who gave you all your powers in the first place."

"She has no connection to me," Aisling corrected. "I've never seen her, but she's awakened and is speaking with my people, harming my people, and I won't stand for it. I want to end this now, regardless of what happens to me. I won't let her touch the sluagh again."

The questing beast stood as well, heaving to its feet, suddenly slow and clumsy. "You do share a connection with her. Haven't you figured it out yet? Carman was the first Raven Queen. It's why she could never be killed in the first place. Underhill is her home because she *is* Underhill."

The foundation of the world Aisling stood on shifted to the side. She stumbled, catching herself at the last moment but, *of course, this all made so much more sense.*

Carman was Underhill—she was the first, she would be the last. That was why she could speak with the sluagh so easily. It was why she could fight against Aisling and Bran without even lifting a finger.

It was why she had never died.

"The first Raven Queen," Aisling repeated. "She's the woman in the lake beneath the Unseelie Castle?"

The questing beast shrugged. "Perhaps that's where they keep her these days. The body doesn't really matter. It's where her power and soul lie that you want to watch out for. Bodies are easily moved and tampered with. The soul, the magic, the essence that makes us who we are... Now that's something that does not stay attached to the physical form."

"Necromancers disagree with you."

It scoffed, barking out thirty voices before calming itself. "Necromancers are parlor tricks compared to what I know. Come here, witch queen. Now that you have proven yourself worthy, I would like to offer my help."

She didn't know what the creature could do. She needed to speak with Lorcan. Perhaps he would have an idea of how to move forward. The Raven Queen? She had to kill the first Raven Queen? What would that even do to this land, these people?

Aisling rocked forward, caught in the stare of the questing beast. It lifted a hoof and beckoned her forward, eyes swirling with hundreds of colors she hadn't noticed before. Step by step, she drew closer to its grasp before it reached out and dragged her forward with a long leg.

"The Duchess gave you this?" it asked.

"She did. She said it was the beginning of a spell which might save us all."

"Hmmm." The questing beast looked it over then ran the tip of its tail down the two new knots that had appeared after she saw Bran. "These two will help you even more than the banshee. Do you know who they are?"

"I don't know where they came from, though I suspect they were the Raven King's doing."

The questing beast looked up and nodded. "There are more

forces at work here than either you or I could ever understand. The first knot, the start of the spell, comes from the dead." It traced over the first, then moved onto the others. "The second and third come from what once was."

"The past?" she asked.

"All that once was, all the stories and the legends wrapped up into two knots that control time itself."

Aisling stared down at the magical threads and wondered again what Bran was up to. Who had he spoken to that was so powerful they controlled the past? She wanted to try to connect with him again, to pry the information out of him, but knew he wouldn't be interested in telling her. Not without bargaining something, and that something would be her whereabouts.

She cleared her throat then forced the thoughts out of her mind. "The Duchess of the Dead seemed to think *you* were the next piece that could help me."

"I am." It continued to stare down at the hemp rope looped over her arm.

"Will you?" AIsling asked, daring to reach out a hand and touch it underneath the questing beast's chin. Cool scales scraped over her palm as she tilted its head up. "Will you help me?"

"What will you do with this newfound power? Once you defeat Carman, you will never be the same again."

She'd had a feeling that was the way this would end. Aisling shrugged. "Life has never been kind to me. I had considered this quest would change me, but I won't let it force me to become someone other than who I already am. I refuse to let power or magic make me lose my way. The path I have chosen for myself is the only path I will ever accept."

An answering fire burned deep in the questing beast's eyes. "Then I will help you."

"What part of the spell are you?" she asked.

"I am what *is*," it replied. "I am the pain, the disgust, and the shame that runs through the hearts of so many. I am the present and all the struggle that comes with existing in the now."

Gods, it didn't deserve that fate. It had been born a monster, but that didn't make its heart impure. She set her jaw and shook her head firmly. "No longer. I will not stand by and let you linger here in the shadows while the world continues on. You will never become the past, and you will not remain stuck in this present, because time changes, the *world* changes."

"Not as quickly as you think, witch queen."

She reached out and stroked a hand over the broad plane of its cheek. "Magic comes in many forms, and if you believe, sometimes it can be forgiveness."

"Are you sure you want to go through with this? My part in this spell brings more power than you may know how to handle."

"I am certain," she said with a nod. "I refuse to give up on you, my people, or the kingdom I have come to love so thoroughly."

The questing beast leaned down, opened its mouth over her arm and whispered, "By knot of four, this power I store. By knot of five, the spell's alive."

Blinding magic, so strong it lit the entire chamber to pure white, blasted through Aisling. She couldn't feel her body because it didn't exist anymore. All that remained of herself was the memories of raven feathers stroking her cheek and the whisper of a man who loved her saying, *"Aisling, Aisling come back!"*

All the magic the questing beast had given her snapped back into the form of a woman who wasn't her anymore. The form of a woman who was suddenly more witch than fae.

Heaving out a cough that rocked her forward, she finally relaxed and let her body sink back onto the floor of the chamber. Aisling slumped there for a few moments, catching her breath and her bearings. The questing beast laid down nearby.

The heat from its body sank into her skin. The sound of its heartbeat grounded her when all her thoughts wanted to fracture and spiral out into the ether. Even the quiet rhythm of its breath helped measure her own.

Finally, she coughed out a croaking sound that wasn't her voice, yet was. "Thank you."

"Don't thank me yet, witch queen. I wish there was more I could do for you than just the gift of strength. Should you reach the Witch Queen, you may draw upon my power as well as your own."

"What did the banshee gift me?"

"All the knowledge of the dead, should you need it."

"And the Raven King's friend?"

"Ancient wisdom from the druids." The questing beast snorted. "And likely a weapon that might kill Carman, potentially the rest of us as well."

"A weapon?" Her brows furrowed. "Do I not want to kill her?"

"You should try not to. Underhill lives in her veins so, without Carman, there is no kingdom at all."

What would happen to the faeries who lived here? Aisling

didn't have to ask. She could already see the answer written in the dust around them. They would die along with the kingdom, which had already been rotting from the inside out. Carman had made herself the lifeblood of Underhill and thus the creatures as well.

She couldn't let them die. There had to be another way.

Slowly, achingly, she forced herself back onto her feet. The curse of the Raven Queen pressed down on her shoulders, and she realized an entire night had passed. The sun rose on the horizon, and her time here with the questing beast was nearly finished.

"How do I find Carman?" she croaked, arms stretching out and fingers spreading as feathers unfurled down her wrists. "Where I do I find the Witch Queen?"

"The banshee gave you a map, didn't she?"

Aisling nodded before the curse swallowed her body. Somehow, the sun had risen on the horizon far sooner than she expected. She lay at the questing beast's feet, long neck outstretched. Breathing hard, she looked up and hoped she somehow conveyed she wished it would continue to speak.

Gently, the beast slid a hoof underneath her prone form and helped her onto her feet. "There's a burned corner of the map. That is where Carman and her sons reside."

Aisling opened her wings and flew away from the labyrinth out the same hole where she'd fallen. A sick feeling made her shiver, but she also felt a tingle of anticipation.

Aisling hoped the Witch Queen was prepared to meet another of her own making.

CHAPTER 15

DRUID GRAVEYARD

Bran stepped through the portal Elva had made and shuddered as the lingering effects of her magic stuck to his shoulders. It didn't feel right anymore, using anyone but Aisling's magic to move between the realms.

"Remind me why we had to go to the human realm?" he asked, shaking his shoulders to free himself from the feeling of Elva's magic. "It seems like we should be able to get everything we need in Underhill, or the Otherworld at the very least."

"Because Tlachtga was not born, nor lived, in our world."

"And the map she gave us said we had to come here?"

"Yes." Elva clutched the paper close to her chest. "Although I haven't been entirely truthful with you on where she's sending us."

He rolled his eyes and held out his hand. "Is she making us fight a dead thing again? I don't want to kill any more necromancers. The last time I tried to do that I had nightmares about the living dead for almost a century."

"I don't think it has anything to do with a necromancer." She opened the map in front of her and tilted it. "Although, it might. I'm honestly not sure. We do have to dig up Tlachtga's grave."

He let his head roll back on his shoulders and stared up at the sky. "I hate digging graves. It's just messy work."

"When have you been afraid of a little mess?"

Without moving his head, he gestured up and down his body. "King now. Clothes are much nicer."

"Gods, I forgot how much I hated your arrogance."

"Low blow," he replied with a slight growl then dropped his head to look at her. "I'd forgotten how rude you were. You should be nicer now that I have a throne. Wasn't that what you wanted all those years ago?"

Elva let the map fall and leveled him with a gaze that might have burned him if she had shown more interest in magic. "You made my *sister* your queen."

Well, she did have him there. She could be as rude as she wanted, but that wouldn't change the fact that he went home to Aisling every night. Or would have if the curse wasn't keeping them apart. Regardless, he still knew what her sister looked like when the stars rained down on her head because he had touched her the way she liked to be touched.

Bran cleared his throat. "Fine then. Where are we going?"

"Oh, I'm sorry. Are you trying to distract the conversation, or are you actually interested in helping?"

"Why don't you give me the map, and then you can do all the digging."

Elva folded the vellum and tucked it into her waistband. "I think I'm going to enjoy this, Unseelie. All those clothes you think are so fancy will be ruined by the time I remember where you need to dig for this."

He narrowed his eyes. "We don't have time for this."

"Then I suggest you start digging sooner rather than later."

"Elva," he growled.

Their gazes caught in a bid for power before she finally caved. "There's a grave around here marked with a single leaf."

"The Green Man?" Bran asked. "What does he have to do with any of this?"

"Maybe Tlachtga made a deal with him for immortality. I don't know, Bran. You're asking questions that I don't have time to answer. Why don't you look around that half of the graveyard" — she waved away from her — "and I'll take this side."

"You want to get away from me already? My, my, I didn't think I could still get under your skin this easily now that you've been trained by a legendary warrior."

"Some things don't change," she snarled through gritted teeth, then stomped away from him.

Bran wondered what Tlachtga's son had said. Elva had been managing quite well before the burly man had taken time to "talk" with her. Though Bran doubted the man would ever lay a finger on Elva — not because he didn't want to but because Elva wouldn't let him — he also wondered what words had transpired.

There was a lot *he* wanted to say to her. Men weren't the devil, although she seemed certain they were. She didn't have to earn Aisling's trust back by saving her from Carman; she could do that just by coming to the castle every now and then to visit. And she didn't have to be so afraid of living just because she'd made a poor choice once in her life.

Bran didn't know her story. He didn't know the history

that had led her to this place in her life. He found, even after all this time, he wanted to know.

Elva would forever remain a special person in his mind. She had been his first love, his first taste of what life would be like if he had been something more than just the spider queen's son. In some small way, she'd led him to this place where he stood now.

Scrubbing a hand over his face, he looked out over the misty graveyard. Even the sun couldn't burn through the clouds. Stone markers cast long shadows on the ground that wavered as the mist obscured the light around them. Each was different, names that blurred until he couldn't really make them out.

Did he want to waste his time searching for the right grave? Or did he want to get to the bottom of Elva's story so he could sleep at night?

There was no contest. The tempting call of a story made his mouth salivate.

Bran waved a hand and sent out the long shadows of the sluagh to meld with the gravestones. "Find the one marked by the Green Man," he murmured. "It's around here somewhere. Then let me know."

The dark mass undulated in agreement, pausing only when he clicked his tongue.

"And don't get yourselves in trouble." The addition seemed important. He forgot so easily that the sluagh always wanted to add more souls to their collection. They desired nothing more than to make something bleed then steal its soul away to "save" it. Although it didn't feel like saving if the human soul was brought back to Underhill when it didn't want to be.

The form sagged, then sluggishly made its way over the ground, hovering over each stone for a moment before moving on.

Who had taught the sluagh to sulk? Aisling, most likely. The ridiculous woman was giving them far too many human qualities.

"Faster," he told them, trying to hide the smile on his face. "We have to find Aisling, remember? This will help us."

That sped them up. The sluagh loved Aisling almost as much as they needed to add people to their own collective. They would do anything for his queen. He felt the same.

Bran spared a moment to make sure the sluagh were doing what he'd told them to. Once he confirmed they were looking at each grave with a speed that satisfied him, he turned on his heel and strode back to Elva.

She was bending over a grave, carefully running her fingers over each corner as if the leaf might be hidden somewhere. It didn't seem like a high possibility that Tlachtga would need to hide her own grave. The humans here worshiped her already. They weren't going to dig up her final resting place.

Humans were strangely attached to graves. They seemed to think that the physical body stayed attached to the soul, or perhaps they just wanted a symbol of where their loved ones lay.

Faeries knew that wasn't the case. The physical body could be set to nourish the land where the faerie had most loved it, but their magic wouldn't remain for long, if even a few moments after the final death. Faeries drifted back to their favorite places, their favorite people, continuing their life in a different way than before.

He stepped closer to Elva and tucked his hands into his pant pockets. "Are you going to tell me what happened to you?"

"We don't have time for stories. We have to find Aisling." She ran her fingers along the edge of the nearest stone, knocking ancient moss and dirt from its top.

"The sluagh are searching the graves for us. They'll do it much faster and much more thoroughly than you or I could. So we have a few moments to speak."

"I don't want to talk about it, Bran."

"Seems to me that you might need to. You've been flinching away from everyone who comes close enough to touch you, and then when you have a few moments away with a dead druid's son, you act far touchier than I've ever seen you act. So, yes, I think we do need to talk."

Elva huffed out an angry breath, abruptly stood, and placed her hands on her hips. A strand of hair fell in front of her eyes, the golden curl swinging every time she breathed. "Bran, there isn't much to say."

"Of course, there is. You aren't the same girl I remember, and something sent you running off to an isle where they breed warrior women. Out with it."

"I told you, there isn't anything to tell. I never married him, I stayed a concubine, and then he was banished. I've always been interested in fighting—"

A laugh erupted from his chest. "No, you weren't! You were interested in courtly intrigue, how to bat your eyelashes at the right man, and what dress made your form look particularly lovely depending on the light. You didn't give a wit about fighting."

"People change."

"You keep saying that, and I keep having a hard time believing they change *this much*."

She moved away from him, wrapping her arms around her waist. For the first time since he'd seen her again, she looked more like the little girl he remembered. "Stop pushing, Bran."

"I'm not going to stop pushing. You need someone to push you, Elva. Hiding away on that isle isn't going to help, you know that? Because now you're trying to connect back with family. Aisling doesn't like weaklings. I've never thought of you as weak before, but now I see that maybe you *have* changed. The Elva I knew would have never hesitated to tell someone a story about her life, regardless of how embarrassing it was, because you loved the attention. Now open your mouth and—"

"I don't trust myself anymore!" she shouted. Her words rang through the graveyard, bouncing off stones and mist until it reverberated between them.

He froze, muscles locking in place as he tried to understand what she meant. Trust herself? That was easy enough; she hadn't done anything wrong.

"Pardon?" he asked. "You're going to have to explain that to me, sweetheart. The way I see it, you had a decent enough life even if it was spent with a selfish prick."

She brushed the strand of hair behind her ear, shifted, and then leaned against the nearest gravestone. One of the sluagh moved past her. Bran watched as it touched a gentle strand of mist to her ankle, then continued on its way.

A few moments passed before Elva managed to speak. Her words were halting, hesitant, as if she hadn't told anyone her thoughts before. "I loved him, you know. More than anything else in this world. He was everything I wanted and more. A king. A throne. A golden man who outshone the sun when he smiled.

"Then, everything changed. He became king, and the Seelie courts were not what he expected. They didn't want to listen to him, and when they did, it was with ridicule. Fionn didn't take that well." She paused on his name, as if saying it hurt. "I watched him go from the kind, dedicated man that I knew to someone who was a stranger.

"He didn't want to make me his queen because he was afraid they would attack me like they attacked him. They thought him foolish, holding tight to the old ways because that was all he knew. And then he became addicted to opium and...worse."

Her fingers tangled in the hem of her white shirt. "I didn't know how to help him other than to partake myself. And then things just deteriorated from there. We became strangers, trying to learn each other but not knowing how, and we didn't like the new versions of ourselves, let alone each other.

"I shouldn't have stayed. But I did. I stayed, and I worked to try and make him see that I could be a good queen because that was what my mother wanted.

"We made monsters out of each other. We hated the world we lived in, and that hatred bled out into each other and then... Where could we go from there? How did we piece together something that had once been so great without even knowing who we were anymore?"

She looked up at him then, and Bran drowned in the deep blue ocean of her eyes. Her sorrow nearly swallowed her up, and he now realized just how bad it had been for her.

He cleared his throat. "Not trusting yourself? I still don't know where that came from."

"I stayed," Elva said, her words thick with emotion. "I stayed for centuries because I thought that was the right thing to do. And it wasn't. I should have left so many times, and I never did. I don't know *why* I stayed. And that frightens me."

Gods, that was so much larger than he expected. He'd thought maybe this was about Fionn not appreciating her, hitting her, or doing whatever it was Seelie king's did to punish their concubines. He hadn't thought it would be this. That she had forgotten her own way because she'd loved him.

Sighing, he walked over to the nearest gravestone and took a seat. Running his fingers through his hair, he took a deep breath and prepared himself to say something she might not like.

She needed to hear it. Anyone in this situation would need to hear it.

"You stayed because you thought you loved him. Hell, I thought I loved you. The mind tells us what we want to hear, and it's not because that's how we thought our future should go or something foolish like hat. He was what you wanted, and you convinced yourself you'd take it in any way possible.

"This wasn't your fault, Elva. It sounds like it might not have been his fault either. We do horrible things in our lives, but we can't focus on them and forget to live for the future. You'll find someone else, someone better who will treat you the way you deserve to be treated."

When she opened her mouth to interrupt, he held up a hand, silencing her. "Not yet, I'm not done. I can't tell you what is the right way to be treated. It's not what Aisling and I have. That's ours and no one else's. You have to find what makes *you* happy. What you want from another person and what they can give you that will make your life better.

"That might be no one. You might be destined to live your life on your own two feet, and there's nothing wrong with that. If you don't want another man in your life, no one can judge you for that. It's a choice that you alone can make and should make. Happiness is not something you find in the arms of another person. Happiness comes from within, and that is not dependent on another body helping you find self-worth. You have to do that yourself."

Finally, he looked up and met her gaze. Tears welled in her eyes, staying put by the sheer force of her will alone. He'd never seen her cry, only on show, and even then she'd turned around once she got what she wanted with a bright smile on her face. That was the Elva he knew. Not this woman who didn't know how to be sure of herself.

He leaned forward and took one of her hands in his. "You'll find yourself again. I'm certain of that. I don't know if it's the spoiled brat I knew as a child, the warrior you've become, or something new and far greater than both of them. That's up to you, and I can't tell you where your path will go. I hope that I will be included in it. Watching you grow and turn into this magnificent, intimidating woman that you have the capability to be would be a gift."

She bared her teeth, pretending to grin. "Intimidating? What about that will draw a man to my side? However will I convince someone to marry me?"

"Those are your mother's words. If you don't marry, then I will make you the most incredible aunt the world has ever seen." He cleared his throat and released her hand. "Who cares if you marry, Elva? If that's not what you want, then dust off the opinions of others and continue on."

"I don't know what I want anymore," she replied quietly. " I'd like to find out."

"You will, and I'll help. Your sister, too." He stood, brushed the dirt off his clothing, and held out a hand for her to take. "First, we have to find her."

Elva reached up and let him draw her to standing. She stepped back immediately, and he didn't miss that she wiped her hand on her pants. Even the feeling of his touch made her shiver in disgust, but he hoped someday that would stop.

He didn't want to touch her, now or any other time. Hell, he didn't want to touch her at all if she didn't like it. He hoped that someday she would accept *someone*. Physical healing could go so much farther than she likely wanted to admit.

He cleared his throat again and rocked back on his heels. "Four graves to the right and five up."

"What?"

"The sluagh found Tlachtga's grave," he said. "There's only one in the entire graveyard that has the symbol of the Green Man. Rather easy to find."

She drew the mantle of composure around her, her emotions disappearing from her expression and wiped clean until he might have sworn they'd never had a difficult conversation at all. "Then you need to find a shovel, Unseelie."

"Shovel?" He lifted a brow. "Who needs a shovel when

you're the Raven King?"

"I'm not digging this hole for you."

He rolled his eyes and strode down the rows. "Oh, ye of little faith! How many times did I tell you learning how to use magic would be helpful someday in your life?"

"I like to work for the things I want."

"Well, I don't. I'd rather have them handed to me on a golden platter." He reached the grave and lifted his hand. Muttering a spell under his breath, he encouraged the earth to shift apart from the coffin deep within its grip.

It wasn't particularly easy. For some reason, the ground here wanted to keep Tlachtga deep within its belly. Like the humans of this realm, it was feeding off her power. Perhaps she wasn't just encouraging the crops to grow, but the land itself.

"Come on, now," he grumbled. "I'm not removing her entirely. She's left something in the coffin for me, and then you can have her back."

With a deep, rocky groan, the ground shifted and moved for him. Nine feet down, deeper than most graves, a plain wooden coffin nestled in the dirt. Again, unexpected. He'd thought the humans would have buried her with much more fanfare than a simple wooden coffin. Marble at the very least, or a stone that wouldn't have rotted away. A few of the boards were already softened by worms.

He glanced up to Elva and gestured down. "Go on then."

"I'm not hopping into that grave."

"Well, I'm not doing it."

"Then have your magic lift it out. I heard the sound the ground made." She pointed at the mounds of earth on either side. "It doesn't want us to be anywhere near that coffin.

Besides, that's far too deep for me to climb out of, and you're the one with the magic. You can hop right back out without any trouble."

"Damn it." He stared down at the earth and hoped to hell it didn't close over his head. The last thing he needed was to be buried alive.

This was a nice suit.

He pressed a hand to his chest and dramatically looked up at the sky. "I wish there were more women around me who wanted to take care of me. I heard that's what women were supposed to do. Instead, all they've done is made my life more difficult."

"You're so dramatic," she said with a chuckle. "And acting far more like yourself than I remember seeing you at the beginning of this journey. For a second there, I thought you might have grown up."

"Please, put an arrow through my skull if that ever happens." He looked back into the grave and hesitated for a brief moment. She'd bared her soul to him and, strangely, he felt like he owed her. Bran licked his lips nervously then said, "I feel more like myself out here. Thrones do strange things to people, but the wilderness has a different feel to it."

"I remember that. You know, you don't have to change just because you're a king now. I don't think Aisling would want you to."

Maybe that's what she was saying. He wasn't trying to break her curse because he was overwhelmed. And yet, now, he could see that wasn't all she'd wanted. She wanted *him*, even though they had a kingdom and people.

Maybe, just maybe, his people wanted him to be the same

as he always had been.

He wouldn't find out if he never jumped into this grave and pulled the boards off a dead woman's coffin. He forced his body to move and leapt into the darkness.

His booted feet hit the ground on either side of the coffin, and he took care not to land directly into Tlachtga's lap. He had a feeling her soul would feel that if he did. And the last thing he needed was an angry, undead druid coming after him. He already had an undead witch doing exactly that.

How many undead things was he going to have to deal with in his lifetime?

Grimacing, he sank his hands into the rotten wood and began to pull them away. "This is disgusting, you know."

"Oh, I thought maybe you'd died," Elva called back. "A shame. Maybe something down there will sew your mouth shut and spare us all the misery."

He grinned. "Doubtful. If my mother hasn't sewn it shut, then a druid certainly won't manage it."

Although, his mother had certainly threatened to more times than he could count. When he was little, she would even start pulling threads out of her abdomen and start advancing on him.

Bran paused for a moment, wondering if other Unseelie had childhood memories like that. He'd never ask another, quite certain they wouldn't have. That would have made him feel as though he'd missed out on something.

The board he was tugging came loose and revealed the skeletal body carefully laid to rest within. They hadn't placed her as he might have expected. Laying on her back with her arms over her chest, that would have been the normal way for humans to place their dead.

Instead, they had laid her curled on her side, as if she had fallen asleep that way, one hand tucked underneath her head, the other carefully placed at her belly. Her hair was still intact, red curls spread out around her skeletal head and decorated with the ancient remains of white flowers.

They had loved her, very much so it seemed.

"Your grave is significantly nicer than the last dead god I saw," he murmured, gently placing a hand atop her head. He wondered for a moment if Tlachtga could hear him. He'd thought they taught that in school. Small gods were still connected to their physical form, at least slightly. That was why the humans took care of their corpses so well.

A flare of magic responded to him. Deep within the sockets of her missing eyes, light glowed. Her hand on her abdomen uncurled, then stilled once more.

He shivered. There was nothing worse than seeing a corpse move, and it didn't matter he knew she wasn't *precisely* dead. "Well, you are much prettier than the last one as well. Pretty graves for pretty women, that's what I always say."

Bran leaned back to find the artifact Tlachtga'd mentioned. A knife, there had to be a knife in here somewhere, and he hoped like hell it wasn't inside her. He'd met the woman. Plunging his hand into her chest cavity seemed wrong somehow.

Scooting back, he pulled a few more boards loose until the entire top of her coffin was free. "Sorry, Tlachtga. I'm sure the top of this coffin had a purpose, but you don't mind going back to the earth entirely, do you? I'm sure it would like to consume the rest of your body. The earthworms in particular will love it."

Elva called out from above, "Are you talking to the corpse?"

"Don't say it like that. She doesn't look a day over three hundred." He leaned up and patted a hand to her bones. "Don't listen to her. She doesn't know what she's talking about. Always had a jealous streak, that one. Did you know I'm marrying her sister? Or married already, really. She's my queen. I should talk to her about making that official. Aisling, not Elva."

"Would you stop trying to get advice from a dead woman and actually look for the knife?"

"I'll take good advice wherever I can get it!" he called back, running his hands along the edges of the coffin where the human's had folded white fabric underneath straw. "It's not exactly easy to find something that was hidden in here. Do you want me to pick up the skeleton?"

"Gods no." The horror in Elva's voice made him chuckle. "Do you want her to hunt you down? That's what she'll do. Don't *touch* her body."

He looked down at the sunken skull. "Tlachtga, my love, should we tell her it's already too late for that? You don't mind a little touch, I'm guessing, but you're probably going to need to move for me."

Perhaps Tlachtga had finally had enough of his antics because her corpse let out a long sigh and then shifted slightly to the side, just enough so he could see the glimmering handle of a knife that protruded from beneath her body.

"There you are." He leaned over, balancing on either edge of the coffin with both hands. "That wasn't too hard, now was it? Thank goodness you had a father who knew magic well. That faerie up there thinks magic has no place in this world, and we're going to prove her wrong together."

He leaned his weight to the side, crouched over her body, and drew the knife out from underneath her.

It wasn't precisely what he had expected. Faeries like to make cursed and powerful objects easily recognizable. If someone picked up a golden piece encrusted with jewels, they knew it was a powerful, magical object.

He turned it in his hands, seeing the wickedly sharp edge as something far more than an instrument to cut with. Black magic was forged into the very metal of the blade. It was a dangerous weapon, far more because it wanted blood. It thirsted for pain and anguish so much that it called out to the powers inside him.

This wasn't something he wanted to handle for very long. Not right now, at least.

Wincing, he called out, "Elva, tell me you have something I can put this in?"

No one responded to him.

He looked up but didn't see her face peering down at him anymore. Frowning, he stood up. "Elva?"

Nothing.

"Damn it," he cursed, then looked down at the corpse. "Was this you? Really? Some kind of protection spell for your own body? I thought you would play a little more fair than that, considering *you* were the one who gave us the map to get here."

He was tempted to kick a little dirt onto her body for good measure, but didn't want to get cursed from afar. This was her land, and the earth itself was filled with her magic. The last thing he needed was to be buried.

Muttering about meddling women and their ridiculous grudges, he launched himself out of the grave. Leaping high into the air, he landed in a crouch with shadows billowing from his fingertips.

The sluagh were prepared for a fight. They tasted it in the air, in the anger that surged through his veins, and longed for nothing more than to be set free so they, too, might find their own blood. The blade hummed in his hand, pommel nearly shaking with anticipation.

It was not the undead army he expected. No corpses were digging themselves out of graves to protect their small goddess.

Instead, Elva was bowed low to two women who stood at the edge of the graveyard.

Impossibly tall, nearly too perfect to look at, they were the first of the ancient Tuatha de Danann that he'd ever seen in his life. He'd met old faeries before. Hell, he lived with them in the Unseelie Castle.

But the originals? The first who created their bloodlines and passed down their lineage throughout all the creatures he now knew?

The breath was pulled from his lungs at their presence. He quickly snuffed his magic, then tucked the blade in the waist of his pants for good measure. The courtly bow he gave them would have made even the Seelie King proud.

"Ladies of magic," he said reverently.

The nearest woman, so tall she looked down on him, smiled. Freckles dotted her face, wild red hair tumbling down her back like a river of fire. She didn't wear a traditional dress, but men's leggings and a soft green, dappled tunic. As if the sun never stopped filtering through leaves, even when she wasn't near the trees.

"Bran," she replied. "It's an honor to meet the new Raven King."

His voice shuddered as he replied, "Macha, the honor is all mine."

The other woman, speckled like the egg of a robin, chuckled. "And yet it is me whom you should be thanking."

"Lady Badb?" he questioned, ducking his eyes low to the ground. "Please, tell me what I should thank you for, and I will lay my sacrifices at your feet."

"Your queen is my granddaughter, and I helped you both arrive at the Duchess of Dusk. Although, I will admit, I didn't want her to be your queen."

He shook at the anger in her voice. How had he managed to piss off a Tuatha de Danann this powerful? "My lady?"

"If I asked you to give her up so that I might train her to become the woman she could have been, would you?" Badb asked.

"No," he said, then looked up to meet her gaze. "My apologies, but no. I would never give her up unless it's what she wanted. With all due respect, she chose me. I think that says more than anything else."

He stared into Badb's eyes and thought for a moment that the speckled being would destroy him where he stood. The rage in those depths rivaled his own at her asking the question. Was this creature angered that Aisling wasn't doing as she wished? Or was she simply angry because the world didn't agree with her? That times had changed so much that even the faeries didn't see her as a goddess anymore?

Macha chuckled. "My dear sister, it seems as though you have lost your flock. I'm surprised the faeries aren't listening to you anymore. The druids have begun listening to me."

"I have not lost anything. And I find I did not miss working with you, Macha."

"Oh, don't say that. We're so much more powerful when we're together."

Bran listened intently. So the stories were true. Macha, Badb, and Morrighan were three sisters of the Tuatha de Danann. When they were together, they were unstoppable. Long ago, they used to wander the battlefields and absorb all the emotion and magic that drained out through death and bloodshed.

This was Aisling's grandmother? No wonder Aisling was capable of so many great things.

Elva shifted at his side, reaching out and placing a hand against his leg. "Bran? Perhaps we should ask the maidens of magic why they are here."

"Maidens?" he repeated. "They made us. Their blood runs through our veins. I don't think we can call them maidens anymore."

The redheaded Tuatha de Danann burst into laughter. The infectious sound eased his mind, although he was still uneasy being in their presence. "The term is respectful, Raven King. Your companion seems to understand the old ways far better than you."

"I renounced the old ways when I discovered they no longer were useful for the world I choose to live in. I find I am just as intrigued as she is. Why *are* you here?"

The sisters paused and looked at each other. A thread of magic tied them together, so faint he almost couldn't see it. It was there, a magical link that intertwined powerful creatures who shared blood.

The glowing thread suggested they used magic to talk so no one else could listen. And try as he might, he couldn't snoop no matter how much the Raven King's power looped around the thread. They were far stronger than he was, and far more capable.

Sometimes, he would admit, the old magic proved itself to be more useful than the new.

Finally, Badb turned back to him. "Regardless of your claim on my progeny, I must admit I do not want to see her die. Carman is a threat to us all. We banished her long ago, and it was our mistake that she still lives. We would like to rectify that."

"You're here to help?" he said, startled they would even think to offer such a thing. "I thought the ancients no longer wished to meddle in the current affairs of our kind?"

"No one can know that we helped you," Macha replied. "This is outside of our realm, and no other Tuatha de Danann can discover we've assisted you. If they do, then we will personally take your kingdom and all that you love away from you."

He recognized the threat. He could care less about the kingdom, although he would be sad to say goodbye to his people. The love he felt for them burned in his veins now; it was as much a part of him as the magic he called his own. But there were others in this world who would treat them better, who would be a far better king than he could ever hope to be.

Still, he inclined his head. "I have no interest in angering the Tuatha de Danann who helped create me. If you wish to help, I will accept it gladly."

Macha gestured with a hand, and the mist suddenly parted. Behind them, Bran saw a small garden and a fountain where a stone woman poured water out of a vase. It was a quaint little place, and Bran had seen this before.

"The fountain of Hy-Brasil?" he asked, stepping forward and walking into the garden where he'd been before. Every time he used to visit Eamonn, now the Seelie King, he'd come to this place because it felt like peace had sunk into the earth. "Why here?"

"This is my sanctuary," Macha said quietly, walking around to the other side of the fountain. "It is here where those who search for kindness will come. Sorcha came here when she was working to free Eamonn from his self-imposed chains. *You* came here when you missed your family."

He had and whispered secrets to the stone woman. Cheeks flaming, he nodded at Macha. "I said a lot of things here that I didn't want anyone else to hear."

"There's always someone listening. That's why I knew, even when my sister didn't, that you would make a wonderful Raven King."

Badb snorted behind him before joining her sister and dipping her fingers into the cool water. "I think we're still finding out whether or not he will make a good king. For the time being, I will agree he's done more for his people than any other king."

He sat on the edge of the fountain and stared up at the women. "What help will you offer me? Guidance on how to find her?"

"We will open a portal that will bring you to her side. But first, let us add our power to the spell that will assist Aisling in her journey."

Somehow, Bran knew what they were talking about. He reached out his arm and let Macha and Badb both finger the rope wrapped around his wrist.

"What can you offer her?" he asked.

Warm, speckled hands surrounded his arm. "Our knowledge of what the future could be and our hopes for her."

Both sisters quietly murmured in unison, "By knot of six, this spell I fix. By knot of seven, events I'll leaven."

The rope twisted underneath their grip, coiling against his skin and knotting two more times. This felt far more powerful than he could have ever imagined.

Then Badb sighed, released her hold on his arm, and set her hand palm up on the fountain stone. "I offer you now your history. These memories are ones I have personally held for many years. I give them back to you and all the remains of Raven Kings of old. Perhaps you will understand why we've worked so hard to keep the queen away."

He stared down at her hand and wondered just how much he wanted to know. Was it worth it? He could deny this knowledge, knowing it had the power to change their fate.

And yet...he was so curious. There were so many souls in his head, so many sluagh and ancient Raven Kings, who wanted to know why their lives were cursed. Why they were forced to devour souls and *hate*.

Magic danced on Badb's fingertips, memories that were his and not his. Suddenly, it wasn't a question of whether or not he wanted to know.

He needed to.

Bran reached out and took her hand.

CHAPTER 16

THE RAVEN KING AND QUEEN

Bran was in his body, but not. He lifted his hands, looking down at them and seeing another man's. He couldn't quite control this body either, almost as though he was nothing more than a passenger in this moment.

He stared into a mirror before him. Another man looked back, one who took control of the body and shook himself as though Bran's consciousness was nothing more than a flicker of magic.

Long dark hair reached his waist, no feathers to bisect it. He wore ancient clothing that somehow seemed familiar. Black fabric, straps of leather across his chest, and tight-fitting leggings with no adornment at all. No embroidery, nothing but a quiet, calm appearance that didn't seem to fit the legend of the Raven King as he knew it.

The first Raven King smoothed a hand down his chest, stepped away from the mirror, and made his way through the castle of Underhill.

It was new, every stone still perfectly in place, no holes in the walls, no cobwebs decorating the corners. It shone with a dark power that threaded throughout the walls. Magic that Bran recognized.

A creature stepped forward, human in appearance and cloaked in black shadows. "Your Highness, are you ready?"

"It's my wedding day," he replied. A grin split his face, and elation spread from the top of his head to the tip of his toes. "I've been ready for this my entire life."

The sluagh smiled in response. "The maiden has said the same. She's waiting for you in the great hall. I apologize again, master. I wish we could have done this with all the faeries in attendance."

"I don't care how many people see us marry. I don't care they disapprove." Again, he smoothed a hand down his chest. "They will agree that we are married once there is nothing they can do about it. My parents might never understand, even though it's not for them to understand. I love her. Nothing will ever change that."

"Very good, Highness. If you'll follow me?"

Bran stayed with the Raven King as they passed through hallways he'd walked many times. Seeing them new nearly made him lose his mind. *This* was what the castle had once looked like? This opulence was something he never would have guessed.

Even the sun was shining through the windows. Bran had never clearly seen the sun while in Underhill. It was always hidden by a haze of clouds, and he thought it impossible to show its face. What had changed? How had something like this happened to the kingdom he loved so much?

The Raven King stepped through a doorway, and they

arrived in the great hall. Murals painted the room from floor to ceiling, depicting every story the Tuatha de Danann remembered. Stories from Bran's childhood, perhaps new at this point, and stories he'd never heard before. The paintings had long since faded in the castle he knew. Now, he wanted to have an artist paint them again.

A woman stood in the center of the room. Both Bran and the Raven King lost their breath at the sight of her.

She wore a dress made of gossamer and alabaster fabric. Pearlescent and shimmering with magic, it poured down her body like the mist of a waterfall. Her dark, obsidian hair flowed down her back, unbound and smooth as the night sky. Tiny diamonds were woven through the strands and winked at every movement.

She slowly turned, hands clasped at her waist, and Bran nearly fell to his knees for love of her.

Aisling. She looked exactly like Aisling.

"My love," she said, her voice chiming like bells. She held out her hands for the Raven King to take, and both Bran and the other raced to her side with love burning in their chests.

The Raven King drew her close and ran a hand down the side of her face. "I love you," he whispered, eyes drinking in the sight of her. "I love you more than I could possibly say."

"And I you. I cannot wait to bind myself to you for all eternity. As it should be and forever will be."

He pressed his lips to hers and breathed in the scent of wild moors and honeysuckle. "No one is here to stop us now."

A sense of foreboding filled the great hall, and Bran knew this was the instant when everything changed. When this world disappeared and *his* began.

The front doors to the main hall burst open. When they slammed against the walls, it rained down plaster and pieces of mural. An eye drifted on a single piece of parchment, flipping to stare at the Raven King before falling to the floor.

He spun and put the woman who looked like Aisling behind him with a snarl.

The mirror image of the dark woman stood in the doorway. She wore a dress made of shadows, hair as white as snow. Like an inky cloud, her dress shifted on its own as she strode forward.

Her face was a portrait of beauty. Simple and clean lines made a heart-shaped face perfect except for a single scar over her left eyebrow. Plump lips were stained crimson and beautiful blue eyes flashed with anger.

"How dare you?" the woman shouted, her voice shaking with anger and a power that cracked the floor in front of her. "How dare you!"

The Raven King's hands clenched onto the woman behind him. "Carman. What are you doing here?"

"I should ask the same of *you*," the witch said with a laugh. "Or did you forget today was our wedding?"

"I did not forget."

"And yet you are *here*." Carman pointed just to his left. "With *her*."

"You know I never wanted to marry you. We've spoken of this, and we both agreed the marriage would only be in appearance alone."

"That did not mean you could disgrace me. That you could leave me at the altar and instead be here marrying another woman." Her voice vibrated, and Bran could almost hear her heart shattering. *"I love you.* And you insist on choosing another over me. Every time."

"I am sorry, Carman, but I will not marry a woman whom I do not love."

"You could have loved me," she said with a whimper. "If you tried hard enough, you could have loved me."

"I couldn't. Not when my heart belongs to another."

Bran realized the Raven King did not think for one instant that Carman would ever attack him. He didn't think she would kill the woman behind him either, and perhaps he was right, but Bran never would have taken such a chance.

The woman who looked like Aisling stepped out from behind the Raven King and stretched out her hand. "Sister, I'm sorry."

"Keep your mouth shut," Carman said, her voice deep and thick. "I don't want to hear any more of your betrayal."

"I never meant to hurt you! I don't know how to stop loving him, though. Surely, you can understand that."

"I cannot!" The cry echoed in the room, and Carman stumbled, fell to a knee, and pressed her hand onto the floor. "I cannot forgive the man I love and my sister. You left me alone! The only two people I have ever loved in my life, and you – you betrayed me."

His vision skewed, and he suddenly couldn't make out whether or not Carman was Elva and the other woman was Aisling. They melded together, two timelines of different people who had ended up in different places but whose story was the same.

The woman who looked like Aisling stepped forward,

hesitating to go to her sister and leave the Raven King's side. "You can forgive us, Carman. You can forgive all of this."

"I cannot. I cannot stop what I have started, and I don't know if I want to."

The Raven King lunged forward and grabbed onto the woman he loved, pulling her against his side and away from her sister. "What have you done?"

Carman looked up. Tears streaked her cheeks, leaving tracks of glistening darkness as she leaked out shadows. "How do you live with yourself after this? Perhaps you can answer, Raven King, after all the lives you have taken. How do you forgive yourself for doing something so awful that the world will forever be changed?"

"What have you *done*?"

"Perhaps you simply forgot. Somehow you managed to wash away the guilt of all the ruin you have wrought."

"Carman!"

The witch shook her head, and the floor cracked beneath her feet. The walls crumbled under an attack of magic that cleaved through the stone like a giant's sword. Three men stepped through the rubble, two lifting their mother from the ground.

Her three sons, Dain, Dother, and Dub propped her up even as she seemed to shatter from within.

The Raven King held out his hand, summoning the sluagh, but it was far too late. Carman hurled a curse through the air that caught her sister between her breasts.

The woman stumbled, ripped from his arms by the sheer force of Carman's magic, and then fell onto her knees. Blood streaked her skin. It wasn't just a curse, it was a death wish.

"*No.*" The word ripped form his mouth, and he reached for the woman he loved.

Magic vibrated the air around her with heat, and her hair turned white as snow. "My love," she whispered.

Their hands nearly touched, then she disappeared.

The scream that ripped from his lungs tasted like blood and black magic. The power inside him roared to the forefront but not by his own doing. Instead, it felt as though it were trying to consume him.

His dark gaze found Carman even as she set her sons loose to destroy Underhill forever. The sad smile on her face felt wrong, even through the centuries.

"I will tear your kingdom apart until my fingers bleed," she said. "I will ruin your world, the Otherworld, and the human realm until you say you love me."

"That's not how you win someone's love, Carman."

"Is it not?" Another tear slid down her cheek. "I've seen my future. I've seen how they will spill my blood on these steps. I've already cursed you, don't you see? You cannot be free of me because I am now part of you, of this land, and never again will Underhill prosper *until you love me.*"

Pain rippled through his body, tearing flesh and bone. His head jerked back, and he let loose a scream of primal rage. Feathers unfurled down his arms, bones cracked and realigned, then he wasn't himself anymore. Not even the slightest.

Wings flapping, he tried to right himself, but she caught him quickly in her hands. Claws dug into his sides as Carman forced him to look into her eyes.

"You will never find her again," she said. "And if you do, I will destroy her. Your magic will be passed through generations unrelated by blood and you never have true lineage. I will destroy everything you are, everything you would be, until you love me."

Both the Raven King and Bran felt nothing but dread.

CHAPTER 17

CARMAN

"Aisling?" Lorcan asked quietly, holding the map in his hands and staring at her. "Are you certain you want to do this?"

No, a void inside her screamed. She wanted to go home, to return to Bran's side, to forget this foolish adventure that might very well end in her death or possession. She wanted to go back to the way things were. Flawed and strange they certainly were, but they had a life. And a life was better than nothing at all.

She blew out a breath, stood, and nodded. "Yes, I'm ready."

"The questing beast was right," he said and pointed at the map. "The edge that was missing is there now. She's just over the rise."

"And she's waiting for me."

"No. I've gone through a lot of trouble to make certain she has no idea where we are."

Aisling shook her head in denial. She could feel it on the wind, the way her hairs raised on her arms, like someone was constantly watching her. Carman was here. More than that, she knew exactly where Aisling was and what she was planning on doing.

No one could sneak up on a woman who was a witch queen. Just as they could not sneak up on Aisling.

A surge of power jolted through the rope around her wrist. It was familiar energy, one she had not expected to feel during this journey.

Fingering the edge, she smiled and whispered a prayer to her grandmother. The ancients had found Bran, so it seemed. Whatever magic they could give her, she hoped it would be enough once she walked over the rise and found whatever Carman had waiting for her.

Lorcan stood and let the map drop to the ground. A cool breeze picked it up, flipping it over and over until the magic disappeared from the page and it was nothing more than an aged piece of vellum once more.

"Something feels wrong," he said.

"No, it doesn't. It just feels like you hadn't planned this far, and now you don't know what to do or what to expect." She stepped forward, placed a hand on his cheek, and smiled up at him even though she felt fear freezing her heart. "We cannot control what is going to happen, Lorcan. Not to us, not to the world. We can spin the wheel of fate and watch it turn."

"I don't want to risk your life," he said quietly. His gaze drifted away from hers, staring down at the ground with her hand still on his face. "I thought this would be easier in the end. That I would feel more confident, but..."

"I know," she whispered. "This is something I have to do."

"We could disappear, you know. Go back to the human realm where she can't find you, start our life all over again.

We've done it before. We could do it again."

Aisling pondered the thought for a moment. It would be so easy to leave, to let this world fall back into the hands of Carman and simply exist with the curse. Was being a swan really all that bad?

Then she remembered the faces of the sluagh, their hopeful gaze and the way they reached out to touch the edge of her skirts every time she passed. They loved her, and more than that, they depended on her. She couldn't leave them.

"No," she said. "We can't. We've moved so far past that."

"I don't know how much I can help you now." He swallowed hard and pulled away from her. "I'm no soldier, but I will try."

She tried to imagine Lorcan fighting with anyone, but could only think of the times he had as a cat. They'd gone rather splendidly well. The element of surprised helped him far more than he gave himself credit for.

Aisling had never asked him how many lives he had left, although she doubted it was really that many. Nine lives. That's all a witch had, and she wasn't willing to risk anymore of his. Not for her. Not for a witch who would undoubtedly try to kill him.

"You won't have to try at all," she replied. "This is the first time I don't need you by my side."

"If you think for one second I'm letting you go in there alone—"

"That's not your choice." She lifted her hands and cast a quick spell that locked his legs. Lorcan let out a shout of anger before she tightened her grip on his mouth as well.

Aisling caught him as he listed to the side and gently

guided him to the ground. He glared at her with wide eyes, but there was nothing he could do now. She'd used a witch's prison, perhaps a cruel fate. Any other witch could unlock him. Bran would have to find one, and would, if things didn't go as she planned.

She patted his shoulder. "You're going to be fine. And I'm going to be fine. Trust me."

The anger that burned in his glare suggested that he didn't. Aisling stood up and shook her head, then turned and made her way over the rise.

She didn't want him to see the tear dripping down her cheek. She had to have more control than this. Right now wasn't the time to let her emotions get the better of her.

Still, her mind seemed hyper focused on all the good things that had happened to her. How much she loved Bran, how all her people had supported her, that even Lorcan would give up another life just to see her happy and safe.

Did she deserve them? Sometimes, she thought she didn't. Other times, like now, she thought that perhaps all the good things she'd done in her life were coming back to her. She wanted to help people, had never given up on them, even when they threw rocks and sticks to harm her. Now?

Now she had people who loved her and would never, ever want to see her hurt. That was a blessing, and she'd lived a good life to find them.

Stones shifted underneath her feet, and she pulled herself up and over the small hill. At the peak, she stared down into the valley below where a monster lay in wait.

A mausoleum stood before her, supported by smooth pillars and made out of an obsidian so dark it seemed to absorb the light. It wasn't a prison, as she had suspected.

This was a tomb.

She slid down into the valley, shocked at how large the building was. Everything else in Underhill was smaller, simple, and showed the cracks of time. Not a speck of dirt or dust marred the outside of Carman's tomb.

The signs of travel stained her linen pants and plain white shirt stolen from Lorcan's pack. When she stepped onto the ebony stairwell leading into the square monolith, her footprints remained in chalky, white earth. She refused to feel shame for her appearance. She had worked hard to get here, and if that required a little dirt to do so, then she would wear it with pride.

She reached the top of the stairs and looked upon the door, three men high. No carvings adorned its surface, no words to confirm this was the final resting place of Carman. Instead, it was as smooth and dark as the rest of the building. As if the door wasn't there at all.

Aisling lifted her hand and placed it on the cold surface, fear slithering up her arm and digging claws into her heart. This was it. She could still turn back. She could still leave and find her old life.

She pushed hard, and the door opened without a sound.

For a moment, it seemed as though she stared into an abyss. There was nothing in the darkness beyond. Nothing but the absence of light with something deep inside that stared back at her.

A grating echo of stone against stone rocked through the mausoleum, and a small square appeared on the ceiling. A beam of moonlight speared down and filtered through the impossibly high room. It landed on the shoulders of three stone giants, each frozen in time. One held a bow, one a spear, and the other lifted a sword above its head, unable to bring it down on the enemy.

The light moved past them and finally settled on a figure crumpled at the feet of the stone giants. Two chains held her arms stretched out taut at her sides, her back to Aisling. Her head dangled limp, staring at the ground.

Aisling's eyes gradually adjusted. She remained where she was, taking in all the details that she could find. No one spoke, although she was certain they knew she was there.

This was the great Carman, the witch who had nearly destroyed all of Ireland, and she remained here, hidden in Underhill, while all others thought she was dead.

She wore a white gown, and that started Aisling. Why white? Why something that spoke of innocence when she might have worn something dark instead?

All the paintings Aisling had seen of Carman placed her in dark fabric. She was something that came out of the night, a creature no one saw until it was too late. But here, they allowed her to remain in something virginal, even at the feet of her sons.

When Aisling stepped forward, the sound reverberated through the hall. No torches lit her way. No goblins or familiars appeared to guide her to their mistress. Even the witch queen herself remained silent as Aisling made the long walk down the hall.

Darkness crept into her vision. It seemed that even the shadows moved with a mind of their own here. They weren't like the sluagh. They didn't reach out for her, or seem to be individual creatures at all.

Aisling stretched out a hand to let one touch her. An

electric feeling danced along her fingertips and then the shadow disappeared, leaving behind nothing more than a smudge of ash. Magic. Pure magic that swirled in the shadows like a wind.

So that was how they had imprisoned her. It wasn't just chains; it wasn't a curse. They had placed her in a tomb filled with magic to bind her.

She paused ten paces behind Carman, somehow not able to move forward.

What did one say to a witch queen? How could she ever say the right words that expressed how horrifying this fate was but also demand Carman remove the curse she had started?

Before Aisling could speak, Carman herself slowly lifted her head. "So, you have finally come."

The witch had gumption, but Aisling had known she would be arrogant. Weren't they all?. "I take it you were expecting me?"

"I've been watching you since you stepped foot in Underhill. I could feel you, and I've been calling you to my side ever since."

Gods, she didn't want to hear that. She didn't want to know that Carman had found her so easily. There were suddenly a thousand questions rocketing through her mind, all questions she shouldn't be focusing on. She should order the witch to remove the curse immediately.

But she couldn't.

Carman's voice sounded so familiar, like the whistle of a lark and the quiet burble of a creek. Even more than that, it somehow sounded exactly like the voice of her mother.

Magic was at work here, and even Aisling couldn't part

through the web that tangled her mind. Carman had ensnared her already. She could tell. She couldn't do anything to pull herself away from the stickiness of the witch's control.

"Come around me, child," Carman said. "There is a stone step in front of me. The Tuatha de Danann used to visit more often than now. Sit and let us speak."

Aisling's feet moved of their own accord. They carried her the remaining paces, her body sat down on the obsidian block, and she stared into the eyes of the first witch queen.

Carman was beautiful. Eyes so dark they appeared black, a heart-shaped mouth, and hair as white as snow. The long length touched the ground, smooth and straight as a waterfall.

The witch queen smiled at her. "You look so very much like my sister."

"Pardon?" Aisling replied. "What do I have to do with your sister?"

"As much as you have to do with my curse. Magic has a price that witches don't like to admit. One cannot simply have all the power in the universe and not expect it to snap back at us like a rope. You have the eyes of my sister, the face of my mother, and the knowledge of all my grandchildren." Carman shifted, and the chains on her hands rattled. "I didn't think you'd look quite so much like her."

"Why?" The question burned Aisling's tongue. "Why do I look like her?"

"Because you are her descendent. I took away everything from her, and to spite me, she passed down her magic and her line through generations that I could no longer control. I couldn't kill her, you see. She was still my blood. And now, so are you."

Aisling shook her head, hands twisting in her lap. "I'm not your blood."

"You are. I couldn't find your little familiar because that magic hid him from me, but you? I've always been able to find you, Aisling."

"The Raven Queen's curse?"

"Only applies when my sister gets too close to all that I will never let her have."

"Why?" Aisling asked, the words blurting out of her mouth so powerfully she felt the chains of Carman's magic loosening. "Why would you curse your sister? Why would you hurt someone who meant so much to you?"

"Did she really mean that much?" Carman's eyes welled up with tears, and Aisling didn't know if she could believe that Carman was affected at all.

How could a creature like this, who had doomed not only her sister but all in her sister's line, care at all? Those were the actions of a person who did not care what happened in the future. Not someone who would feel regret or remorse.

"She was your sister, yet someone who meant enough to you to curse. She must have hurt you if you reacted in such a way, which means *yes*. She did mean that much."

"You see much for a witch whom the world has forgotten," Carman said, her voice deepening. "My sister meant something, yes. But so did the man she stole from me. So did the life she took that should have been mine."

"And now you're here," Aisling replied. "Now you will spend the rest of your existence in chains because you could not bear to see another where you wished to be."

"It must seem as though I'm a monster to you."

Of course, it did, Aisling wanted to shout. No one was so petty, so disgusting that they would try to end the world just because a man spurned her. She opened her mouth to say just that when Carman let out a soft laugh and shook her head.

"No," the witch queen said, "don't say those words just yet. Would you not have done the same for your Raven King? Would you not destroy the world if someone tried to take him from you?"

She tried to lie, but the words stuck on her tongue and burned her throat. Aisling couldn't even shake her head. The curse of faerie truthfulness prevented her from responding at all. Instead, she glared at Carman and hoped her eyes portrayed her anger.

"You see?" Carman asked. "We are not so different after all."

"I would never do what you have done."

"And yet you are here, risking everything just to see if you can break a curse that turns you into a swan during the day. There are many more things a queen could be doing, so many more you could help. Instead, you've decided to run away from them all for a selfish quest. Are you so certain you wouldn't walk in my footsteps if our stories were the same?"

No, she wasn't, and that made Aisling's stomach twist in knots. Vomit rose in her throat, threatening to project from her lips across the room. She shook her head firmly. "Take away the curse, Carman."

"Why should I? You've already made your mind up about me. You already want to condemn me as a beast, a monster, a creature who is worth no help at all."

"I want to be free," Aisling replied. "You've cursed your

sister, and her life was forfeit. The curse ends with me."

"No, the curse ends when I sit on the throne that was promised to me."

"You will *never* sit on my throne." Aisling's words rang in the chamber, bouncing off dark walls and reflecting back upon them a thousand-fold. Over and over again, her voice proclaimed the same declaration.

And though it should have made Carman flinch or feel fear, the witch queen simply smiled.

"Why do you think I called you here, Aisling? Did you think it was because I wished to see my sister's visage again? Or perhaps because I wanted to see just how powerful Badb's progeny was?" Carman chuckled. "No, my dear. I called you here because we are the same person, and because you have no other choice but to do exactly as I say."

"I will not."

"You will, though you won't like it."

Aisling swallowed hard. The determined set of Carman's jaw suggested the witch knew something that Aisling didn't. That did not bode well.

She shifted on the stone only to feel dark magic tighten around her ankles and force her to stay still. "What is it that you want?"

"We will join together, you and I. A shared body but two, powerful minds that can rule Underhill the way it should be ruled. By strong women who will no longer allow anyone to tell us how the world should look."

The breath rushed from Aisling's lungs. "You want to possess me."

"Yes."

"Never," she said, shaking her head vigorously. "I would never let you violate my mind and my body in such a way."

"You don't really have a choice, Aisling."

"Of course, I do. This is my body and my people. You are locked up in chains, or have you not looked around you recently? This is your world. And you will never, ever get out."

Carman cocked an eyebrow, and Aisling knew there was far more to the witch than she understood. "The questing beast told you I was connected to the land, didn't he? That's what his purpose is in that maze. If someone is searching for me, they always end up in his labyrinth. He waits for someone just like you so that he can tell a little story and decide whether or not he wants you to meet me."

When Aisling didn't respond, Carman smiled.

"You see, Aisling, there's so much more to this story than you know. I am connected to Underhill; I am Underhill. And if you don't allow me to possess you and take back my throne, then this land will continue to die. More and more of the sluagh will fall to madness, and you will have to kill them over and over again until your little mind snaps in half like a twig underneath my heel. You'd be smart to just let me rule them."

Aisling couldn't imagine what Carman would do to this land. Already, she drained it of power and tried her best to destroy the world just for a petty hatred that was centuries old. What would she do with a throne and with all the power that the name of queen could provide?

She shook her head again. "No, I'm not willing to risk what the future might hold with you as the queen. The land might rot away into ruin, but at least the people who are here will still be happy and alive. I cannot promise them that if you are ruling this body. I know damned well that you will push me aside. It won't be me. I won't have any say over what we do or how we do it."

That future was far worse than what they were currently suffering. Aisling would gladly sit on this stone staring at her great great aunt without ever returning home if that meant that her people would live. She would do it for the rest of her life.

She had promised the sluagh they would be accepted and loved. In no timeline would she ever give up so easily just because a witch queen threatened her.

Aisling gritted her teeth, muscles bouncing on her jaw, and stared back at the witch who looked at her with a calculating expression.

Carman was thinking. Aisling could see the gears turning in the witch queen's mind, and of course there would be another barrage of information that was meant to tear her down.

"Shall we speak of your lover then? I stole the first Raven King away. Do you think I wouldn't do it to him as well? I haven't cursed him yet, you know. I loved the first far too much to hurt him even more than I already did, and then those who came after him were already beasts. But yours?" Carman smiled. "Yours is kind, he has a good heart, and one that is easily swayed."

"He doesn't. He's the most loyal man I have ever met."

"That's because you're a witch and naturally people despise you, distrust you, think that you are little more than a shadow in the night sent to steal their soul. But he's a man, darling, and easily swayed. Even now, he journeys with your sister because she thinks she wants to save him.

"What do you think, little witch?" Carman let out a laugh that was both evil and sad. "What if I turn your sister's heart just a little bit, back to where it was so many years ago when she first caught your Raven King's eye? Perhaps that's the difference in our story. Your sister met him first, and he fell in lust then. Maybe that was where I went wrong all those years ago. Regardless, if I turned back the wheel of time just a little bit, your sister would fall in love with him again.

"Do you think she would sway him? Do you think he would turn his gaze from you the moment she allowed him the time of day?"

Aisling swallowed the beginning of panic. "No."

"You seem to think that, but I'm not sure if your tongue just curled in on itself. Perhaps you don't entirely believe that he is so loyal to you? Men are not loyal, my dear. They see something they want and they take it. *That* is our history and our path to walk. If you don't believe me, just look at all the other women who have fallen in love with the wrong person who tore their heart out of their chest."

The fire in Carman's eyes made Aisling's burn as well. She knew what she meant, but it wasn't a disbelief or blind eye that she turned toward Bran. "You misunderstand me, witch queen. I say 'no' even if you turn him from me. You may take my lover and my sister from my side but I will always walk with the sluagh, the dearg due, the dullahan, the beasts that have been disgraced by their families. I have survived loss before, and I will survive it again. Take everything from me. Do it. I will still stand by those who others think are *nothing* because I, too, have been called nothing, and they will never suffer as I did again."

Once more, her words rang true and clear in the

mausoleum. Carmen thrust her hands toward Aisling in a moment of pure rage, her chains rattling like air in dying lungs. Aisling had never seen anything like it before.

The woman moved as though she hated Aisling. As though every fiber of her being couldn't help but reach for a throat that she wanted to tear out with claws that suddenly grew from her fingertips.

Arms stretched taut, muscles straining, Carman still reached for her, but then sagged on a breath, as though she had given up entirely. Her head hung limp, swaying even as her body listed to the side.

And for the first time since entering the tomb, Aisling felt a small twinge of pity in her heart. This woman was once the most powerful witch to ever exist. The world bent a knee to her and her sons who could have destroyed everything if they wished, and they almost did.

Now, she was little more than a sad excuse for a woman, holding onto life by a thread of anger and hatred that she couldn't let go. If Aisling hadn't found Bran, if she hadn't had Lorcan in her life to guide her, this was where she might have ended up, allowing hatred to overwhelm her, to swallow her whole. She was infinitely glad that the world had pitied her, had given her more than just a sister who betrayed her and sons who died in front of her eyes.

Aisling reached forward and touched a finger to Carman's chin, lifting the witch queen's head. "I am sorry, for what it's worth. This life that you lived was not one that should have been. Now, I need you to lift my curse."

Carman sagged, tilting her head into Aisling's touch. "Don't you feel them?"

"Who?"

"All the people we're letting down? I didn't do all this for my sister. That was never the plan. I was going to destroy the world regardless of my sister and the Raven King." When she looked up, tears slid down her cheeks. "You and I walked the same path. The witch who was cast aside from her family, who grew up in the gutter and desired nothing more than to live the way everyone else did."

Aisling shook her head. "You aren't going to distract me with pity. I know this is not a life someone should have, but I don't agree the only way to fix it is to destroy it."

"You are so *young*. You haven't even tried all the things that your magic can do. You haven't looked into the future with tarot cards, let alone dove into the blackness that is your soul. *I looked into our future and saw death.*"

Her breath caught in her lungs. Aisling had heard other witches say the same thing. They dreamed in fire and felt the tightening of a noose long before they were ever caught by another person. She'd heard it before, understood the fear and the anger. But she knew what these visions were.

She smoothed her thumb over Carman's cheek. "Death walks beside you, witch queen. Perhaps you should allow him to guide you far from this place."

"It's not death," Carman replied with a sinister laugh. "I ripped open the veil of time. I reached forward to all the powerful witches and women who were, are, and will be. Every single one of them that died a horrific death at the hands of men who could never understand them. I *promised* them a queen who would lead them from the shadows and guide them into the light. And that queen, of course, *was me.*"

A shiver traveled down Aisling's spine. Magic pressed her forward, closer to Carman, until her chin rested on the witch queen's shoulder. "Unchain me, child, and together we will save not only your faeries but all the witches who need us."

"No," she said in a whimper, struggling against the magic that would not release her.

Carman pressed her lips against Aisling's ear. "Then feel their pain."

A rushing wave of sensation poured from the witch queen through Aisling's senses. Anguish unlike anything she'd ever felt in her life threatened to overwhelm her. Her back arched, forcing her closer into Carman's arms.

Where were the chains? But she only had a moment to even consider it before she was overwhelmed again. Hatred, pain, sadness, all emotions she'd felt before but somehow couldn't recognize because they were infinitely more painful than she had ever felt in her short life.

Aisling couldn't think. She could hardly breathe through the emotions that swallowed her own until she couldn't tell where she started and they began.

"Feel them," Carman's voice whispered in her ear. "Feel the witches whom you are denying happiness, peace, and contentment. It is their lives you are destroying, not just those of the faeries."

Aisling gritted her teeth and moaned through the pain. She refused to believe these words. They were just a story that Carman was telling her. Pain was easy to replicate. Emotions were simple to manipulate. She would not bow to the witch who wanted her to fall at her feet.

Lips pressed against her ear, words tumbled from a

honeyed tongue, "Lilith, the first of us and the one who was killed by her own god for being too much of a woman. She died alone and in pain, and the darkness devoured her."

Spikes of pain shot down her spine like someone had ripped wings from her back. Aisling flinched forward, shoulder blades flexing, trying to get away from the burning ache.

"Pandora, too beautiful and too curious for her own good. She opened a box full of secrets and knew them all as no woman was ever meant to know. They locked her away, but she can't die. They gave her *immortality* so that she would forever know what it felt like to be alone."

Sadness, an aching desire for love, burst through her chest and forced tears from her eyes. She wanted someone, anyone, to love her, if even for a few moments. *Please, god, don't let her be alone anymore.*

"They called her witch but her name was Hecate, mother of the moon, goddess of magic, and she gave us all the power that we desired and they burned her. You've felt the flames before, and you know the pain she felt as she stood on that stake and watched all the people who professed to love her watch and laugh."

Aisling felt the flames on her legs again, but this time there was no Unseelie to save her. The skin of her legs peeled back in the wake of pain so profound no words could ever describe it.

"Cleopatra and Helen, the most beautiful women to ever live. They weren't even witches but simply knew what it meant to be powerful because they were beautiful. They made men bend a knee before them, and because of that, they were murdered with a knife between their breast. They stared up at the stars and begged for someone to save them, but no one wanted to." Carman's lips pressed against her ear again, leaving a kiss that scorched her to the bone. "They ravaged their bodies before they buried them because beautiful things were meant to be possessed and not exist without the bruises left by a man's hand."

Aisling shook her head, trying to shake free from the ancient sadness that came not only from her magic but also her sex. "*Stop.*"

"Morgana le Fay, Joan of Arc, Tiamat, Circe, Medusa, women over the ages who will be born, were born, lived and died, because *you* will not help them. We can rip through the fabric of time and spare them the pain, the harm, the destruction of their minds and bodies. *You are denying them this life.*"

"*Enough!*"

Aisling's words shattered through the magic that Carman held her with and blasted through the mausoleum. Obsidian stone tiles rained down on them from the ceiling and cracked against the skull of one of her sons.

A deep groan rattled within the frozen giant. He shifted, breaking through the spell that held his hands still, but then paused when magic took hold once more.

Aisling stumbled back from the witch queen, tripped over the stone tablet behind her, and landed hard on her back. She stared up at the light filtering from the ceiling and tried to remember where she was.

She lifted a hand to the blackness, hoping that her eyes might focus on something closer, but she couldn't distinguish her own body from the darkness. The eye on her palm blinked, then bled out until all she could see was more darkness, pain, and hurt.

Where had she gone? Her body was there, she could feel it, but it wasn't. Not even the fingers she knew so well. Just a lingering shadow that sometimes moved when she looked at it.

The memories of the women in her bloodline and those that simply shared a soul with her called out from beyond. Some had already met their demise in the branches of the hanging tree, others knew they were headed there, while some hadn't even breathed their first breath.

There were thousands of them. Women who would be hated no matter how much they tried to explain their worth. Women who would always be seen as nothing more than dangerous.

The soft sound of a sigh filled her ears, and Carman whispered, "How were you to know, child? Poets will sing for ages of women limp on the end of a spear. Our journey in life always ends in a river of tears we weep for each other, our children, those we love, and they say there is nothing we can do to stop the tidal wave. *I say there is.*"

"Eternal glory is not worth the price of blood," Aisling said, her tongue thick and sticking to the roof of her mouth. "What will you do when we all burn at the pyre? When there is nothing left of us but ashen bones?"

"Then I will remind them there are always grandchildren of witches who burned. That magic passes not through blood but through a desire to see change. I see into your heart, Aisling, and know you understand. We are not just women; we are witches. We will pull ourselves on bellies through hardship, we will crawl through pain, and we will rise with rage and devour all those who stand in our way."

Something in her mind broke. All the weight she carried on her shoulders as a woman, as a witch, pressed down upon her soul until she shattered into a million pieces at the feet of a witch queen who wanted to stop it all.

"What do you want me to do?" she whispered, shifting until she knelt before Carman.

Carman stared down at her and smiled softly. "We will destroy everyone who stands in our way. But there are many who are gods, who fear our power, what we can do. And there is only one way to kill a god."

"How?"

"With another god. Strip the ichor from their veins, drink it, and let it slide down your throat until you are more than they could ever be."

Sadness made her shoulders heavy. Her fingers felt fragile and weak as she reached out and touched the chains that held Carman prisoner. They fell from the witch queen, who reached out and took Aisling in her arms.

Carman pet her hair, smoothing the dark locks down her shoulders to her waist. "You've made the right choice, my child. Now finish it."

Aisling looked down at the rope around her wrist and saw it for what it truly was. A witch's ladder. A spell impossible to break other than by death itself.

She knotted two more loops, fingers shaking. "By knot of eight, I accept my fate. By knot of nine, what's done is mine."

CHAPTER 18

THE HANGING TREE

Bran launched himself through the portal made by the ancient Tuatha de Danann and landed in a crouch. They had said this would take him to Carman. He wasted no time, pulling his sword from his waist and letting out a snap of magic that arced like a whip in front of him.

The portal shimmered again, and Elva stepped out, her armor manifesting down her body like a second skin. The glimmering gold reflected the moonlight and cast its own light upon the ground.

He let the armor of the Raven King swarm down his body like a thousand black beetles trailing across his skin. They solidified, grouped together, and moved with his body like no metal ever could. The blade in his hand was thin, made out of dark metal that dripped black magic as it moved through the air. *Poison*.

"Carman!" he called out, his voice lashing through the air. "Where are you, witch?"

No one responded to him. There was nothing here but the pale, gray clay of the earth, a sprinkling of dead trees, and a black box so tall he didn't think any man could scale it. He looked at the monolithic building and tilted his head to the side.

"A tomb," he asked, "or a prison?"

"Both," Elva replied, stepping closer to it. "They wouldn't have put her in there, would they? They can't control who walks into this place. It's too easy."

He agreed and might have replied if he didn't hear the distinct sound of whimpering. He knew that voice. It haunted his dreams and sung him lullabies at night.

"Aisling," he whispered in horror.

They shared a glance before bursting into motion. They raced across clay that puffed up behind them in dead, dried earth. Bran edged ahead of Elva, struck the door with his shoulder, and burst into darkness so profound that he had never seen its ilk before.

It was as if he no longer existed.

So this was how they tried to curse the witch. They placed her in a black box and filled it with magic that replicated the horrors of death. They created a living hell for Carman to exist in. A single ray of light beamed down upon her and the woman he loved.

Bran slowed, then stood still in the center of the mausoleum. He called out her name, but she didn't react.

His heart clenched and stomach rolled as he watched Aisling kneel at the feet of the most dangerous witch to ever exist, release her from the chains, and then fall. His breath hitched as Carman drew his greatest love into her arms and whispered something in her ear.

"Don't listen!" he called out, but Aisling couldn't hear them.

Elva raced forward, but he already knew they were far too late. Whatever Carman had done, or said, had convinced the Raven Queen that Carman was right. Aisling wouldn't fall under Carman's spell so easily, but she would give her own life to save their people. Their lives, their safety, meant far more than her own to her.

More than him.

It felt as though his heart cracked down the middle. Something in him broke as yet another woman chose her own future over him. And he knew he shouldn't feel that way. Hadn't he promised Elva that she would get over such a heartbreak? That this was just a stepping stone in life?

He was a hypocrite. Losing Aisling meant more to him than a kingdom, than life, than anything else he could even fathom.

"Bran!" Elva shouted, lifting her blade above her head. She launched herself toward Carman and Aisling as though she could plunge her sword into the witch's heart.

He knew better. Carman melted into Aisling's skin, forming to her body as if it were a gift created just for her.

Aisling arched, arms open wide, back curved almost poetically. Her head was tilted back, berry colored lips open in a gasp.

And then all hell broke loose.

The stone holding the three giants at bay cracked down the center. Large shards rained down and snapped the stone tiles. A groan cracked through the room as the sons of Carman were freed to roam the lands once more.

The one nearest to Bran held a spear. He shook his great shoulders, opened his mouth wide, and let out a primal scream that made the very air shake. His brothers shifted forward, one reaching behind him for an arrow the size of a man that he then notched at his bow. The other drew back his sword and a wicked grin spread across his wide, square face.

But Bran wasn't looking at the beasts. He was looking at his queen whose hair had lifted as if she were underwater.

"Aisling," he called out, stumbling forward a step before telling himself it wasn't her. But it looked like her, and he wanted to preserve that last lingering impression for as long as possible.

He tried again, lifting his voice and calling out for her to see him one last time. "Aisling, my love!"

Miraculously, her head tilted as if she had heard him. She opened her eyes, those beloved eyes that filled with tears he knew were meant for him. Bran stretched out a hand, too far away to touch her and too late to help her.

"Bran." Her voice crossed the room, impossible for him to hear and yet he heard his name. "I lo—"

Magic blasted her head back again, hair raised in static, raven locks turning to white as too much power ran through her veins that she could not control. He'd seen such effects before, in a faerie who had touched a magical object that was too powerful for it to wield. The creature experienced an entire lifetime, aging and then exploding into a red mist before it disappeared from the world forever.

He couldn't watch her die like that. He couldn't see Carman win, but he couldn't be there for her in this moment when she was dying and it was his fault.

Still. Bran kept his eyes forward, forcing himself to live this with her because even though he was a coward, he was *hers*. And she would not die alone.

White flames licked her fingertips, stretching out from her body as it leaked magic. And still he stared, watching as the woman he loved became something else entirely.

Power pooled at her feet in the form of liquid fire then a great clap of thunder boomed through the mausoleum and everything sucked back into her. Her body seized, her skeleton lighting up beneath her skin until he could count her ribs even through her clothing.

And then all fell silent.

Aisling's body relaxed on a heaving sigh. Her shoulders curved forward, her hands limp at her sides, every bit of her suddenly calm.

Carman's three sons paused, seemed to hold their breath, and looked down at the woman who barely stood to their knee.

The one who held a sword knelt at her side and said, "Mother?"

"No," Bran said with a curse. "Anything but that."

Aisling's head lifted, and she stared up at the giant whose eyes widened in shock. "Hello, my son," she whispered. "It's good to be back."

And damned if he didn't feel a chill trace down his spine at the words. She had no right to possess the woman he loved. The Raven Queen was far too strong to allow someone else to take control of her body like that so easily. Aisling wouldn't allow her; she would fight. But when she turned to look at him, there was not even a single speck of Aisling left in her eyes.

Bran shook his head and took a step back. "No," he said again.

"What, you don't recognize me?" Carman lifted her hands, so familiar and yet so strange as claws grew from their tips.

"This body is one you love, Raven King. And we all know men love only the body, not the being within them. Such a change should be agreeable to you."

"I loved her, not you." He noted Elva stood frozen with her sword lifted over her head. He nodded toward her body. "What have you done to her?"

Carman gestured toward the shadows around them. "This place requires a sacrifice. None can leave it without one remaining. She shall do nicely, just as I did for my sister so long ago."

She waved a hand, and Elva's body launched to the chains. They snapped up, hovering in the air like snakes, then lashed out when she got close enough. The damning sound of locks clicking into place made his head ache.

"How dare you?" he growled, stepping forward ominously but hesitating. He didn't know how close he could get to her or how powerful her magic was now. "That was my wife you possessed."

"Was she? Not even in name from what I've heard. You never really made her your queen, did you, *Bran*?"

The sound of his name was the worst nightmare he could ever have dreamt. She knew the word that could control him. The one thing in the world faeries were weak to was their own name. Damn his mother for giving him one that was so obvious.

Carman grinned, her teeth suddenly sharp and feral. "Oh, don't worry, Unseelie. I've known your name since the first day you were called the Raven King's successor. I know all their names."

"Then why didn't you summon one before now?"

"I'm not interested in you. I'm interested in your queen.

And *you* are the very first to ever find her." She smoothed a hand down her chest. "Such a pretty little thing this witch is, and powerful as well. She'll do very nicely for all the plans I must set into motion now."

"What plans?" he snarled.

"You'll find out soon enough." She snapped her fingers, and all three of her sons lunged forward.

Bran swept up his blade and raced into battle. This was something he knew how to handle, something he'd done time and time again. His mind didn't need to think in moments like this. His body did it for him.

The first son brought down his sword, swinging in a deadly arc that might have cut off Bran's head if the giant had been faster. But giants weren't quick, and Bran was. He dodged out of the way, landed on one knee, and spun in a circle with blade outstretched. It caught the giant at the heel who stumbled past Bran as Bran prepared for the second brother with the spear.

He launched himself forward, racing as quickly as he possibly could. Leaping into the air, Bran put a foot to the first brother's back, pushed himself off, and lifted his blade as his momentum carried him up into the air.

The spear came dangerously close to his torso, but Bran managed to twist at the right second. He drew his sword across the giant's cheek and then rolled when he landed on the ground.

An arrow sank into the stones next to him, just barely missing his head.

Turning, he bared his teeth in a grimace and watched the third brother notch an arrow in his bow. That one was

339

dangerous, perhaps more dangerous than his brothers. Bran would need to plan appropriately to catch him the next time he loosed an arrow.

A dark thread of magic wiggled in his mind, shifting with purpose and desire. He'd never fully allowed the Raven King's power to dictate what he did. Bran thought it was far too dangerous, too desiring of pain and dismemberment, to ever allow it freed. But in this instant, he couldn't think of any reason why the Raven King couldn't be free.

Aisling was no longer here to ground him, and though he could still feel the binding curse, it was on her body not her mind. She wasn't here, not really. Instead, Carman controlled her like a puppet.

Why had she allowed it? It hadn't seemed as though Aisling fought at all. She'd simply given in to the witch who had destroyed so much.

Anger surged forth, taking hold of his sound mind and turning it into that of a mad man. Bran tilted his head back and let out a primal roar that sizzled at his fingertips. Black shadows boiled beneath his eyelids, then oozed out of his pores and raced from his body in rivers of black ink.

A murder of crows burst from his body, flying forward to attack the brother with the bow. They went for his eyes, pecking and screaming. He slapped a few to his face, but he couldn't control all of them. They weren't real birds, but simply shadows at the beck and call of a man who wanted nothing more than to see blood streaming from the giant's face.

More flooded from Bran's body, detaching themselves from his chest and taking with them pieces of himself until he didn't know where he started and they ended. Each murder of crows had a single raven within them, and that bird was *him*. Through countless eyes, he surveyed with cool detachment the damage upon each giant.

He hadn't ever wanted to hurt someone like this. He hadn't wanted to be so close to the destruction of a person's form. And yet, he enjoyed nothing more than hearing them scream.

The giants clawed at their eyes, screaming into the dark void of the mausoleum and begging for help. They would find none, not from him.

Bran's soul darkened, and his mind filled with an ache that he'd never felt before. For the first time in his life, he'd lost something. *Someone*. And he didn't like how it felt in the slightest.

For Aisling, he raged. For Aisling, he tore apart the giants and watched them bleed in rivers that leaked onto the floor like fountains. Through it all, Elva was hunched over herself, chained to the walls with her arms outstretched. Carman stood in the center of the room, watching him with cold eyes that only heated the moment he felt his heart shatter.

Carman clapped her hands slowly, the sound cracking through the air like a whip. "So you are capable of it," she whispered in awe.

"Capable of what?" The sound of his voice whipped through the chamber, deep and aching with emotions he did not know how to express. He wanted more pain, more anguish, more screams.

"Everything that you are, everything that she was, came from a place of emotion and terror. She was powerful because she *felt* things deeper than you or I could imagine. But now I see you are capable of it. You can feel as so few faeries can feel."

Hips swaying, she strode toward him. Her white hair curled slightly at her hips, and though he knew it was meant to be seductive, all he saw was a viper wearing the clothes of the woman he loved. She had no right to those clothes, to that form, to have any semblance to the woman who had changed him so thoroughly.

Bran bared his teeth in a snarl. "Step lightly, witch. I'm in no mood for your games."

"No, I imagine you're not. After all that I've done..." Carman tsked. "You want to kill me, don't you?"

"Very badly."

"And yet, you won't." She gestured up and down her body. "This is too precious to you, the woman you love. Your first true love, isn't that right? The woman who replaced me, the woman in chains, was someone you felt deeply for, but not like this. Not the love that tore you apart and made you a new man."

Bran imagined himself slitting her throat and watching the blood drain from her body in rivers. But the image made him nauseous, his heart thumping with the pain it would then feel. At least now she was alive. In some sense, Aisling was still alive.

Could he kill her?

He shook his head and took a step away from Carman. Perhaps he could. She wouldn't want to live like this, not when so much of her life was dedicated to being good. She might have been a witch, but Aisling hadn't wanted to hurt anyone.

He ran a hand over his face, the mere idea of murdering her hurting his very soul. He missed her already, and it had only been a few moments since he saw her consciousness glimmering in her gaze.

"I could kill you," he finally said. "I wouldn't enjoy it, I wouldn't want to do it, but if you don't release her body and allow her to return to me, then I will not let you win."

"You like to think that." Carman trailed a finger between her breasts. "This body means far more to you than the mind within it. Come to me."

"I have no interest in being your king. Leave, witch, or I will banish you from that body."

Before Carman could respond, the dark magic behind her stirred. She glanced over her shoulder with a frown.

The shadows parted like a curtain, and a man stepped out of them. Tall and lean with a hawkish nose, he was a stranger in these lands when Bran had thought he'd seen them all. A tendril of the Raven King's magic tasted him, running shadows along his arms, and he realized this was not a faerie.

The feel of this man's magic was familiar, though strange. Bran narrowed his eyes, staring at the man as if trying to look through a glamour. When he looked hard enough, the man's eyes shifted from black to slitted yellow.

"Lorcan?" he asked.

A grin spread across the man's face, feral and toothy. "I'm surprised you could recognize me without the fur."

Though he wished there was more time, Carman spun on her heel and shot a dart of magic toward Lorcan with surprising ease. The shadows burst from her fingers, rocketing through the air that shimmered like a heat wave around the bolt.

Lorcan calmly stepped aside. Her magic hit the wall of darkness behind him, which rippled at the impact.

The witch queen growled, "What magic is this?"

"The same as yours," Lorcan replied. "The same as yours

has always been."

"Never the same. I was the first, young witch," she snarled in return. "You have no idea who you're dealing with."

"But I do, Carman of Greece."

She flinched at the words. One hand lifted as if she wanted to cover her face. Bran wondered if she were ashamed of where she'd come from, but that didn't seem right. The legends all claimed she was proud to have been Grecian and wore her heritage like a badge.

Lorcan stepped forward. "You are not welcome in that body, and it's far past time for you to allow the original owner control over her own form."

"She is locked away in the darkness where she will remain."

"No," he said, then shook his head. "She won't."

Carman's head snapped back, rocking side to side as if in pain. A low whine erupted from her lips.

Once again, Lorcan called out, "Witch, you cannot control the body of the Raven Queen. Not for long. You're only hurting yourself in this struggle."

Her head snapped to the side, ear pressed to her shoulder, and she wheezed out a long breath. Then her eyes slowly closed.

Lorcan caught Bran's gaze and nodded toward her still body. "Now, Raven King. While you have the chance."

The knife he had in his belt seemed to burn against his thigh. Could he kill her? Damn it, he didn't want to. But he couldn't stand to see her where she was, with another woman looking out from her beloved eyes.

He stepped forward as if underwater, slowly making his

way to her side, while pulling the knife free from its sheath. The metal gleamed in the dim light. Bran wrapped an arm around her waist, pulled her against him, and slowly slid the knife between her ribs.

Bran held his breath, hoping beyond hope that Lorcan was right. He hadn't called out to her, damn it. Why hadn't he thought to call out to her? Of course Aisling was strong enough to banish this witch who had claimed her body. She was far stronger than he'd ever given her credit for.

"Come back to me," he said quietly. "I'm here, my love. I'm fighting for you, and now I need you to fight for me. *Please*, Aisling. We all need you."

Heartbeats passed, and then her eyes drifted open. She lifted her head, blinking at him as if he were a shining light in this darkness.

"Bran?" she asked. And it was *her* voice, not anyone else's.

Her eyes stared back at him and recognized him. Bran nearly fell to his knees as a wave of relief poured over him. It was *her*. She was still here, even though somehow Carman had taken over. But Aisling, his love, was *still here*.

He lifted a hand and cupped her cheek, staring at her as though she might disappear any second.

"It's you?" he asked.

A breathy sigh brushed against his wrist. "I'm so sorry, Bran."

"For what? You have nothing to be sorry for." But she did, and he knew it as well as her. Allowing Carman to take over her body was irresponsible for someone like them. They were too powerful for something like that to happen.

Lorcan cleared his throat. "She does, you just don't know it yet."

He didn't look over at the cat, but a sense of dread settled deep in his belly. Bran stared into Aisling's eyes and asked, "What did you do?"

"A witch always has another plan," she replied, "just in case anything goes awry."

"Aisling, what *did you do*?"

The soft smile on her face wasn't reassuring. She pushed herself out of his arms, stumbling backward once, twice, three times until he could no longer reach her. Throughout it all, she held his gaze even as blood bloomed on her chest and the knife blinked in the light.

He'd never seen anything like this: a woman with arms outstretched, the shadow of white wings overlaying her form from shoulder to fingertip. The darkness couldn't touch her. It reflected from the edges of her feathers like they were made of metal.

When she stepped back again, he realized she was barefoot. How long had she been like that? Pale, elegant feet stepped through a pool of blood and the red smears looked like the end of a war. Each step left a smudge on the darkness of the floor, golden and glimmering with her magic.

It poured from her in waves. A dangerous woman, made of the void and something more, something infinitely more.

"Aisling?" he asked again, but knew she wouldn't respond.

Her eyes left his and she smiled at Lorcan. "Thank you."

Bran had been warned of women like this. Whose grin was made for fighting and whose teeth were hiding fangs. "Aisling?"

A wave of her hand sent ripples through the shadows. The

darkness disappeared in the wake of a blazing light that filled the mausoleum. Bran lifted a hand to his eyes.

The hanging tree stood in the center of the room, its branches ablaze. A rope hung from a branch and seemed to shift in a breeze he could not feel.

"No," he whispered. "Anything but that."

Aisling looked back at him then. "If I could have spared you this, I would have. I'm so sorry, my love. Infinitely sorry."

"Aisling, don't do this."

Her eyes shifted, flickering from dark to light as Carman fought to the surface. Perhaps, for the first time in the Witch Queen's life, she felt fear.

Aisling lifted a hand, and the rope from the hanging tree snapped out. It lashed around her throat and looped around itself.

"There wasn't any other way," she said, voice choking as the rope tightened its grip. "Just like she said. Only a god can kill a god."

The rope tightened and then drew taut.

CHAPTER 19

DEATH OF THE QUEEN

A isling crouched in a field of nothing, her palm pressed to the ground she couldn't quite feel. This wasn't reality, or even a place, just the space of her mind where only she should exist.

And yet, there was another.

A darker energy that gathered in the corners. A witch queen who screamed into the darkness that she refused to die. Aisling was pleased that she would fight. She wanted to feel the witch's anguish as she squeezed the life from her throat.

Slowly she stood, stretching her body, feeling the ache of exhaustion building in the muscle of her lower back. Carman's magic forced her to constantly shield her mind. She'd allowed her to take control for a few moments, knowing that the witch would get too confident, being thrown into the void of her own mind had been unsettling.

No more. Carman might be the witch queen of old, but she hadn't learned any new tricks.

The bubble of her shield extended outward. White mist swirled around her legs as she walked to the very edge where

Carman slammed her fists against the wall over and over again.

Aisling could finally hear her enraged screams.

"Let me out!" she shouted. "You're killing us both. Give me control!"

"No."

"You foolish girl! My life is not worthy of death. Let me out or take control over your body again. You are going to *die*."

Aisling nodded, tucking her hands behind her back. "Yes, I likely will. But so will you. And the world will be a much better place without you."

"How dare you?" Carman pressed herself nearly flat against Aisling's shield, teeth bared in a snarl. "I am the Witch Queen of Greece who razed these lands to the ground. I have destroyed many witches before you. You will *never* defeat me."

Anger made Aisling's heart beat faster. Sweat slicked her palms, and a menacing grin spread across her face. She stepped closer and pressed her hand to the shield, mirroring Carman's position. "I am the descendent of a thousand witches *you let burn*." Her lips twisted into a weak grin. "And now, so shall you."

Green spears of light slammed down from the sky. They imbedded in the ground around Carman, creating a cage around her. More and more fell, each new spear forcing her closer to Aisling's shield until she was pressed against it entirely, her cheek next to Aisling's hand.

And yet, through it all, Aisling only felt pity. This was a woman who had never experienced love. Not truly. Even her sons hadn't expressed their love when they came back alive. They just fought for her, blindly and loyally, but without any true connection at all.

Aisling stroked her finger against the shield. "I'm sorry, my sister. There is no other way."

"Aisling, we're dying!" Carman screamed.

She could feel it. The way even her mind seemed to blur. The mist was more than just mist now, but a white light dragging her away to another place.

"I know," she whispered. "I know."

It didn't matter if she had to destroy herself to rid the world of Carman. Aisling knew her kingdom would live on without her. They would find shelter tucked under Bran's wing, kindness at Lorcan's side, and love within their ranks, all without a queen to assist them. The world would continue on without a witch with them.

Sometimes, it stung how little she mattered. In the grand scheme of things, a life like hers was only a heartbeat in time.

Carman had been alive much longer. A woman made of magic that came deep from within the earth always was an ancient. Perhaps it was harder for her to let go of life.

The witch queen stared at her with wide eyes, reaching her hand through a small hole in the green spears to press against the shield. "Please," she begged, "don't do this to us. You don't really want to die."

"I don't," Aisling said. "But is there another way?"

"I have seen countless kingdoms fall, watched men take thrones and lose them in a breath of time. I have seen dreams shattered and prideful men lose everything. In every end, there was another choice that would have led to a different path. There is another way." Her hand pressed harder against Aisling's shield, slipping through the magic until she could hold her fingers out for Aisling to take. "We are *witches*, Aisling.

We are fateless, deathless, and immortal if we wish to be."

The words were tempting, but the meaning behind them shallow and weak. Aisling shook her head, reached out, and laced her fingers with Carman's.

"Close your eyes with me," she whispered, letting her lids drift shut. "Let us sink deep into ourselves, into the magic that builds around us."

"No," Carman replied. "Don't do this to us."

"A witch never dies. We return to the magic from whence we came. We *become* the magic. Come with me, sister. Redeem yourself in the eyes of all you have failed."

"We have failed because of *you*."

A white light fell over them both, glimmering with magic and power. To Aisling, it felt like the most comforting blanket spreading over her shoulders and pulling her back into kind arms. It was quiet happiness, light and beautiful and all that was good in the world.

She breathed in the essence and sighed, "Oh Carman, we haven't failed them at all. We've simply given them space to grow."

She felt her body take its last breath. A gasping inhale rocked her form and that of her soul trapped in her mind with Carman. The witch queen sobbed, fell forward into Aisling's waiting arms, and together they held each other as their shared physical form died.

The form of Carman melted away into white ash that drifted out of her arms on a breeze. Aisling waited for her own time, staring into the white mist that swirled around her, then closed her eyes with a sigh. This wasn't where she thought she would die.

Perhaps it was childish to hope she would die in the arms of someone who loved her. She'd thought she would die in Bran's arms, where he would pour love and kindness into her last moments until she forgot how painful death was.

But she discovered now that death wasn't painful at all.

It was just sad.

She waited for the moment when all the weight of responsibility would lift from her shoulders. Waited for the next stage of her afterlife, the unknown world she'd heard the humans talk about so much. Was there a heaven for faeries? She didn't know.

A hand touched her shoulder. She opened her eyes and turned to stare at the woman who grasped her shoulder. Tall and lithe, the blonde wore a diaphanous robe that undulated around her body. She smiled softly, light glowing from within her body, then gestured behind Aisling.

She was surrounded by women who all looked remarkably similar. Each with hair as white as hers, silken robes, and a smile on their face that was both proud and kind.

"Aisling," they said as one. "You've saved us."

"Who are you?" she asked. But she didn't really need to ask at all.

These were the numerous Raven Queens who had come before her, or should have been. They smiled at her because, finally, after all this time, the curse was truly broken.

Aisling let her head fall back in relief. "Then it's done."

"It's done."

"Am I to go home with you?" she asked. She didn't really want to. She wanted to return to her home with the man she loved, to a kingdom that should prosper. That should have prospered for hundreds of years if not for the effects of Carman.

"No. Your time in here is limited."

Aisling frowned. "Limited? But I died. I could feel my own death."

"A true Raven Queen cannot die. She's connected to the earth, to Underhill itself. Carman stole that from us long ago." One of the women reached out and touched her cheek. "You have taken that magic back. The land heals you, Aisling. It feeds you; it gives you power. And it would *never* let you die."

Power surged into her body, lacing through her veins, like a bolt of lightning striking a tree. She was on fire, burning with magic, flaming with the possibilities. It wasn't just her sisters, and it wasn't just the excitement of life flooding through her. The magic was threading through her like the land was stitching itself into the fabric of Aisling's being.

Underhill was pleased to have her home.

Magic sizzled hot and powerful, pulling her from the space of her mind. It dragged her back into a physical form that was the same, but not. Now, there was so much more to her than just Aisling the witch, Aisling the Raven Queen. She was Underhill itself. A small goddess, but powerful beyond measure.

The rope around her neck was uncomfortable, but no longer burned. She lifted a hand, touched a finger to the burlap, and felt the weaving unravel immediately.

The hanging tree let her go with a sigh of relief and pleasure. It hadn't wanted her to swing in its branches with the rest of the condemned souls. She was suited here, watching over this land and its people, alongside her king who would now become infinitely more powerful when he fed off her power. She wasn't just a witch now; she was Underhill itself.

Together, they would bring Underhill back to its former glory. They would bring their people to prosperity. But most of all, Aisling knew they would live their lives together with so much love they would feel full to bursting.

Aisling's feet touched the ground, toes sinking into soft loam that suddenly felt squishy with life. She sank deep into the earth. It breathed beneath her, flexing with new life that it hadn't had before. Underhill sighed with relief as a new era began in the heart of a Raven Queen.

She spread her fingers wide. This body, although the same, felt different. Far more different than she'd expected. It was hers but it was...more.

Earthen magic flowed in her veins. Greenery blossomed at her feet, spreading like a wave everywhere she looked. Dead, dried dirt turned into chocolate-colored loam that rolled in great waves farther and farther from her.

Although it felt strange to share so much of her power at once, it also felt right. A weight lifted off her shoulders, and she finally found relief after struggling for so long.

Aisling looked down at the knife buried in her chest. Blood still leaked from the wound, but far slower than it had before. She grasped the hilt without thought and slid it from the hole in her chest.

The wound closed as soon as the air touched it.

Aisling dropped the knife to the ground and pressed her hand against what had been the wound. Was it possible that Underhill could heal even a mortal wound? She hadn't expected the magic to be quite so powerful. Defying death had always seemed impossible, even to a witch.

"Aisling?" the words were carefully said, as if the speaker didn't believe it was her. "How?"

When she looked up, her gaze caught on a dark one, eyes as deep and expansive as the night sky. It took a moment for her to recognize him. The dusted black feathers over his right eye that stretched back over his head. The same side held a yellow eye that whirled wildly over the length of her body. But the other, the dark eye, was the one that watched her with a fascination that put the memory back in place.

"Bran?" she asked quietly, her voice wavering slightly.

It was him. She knew it was him, even though it felt like she was looking at him with new eyes. This was the man she loved, the one who had given her so much freedom and had stolen her heart on a journey that would change her life forever. How could she have forgotten him?

He stepped forward, halting and stiff. His face was white as snow and his hand shaking as he lifted it. "Is it you behind those eyes or Carman?"

"The witch queen is dead." She could say that with certainty. She'd feel the witch if she wasn't. Her presence had lurked in Aisling's mind long enough that she knew the acidic flavor of her dark magic. "She won't return."

Bran blew out a disbelieving breath, still hesitant in his movements. "How are you doing all this?"

The earth had changed in the mere moments they'd been speaking. The mausoleum had melted away until the hanging tree stood in first a desert, then a meadow, as her magic spread throughout Underhill.

Aisling lifted her hands and reached for him. "This is what was stolen so long ago from the Raven King and Queen. You look out for the people and are tied to them. To the sluagh. The Raven Queen is tied to the land, and she ensures its survival."

And how good it felt. Finally, after all these years, she had a purpose in life. It wasn't just to be a witch, to heal, to keep others safe. She was here to keep Underhill alive.

Bran let out a choked sound, stumbled forward, and then rushed forward like a storm racing across the plains. He crashed into her, harshly pulling her against him and sealing their mouths together. He tasted her like a starving man, like a man denied the world who then had it given to him on a platter.

The magic of the Raven Queen drifted away on the taste of wine that poured from his tongue. Their teeth clashed in battle, but she didn't care if he drew blood from her lips. Let him have it since he already had everything else. Her respect, her dedication, her love.

She pulled back slightly, out of breath and with worry making her hair stand on end. She stared up into his eyes and noted the mulberry bruises surrounding them. How his lips were chapped when she remembered them velvet smooth. He looked tired. Bone tired, the kind that made a man not think straight.

His body shook under her hands so she drew him closer. He trembled in her arms, ribs shaking with breaths, knees shivering with emotion so strong she didn't know how to comfort him. Aisling ran her hands up his sides. "What's the matter, my love? You looked troubled."

"Troubled?" he said on a huffing breath of disbelief. "You just died in front of me, *because of me*, and I didn't know if I could—"

When he paused, she saw the panic in his gaze. He

searched hers for signs of life. She was certain he needed to remind himself she was there so she touched her fingertips to his ribs again.

"I'm here," she whispered. "I'm here, and I'm not going anywhere again."

Bran reached up and feathered a fingertip over her lower lip. "I promised you a thousand sunrises, and a thousand more after that, until the sun no longer rises from the sky and the world falls into darkness that only *we* could love. And I thought I'd have to break that promise. It nearly ruined me, you reckless woman."

"I knew it wouldn't," she replied.

"How?"

"Because there is no darkness powerful enough in this world to take me from your side." She leaned up and pressed her lips to his. "I love you. Every aching inch of your moonlight soul."

He pressed a hand onto her lower back and drew her closer. "And I every part of your wildflower heart."

CHAPTER 20
WHEN THE WORLD WAS BORN ANEW

Flowers hung in drapes of color from the window, spilling down the tower and landing in a pile of orchids at the ground. Aisling leaned out the opening and eyed the ridiculous show Underhill was putting on for all the Seelie faeries who were coming to visit them.

Aisling had insisted the Seelie King and Queen have the coronation somewhere else. There were hundreds of other options, far better than Underhill, far more appropriate to crown the new prince of the Seelie Fae. They had continually batted aside her arguments, insisting they wanted their son to be crowned in the new land that would soon become an ally all courts could consider friend.

It wasn't fair, and it certainly wasn't good for her nerves.

She again smoothed a hand down her now white hair. The strands stuck to her fingers and seemed to glow with an otherworldly light that was entirely embarrassing. It gave away her emotions far better than her face.

Glowering at the strands, she dropped them with a disgusting sound. "You could try to behave, you know."

A few of the flowers tilted their heads up and down in agreement. Underhill knew it could behave, but it also wanted to do its mother proud.

Aisling hadn't ever thought she'd consider herself mother to what was essentially a section of earth. Even when the power first blossomed in her chest, she'd thought it would be a little easier. Plant some seeds, watch them grow, convince the land with a little green magic that it should do what she wanted. She even knew a few green spells from her time helping farmers. It should have been easy.

Nothing in Underhill was that easy. The land was a being all its own, and as stubborn as a child.

The sluagh had tried to explain it to her. Each Raven Queen was supposed to teach the land to do what she wanted. It *was* a child. Nothing more than a baby who needed someone to teach it how to live, what was appropriate, and how to act. Aisling wasn't doing a great job at that.

"Mistress?" a voice asked from the doorway, "are you ready to go to the great hall?"

"No." She glowered. "I don't want to entertain the Seelie Fae when I have far more important things to do." Like teach those flowers that they couldn't grow so ridiculously large just because they had visitors.

The sluagh coughed behind its feathered hand. Now that Carman was no longer siphoning off their magic, they were much better looking. They'd all filled out, leathery wings changing to feathered, midnight wings that spread out from them in graceful arches. She'd never seen anything like them in nature, but was proud to see that her people, though still intimidatingly ugly, were far healthier than they were before.

"Mistress," the sluagh said, clearly trying to hide its laughter, "they're here for *you*."

"They're here for the crowned prince," she corrected. "They care little if I'm here, only that Underhill is pretty enough for the ceremony."

Another voice joined the other, dark and feathered with power. Bran stepped out of the shadows of the corridor and into the room. A grin split his face, sharpened teeth gleaming in the light. "I can take it from here. Thank you, sluagh."

"As you wish, Highness."

They waited until the door closed behind their bird-like subject before they raced to each other's side. Aisling didn't know who moved first. She only knew she was in his arms and the taste of honeyed wine filled her mouth once more.

"I missed you," she whispered against him. "Why did you have to leave for such a long time?"

"There were a few things I wanted to do before I returned."

"The Seelie Fae are already here. They're all waiting for us in the great hall, and I don't know what to say to them. What they'll think of me."

He tucked a strand of white hair behind her ear. "They'll think you're the most beautiful woman they've ever seen. They'll be thankful you saved one of their own. Elva's still waiting to speak with you, you know."

She bit her lip. There were a lot of things unsaid between Aisling and her sister, but she didn't know where to begin. *You left me* was perhaps the right place to start, but it somehow felt so meaningless when there was a world between them.

Elva had been her idol growing up, and now there was simply a lot of growth between them. Aisling didn't know how to bridge the gap that had spread into a chasm after years of discontent between them.

Could she love her sister? Maybe someday. But that wasn't necessary, not anymore.

She had a family again. This place was filled with people who not only needed her, or loved her, but that knew her innermost thoughts and didn't judge her for them. She wasn't a cast-off, a family member who was too odd or uncomfortable to understand.

She was simply Aisling. A witch sometimes. A woman most times. And always the Raven Queen who loved her subjects more than the air she breathed.

Bran let out a soft chuckle, the grin on his face burning into her like the sun.

"What?" she asked.

"You're happy," he said. And she saw the same emotion reflected in his own eyes.

"How do you know that?" Of course, she was. He was always right when he observed something like that. How could she be anything else? Aisling finally had everything that she wanted, minus a few lingering curses that took her husband away from her during the day. But the nights... Oh, the nights were well worth the wait.

He reached behind her. A soft snapping sound surprised her, and then he pulled a lily between them. "Because Underhill always blooms when you're happy."

She snorted at the white flower. "And apparently whenever I'm nervous. It blooms at every emotion it can. The entire place is like an unruly teenager that just found color. I swear, Underhill is insistent on painting every surface it can with color."

"Then let it," he said, hooking a leg behind hers to pull her off balance. "I don't mind the color after so much time in the dark."

"But I like the dark."

Bran leaned down to kiss her, then growled against her lips, "So do I."

Her cheeks burned in a blush. They'd spent far too much time in the darkness lately, and she refused to complain in the slightest.

"We have to go to the great hall," she murmured. "They'll miss us."

With a groan, he helped her straighten then let out a sigh that could have shaken the rafters. "Ridiculous Seelie Fae. Why are they in our home again?"

"Coronation."

"It's not even one of ours."

"Oh, suddenly you agree with me there's something else we could be doing."

Bran winked. "Something far more pleasurable than entertaining a bunch of stuffy Seelie Fae who are only here to see what gift we give to the boy."

"How about a tail?" Aisling wiggled her eyebrows, stepping away so she could finish getting ready. "Or perhaps ears. I think a little redheaded boy with mouse ears would be rather cute, don't you think so?"

Bran's laughter sounded like music. She had heard few symphonies in her life, but she was certain this was what poets waxed on about. No one could make a song so beautiful, a sound so lovely, as the man who had stolen her heart.

She made her way to the small mirrored table where the sluagh kept her brushes. They were supposed to have put her hair up in some pretty style that would make the other Seelie faeries think she was like them. But her new hair refused to be braided or twisted into an updo at all.

Instead, the strands liked to make a scene. They slipped out of every bun. They tangled in braids until she had to take them out. They even flicked her ears if she put them up in a simple tail.

So she'd given up. Aisling let them have their own way, and the strands were much happier. Strangely, her hair didn't seem so much to be part of her body anymore. Every strand was as much part of Underhill as was the rest of her.

On the table sat a crown made of thorns. Slightly smaller than Bran's, it was no less intimidating.

He strode up behind her, appearing in the reflection of the mirror as a dark shadow that hovered behind her. His feathers scraped against her back, the warmth of his body heated her spine, and that yellow raven eye whirled in its socket.

He reached around her, took hold of the crown, and slowly lifted it to her head. Individual strands of her hair reached up and looped around the metal. The glowing white strands would hold it against her head, and they certainly wouldn't let it fall.

With a happy sigh, Bran leaned down and pressed his chin to her shoulder. He wrapped his arms around her waist, fingers tightening on the simple black silk of her gown. "You look every inch a queen."

She looked at their reflection in the mirror, how perfect a pair they were. He, the raven, and she, the swan. The night and moon were who they were, and she'd never seen it before this second. Together, they were the universe and all the stars together in one beautiful, infinite moment.

Aisling breathed out a sigh that mimicked his. "And for the first time, I feel it."

He grinned, all feral smile and wild abandon, and she fell in love with him all over again.

"Ready to go give a Seelie prince a tail?"

"Are we finally agreeing to that?"

With laughter bubbling at their heels, they chased each other down the halls of their castle. Aisling caught the grins of sluagh as they ran by and the sound of laughter as a dullahan tossed his head up in glee.

They were finally in a place where all these misfits could be happy, and she was so proud.

Lorcan had settled on staying with the hanging tree as a guide of sorts. Aisling missed him, but he visited whenever he could. That usually meant at inopportune times, mostly whenever she wanted to be alone with Bran, but at the very least, she saw her dear friend.

Life had changed drastically since she'd taken on the full powers of the Raven Queen, but she wouldn't change it for the world, no matter how uncomfortable it made her.

She skidded to a halt in front of the great hall doors, taller than a person and ominously high over their heads. Aisling blew out a breath and stared at the worn wood, knowing this wasn't something she could step back from. Through those doors were the people who had rejected her all those years ago. The faeries who hadn't wanted her, but now somehow wanted to make amends.

Could she do it? Suddenly, happiness drained from her,

replaced by a sense of dread so profound she could hardly think. What if they did it again? What if she trusted them, let them back into her life, and then they threw her away again?

Warm hands curved around her waist and drew her against a chest that was sturdy and strong. "Together," Bran murmured in her ear. "As always."

And all her worries disappeared. No matter what, he'd be with her. He always was.

She took a deep breath, nodded, and the doors before them opened. The great hall was filled with faeries from all walks of life. Golden beings with dragonfly wings. Tall, strong women with equally powerful men standing side by side, swords strapped to their waists. Brownies, pixies, Tuatha de Danann all gathered together, awaiting their hosts.

All eyes turned to them. They drank in the sight of the Raven King and Queen, how they stood wrapped around each other even when decorum should have been recognized.

She didn't care. After all this time worrying that she would say something or do something embarrassing, Aisling realized she didn't care. It didn't matter what they thought of her as long as Bran was beside her, the kingdom prospered, and those she valued above all else were happy and whole.

The amount of relief she felt from the realization nearly sent her to her knees. Who cared what the Seelie Fae thought with all their rules and opinions? She had a kingdom of people who saw those rules and discarded them. A kingdom of people who had renounced the ways of Seelie and Unseelie forever more.

Together, they would continue to strengthen this kingdom that valued them when all others didn't. That was her life now, the Seelie Fae be damned.

"Ready?" Bran asked.

"More than ready. I've never seen a faerie baby before."

He let go of her waist and stepped up to her side, holding out his arm for her to take. The smile on his face nearly blinded her. "They look very much like every other baby you've seen."

"Human?"

"In a way."

Aisling wrinkled her nose and stepped forward into the great hall with him. "Maybe I really will give him a tail then. Poor thing, he's a faerie and no one would even know it."

The crowd parted like a wave in front of them, revealing the Seelie King and Queen at the center of the great hall. They'd set up a makeshift stage, although only a step up from the ground. She appreciated they at least abstained from using her and Bran's throne. They were welcome to it, of course, but she noticed the olive branch they extended.

Of all people, she hadn't thought to find peace with the king and queen of the faeries who'd found her lacking. But Sorcha and Eamonn were kindhearted and far more amiable than she ever expected.

Sorcha beamed at them from her place beside Eamonn. A golden dress spilled down her sides like liquid, pooling at her feet and reflecting bits and pieces of the room. She could see the Seelie faerie's faces in the dress, and wondered at the design. It was as if the Seelie Queen had absorbed her people. Of course, that was what Sorcha had done with her *own*, the druids, and was trying to do with the faeries.

Eamonn was dressed entirely in white silk edged in gold. Aisling noted it was unusually simple for a king. That seemed to fit the Seelie faerie, though. He wasn't one for pomp and circumstance and much preferred to blend into the crowd.

In that, they matched. Aisling felt their eyes on her like a physical touch and might have turned around if Bran's hand wasn't warm against her lower back.

Between the two Seelie faeries was a cradle that rocked back and forth under a magical touch. Inside, she knew she would see their new baby. The sluagh had spoken of the birth in great lengths. It was the first Seelie prince born in over three centuries, and they were certain this was a great omen that must be heeded.

Aisling wasn't so sure of that. She stepped up onto the stage and walked toward the cradle. She rested a hand against the edge and stopped the rocking.

The baby lay underneath a cream woolen blanket. He looked up at her with bright green eyes that were far too aware for a human child of only a few days old. Freckles dusted his cheeks, so many she couldn't count them. He smiled a toothless grin and reached up a hand for her.

"Sorcha," she said with a smile, holding out her finger for the baby to take. "He's lovely. No red hair?"

His mother scowled. "No, it does appear that he might take after his father in that aspect."

Difficult as it was, Eamonn somehow managed to puff his chest out even farther. "I don't see what's wrong with that."

"I wanted him to have red hair like me," his wife grumbled. "There are far too many blondes in the Seelie kingdom. I think a little color would do you all good."

"He's got your freckles."

"And your stubborn jaw."

As they continued arguing, Aisling leaned down to get a good look in the prince's eyes. He was a remarkably beautiful child, although she'd expected no less from good-looking parents, but there was something else in his gaze, something she recognized deep in the belly of her being.

Mischief already flickered there. Mischief that wasn't quite Seelie fae at all.

"You're going to cause so much trouble, aren't you?" she asked the child. "Maybe I won't give you a tail after all."

Bran's hand settled next to hers, tilting the crib further so he could peek in as well. "Handsome boy."

"Bigger than I thought."

"Hearty."

"Likely to follow in his mother's footsteps."

Bran snorted. "No, he'll follow in his father's footsteps. Look at the set of his jaw, the look in his eye. That's clearly a lust for adventure, just like Eamonn had when he was first born. He'll be quite the Seelie prince."

"Look closer," Aisling said with a raised brow.

The Raven King leaned close to the child then reared back in surprise. Wide-eyed, he looked back at her. "Is that?"

"Mm-hmm."

"Oh no." He glanced over at Sorcha and Eamonn who were still arguing about who was more reflected in their son's features. "Do you think they have any idea?"

"Let's just not tell them. We'll get the boy later." She reached forward and touched a finger to his forehead. "I gift you with luck, little prince. For the rest of your life, lady luck will follow in your footsteps and keep you safe from all harm."

The entire crowd fell silent at her words, holding their

breath as if they had sucked the gift into themselves. Aisling looked up, afraid she'd done something irreversible. Faerie gifts were permanent. Once given, they would forever remain with the child. Luck seemed like a good gift, but in hindsight...

Sorcha cleared her throat, and tears glimmered in her eyes. "That's quite the gift," she said with thick words. "You can only give that to one child you know."

"Then it will be my greatest accomplishment to give it to your son." She didn't add that she thought it likely he'd need it. The boy had a strand of Unseelie in his blood, and he'd have to tread carefully. She'd never heard of a Seelie prince who varied from the throne. Perhaps he was the future.

She looked down at the bright child with all his freckles and green summer eyes. Maybe he was the future after all. Maybe, just maybe, the courts would disappear forever with one boy who could bring them together for good.

How would she know? Aisling refused to peek into the future, no matter how much Underhill wanted her to.

Sorcha stepped up and took her hand. She pressed it tight against her ribs, as close as two queens could get in front of their subjects. "It's an honor, Raven Queen."

With a smile, Aisling squeezed the Seelie Queen's hand. She looked over at Bran and felt her heart warm with the love reflected in his eyes. Finally, this was what *family* felt like.

"The honor is all mine, Seelie Queen."

As the crowd cheered behind them, thankful for the gift Underhill had given, Bran mouthed the words, *I love you.*

This was what immortality felt like. Not the weight of centuries passing. Just the love of one man who had given her *his* forever.

ACKNOWLEDGEMENTS

Thank you so much to everyone who helped this book come to life. To my family who believed in me every step of the way, and to all those who breathed life into me when I was struggling.

This one's for you.

ALSO BY EMMA HAMM

Heart of the Fae

The journey began in *Heart of the Fae*, a Beauty and the Beast retelling.

Veins of Magic

Continued in *Veins of Magic*, the second book in the Beauty and the Beast Duology.

Bride of the Sea

Dove beneath the waves in *Bride of the Sea*, an Otherworld Companion Novel and retelling of The Little Mermaid.

The Faceless Woman

We met the Unseelie Prince and Witch in *The Faceless Woman*, the first book in the Swan Princess Duology.

ABOUT THE AUTHOR

Emma Hamm grew up in a small town surrounded by trees and animals. She writes strong, confident, powerful women who aren't afraid to grow and make mistakes. Her books will always be a little bit feminist, and are geared towards empowering both men and women to be comfortable in their own skin.

To stay in touch
www.emmahamm.com
authoremmahamm@gmail.com